Joanne Rock credits her decision to write romance after a book she picked up during a flight delay engrossed her so thoroughly that she didn't mind at all when her flight was delayed two more times. Giving her readers the chance to escape into another world has motivated her to write over eighty books for a variety of Mills & Boon series.

Sophia Singh Sasson puts her childhood habit of daydreaming to good use by writing stories that will give you hope, make you laugh, cry and possibly snort tea from your nose. She was born in Mumbai, India, and has lived in India and Canada. Currently she calls the chaos of Washington, DC, home. She's the author of the Welcome to Bellhaven and State of the Union series. She loves to read, travel to exotic locations in the name of research, bake fancy cakes, explore water sports and watch Bollywood movies. Hearing from readers makes her day. Contact her through sophiasasson.com

Also by Joanne Rock

Harlequin Desire Dynasties: Mesa Falls

The Rebel
The Rival
Rule Breaker
Heartbreaker

Texas Cattleman's Club: Inheritance

Her Texas Renegade

Also by Sophia Singh Sasson

Marriage by Arrangement
The Senator's Daughter
Mending the Doctor's Heart
First Comes Marriage

THE RANCHER

JOANNE ROCK

RUNNING AWAY WITH THE BRIDE

SOPHIA SINGH SASSON

MILLS & BOON

First Published in Great Britain 2020
by Mills & Boon, an imprint of HarperCollinsPublishers,
1 London Bridge Street, London, SE1 9GF

ISBN: 978-0-263-28278-8

0121

MIX
Paper from responsible sources
FSC™ C007454

This book is produced from independently certified FSC™ paper to ensure responsible forest management.

For more information visit: www.harpercollins.co.uk/green

Printed and bound in Spain
by CPI, Barcelona

THE RANCHER

JOANNE ROCK

To the Rockettes,
for keeping me company
while I write.

One

Chiara Campagna slipped into her host's office and silently closed the heavy oak door, leaving the raucous party behind. Breathing in the scents of good bourbon and leather, she held herself very still in the darkened room while she listened for noise outside in the hallway to indicate if anyone had followed her.

When no sounds came through besides the pop song people danced to in the living room of Miles Rivera's spacious Montana vacation home, Chiara released a pent-up breath and debated whether or not to switch on a lamp. On the one hand, a light showing under the door might signal to someone passing by that the room was occupied when it shouldn't be. On the other, if someone found her by herself snooping around in the dark, she'd be raising significant suspicions that wouldn't be easy to talk her way around.

As a prominent Los Angeles-based social media influencer, Chiara had a legitimate reason to be at the party given by the Mesa Falls Ranch owners to publicize their environmental good works. But she had no legitimate reason to be *here*—in Miles Rivera's private office—snooping for secrets about his past.

She twisted the knob on the wall by the door, and recessed lighting cast a warm glow over the heavy, masculine furnishings. Dialing back the wattage with the dimmer, she left it just bright enough to see her way around the gray leather sofa and glass-topped coffee table to the midcentury modern desk. Her silver metallic dress, a gorgeous gown with an asymmetrical hem and thigh-high slit to show off her legs, moved around her with a soft rustle as she headed toward the sideboard with its decanter full of amber-colored liquid. She set aside her tiny silver handbag, then poured two fingers' worth into one of the glasses beside the decanter. If anyone discovered her, the drink would help explain why she'd lingered where she most definitely did not belong.

"What secrets are you hiding, Miles?" she asked a framed photo of her host, a flattering image of an already handsome man. In the picture, he stood in front of the guest lodge with the five other owners of Mesa Falls Ranch. It was one of the few photos she'd seen of all six of them together.

Each successful in his own right, the owners were former classmates from a West Coast boarding school close to the all-girls' academy Chiara had attended. At least until her junior year, when her father lost his fortune and she'd been booted into public school. It would have been no big deal, really, if not for the fact that the public school had no art program. Her dreams of attending a prestigious art university to foster her skills with collage and acrylic paint faltered and died. Sure, she'd parlayed her limited resources into fame and fortune as a beauty influencer thanks to social media savvy and—in part—to her artistic sensibilities. But being an Instagram star wasn't the same as being an artist.

Not that it mattered now, she reminded herself, lingering on the photograph of Miles's too-handsome face. He stood flanked by casino resort owner Desmond Pierce and game developer Alec Jacobsen. Miles's golden, surfer looks were a contrast to Desmond's European sophistication and Alec's stubbled, devil-may-care style. All six men were wealthy and successful in their own right. Mesa Falls was the only business concern they shared.

A project that had something to do with the ties forged back in their boarding school days. A project that should have included Zach Eldridge, the seventh member of the group, who'd died under mysterious circumstances. The boy she'd secretly loved.

A cheer from the party in the living room reminded Chiara she needed to get a move on if she wanted to accomplish her mission. Steeling herself with a sip of the aged bourbon, she turned away from the built-in shelves toward the desk, then tapped the power button on the desktop computer. Any twinge of guilt she felt over invading Miles's privacy was mitigated by her certainty the Mesa Falls Ranch owners knew more than they were telling about Zach's death fourteen years ago. She hadn't been sure of it until last Christmas, when a celebrity guest of the ranch had revealed a former mentor to the ranch owners had anonymously authored a book that brought the men of Mesa Falls into the public spotlight.

And rekindled Chiara's need to learn the truth about what had happened to Zach while they were all at school together.

When the desktop computer prompted her to type in a passcode, Chiara crossed her fingers, then keyed in the same four numbers she'd seen Miles Rivera code into his phone screen earlier in the evening while ostensibly reaching past him for a glass of champagne. The generic photo of a mountain view on the screen faded into the more businesslike background of Miles's desktop with its neatly organized ranch files.

"Bingo." She quietly celebrated his lack of high tech cyber security on his personal device since she'd just exhausted the extent of her code-cracking abilities.

"Z-A-C-H." She spoke the letters aloud as she typed them into the search function.

A page full of results filled the screen. Her gaze roved over them. Speed-reading file names, she realized most of the files were spreadsheets; they seemed to be earnings reports. None used Zach's name in the title, indicating the references to him were within the files themselves.

Her finger hovered over a promising entry when the doorknob turned on the office door. Scared of getting caught, she jammed the power button off on the computer.

Just in time to look up and see Miles Rivera standing framed in the doorway.

Dressed in a custom-cut tuxedo that suited his lean runner's build perfectly, he held his phone in one hand before silently tucking it back in his jacket pocket. In the low light, his hair looked more brown than dark blond, the groomed bristles around his jaw and upper lip decidedly sexy. He might be a rancher, normally overseeing Rivera Ranch, a huge spread in central California, yet he was always well-dressed anytime the Mesa Falls owners were in the news cycle for their efforts to bring awareness to sustainable ranching practices. His suits were always tailored and masculine at the same time. Her blog followers would approve. She certainly approved of his blatant sexiness and comfort in his own skin, even though she was scared he was about to have her tossed out of his vacation home on the Mesa Falls property for snooping.

His blue eyes zeroed in on her with laser focus. Missing nothing.

Guilty heart racing, Chiara reached for her bourbon and lifted it to her lips slowly, hoping her host couldn't spot the way her hand shook from his position across the room.

"You caught me red-handed." She sipped too much of the drink, the strong spirit burning her throat the whole way down while she struggled to maintain her composure.

"At what, exactly?" Miles quirked an eyebrow, his expression impossible to read.

Had he seen her shut off the computer? She only had an instant to decide how to play this.

"Helping myself to your private reserves." She lifted the cut-crystal tumbler, as if to admire the amber contents in the light. "I only slipped in here to escape the noise for a few minutes, but when I saw the decanter, I hoped you wouldn't mind if I helped myself."

She waited for him to call her out for the lie. To accuse her of spying on him. Her heartbeat sounded so loud in her ears she thought for sure he must hear it, too.

He inclined his head briefly before shutting the door behind him, then striding closer. "You're my guest. You're welcome to whatever you like, Ms. *Campagna*."

She sensed an undercurrent in the words. Something off in the slight emphasis on her name. Because he knew she was lying? Because he remembered a time when that hadn't been her name? Or maybe due to the simple fact that he didn't seem to like her. She had enough of an empath's sensibilities to recognize when someone looked down on her career. She suspected Miles Rivera was the kind of man to pigeonhole her as frivolous because she posted beauty content online.

As if making women feel good about themselves was a waste of time.

"You're not a fan of mine," she observed lightly, sidling from behind his desk to pace the length of the room, pretending to be interested in the titles of books on the built-in shelves lining the back wall. "Is it because of my profession? Or does it have more to do with me invading your private domain and stealing some bourbon? It's excellent, by the way."

"It's a limited edition." He unbuttoned his jacket as he reached the wet bar, then picked up the decanter to pour a second glass, his diamond cuff-link winking in the overhead lights as he poured. "Twenty-five years old. Single barrel. But I meant what I said. You're welcome to my hospitality. Including my bourbon."

Pivoting on his heel, he took two steps in her direction, then paused in front of his desk to lean against it. For a moment, she panicked that he would be able to feel that the computer was still warm. Or that the internal fan of the machine still spun after she'd shut it off.

But he merely sipped his drink while he observed

her. He watched her so intently that she almost wondered if he recognized her from a long-ago past. In the few times they'd met socially, Miles had never made the connection between Chiara Campagna, social media star, and Kara Marsh, the teenager who'd been in love with Miles's roommate at school, Zach Eldridge. The old sense of loss flared inside her, spurring her to turn the conversation in a safer direction.

"I noticed you neatly sidestepped the matter of my profession." She set her tumbler on a granite-topped cabinet beside a heavy wire sculpture of a horse with a golden-yellow eye.

He paused, taking his time to answer. The sounds of the party filtered through to the dim home office. One dance tune blended seamlessly into another thanks to the famous DJ of the moment, and voices were raised to be heard over the music. When Miles met her gaze again, there was something calculating in his expression.

"Maybe I envy you a job that allows you to travel the globe and spend your nights at one party after another." He lifted his glass in a mock salute. "Clearly, you're doing something right."

Irritation flared.

"You wouldn't be the first person to assume I lead a charmed life of leisure, full of yachts and champagne, because of what I choose to show the world on social media." She bristled at his easy dismissal of all the hard work it had taken to carve herself a place in a crowded market.

"And yet, here you are." He gestured expansively, as if to indicate his second home on the exclusive Mesa Falls property. "Spending another evening with Hollywood celebrities, world-class athletes and a few heavyweights from the music industry. Life can't be all bad, can it?"

In her agitation, she took another drink of the bourbon, though she still hadn't learned her lesson to sip carefully. The fire down her throat should have warned her that she was letting this arrogant man get under her skin.

Considering her earlier fears about being caught spying, maybe she should have just laughed off his assumption that she had a shallow lifestyle and excused herself from the room. But resentment burned fast and hot.

"And yet, you're at the same party as me." She took a step closer to him before realizing it. Before acknowledging her own desire to confront him. To somehow douse the smug look in his blue eyes. "Don't you consider attendance part of your job, not just something you do for fun?"

"I'm the host representing Mesa Falls." His broad shoulders straightened at her approach, though he didn't move from his position leaning his hip against the desk. "Of course it's a work obligation. If I didn't have to take a turn being the face of Mesa Falls tonight, I would be back at my own place, Rivera Ranch."

His voice had a raspy quality to it that teased along her nerve endings in a way that wasn't at all unpleasant. He was nothing like the men who normally populated her world—men who understood the beauty and entertainment industries. There was something earthy and real about Miles Rivera underneath the tailored garments, something that compelled her to get closer to all those masculine, rough edges.

"And I'm representing my brand as well. It's no less a work obligation for me."

"Right." He shook his head, an amused smile playing at his lips, his blue eyes darkening a few shades. "More power to you for creating a brand that revolves around long-wearing lipstick and international fashion shows."

This view of her work seemed so unnecessarily dismissive that she had to wonder if he took potshots as a way to pay her back for invading his office. She couldn't imagine how he could rationalize his behavior any other way, but she forced herself to keep her cool in spite of his obvious desire to get a rise from her.

"I'm surprised a man of your business acumen would hold views so narrow-minded and superficial." She shrugged with deliberate carelessness, though she couldn't stop herself from glaring daggers at him. Or taking another step closer to hammer home her point. "Especially since I'm sure you recognize that work like mine requires me to be a one-woman content creator, marketing manager, finance director and admin. Not to mention committing endless hours to build a brand you write off as fluff."

Maybe what she'd said resonated for him, because the condescension in his expression gave way to something else. Something hotter and more complex. At the same moment, she realized that she'd arrived a foot away from him. Closer than she'd meant to come.

She couldn't have said which was more unnerving: the sudden lifting of a mental barrier between them that made Miles Rivera seem more human, or her physical proximity to a man who…stirred something inside her. Good or bad, she couldn't say, but she most definitely didn't want to deal with magnified emotions right now. Let alone the sudden burst of heat she felt just being near him.

Telling herself the jittery feelings were a combination of justified anger and residual anxiety from her snooping mission, Chiara reached for her silver purse on the desk. Her hand came close to his thigh for an instant before she snatched up the handbag.

She didn't look back as she stalked out the office door.

Still shaken by his unexpected encounter with Chiara Campagna, Miles made a dismal effort to mingle with his guests despite the loud music, the crowd that struck him as too young and entitled, and the text messages from the other Mesa Falls Ranch owners that kept distracting him. Trapped in his oversize great room that took "open concept" to a new level of monstrosity, he leaned against the curved granite-topped cabinetry that provided a low boundary between the dining area and seating around a stone fireplace that took up one entire wall. Open trusswork in the cathedral ceilings added to the sense of space, while the hardwood floor made for easy dancing as the crowd enjoyed the selections of the DJ set up near the open staircase.

Miles nodded absently at whatever the blonde pop singer standing next to him was saying about her reluctance to go back on tour, his thoughts preoccupied by another woman.

A certain raven-haired social media star who seemed to captivate every man in the room.

Miles's gaze followed Chiara as she posed for a photo with two members of a boy band in front of a wall of red flowers brought into the great room for the party. He couldn't take his eyes off her feminine curves draped in that outrageous liquid silver dress she wore. Hugged between the two young men, her gown reflected the flashes of multiple camera phones as several other guests took surreptitious photos. And while the guys around her only touched her in polite and socially acceptable ways, Miles still fought an urge to wrest her away from them. A ludicrous reaction, and totally out of character for him.

Then again, *everything* about his reaction to the wildly sexy Chiara was out of character. Since when was he the kind of guy to disparage what someone else did for a living? He'd regretted his flippant dismissal of her work as soon as he'd said the words, recognizing them as a defense mechanism he had no business articulating. There was something about her blatant appeal that slid past his reserve. The woman was like fingernails down his back, inciting response. Desire, yes. But there was more to it than that. He didn't trust the femme fatale face she presented to the world, or the way she used her femininity in an almost mercenary way to build her name. She reminded him of a woman from his past that he'd rather forget. But that wasn't fair, since Chiara wasn't Brianna. Without a doubt, he owed Chiara an apology before she left tonight.

Even though she'd definitely been on his computer when he'd entered his office earlier. He'd seen the blue glow of the screen reflected on her face before she'd scrambled to shut it down.

"How do you know Chiara Campagna?" the woman beside him asked, inclining her head so he could hear her over the music.

He hadn't been following the conversation, but Chiara's name snagged his focus, and he tore his gaze away from the beauty influencer who'd become a household name to stare down at the earnest young pop singer beside him.

He was only on site at Mesa Falls Ranch to oversee things for the owners for a few weeks. His real life back at Rivera Ranch in central California never brought him into contact with the kind of people on the guest list tonight, but the purpose of this party—to promote the green ranching mission of Mesa Falls by spreading the word among celebrities who could use their platforms to highlight the environmental effort—was a far cry from the routine cattle raising and grain production he was used to. Just like his modern marvel of a home in Mesa Falls bore little resemblance to the historic Spanish-style main house on Rivera Ranch.

"I don't know her at all," Miles returned after a moment. He tried to remember the pop singer's name. She had a powerful voice despite her petite size, her latest single landing in the top ten according to the notes the ranch's publicist had given him about the guests. "But I assume she cares about Mesa Falls's environmental mission. No doubt she has a powerful social media platform that could help our outreach."

The singer laughed as she lifted her phone to take a picture of her own, framing Chiara and the two boy band members in her view screen. "Is that why we're all here tonight? Because of the environment?"

Frowning, he remembered the real reason for this particular party. While the green ranching practices they used were touted every time they hosted an event, tonight's party had a more important agenda. Public interest in Mesa Falls had spiked since the revelations that the owners' high school teacher and friend, Alonzo Salazar, had been the author behind the career-ending tell-all *Hollywood Newlyweds*. In fact, the news story broke at a gala here over Christmas. It had also been revealed that Alonzo had spent a lot of time at Mesa Falls before his death, his association with the ranch owners drawing speculation about his involvement with the business.

Tonight, the partners hoped to put an end to the rumors and tabloid interest by revealing the profits from *Hollywood Newlyweds* had gone toward Alonzo Salazar's humanitarian work around the globe. They'd hoped the announcement would put an end to the media interest in the Mesa Falls owners and discourage newshounds from showing up at the ranch. There'd been a coordinated press release of the news at the start of the party, a toast to the clearing of Alonzo's good name early in the evening, and a media room had been set up off the foyer with information about Alonzo's charitable efforts for reporters.

But there was something the owners weren't saying. While it was true a share of the book profits had benefited a lot of well-deserving people, a larger portion had gone to a secret beneficiary, and no one could figure out why.

"So the threat of global warming didn't bring you here tonight," Miles responded with a self-deprecating smile, trying to get back on track in his host duties. He watched as Chiara left behind the band members for one of the Mesa Falls partners—game developer Alec Jacobsen—who wanted a photo with her. "What did? A need to escape to Montana for a long weekend?"

He ground his teeth together at the friendly way Alec placed his hand on the small of Chiara's back. Miles remembered the generous cutout in her dress that left her completely bare in that spot. Her hair shimmered in the overhead lights as she brushed the long waves over one shoulder.

"Honestly? I hoped to meet Chiara," the singer gushed enthusiastically. "Will you excuse me? Maybe I can get a photo with her, too."

Miles gladly released her from the conversation, chagrined to learn that his companion had been as preoccupied with Chiara as he was. What must life be like for the influencer, who'd achieved a different level of fame from the rest of the crowd—all people who were highly accomplished in their own right?

Pulling out his phone, Miles checked to see if his friend and fellow ranch owner, Gage Striker, had responded to a text he'd sent an hour ago. Gage should have been at the party long ago.

Miles had sent him a text earlier:

How well do you know Chiara Campagna? Found her in my study and I would swear she was riffling through my notes. Looking for something.

Gage had finally answered:

Astrid and Jonah have known her forever. She's cool.

Miles knew fellow partner Jonah Norlander had made an early exit from the party with his wife, Astrid, so Miles would have to wait to check with him. Shoving the phone back in the pocket of his tuxedo, Miles bided his time until he could speak to Chiara again. He would apologize, first and foremost. But then, he needed to learn more about her.

Because she hadn't just been snooping around his computer in his office earlier. She'd been there on a mission. And she hadn't covered her trail when she'd rushed to close down his screen.

Somehow, Chiara Campagna knew about Zach. And Miles wasn't letting her leave Mesa Falls until he figured out how.

Two

Chiara grooved on the dance floor to an old disco tune, surrounded by a dozen other guests and yet—thankfully—all by herself. She'd spent time snapping photos with people earlier, so no one entered her personal dance space while she took a last glance around the party she should have left an hour ago.

Normally, she kept a strict schedule at events like this, making only brief appearances at all but the biggest of social engagements. The Met Gala might get a whole evening, or an Oscar after-party. But a gathering hosted by a Montana rancher in a thinly disguised PR effort to turn attention away from the Alonzo Salazar book scandal?

She should have been in and out in fifty minutes once her spying mission in Miles Rivera's office had proven a bust. Finding out something about Zach had been her real motive for attending, yet she'd lingered long after she'd failed in that regard. And she knew the reason had something to do with her host. She knew because she found herself searching him out in the crowd, her eyes scanning the darkened corners of the huge great room hoping for a glimpse of him.

Entirely foolish of her.

Annoyed with herself for the curiosity about a man who, at best, was keeping secrets about Zach and at worst thought her work shallow and superficial, she was just about to walk off the dance floor when he reentered the room. His sudden presence seemed to rearrange the atoms in the air, making it more charged. Electrified.

For a moment, he didn't notice her as he read something on his phone, and she took the opportunity to look her fill while unobserved. She was curious what it was about him that held her attention. His incredibly fit physique? Certainly with his broad shoulders he cut through the guests easily enough, his size making him visible despite the crowd around him. Or maybe it was the way he held himself, with an enviable confidence and authority that implied he was a man who solved problems and took care of business. But before she could explore other facets of his appeal, his gaze lifted from his device to land squarely on her.

Almost as if he'd known the whole time she'd been watching him.

A keen awareness took hold as she flushed all over. Grateful for the dim lighting in the great room, she took some comfort in the fact that at least he wouldn't see how he affected her. Even if he had caught her staring.

Abruptly, she stepped out of the throng of dancers with brisk efficiency, determined to make her exit. Heels clicking purposefully on the hardwood, she moved toward the foyer, texting her assistant that she was ready to leave. But just as the other woman appeared at her side to gather their entourage, Miles intercepted Chiara.

"Don't go." His words, his serious tone, were almost as much of a surprise as his hand catching hers lightly in his own. "Can we speak privately?"

It might have been satisfying to say something cutting now in return for the way he'd behaved with her earlier. To hold her head high and march out his front door into the night. She looked back and forth between Miles and her assistant, Jules Santor, who was busy on her phone assembling vehicles for the return to their nearby hotel. But the reason Chiara had come here tonight was more important than her pride, and if there was any chance she could still wrest some clue about Zach's death from Miles after all this time, she couldn't afford to indulge the impulse.

"On second thought," she told Jules, a very tall former volleyball player who turned heads everywhere she went, "feel free to take the rest of the evening off. I'm going to stay a bit longer."

Jules bit her lip, her thumbs paused midtext as she glanced around the party. "Are you sure you'll be okay? Do you want me to leave a car for you?"

"I'll be fine. I'll text if I need a ride," Chiara assured her before returning her attention to whatever Miles had in mind.

At her nod, he guided her toward the staircase behind the dining area, one set of steps leading to an upper floor and another to a lower. He took her downstairs, never relinquishing her hand. A social nicety, maybe, because of her sky-high heels, long gown and the open stairs. Yet his touch made her pulse quicken.

When they reached the bottom floor, there was a small bar and a mahogany billiards table with a few guys engaged in a game. He led her past a smaller living area that was dark except for a fire in the hearth, through a set of double doors into a huge room with a pool and floor-to-ceiling windows on three sides. Natural stonework surrounded the entire pool deck, making it look like a grotto complete with a small waterfall from a raised hot tub. The water was illuminated from within, and landscape lights showcased a handful of plantings and small trees.

"This is beautiful." She paused as they reached two easy chairs flanking a cocktail table by the windows that overlooked the backyard and the Bitterroot River beyond.

Withdrawing her hand from his, she took the seat he gestured toward while he made himself comfortable in the other.

"Thank you." He pulled his gaze from her long enough to look over the pool area. "I keep meaning to come here during the summer when I could actually open all the doors and windows and feel the fresh air circulating."

"You've never visited this house during the summer?" She wondered if she misunderstood him. The house where he was hosting tonight's party was at least fourteen thousand square feet.

"I'm rarely ever in Montana." His blue eyes found hers again as he leaned forward in the wingback, elbows propped on his knees. "Normally, my brother oversees Mesa Falls while I maintain Rivera Ranch, but Weston had his hands full this year, so I'm helping out here for the month." His jaw flexed. "I realize I did a poor job in my hosting duties earlier this evening, however."

Surprised he would admit it, she felt her brows lift but waited for him to continue. The sounds of the game at the billiards table drifted through the room now and then, but for the most part, the soft gurgle of the waterfall drowned out the noise of the party. The evening was winding down anyhow.

"I had no right to speak disparagingly of your work, and I apologize." He hung his head for a moment as he shook it, appearing genuinely regretful. "I don't know what I was thinking, but it was completely inappropriate."

"Agreed." She folded her fingers together, hands in her lap, as she watched him. "Apology accepted."

He lifted his head, that amused smile she remembered from earlier flitting around his lips again. "You're an unusual woman, Chiara Campagna."

"How so?" Crossing her legs, she wished she didn't feel a flutter inside at the sound of her name on his lips. She couldn't have walked away from this conversation if she tried.

She was curious why he'd sought her out for a private audience again. Had she been in his thoughts as much as he'd been in hers over the last hour? Not that it should matter. She hadn't decided to stay longer at the party because he made her entire body flush hot with a single look. No, she was here now because Miles knew something about Zach's death, and getting to know Miles might help her find out what had really happened.

"Your candor, for one thing." He slid a finger beneath his bow tie, expertly loosening it a fraction.

Her gaze tracked to his throat, imagining the taste of his skin at the spot just above his collar. It was easier to indulge in a little fantasy about Miles than it was to reply to his opinion of her, which was so very wrong. She'd been anything but truthful with him this evening.

"I appreciated the way you explained your job to me when I made a crack about it," he continued, unbuttoning his tuxedo jacket and giving her a better view of the white shirt stretching taut across his chest and abs. He looked very…fit. "I had no idea how much work was involved."

Her gaze lingered on his chest as she wondered how much more unbuttoning he might do in her presence tonight. She didn't know where all this physical attraction was coming from, but she wished she could put the lid back on it. Normally, she didn't think twice about pursuing relationships, preferring to focus on her work. But then, men didn't usually tempt her to this degree. The awareness was beyond distracting when she needed to be smart about her interaction with him. With an effort, she tried to focus on their conversation.

"I'm sure plenty of jobs look easier from the outside. You're a rancher, for example, and I'm sure that amounts to more than moving cattle from one field to the next, but that's really all I know about it."

"Yet whereas you have the good sense to simply admit that, I made presumptuous wisecracks because I didn't understand your work." He studied her for a long moment before he spoke again. "I appreciate you being here tonight. I do recognize that our ranch party probably wouldn't be on your list of social engagements if not for your friendship with Jonah Norlander's wife, Astrid."

"Astrid is one of my closest friends," she said, wary of going into too much detail about her connections to the Mesa Falls partners and their spouses. But at least she was telling the truth about Astrid. The Finnish former supermodel had caused Chiara's career to skyrocket, simply by posting enthusiastic comments on Chiara's social media content. Because of her friend, she'd gone from an unknown to a full-blown influencer practically overnight. "As someone who doesn't have much family, I don't take for granted the few good friends I have in my life."

Another reason she planned to honor Zach's memory. She counted him among the people who'd given her the creative and emotional boost she'd needed to find her professional passion.

"Wise woman." Miles nodded his agreement. "I guess you could say I'm here tonight because of my good friends, too. I do have family, but I don't mind admitting I like my friends better."

His grin was unrepentant, giving his blue eyes a wicked light.

"What about Weston?" She wondered what he thought of his younger brother, who held a stake in Mesa Falls with him.

"We have our moments," he told her cryptically, his lips compressing into a thin line as some dark thought raced across his expression.

"Does owning the ranch together make you closer with him?"

One eyebrow arched. "It does."

His clipped answer made her hesitate to probe further. But she couldn't stop herself from asking, "If you're close to the other Mesa Falls owners, why don't you spend more time here? I know you said you run Rivera Ranch, but why build this huge, beautiful house if you didn't ever plan on making time to be in Montana?"

She wondered what kept him away. Yes, she was curious if it had anything to do with Zach. But she couldn't deny she wanted to know more about Miles. With luck, that knowledge would help her keep her distance from this far-too-sexy man.

He took so long to answer that she thought maybe he'd tell her it was none of her business. He watched the spillover from the hot tub where it splashed into the pool below, and she realized the sounds had faded from the other room; the billiard game had ended.

"Maybe I was feeling more optimistic when we bought the land." He met her gaze. "Like having this place would bring us together more. But for the most part, it's just another asset we manage."

Puzzled why that would be, she drew in a breath to tease out the reason, but he surprised her into silence when his hand landed on her wrist.

"Isn't it my turn to ask you something?" Mild amusement glinted in his eyes again.

Her belly tightened at his attention, his touch. There was a potent chemistry lurking between them, and she wanted to exercise extreme caution not to stir it any further. But it was incredibly tempting to see what would happen if she acted on those feelings. Too late, she realized that her pulse leaped right underneath the place where his hand rested. His thumb skated over the spot with what might pass for idleness to anyone observing them, but that slow caress felt deliberate to her.

As if he wanted to assess the results of his touch.

"What?" she prodded him, since the suspense of the moment was killing her.

Or maybe it was the awareness. She was nearly brought to her knees by physical attraction.

"I saw you dancing alone upstairs." His voice took on that low, raspy quality that sent her thoughts to sexy places.

She remembered exactly what she'd been thinking about when he'd caught her eye earlier. She would not lick her lips, even though they suddenly felt dry.

"That's not a question," she managed, willing her pulse to slow down under the stroke of his thumb.

"It made me wonder," he continued as if she hadn't spoken. "Would you like to dance with me instead?"

The question, like his touch, seemed innocuous on the surface. But she knew he wasn't just asking her to dance. She *knew*.

That should have given her pause before she answered. But she gave him the only possible response.

"I'd like that." She pushed the words past the sudden lump in her throat. "Very much."

Even before he'd asked her to be his dance partner, Miles knew the party upstairs had ended and that this would be a private dance.

The Mesa Falls PR team excelled at keeping events on schedule, and the plan had been to move the late-night guests into the media room to distribute gift bags at midnight. His public hosting duties were officially done.

His private guest was now his only concern.

Which was a good thing, since he couldn't have taken his eyes off her if he tried. He needed to figure out what she was up to, after all. What would it hurt to act on the attraction since he had to keep track of what she was doing anyway? Keep your friends close and your enemies closer. Wherever Chiara ended up on the spectrum, he'd have his bases covered.

Helping her to her feet, he kept hold of her hand as

he steered her toward the billiards room, now empty. Stopping there, he flipped on the speaker system tucked behind the bar, then dimmed the lights and pressed the switch for the gas fireplace at the opposite end of the room. Her green eyes took in the changes before her gaze returned to him.

"Aren't we going upstairs?" she asked while the opening refrain of a country love song filled the air.

Miles shrugged off his tuxedo jacket and laid it over one of the chairs at the bar. If he was fortunate enough to get to feel her hands on him tonight, he didn't want extraneous layers of clothes between them.

"The DJ is done for the night." He led her to the open floor near the pool table and pulled her closer to him, so they faced one another, still holding hands. He waited to take her into his arms until he was certain she wanted this. "I thought if we stayed down here we'd be out of the way of the catering staff while they clean up."

"I didn't realize the party was over." She didn't seem deterred, however, because she laid her free hand on his shoulder, the soft weight of her touch stirring awareness that grew by the minute. He was glad he'd ditched his jacket, especially when her fingers flexed against the cotton of his shirt, her fingernails lightly scratching the fabric.

"It's just us now." He couldn't help the way his voice lowered, maybe because he wanted to whisper the words into her ear. But he still didn't draw her to him. "Are you sure you want to stay?"

"It's too late to retract your offer, Miles Rivera." She lifted their joined hands, positioning them. "I'll have that dance, please."

Damn, but she fascinated him.

With far more pleasure than a dance had ever inspired in him, he slid his free hand around Chiara's waist. He took his time to savor the feel of her beneath his palm, the temperature of her skin making her dress's lightweight metallic fabric surprisingly warm. Sketching a touch from her hip to her spine, he settled his hand in the small of her back where the skin was bare, then used his palm to draw her within an inch of him.

Her pupils dilated until there was only a dark green ring around them.

"That's what I hoped you'd say." He swayed with her to the mournful, longing sound of steel guitars, breathing in her bright, citrusy scent.

Counting down the seconds until he kissed her.

Because he had to taste her soon.

Not just for the obvious reasons, like that she was the sexiest woman he'd ever seen. But because Chiara had gotten to the heart of the loneliness he felt in this big Montana mansion every time he set foot in the state. With her questions and her perceptive gaze, she'd reminded him that Mesa Falls might be a testament to Zach Eldridge's life, but it remained a hollow tribute without their dead friend among them.

He'd hoped that ache would subside after they'd owned the property for a while. That Mesa Falls could somehow heal the emptiness, the pervasive sense of failure, that remained in him and his partners after they'd lost one of their own. But for Miles, who'd defined his whole life by trying to do the right thing, the consequences of not saving his friend were as jagged and painful as ever.

"Is everything okay?" Chiara asked him, her hand

leaving his shoulder to land on his cheek, her words as gentle as her expression.

And damned if that didn't hurt, too.

He didn't want her sympathy. Not when her kiss would feel so much better.

With an effort, he shoved his demons off his back and refocused on this woman's lush mouth. Her petal-soft fingertips skimming along his jaw. Her hips hovering close enough to his to tantalize him with what he wanted most.

"Just wondering how long I can make this dance last without violating social conventions." He let his gaze dip to her lips before meeting her gaze again.

She hesitated, her fingers going still against his cheek. He could tell she didn't buy it. Then her hand drifted from his face to his chest.

"You're worried what I'll think about you?" she asked lightly, her forefinger circling below his collarbone.

The touch was a barely there caress, but it told him she wasn't in any hurry to leave. The knowledge made his heart slug harder.

"A host has certain obligations to the people he invites under his roof." He stopped swaying to the song and looked into her eyes.

He kept one hand on the small of her back, the other still entwined with hers.

"In that case—" Her voice was breathless, but her gaze was steady. Certain. "I think you're obligated to make sure I don't dance alone again tonight."

Three

She needed his kiss.

Craved it.

Chiara watched Miles as he seemed to debate the merits of continuing what he'd started. He was a deliberate, thoughtful man. But she couldn't wait much longer, not when she felt this edgy hunger unlike anything she'd felt before.

She simply knew she wanted him. Even if what was happening between them probably shouldn't.

Maybe the impatience was because she'd had very little romantic experience. In her late teens, she'd mourned Zach and wrestled with the mix of anxiety and depression that had come with his death. Her lifestyle had shifted, too, after her father went bankrupt and she'd been forced to change schools. Giving up her dream of going to an art school had changed her, forging her into a woman of relentless ambition with no time for romance.

Not that it had really mattered to her before, since she hadn't been impressed with the few relationships she'd had in the past. The explosive chemistry other women raved about had been more of a simmer for her, making her feel like she'd only been going through the motions with guys. But tonight, dancing with Miles in this huge, empty house now that all the party guests had gone home, she felt something much different.

Something had shifted between them this evening, taking them from cautiously circling enemies to charged magnets that couldn't stay apart. At least, that's how she felt. Like she was inexorably drawn to him.

Especially with his broad palm splayed across her back, his thumb and forefinger resting on her bare skin through the cutout in the fabric of her gown, the other fingers straying onto the curve of her ass. A touch that made her very aware of his hands and how much she wanted them all over her without the barrier of clothes.

Determined to overcome his scruples, or host obligations, or whatever it was that made him hesitate, Chiara lifted up on her toes. She was going to take this kiss, and whatever else he was offering, because she needed it. She'd worry about the repercussions in the morning. For now, she grazed her mouth over his. Gently. Experimentally.

Hopefully.

She breathed him in, a hint of smoky bourbon enticing her tongue to taste his lower lip.

The contact sparked through her in unexpected ways, leaping from one pulse point to the next until something hot flamed to life. Something new and exciting. And as much as she wanted to explore that, she hesitated, worried about compounding her subterfuge with this man by adding seduction into the mix. Or maybe she just feared she didn't have the necessary skills. Either way, she needed to be sure he wanted this, too.

Just when she was about to pull back, his fingers tangled in her hair, anchoring her to him and deepening the kiss. And every cell in her body cried out a resounding *yes*.

The heat erupted into a full-blown blaze as he took over. With one hand he drew her body against his, sealing them together, while he used the other to angle her face in a way that changed the trajectory of the kiss from sensual to fierce and hungry. She pressed her thighs together against the sudden ache there.

From just a kiss.

Her body thrilled to the new sensations even as her brain struggled to keep up with the onslaught. Her scalp tingled when he ran his fingers through her hair. Her nipples beaded, skin tightening everywhere. A soft, needy sound emanated from the back of her throat, and the noise seemed to spur him on. His arm banded her tighter, creating delicious friction between their bodies as he backed her into the pool table. She wanted to peel off her gown and climb all over him. She simply *wanted*.

Her hands went to his shirt, ready to strip away the barriers between them, her fingers taking in the warm strength of all that delectable male muscle as she worked the fastenings. He lifted her up, seating her on the pool table as he stepped between her knees, never breaking the kiss. The long slit in her silver gown parted, making the fabric slide away as it ceased to cover her. The feel of him against her *there*, his hips pressing into the cradle of her thighs, made her forget everything else. Her fingers fell away from the shirt fastenings as she raked in a gasp, sensation rocking her.

Miles edged back, his blue eyes now a deep, dark ultramarine as his gaze smoked over her, checking in with her.

"I need to be sure you want to stay." His breathing was harsh as he tipped his forehead to hers, his grip going slack so that his palms simply rested on her hips. "Tell me, Chiara."

She respected his restraint. His concern for her. Things had spiraled out of control in a hurry, but she didn't want to stop now, no matter how it might complicate things down the road. She wanted to know real passion. What it was like to be carried away on that wave of hot, twitchy, need-it-now hunger.

"I've never felt the way you're making me feel tonight," she confided in a low voice, her hands gripping the side rails of the table, her nails sinking into the felt nap. "But I've always wanted to. So yes, I'm staying. I have to see what I've been missing all the years I chose work over…fun."

His lips quirked at that last bit. He straightened enough to look into her eyes again. The flames from the fireplace cast his face half in shadow.

"It's going to be more than fun." His thumbs rubbed lightly where they rested on her hips, the certainty in his tone assuring her he knew how to give her everything she craved.

She resisted the urge to squeeze his hips between her thighs and lock her ankles so he couldn't leave her. "Promise?"

His fingers clenched reflexively, which made her

think that she affected him as thoroughly as he was affecting her.

"If you make me a promise in return."

"What is it?" She would have agreed to almost anything to put his hands in motion again. To experience another mind-drugging kiss with the power to set her on fire. How did he do that?

"I get a date after this." He pressed his finger to her lips when she'd been about to agree, silencing her for a moment while she battled the urge to lick him there. "One where you'll tell me why you've chosen work over fun for far too long," he continued, removing his finger from her mouth so she could speak.

Her conscience stabbed her as Zach's face floated through her mind. She had no idea how she'd appeal to Miles for information about Zach in the aftermath of this. He'd probably hate her when he found out why she'd come to Montana in the first place. He'd never look at her the same way again—with heat and hunger in his eyes. Was it so wrong to chase the feelings Miles stirred inside her?

"Deal," she told him simply, knowing he'd never follow through on the request once he understood what had brought her here in the first place. Her fingers returned to the studs in his shirt, wanting the barriers between them gone.

He tipped her chin up to meet his gaze before he breathed his agreement over her lips. "Deal."

His kiss seemed to seal the pact, and her fingers forgot how to work. All her thoughts scattered until there was only his tongue stroking hers, teasing wicked sensations that echoed over her skin, dialing up the heat. She shifted closer to him, wanting to be near the source of that warmth. He answered by bracketing her hips and tugging her forward to the edge of the table, pressing her against the rigid length beneath his fly.

She couldn't stifle the needy sound she made at the feel of him, the proof of his hunger pleasing her almost as much as having him right where she wanted him. Almost, anyway. A shiver rippled through her while he tugged the straps of her gown off her shoulders.

"I need to see you," he said as he broke the kiss, watching the metallic silver gown slide down her body.

The material teased her sensitive nipples as it fell, since she hadn't bothered to wear a bra. Miles's eyes locked on her body, and the peaks tightened almost painfully, her breath coming faster.

"And I need to *feel* you." She might not have a ton of romance experience, but she believed in voicing her needs. And damn it, she knew what she wanted. "Your hands, your body, your mouth. You pick."

His blue eyes were full of heat as they lifted to hers again. "Let's find a bed. Now."

He plucked her off the table and set her on her feet while she clutched enough of her gown to keep it from falling off. Holding her hand, Miles tugged her through the bar area and past an office to a bedroom with high wooden ceilings and lots of windows. She guessed it wasn't the master suite in a home like this, given its modest size and single closet, yet she glimpsed a pair of boots near the door and toiletries on the granite vanity of the attached bath.

Miles closed the door behind her, toed off his shoes, then made quick work of his shirt, tossing it on a built-in window seat.

She was about to ask why he was staying in a guest

bedroom of his own home when he came toward her. The words dried up on her tongue at the sight of his purposeful stride.

When he reached her, he took the bodice she was clutching and let it fall to the floor, the heavy liquid silver pooling at her feet. Cool air touched her skin now that she was almost naked except for an ice-blue silk thong.

She didn't have long to feel the chill, however, as Miles pressed her body to his. Her breasts molded to his hard chest as his body radiated heat. He took his time wrapping her hair around his hand, lifting the heavy mass off her shoulders and watching it spill down his forearm.

"My hands, my body, my mouth." He parroted the words back to her, the rough sound of his voice letting her know how they'd affected him. "I pick all three."

Oh.

He kissed her throat and the crook behind her ear, then trailed his lips down to her shoulder, letting her feel his tongue and his teeth until she twined her limbs around him, wanting to be closer. He drew her with him to the bed, his hands tracing light touches up her arms, down her sides, under her breasts. When her calf bumped into the mattress, she dropped onto the gray duvet, pulling him down with her into the thick, downy embrace. She wanted to feel the weight of him against her, but he sat beside her on the edge of the bed instead, leaning down to unfasten the strap of her sequined sandal with methodical care.

A shiver went through her that had nothing to do with room temperature. When the first shoe fell away, he slid a warm palm down her other leg, lifting it to undo the tiny buckle on her other ankle. Once that shoe dropped onto the floor, he skimmed his hand back up her leg, circling a light touch behind her knee, then following the line of muscle in her thigh. Higher.

Higher.

She was on fire, desperate for more, by the time he pressed her back onto the bed. He followed her down, combing his fingers through her dark hair and kissing her neck, bracketing her body between his elbows where he propped himself over her. He kissed her jaw and down her neck, tracing a touch down the center of her breastbone, slowing but not stopping as he tracked lower. Lower.

Her pulse rushed as she inhaled sharply. She noticed he was breathing faster, too, his eyes watching the movement of his fingers as he reached the low waist of the ice-blue silk thong that still clung to her hips. As he slipped his fingers beneath the fabric, the brush of his knuckles made her stomach muscles clench, tension tightening as he stroked a touch right where she needed it. His gaze returned to her face as a ripple of pleasure trembled through her. She was already so close, on edge from wondering what would happen between them. Her release hovered as she held her breath.

He must have known. She didn't know how he could tell, but he leaned down to speak into her ear.

"You don't need to hold back." That deep, suggestive voice vibrated along her skin, evaporating any restraint. "There's no limit on how many times you can come."

His fingers stroked harder, and she flew apart. She gripped his wrist, whether to push him away or keep him there, she didn't know, but he didn't let go. Expertly, he coaxed every last shudder from her while waves of pleasure rocked through her. Only when she went still, her breathing slowing a fraction, did he slide off the bed.

She would have mourned the loss, but he shoved off his pants and boxers, reminding her how much more she had to look forward to. He disappeared into the bathroom for a moment but returned a moment later in all his delectable naked glory, condom in hand. Yet even as she tried to memorize the way he looked, to take in all the ways his muscles moved together so that she'd never forget it, she experienced a moment's trepidation. Just because he'd known how to touch her in a way that had made the earth move for her didn't mean she could return the favor.

But when he joined her on the bed, handing her the condom and letting her roll it in place, the worries faded. Having him next to her, covering her with all that warm male muscle as he kneed her legs apart to make room for himself, made it impossible to think about anything but this.

Him.

The most tantalizing encounter she'd ever had with a man.

He kissed her as he eased his way inside her, moving with her as easily as if they'd done this a thousand times before. Closing her eyes, she breathed in his cedarwood scent, letting the heat build between them again, hotter and stronger this time. The connection between them felt so real to her, even though she knew it could only be passion or chemistry, or whatever that nameless X-factor was that made for amazing sex.

Still, when she opened her eyes and found his intense gaze zeroed in on her, she could have sworn he'd seen deep inside her, past all the artifice that was her whole life and right down to the woman underneath. The thought robbed her of breath, stirring a hint of panic until he kissed her again, shifting on top of her in a way that created heart-stopping friction between their bodies.

He thrust again. Once. Twice.

And she lost all her bearings, soaring mindlessly into another release. This time, she brought him with her. She could feel him going still, his shout echoing hers, their bodies utterly in sync. For long moments, all she could do was breathe, dragging in long gulps of air while her heart galloped faster.

Eventually, everything slowed down again. Her skin cooled as Miles rolled away, but he dragged a cashmere throw up from the base of the bed, covering them both. He pulled her against him, her back tucked against his chest, as he stroked her hair in the darkened room. Words failed her, and she was grateful that he didn't say anything, either. She was out of her depth tonight, but she wasn't ready to leave. The only solace she took was that he didn't seem to want her to go.

In the morning, she'd have to come clean about what she was doing here. She hoped he wouldn't hate her for sleeping with him after she'd tried spying on him. Chances seemed slim that he'd understand the truth—that the two things were entirely unrelated.

Who was she kidding? He'd never believe that.

Guilt and worry tightened in her belly.

"Whatever you're thinking about, stop," came Miles's advice in her ear, a warm reassurance she didn't deserve. "Just enjoy it while we can."

How had he known? Maybe he'd felt her tense. Either

way, she didn't feel compelled to wreck what they'd just shared, so she let out a long breath and tucked closer to his warmth.

The morning—and all the consequences of her decision to stay—would come soon enough.

Miles awoke twice in the night.

The first time, he'd reached for the woman in his bed on instinct, losing himself in her all over again. She'd been right there with him, touching him with the urgency of someone who didn't want to waste a second of this time together, as if she knew as well as he did that it wouldn't be repeated. The knowledge gave every kiss, every sigh a desperate need that only heightened how damned good it all felt.

The second time he'd opened his eyes, he'd felt her stirring beside him, her head tipping to his chest as if she belonged there. For some reason, that trust she would have never given him while awake seemed as much a gift as her body had been.

Another moment that he wouldn't be able to repeat.

So when daylight crept over the bed, he couldn't pretend that he felt no regrets. Not about what they'd shared, because Chiara cast a long shadow over every other woman he'd ever been with. No, he didn't regret what had happened. Only that the night was a memory now.

And that's what it had to remain.

He guessed Chiara knew as much, since the pillow next to his was empty. He heard the shower running and left some clothes for her in the dressing room outside the bathroom. The T-shirt and sweats with a drawstring would be huge on her, but a better alternative than her evening gown.

He grabbed cargoes and a Henley for himself before retreating to the pool to swim some laps and hit the shower there. Afterward he retreated to the kitchen to work on breakfast, making good use of the fresh tortillas from a local source his brother, Weston, had mentioned to him. While he and Wes had never been close, they shared a love for the food from growing up with their *abuela* Rosa's incredible cooking on Rivera Ranch. Miles scrambled eggs and browned the sausage, then chopped tomatoes and avocadoes. By the time Chiara appeared in the kitchen to help herself to coffee, the breakfast enchiladas were ready.

"Morning." She pulled down a mug from a hook over the coffee bar and set it on the granite. "I didn't mean to wake you."

At first look, there was something soft and vulnerable about her in the clothes he'd left for her. She'd rolled up the gray sweats to keep them from dragging on the floor; he saw she was wearing his gym socks. The dark blue T-shirt gaped around her shoulders, but she'd tucked a corner of the hem into the cinched waist of the sweats. Memories of their night together blindsided him, the need to pull her to him rising up again as inevitably as high tide.

Then she met his gaze, and any illusion of her vulnerability vanished. Her green eyes reflected a defensiveness that went beyond normal morning-after wariness. She appeared ready to sprint out of there at the first opportunity. Had her spying mission been a success the night before, so that she could afford to walk away from him now? He hadn't been aware that at least a part of him—and yeah, he knew which part—had hoped she'd stick around if she wanted to learn more about Mesa Falls.

Damn it. He needed to be smarter about this if he wanted to remain a step ahead of her.

"You didn't wake me," he finally replied as he grappled with how to put her at ease long enough to have a conversation about where things stood between them. "At home, I'm usually up before now." Gesturing toward the coffee station, he took the skillet off the burner. "Grab your cup and join me for breakfast."

He carried the dishes over to their place settings at the table for eight. The table felt big for two people, but he arranged things so he'd be sitting diagonally from her and could easily gauge her reaction to what he had to say.

Chiara bypassed the single-cup maker for the espresso machine, brewing a double shot. When she finished, she carried her mug over and lowered herself into one of the chairs.

"You didn't have to go to all this trouble." She held herself straight in the chair, her posture as tense as her voice.

What he couldn't figure out was why she was so nervous. Whatever preyed on her mind seemed weightier than next-day second thoughts. Was she thinking about whatever information she'd gleaned from his study during the party?

"It was no trouble." He lifted the top of the skillet to serve her. "Can I interest you in any?" At her hesitation, he continued, "I won't be offended either way."

Her eyes darted to his before she picked up her fork and slid an enchilada onto her plate. "It smells really good. Thank you."

He served himself afterward and dug in, debating how best to convince her to spend more time in Montana. He didn't want to leverage what happened between them unfairly—or twist her arm into keeping that date she'd promised him—but questions remained about what she was doing in his office the night before. If she knew about Zach, he needed to know how and why.

While he puzzled that out, however, Chiara set her fork down after a few bites.

"Miles, I can't in good conscience eat your food—which is delicious, by the way—when I haven't been honest with you." She blurted the words as if they'd been on the tip of her tongue for hours.

He slowly set aside his fork, wondering what she meant. Would she confess what she'd been doing in his office last night? Something else?

"I'm listening." He took in her ramrod-straight posture, the way she flicked a red-painted fingernail along the handle of the mug.

A breath whooshed from her lungs before she spoke again.

"I'm an old friend of Zach Eldridge's." The name of his dead friend on her lips sent a chill through him. "I came here last night to learn the truth about what happened to him."

Four

Miles didn't remember standing up from the table, but he must have after Chiara's startling announcement. Because the next thing he knew, he was staring out the kitchen window into a side yard and the Bitterroot River meandering in a bed of slushy ice. He felt ice on the inside, too, since numbing his feelings about his dead friend had always been a hell of a lot easier than letting them burn away inside him.

Snow blanketed the property, coating everything in white. Spring might be around the corner, but western Montana didn't know it today. Staring at the unbroken field of white helped him collect his thoughts enough to face her again.

"You knew Zach?" It had never crossed his mind that she could have had a personal relationship with Zach even though he'd seen the search history on his computer. He'd assumed she'd heard an old rumor. If she'd known him, wouldn't she have come forward before now?

Zachary Eldridge had never talked about his life before his stint in a foster home near Dowdon School on the edge of the Ventana Wilderness in central California where the ranch owners had met. The way Zach had avoided the topic had broadcast all too clearly the subject was off-limits, and Miles had respected that. So he didn't think Chiara could have known him from that time. And he'd never heard rumors of her being in the foster system, making it doubtful she'd met him that way. Zach had been on a scholarship at their all-boys boarding school, a place she obviously hadn't attended.

"Dowdon School did events with Brookfield Academy." She clutched the espresso cup tighter, her gaze sliding toward the river-stone fireplace in the front room, though her expression had the blankness of someone seeing another place and time. Miles was familiar with the prestigious all-girls institution in close proximity to his alma mater. "I met Zach through the art program the summer before my sophomore year."

"You were at Brookfield?" Miles moved back toward the table, struggling to focus on the conversation—on her—no matter how much it hurt to remember the most painful time of his life. And yes, he was drawn to the sound of her voice and a desire to know her better.

He dropped back into his seat, needing to figure out how much she knew about Zach's death and the real motives behind her being in Mesa Falls all these years later.

"Briefly." She nodded her acknowledgment, her green eyes refocusing on him as he returned to the table. "I only attended for two years before my father lost everything in a bad investment and I had to leave Brookfield to go to public school."

Miles wondered why he hadn't heard of her connection to Zach or even to Brookfield. While he'd never sought out information about her, he would have thought her school affiliation would have been noted by the ranch's PR department when she was invited to Mesa Falls events.

Questions raced through his mind. How close had she been to Zach? Close enough to understand his mindset the weekend he'd died?

A hollow ache formed in his chest.

"How well did you know him?" He regretted the demanding sound of the question as soon as it left his lips, unsure how it would come across. "That is, I'm interested how you could make friends during a summer program. The school staff was strict about prohibiting visits between campuses."

Her lips quirked unexpectedly, her eyes lifting to meet his. "Zach wasn't afraid to bend rules when it suited him, though, was he?"

Miles couldn't help a short bark of laughter as the truth of that statement hit home. "'Rules are for people with conventional minds,' he once told me."

Chiara sat back in her chair, some of her rigid tension loosening as warmth and fondness lit her gaze. "He painted over an entire project once, just an hour before a showing, even though I was a wreck about him ruining the beautiful painting he'd done. He just kept slapping oils on the canvas, explaining that an uncommon life demanded an uncommon approach, and that he had all-new inspiration for his work."

The shared reminiscence brought Zach to life in full

color for a moment, an experience Miles hadn't had in a long time. The action—and the words—were so completely in keeping with how he remembered his friend.

"He was a bright light," Miles agreed, remembering how often they'd looked up to his fearlessness and, later, stood beside him whenever he got into scrapes with schoolmates who weren't ready for the Zach Eldridges of the world.

"I never met anyone like him," Chiara continued, turning her mug in a slow circle on the table. "Not before, and not since." Halting the distracted movement, she took a sip from her cup before continuing. "I knew him well enough to have a crush on him, to the point that I thought I loved him. And maybe I did. Youthful romances can have a profound impact on us."

Miles searched her face, wondering if Chiara had been aware of Zach's sexual orientation; he'd come out to his friends the summer before sophomore year. Had that been why things hadn't worked out between them?

But another thought quickly crowded that one out. A long-buried memory from the aftermath of that dark time in Miles's life.

"There was a girl who came to Dowdon after Zach's death. Around Christmastime." He remembered her telling Miles the same story. She loved Zach and needed the truth about what had happened to him. But Miles had been in the depths of his own grief, shell-shocked and still in denial about the cliff-jumping accident that had killed his friend.

Chiara studied him now, the long pause drawing his awareness to a clock ticking somewhere in the house.

"So you remember me?" she asked, her words jarring him.

He looked at her face more closely as slow recognition dawned. He couldn't have stopped the soft oath he breathed before he spoke again.

"That was you?"

Chiara watched the subtle play of emotions over Miles's face before he reined them in, regretting the way she'd handled things even more than when she'd first awoken.

But she couldn't back down on her mission. She would have answers about Zach's death.

"Yes." Her stomach clenched at the memory of sneaking onto the Dowdon campus that winter to question Zach's friends. "I spoke to you and to Gage Striker fourteen years ago, but both of you were clearly upset. Gage was openly hostile. You seemed…detached."

"That girl couldn't have been you." Miles's jaw flexed, his broad shoulders tensing as he straightened in his chair. "I would have remembered the name."

Defensiveness flared at the hard look in his blue eyes.

"I was born Kara Marsh, but it was too common for Instagram, so I made up Chiara Campagna when I launched my career." Perhaps it made her sound like she'd hidden something from him, but her brand had taken off years ago, and she no longer thought of herself as Kara. Her family certainly hadn't cared, taking more of an interest in her now that she was famous with a big bank account than they ever had when she was under their roof saving her babysitting money to pay for her own clothes. "I use the name everywhere for consistency's sake. While I don't try to conceal my identity, I also don't promote it."

"Yet you kissed me. Spent the night."

Her gaze lingered on the black Henley he was wearing with a pair of dark brown cargo pants, the fitted shirt calling to mind the feel of his body under her hands.

"That wasn't supposed to happen," she admitted, guilt pinching harder at the accusation in his voice. "What took place between us was completely unexpected."

The defense sounded weak even to her ears. But he'd been there. He had to know how the passion had come out of nowhere, a force of nature.

The furrow in his brow deepened. "So you'll admit you were in my study last night, looking up Zach's name on my computer."

A chill crept through her. "You knew?" She bristled at the realization. "Yet you kissed me. Invited me to spend the night."

She parroted his words, reminding him he'd played a role in their charged encounter.

"You didn't clear the search history. A page of files with Zach's name on them was still open." He didn't address the fact that he'd slept with her anyway.

Because it hadn't mattered to him? Because *she* didn't matter? She stuffed down the hurt she had no business feeling, shoving aside the memories of how good things had been between them. She'd known even then that it couldn't last. She'd told herself as much when Miles had wrested a promise from her that he could have a date afterward. He wouldn't hold her to that now.

Steeling herself, she returned to her agenda. Her real priority.

"Then you know I'm desperate for answers." Regret burned right through all the steeliness. "I'm sorry I invaded your privacy. That was a mistake. But I've been digging for clues about Zach's death for fourteen years. Now that the media spotlight has turned to the Mesa Falls owners thanks to your connection to Alonzo Salazar, I saw a chance to finally learn the truth."

"By using your invitation into my home to spy on me," he clarified.

"Why wasn't Zach's death in the papers? Why didn't the school acknowledge it?" She'd searched for years. His death notice had been a line item weeks after the fact, with nothing about the person he'd been or how he'd died.

"You say you were friends with him, but I only have your word on that." Miles watched her suspiciously. Judging her? She wondered what had happened to the man she'd been with the night before. The lover who'd been so generous. This cold stranger bore him no resemblance. "How do I know this isn't another attempt by the media to unearth a story?"

"Who else even knows about him but me?" she asked, affronted. Indignant. "There was never a public outcry about his death. No demand for answers from the media. Maybe because he was just some foster kid that—"

Her throat was suddenly burning and so were her eyes, the old emotions coming back to surprise her with their force while Miles studied her from across the breakfast table. With an effort, she regained control of herself and backed her chair away from the table.

"I'd better go," she murmured, embarrassed for the ill-timed display of feelings. But damn it, Zach had deserved a better send-off. She'd never even known where to attend a service for him, because as far as she'd known, there hadn't been one.

That broke her heart.

Miles rose with her, covering her hand briefly with his.

"It was a simple question. I meant no offense." He shifted his hand away, but the warmth remained where his fingers had been. "We've safeguarded our friend's memory for a long time, and I won't relax my protection of him now. Not for anyone."

She tilted her chin at him, trying her damnedest to see some hint of warmth in that chilly facade.

"What memory?" she pressed. "He vanished without a trace. Without an opportunity for his friends to mourn him."

"His friends *did* mourn him. They still do." His expression was fierce. "We won't allow his name to be drawn into the public spectacle that Alonzo Salazar brought to the ranch because of that damned tell-all book."

"I would never do that to Zach." She hugged her arms around herself, recalling too late that she wore Miles's clothes. Her fingers rested on the cotton of his sweats. The scent of him. As if she wasn't feeling vulnerable already. "As for his friends mourning him, you weren't the only ones. There were a lot of other people who cared about Zach. People who never got to say goodbye."

For a long minute, they regarded each other warily in the quiet room, the scents of their forgotten breakfast still savory even though no food could possibly tempt her. Her stomach was in knots.

But even now, in the aftermath of the unhappy exchange, awareness of him lingered. Warmth prickled along her skin as they stood facing each other in silent challenge, reminding her of the heat that had propelled her into his arms the night before.

The chime of her cell phone intruded on the charged moment, a welcome distraction from whatever it was that kept pulling her toward a man who was determined to keep his secrets. He was as quick to seize on the reprieve from their exchange as she was. He turned toward the table to begin clearing away their half-finished meal.

She retrieved the device from where it lay on the table, checking the text while she carried her coffee cup to the sink. The message was from her assistant, Jules.

All your platforms hacked. On phone with IG now. Sent help notices to the rest. Some joker who didn't like a post? I'm on it, but knew you'd want heads-up.

She didn't realize she'd gone still until she heard Miles asking, "What's wrong?"

Her brain couldn't quite compute what was wrong. The timing of the attack on all her platforms at once seemed strange. Suddenly feeling a little shaky, she dropped into the closest seat, a bar stool at the island.

"Someone hijacked my social media accounts," she whispered, stunned and not buying that it was the work of a disgruntled commenter. "All of the platforms at once, which seems really unusual."

"Does that happen often?" Miles jammed the food in the huge refrigerator, working quickly to clean up.

"It's never happened before." She gulped back a sick

feeling, tapping the tab for Instagram on her phone to see for herself. "I have friends who have had one platform hijacked here or there, but not all at once."

Miles dumped the remaining dishes in the sink and toweled off his hands before tossing the dishcloth aside. He rejoined her, gripping the back of her chair. "That feels like someone has an ax to grind."

The warmth of his nearness was a distraction she couldn't afford. She scooted forward in her seat.

"Someone with enough tech savvy to take over all my properties at once." She checked one profile after another, finding the photos changed, but still of her.

Less flattering images. Older images. But they weren't anything to be embarrassed about. She'd had friends whose profiles were hacked and replaced with digitally altered pictures that were highly compromising.

"Any idea who'd do something like that?" Miles asked, the concern in his voice replacing some of the animosity that had been there before. "Any enemies?"

"I can't think of anyone." She'd had her fair share of trolls on her account, but they tended to stir up trouble with other commenters as opposed to targeting her.

Her phone chimed again. She swiped the screen in a hurry, hopeful Jules had resolved the problem. But the text in her inbox was from a private number. Maybe one of the social media platforms' customer service used that kind of anonymous messaging?

She clicked open the text.

Today's takeover is a warning. Stay out of Zach's business or your accounts will be seriously compromised.

Her grip on the phone tightened. She blinked twice as the threat chilled her inside and out.

"Are you okay?" Miles touched her shoulder, the warmth of his fingers anchoring her as fear trickled through her.

"I've got to go." Shaky with the newfound realization that someone was keeping close tabs on her, she wondered who else could possibly know she was investigating Zach's death besides Miles.

She slid off the bar stool to her feet, needing to get back to her laptop and her assistant to figure out the extent of her cybersecurity problem. This felt like someone was watching her. Or tracking her online activity.

"You're pale as the snow." Miles steadied her by the elbow when she wobbled unsteadily. "What's going on?"

She didn't want to share what she'd just read with him when he mistrusted her. When she mistrusted him. But his touch overrode everything else, anchoring her in spite of the hollow feeling inside.

"Look." She handed him her phone, unable to articulate all the facets of the new worries wriggling to life. "I just received this." Pausing until he'd had time to absorb the news, she continued, "Who else even knows about Zach, let alone what I came here for?"

His jaw flexed as he stared at the screen, stubble giving his face a texture she remembered well from when he'd kissed her during the night. She fisted her hands in the pockets of the sweatpants to keep herself from doing something foolish, like running an exploratory finger along his chin.

"I didn't think anyone else remembered him outside of my partners and me." He laid her phone on the kitchen island behind her. "As for who else knows why you came here, I can't answer that, as I only found out moments ago."

She hesitated. "You saw my attempt to check your computer last night. So you knew then that I had an interest. Did you share that information with anyone?"

A scowl darkened his expression.

"I texted Gage Striker about an hour into the party to ask how well he knew you, since I thought you'd been going through my files."

She shouldn't be surprised that Miles had as much reason to suspect her of hiding something as she'd had to suspect him. She'd recognized that they'd been circling one another warily the previous night before the heat between them burned everything else away. If anything, maybe it soothed her grated nerves just a little to know he hadn't been any more able to resist the temptation than she had.

"And Gage could have told any one of your other partners. They, in turn, could have confided in friends or significant others." Reaching back to the counter, she retrieved the cell and shoved it in the pocket of Miles's sweats. "So word could have spread to quite a few people by this morning."

"In theory," he acknowledged, though his voice held a begrudging tone. "But Gage didn't even put in an appearance at the party. So he wouldn't have been around anyone else to share the news, and I'm guessing he had something big going on in his personal life that kept him from attending."

"Maybe he needed to hire someone to hack all my accounts." She couldn't rule it out, despite Miles's scoff. Anger ramped up inside her along with a hint of mistrust. "But for now, I need to return to my hotel and do everything I can to protect my brand."

"Wait." He stepped in front of her. Not too close, but definitely in her path.

Her pulse quickened at his nearness. Her gaze dipped to the way the fitted shirt with the Rivera Ranch logo skimmed his broad shoulders and arms. Her mouth dried up.

Maybe he felt the same jolt that she did, because he looked away from her, spearing a hand through his hair.

"Let me drive you back," he told her finally. "Someone might be watching you. And until you know what you're dealing with, you should take extra precautions for your safety."

The thought of spending more time alone with this man was too tempting. Which was why she absolutely had to decline. Things were confused enough between them already.

"I'll be fine. My assistant will send a car and extra security." She withdrew her phone again—a good enough excuse to take her eyes off him—and sent the request. "I just need to get my dress and I'll be on my way."

Still Miles didn't move.

"Where are you staying?" he pressed. "You can't ghost me. You owe me a date."

"I think we both know that's not a good idea in light of how much things have gone awry between us." She couldn't believe he'd even brought it up. But perhaps he only wanted to use that time with her as a way to keep tabs on her while she sought the information he was determined to keep private.

"I still want to see you." He didn't explain why. "Where will you be?"

"I've been in a local hotel, but today I've got a flight to Tahoe to spend time with Astrid. I haven't seen her since she had the baby."

Jonah and Astrid had a house on the lake near a casino resort owned by Desmond Pierce, another Mesa Falls partner. Spending time with Astrid would be a way to keep an eye on two of the ranch owners while removing herself from the temptation that Miles presented just by being in the same town.

Even now, looking into Miles's blue eyes, she couldn't help recalling the ways he'd kissed and touched her. Made her fly apart in his arms.

For now, she needed to regroup. Protect her business until she figured out her next move in the search for answers about Zach.

"I don't suppose it's a coincidence that half of the Mesa Falls partners live around Tahoe," Miles observed drily. "Maybe I should go with you. No doubt we'll be convening soon to figure out who could be threatening you. Zach's legacy is important to us."

She shrugged, averting her eyes because she knew they'd betray her desire for him. "You can look into it your way. I'll keep looking into it mine. But I don't think it's a good idea for us to spend more time alone together after what happened last night."

Just talking about it sent a small, pleasurable shiver up her spine. She had to hold herself very still to hide it. The least movement from him and she would cave to temptation.

"I disagree. And if we both want answers, maybe we should be working together instead of apart." His voice gentled, taking on that low rasp that had slid right past her defenses last night. "You wouldn't have checked my computer files if you didn't think I had information that could help you. Why not go straight to the source?"

For a moment, the idea of spending another day with him—another night—rolled over her like a seductive wave. But then she forced herself to shake it off.

"If you wanted to share information with me, you could tell me now." She put it out there like a dare, knowing he wouldn't spill any secrets.

He and his friends had never revealed anything about Zach. Not then. And not now. Because Miles was silent. Watchful. Wary.

Her phone chimed again, and she didn't need to check it to know her ride was out front.

"In that case, I'd better be going." She turned on her heel. "Maybe I'll see you in Tahoe."

"Chiara." He called her name before she reached the stairs leading back to the bedroom suite.

Gripping the wood rail in a white-knuckled grip, she looked over her shoulder at him.

"Be careful. We don't know who you're dealing with, but it could be someone dangerous."

The reminder brought the anxiety from earlier churning back. She tightened her hold on the rail to keep from swaying.

"I'll be careful," she conceded before stiffening her spine with resolve. "But I'm not backing down."

Five

Miles began making phone calls as soon as Chiara left. He poured himself a drink and paced circles around the indoor pool, leaving voice messages for Gage and Jonah. Then he tapped the contact button for Desmond Pierce, his friend who owned the casino resort on Lake Tahoe.

For fourteen years, the friends who'd been with Zach Eldridge when he died had kept the circumstances a secret. At first, they'd done so because they were in shock and grieving. Later, they'd remained silent to protect his memory, as a way to honor him in death even though they'd been unable to save him.

But if someone outside the six friends who owned Mesa Falls knew about Zach—about the circumstances that had pushed him over the edge that fateful day—then his secrets weren't safe any longer. They needed to figure out their next steps.

A voice on the other end of the phone pulled him from his thoughts, and he paused his pacing around the pool to listen.

"Hey, Miles," Desmond answered smoothly, the slot machine chirps and muted conversation of the casino floor sounding in the background. "What's up?"

"Problems." As succinctly as possible, he summarized the situation with Chiara and the threat against her if she kept looking for answers about Zach's death.

When Miles was done, Desmond let out a low whistle. The sounds of the casino in the background had faded, meaning he must have sought privacy for the conversation.

"Who else knows about Zach but us?" Desmond asked. "Moreover, who the hell would have known Chiara was asking questions within hours of her showing up at Mesa Falls?"

Miles stared out the glass walls around the enclosed pool, watching the snow fall as he let the question hang there for a moment. He was certain Desmond must have come to the same conclusion as him.

"You know it points to one of us," Miles answered, rattling the last of the ice in his drink. "I texted Gage last night when I thought she was snooping in my office."

He didn't want to think Gage would go to the length of hacking her accounts to protect their secrets, but every one of the partners had his own reasons for not wanting the truth to come to light. Gage, in particular, bore a weight of guilt because his influential politician father had kept the truth of the accident out of the media. Nigel Striker had made a substantial grant to the Dowdon School to ensure the incident was handled the way he chose.

Quietly. Without any reference to Zach's connection to the school. Which explained why Chiara hadn't been able to learn anything about it.

Desmond cleared his throat. "Gage could have shared that information with any one of us."

"I can't believe we're even discussing the possibility of a leak within our group." The idea made everything inside him protest. They'd spent fourteen years trying to protect the truth.

Who would go rogue now and break that trust?

"Just because we're discussing it doesn't prove anything," Desmond pointed out reasonably. "Chiara could have confided her intentions to someone else. Or someone could have tracked her searches online."

"Right. But we need to meet. And this time, no videoconferencing." He remembered the way the last couple of meetings had gone among the partners—once with only four of them showing up in person, and another time with half of them participating remotely. "We need all six of us in the same room."

"You really think it's one of us?" Desmond asked. Despite Desmond's normally controlled facade, Miles could hear the surprise in his friend's tone.

"I'm not sure. But if it's not, we can rule it out faster if we're together in the same room. If one of us is lying, we'll know." Miles might not have spent much time in person with his school friends in the last fourteen years, but their bond ran deep.

They'd all agreed to run the ranch together in the hope of honoring Zach's life. Zach had loved the outdoors and the Ventana Wilderness close to their school.

He would have appreciated Mesa Falls's green ranching mission to protect the environment and help native species flourish.

"Do you need help coordinating it?" Desmond asked, the sounds of the casino again intruding from his end of the call.

"No. I think we should meet in Tahoe this time. But I wanted to warn you that Chiara is on her way there even now. She says she's going to see Astrid, but I have the feeling she'll be questioning Jonah, too. She might even show up at your office." Miles couldn't forget the look in her eyes when she'd said she wouldn't back down from her search for answers about Zach.

There'd been a gravity that hinted at the strong stuff she was made of. He understood that kind of commitment. He felt it for Rivera Ranch, the family property he'd inherited and would protect at any cost.

Of course, he felt that way about Zach and Mesa Falls, too. Unfortunately, their strong loyalties to the same person were bound to keep putting them at odds. Unless they worked together. The idea made him uneasy. But did he really have a choice?

The thought of seeing her again—even though she'd only walked out his door an hour ago—sent anticipation shooting through him. He'd never forget the night they'd shared.

"I'll keep an eye out for her," Desmond assured him. "Thanks for the heads-up."

Miles disconnected the call and pocketed his phone. He would hand off the task of scheduling the owners' meeting to his assistant, since coordinating times could be a logistical nightmare. But no matter how busy they were, this had to take priority.

Things were coming to a head for Mesa Falls. And Zach.

And no matter how much Miles didn't trust Chiara Campagna, he was worried for her safety with someone threatening her. Which would have been reason enough for him to fly to Tahoe at the first opportunity. But he also couldn't deny he wanted to see her again.

She'd promised him a date. And he would hold her to her word.

That night, in her rented villa overlooking Lake Tahoe, Chiara tucked her feet underneath her in the window seat as she opened her tablet. The nine-bedroom home and guesthouse were situated next door to Desmond Pierce's casino resort, assuring her easy access to him. The separate guesthouse allowed her to have her assistant and photo team members nearby while giving all of them enough space. Astrid and Jonah lived just a few miles away, and Chiara would see them as soon as she could. She'd already made plans to meet Astrid for a spin class in the morning.

This was the first moment she'd had to herself all day. First there'd been the morning with Miles, then the flight to Truckee and drive to Tahoe Vista, with most of the travel time spent on efforts to stabilize her social media platforms.

She should probably be researching cybersecurity experts to ensure her social media properties were more secure in the future, even though she'd gotten all of her platforms corrected by dinnertime. It only made good business sense to protect her online presence. But she'd spent so many years making the right decisions for her public image, relentlessly driving her empire to keep growing that she couldn't devote one more minute to work today. Didn't she deserve a few hours to herself now and then? To be a woman instead of a brand?

So instead of working, she thumbed the remote button to turn on the gas fireplace and dimmed the spotlights in the exposed trusswork of the cathedral ceiling. Settling back against the yellow cushions of the window seat, Chiara returned her attention to the tablet and found herself scrolling through a web search about Miles Rivera.

She'd like to think it was all part of her effort to find out more about Zach. Maybe if she could piece together clues from the lives of his friends during the year of Zach's death, she would find something she'd overlooked. But as she swiped through images of Miles at the historic Rivera Ranch property in the Red Clover Valley of the Sierra Nevada foothills, pausing on a few of him at galas in Mesa Falls and at the casino on Lake Tahoe, she realized she had ulterior motives. Even on the screen he took her breath away.

He looked as at home in his jeans and boots as he did in black tie, and not just because he was a supremely attractive man. There was a comfort in his own skin, a certainty of his place in the world that Chiara envied. She'd been born to privilege as the daughter of wealthy parents, but she'd always been keenly aware she didn't belong. Her mother had never known what to do with her; she'd been awkward and gangly until she grew into her looks. As a girl, she'd been antisocial, preferring books to people. She'd lacked charm and social graces, a failure that confirmed her mother's opinion of her as a hopeless child. So she'd been packed off to boarding school on the opposite coast, where she'd retreated into her art until she met Zach, her lone friend.

Then Zach died, and her parents lost their fortune.

Chiara transferred to public school and made even fewer friends there than she had at Brookfield. She fit in nowhere until she founded her fictional world online. Her Instagram account had started as a way to take photos of beautiful things. That other people liked her view of the world had shocked her, but eventually she'd come to see that she was good at being social on the other side of a keyboard. By the time she gained real traction and popularity, her awkwardness in person didn't matter anymore. Her followers liked her work, so they didn't care if she said very little at public events. Fans seemed to equate her reticence with the aloofness they expected in a star. But inside, Chiara felt like a fraud, wrestling with impostor syndrome that she'd somehow forged an extravagant, envied life she didn't really deserve.

Her finger hovered over an image of Miles with an arm slung around his friend Alec Jacobsen and another around Desmond Pierce. It was an old photo, similar to the one she'd seen in Miles's office at his house. She thought it was taken around the time the six friends had bought Mesa Falls. She'd known even before she'd restarted her search for answers that the men who'd bought the ranch had been Zach's closest friends at Dowdon. One of them knew something. Possibly all of them. What reason would they have to hide the circumstances of his death?

She'd contacted his foster home afterward, and years later, she'd visited the department of social services for information about Zach. The state hadn't been under any legal obligation to release details of his death other than to say it was accidental and that issues of neglect in foster care hadn't been a concern. She'd had no luck tracking down his birth parents. But Miles knew something, or else he wouldn't have been so emphatic about protecting Zach's privacy.

Staring into Miles's eyes in the photograph didn't yield any answers. Just twenty-four hours ago, she'd been convinced he was her enemy in her search. Sleeping with Miles had shown her a different side of him. And reminiscing with him about Zach for those few moments over breakfast had reinforced the idea that he'd shared a powerful bond with their shared friend. What reason did Miles have to push her away?

When she found herself tracing the angles of his face on the tablet screen, Chiara closed the page in a hurry. She couldn't afford the tenderness of feeling that had crept up on her with regard to Miles Rivera. It clouded her mission. Distorted her perspective when she needed to be clearheaded.

Tomorrow, she'd find a way to talk to Desmond Pierce. Then she'd see if Alec Jacobsen was in town. If she kept pushing, someone would divulge something. Even if they didn't mean to.

Turning her gaze to the moon rising over the lake through the window, she squinted, trying to see beyond her reflection in the glass. She needed to learn something before her anonymous blackmailer discovered she was still asking questions. Because while she was prepared to risk everything—the fame, the following, the income that came from it—to find out the truth of Zach's death, she couldn't help hoping Miles didn't have anything to do with it.

* * *

"Dig deep for the next hill!" The spin class instructor kept up her running stream of motivational commentary from a stationary bike at the center of the casino resort's fitness studio. "If you want the reward, you've got to put in the work!"

Chiara hated exercise class in general, and early-morning ones even more, but her friend Astrid had insisted the spin class was the best one her gym offered. So Chiara had pulled herself out of bed at the crack of dawn for the last two mornings. She'd dragged Jules with her, and Astrid met them there to work out in a room that looked more like a dance club than a gym. With neon and black lights, the atmosphere was high energy and the hip-hop music intense. Sweating out her restlessness wasn't fun, but it felt like a way to excise some of the intense emotions being with Miles had stirred up.

"I can't do another hill," Astrid huffed from the cycle to Chiara's right, her blond braid sliding over her shoulder as she turned to talk. A former model from Finland, Astrid had happily traded in her magazine covers for making organic baby food since becoming a mother shortly before Christmas. "You know I love Katja, but being pregnant left me with no muscle tone."

"I would have chosen the yoga class," Chiara managed as she gulped air, her hamstrings burning and her butt numb from the uncomfortable seat. "So I blame this hell on you."

"I would be *sleeping*." Jules leaned over her handlebars from the bike on Chiara's left, her pink tank top clinging to her sweaty shoulders. "So I blame both of you."

"Please," Chiara scoffed, running a skeptical eye over Jules's toned legs. "You were a competitive volleyball player. I've seen you play for hours."

Chiara's family had lived next door to Jules's once upon a time, and the Santors were more like family to her than her own had ever been. When her business had taken off, she'd made it her mission to employ as many of the family members as she could, enjoying the pleasure of having people she genuinely liked close to her. Even now, back in Los Angeles, Jules's mom was in charge of Chiara's house.

"Spiking balls and attacking the net do not require this level of cardio," Jules grumbled, although she dutifully kicked up her speed at their instructor's shouted command to "go hard."

Chiara felt light-headed from the exercise, skipping breakfast, and the swirl of flashing lights as they pedaled.

"We owe ourselves lunch out at least, don't we?" Astrid pleaded, letting go of her handlebars long enough to take a drink from her water bottle. "Jonah got us a sitter tomorrow for the first time since I had Katja, so I've got a couple of hours free."

"This is the first time?" Chiara asked, smiling in spite of the sweat, the aches and the gasping for air.

Astrid had been nervous about being a mom before her daughter was born, but she'd been adorably committed to every aspect of parenting. Chiara couldn't help but compare her friend's efforts with her own mother's role in her life. Kristina Marsh had handed her daughter off to nannies whenever possible, which might not have been a problem if there'd been a good one in the mix. But she tended to hire the cheapest possible household help in order to add to her budget for things like clothes and jewelry.

"I hate leaving her with anyone but Jonah," Astrid admitted, slowing her pedaling in spite of their coach's motivational exhortation to "grind it out."

"But I think it's important to have someone trained in Katja's routine in case something comes up and I need help in a hurry."

"Definitely." Chiara wasn't about to let her friend hover around the babysitter when she could get her out of the house for a little while. "Plus you deserve a break. It's been two months."

"That's what Jonah says." Astrid's soft smile at the thought of her husband gave Chiara an unexpected pang in her chest.

She hadn't realized until that moment how much she envied Astrid's rock-solid relationship with a man she loved and trusted. Chiara hadn't even given a second thought to her single status in years, content to pursue her work instead of romance when she had difficulty trusting people anyhow. And for good reason. Her family was so good at keeping secrets from her she hadn't known they'd lost everything until the headmistress at Brookfield told her they were sending her home because her tuition hadn't been paid in months.

Chiara shoved that thought from her head along with any romance envy. She cheered along with the rest of the class as the instructor blew her whistle to signal the session's end. Jules slumped over her handlebars as she recovered, clicking through the diagnostics to check her stats.

Chiara closed her eyes for a long moment to rest them from the blinking red and green lights. And, no surprise, an image of Miles Rivera appeared on the backs of her eyelids, tantalizing her with memories of their night together.

She could live to be a hundred and still not be able to account for how fast she'd ended up in his bed. The draw between them was like nothing she'd ever experienced.

Astrid's softly accented words broke into Chiara's sensual reverie.

"So where should we meet for lunch tomorrow?" The hint of Finland in Astrid's words folded "where" to sound like "vere," the lilt as attractive as every other thing about her. "Des's casino has a bunch of places."

Chiara's eyes shot open at the mention of Desmond Pierce, one of Miles's partners. She needed to question him and Astrid's husband, Jonah, too. Subtly. And, ideally, close to the same time so neither one had a chance to warn the others about Chiara's interest in the details of Zach's final days.

"The casino is perfect." Chiara slid off her cycle and picked up her towel and water bottle off the floor, locking eyes with another woman who lingered near the cycles—a pretty redhead with freckles she hadn't noticed earlier. Why did she look vaguely familiar? Distracted, she told Astrid, "Pick your favorite place and we'll meet there."

The redhead scurried away, and Chiara guessed she didn't know the woman after all.

"There's an Indo-Mexican fusion spot called Spice Pavilion. I'm addicted to the tikka tacos." Astrid checked her phone as the regular house lights came up and the spin class attendees shuffled out of the room. "Can you do one o'clock? Jonah has a meeting that starts at noon, so I can shop first and then meet you."

A meeting? Chiara's brain chased the possibilities of what that might mean while she followed Jules toward the locker room, with Astrid behind them.

"Perfect," Chiara assured her friend as they reached the lockers and retrieved their bags. "Is Jonah's meeting at the casino, too?"

"Yes. More Mesa Falls business," Astrid answered as she hefted her quilted designer bag onto one shoulder and shut the locker with her knee. "Things have been heating up for the ranch ever since that tell-all book came out."

Didn't she know it. Chiara had plenty of questions of her own about the ranch and its owners, but she'd tried not to involve Astrid in her hunt for answers since she wouldn't use a valued friendship for leverage.

But knowing that Zach's friends would be congregating at the resort tomorrow was welcome information.

"Then you can leave Jonah to his meeting and we'll gorge ourselves on tikka tacos," Chiara promised her, calling the details over her shoulder to Jules, who had a locker on the next row. "Today I'm going to finish my posts for the week, so I can clear the whole day tomorrow. Text me if you're done shopping early or if you want company."

If all the men of Mesa Falls were in town, there was a chance she'd run into one of them at the casino anyhow. Desmond Pierce had been avoiding her calls, so she hadn't even gotten a chance to meet him. But she needed to speak to all of them.

Although there was one in particular she couldn't wait to see, even though she already knew he had nothing else to say to her on the subject of Zach's death.

Miles might be keeping secrets from her. And he

might be the last man she'd ever trust with her heart because of that. But that didn't mean that she'd stopped thinking about his hands, his mouth or his body on hers for more than a few seconds at a time since she'd left Montana.

No doubt about it—she was in deep with this man, and they'd only just met.

Six

Steering his borrowed SUV around a hairpin turn, Miles pulled up to the massive lakefront villa where Chiara was staying for the week. He'd been in town for all of a few hours before seeking her out, but ever since he'd heard from Jonah that the place she'd rented was close to the casino where Miles was staying, he'd needed to see her for himself.

The property was brightly lit even though the sun had just set, the stone turrets and walkways illuminated to highlight the architectural details. Huge pine trees flanked the building, while a second stone guesthouse sat at an angle to the villa with a path linking them.

Stepping out of the casino's Land Rover that he'd commissioned for the evening, Miles hoped all the lights meant that Chiara was taking her security seriously. He'd kept an eye on her social media sites since she'd left Mesa Falls to make sure no one hacked them again, but that hadn't done nearly enough to soothe his anxiety where she was concerned. Someone was threatening her for reasons related to Zach, and that did not sit well with him. He'd messaged her earlier in the day to let her know he would be in town tonight, but she hadn't replied.

Now, walking up the stone path into the central turret that housed the front entrance, he tucked his chin into the collar of his leather jacket against the chill in the wind. He could see into one of the large windows. A fire burned in the stone hearth of a great room, but he didn't notice any movement inside.

He shot a text to Chiara to warn her he was outside, then rang the bell. No sense adding to her unease during a week that had already upset her.

An instant later, he heard a digital chime and the bolt sliding open, then the door swung wide. Chiara stood on the threshold, her long dark hair held off her face with a white cable-knit headband. She wore flannel pajama bottoms in pink-and-white plaid. A V-neck cashmere sweater grazed her hips, the pink hue matching her fuzzy socks.

She looked sweetly delicious, in fact. But his overriding thought was that she shouldn't be answering her own door while someone was watching her movements and threatening her. Fear for her safety made him brusque.

"What happened to taking extra precautions with your safety?" He didn't see anyone else in the house with her. No bodyguard. No assistant.

Tension banded his chest.

"Hello to you, too." She arched a brow at him. "And to answer your question, the door was locked, and the alarm system was activated." She stepped to one side, silently inviting him in. "I gave my head of security the evening off since I had no plans to go out."

Relieved she'd at least thought about her safety, he entered the foyer, which opened into the great room with its incredible views of the lake. He took in the vaulted ceilings and dark wood accents along the pale walls. The scent of popcorn wafted from deeper in the house, the sound of popping ongoing.

"Right. I realize the level of security you use is your own business, I've just been concerned." He noticed a throw blanket on the floor in front of the leather sofa. A nest of pillows had been piled by the fireplace, and there was a glass of red wine on the hearth. "Early night?"

"My job isn't always a party every evening, contrary to popular opinion." She hurried toward the kitchen, a huge light-filled space separated from the great room by a marble-topped island. "Have a seat. I don't want my popcorn to burn."

He followed more slowly, taking in the honey-colored floors and pale cabinets, the row of pendant lamps casting a golden glow over the island counter, where a popcorn popper quickly filled with fluffy white kernels. The excessive size and grandeur of the space reminded him they moved in very different circles. For all of his wealth, Miles spent most of his time on his ranch. His life was quiet. Solitary. Hers was public. Extravagant.

But at least for now, they were alone.

"I didn't mean to intrude on your evening." He had to admit she looked at home in her sprawling rented villa, her down-to-earth pj's and sweater a far cry from the metallic dress she'd worn to the ranch party. She seemed more approachable. "I'm in town to meet with my partners, and I wanted to make sure there have been no new incidents."

He lowered himself onto a backless counter stool, gladder than he should be to see her again. She'd been in his thoughts often enough since their night together, and not just because he'd been concerned about her safety. Her kiss, her touch, the sound of her sighs of pleasure had distracted him day and night.

"Nothing since I left your house. Can I get you a glass of wine?" she asked, turning the bottle on the counter. "It's nothing special, but it's my preferred pairing with popcorn."

Her light tone hinted she wanted to change the subject from the threat she'd received, but he was unwilling to let it go.

"No, thank you. I won't keep you long." He stood again, if only to get closer to her while she leaned a hip on the island.

The urge to pull her against him was so strong he forced himself to plant a palm on the marble countertop instead of reaching for her.

"Well, you don't need to fear for my safety. My assistant's boyfriend is also my bodyguard, and they're both staying in the guesthouse right on the property." She pointed out the window in the direction of the smaller lodge he'd seen close by. "I'm in good hands."

He'd prefer she was in *his* hands. But he ignored the need to touch her; he was just glad to hear she hadn't taken the threat lightly.

"Did you report the incident to the police?" His gaze tracked her emerald eyes before taking in her scrubbed-clean skin and high cheekbones. She smelled like orange blossoms.

"I didn't reach out to them." She frowned, folding her arms. "I was so busy that day trying to get all my social media accounts secured that I never gave it any thought."

He hated to upset her unnecessarily, but her safety was important to him. "You should let the authorities know you're being harassed. Even if they can't do anything to help, it would be good to have the episode on the record in case things escalate."

She mattered to him. Even when he knew that was problematic. She didn't trust him, and he had plenty of reason not to trust her. Yet that didn't stop him from wanting to see her again. He could tell himself all day it was because staying close to her would help him protect Zach's memory. But he wasn't that naive. The truth was far simpler. Their one night together wasn't nearly enough to satisfy his hunger for this woman.

"I'll report it tomorrow," she conceded with a nod, her dark hair shifting along her sweater. "I can head to the local station in the morning, before I have lunch with Astrid."

"Would you like me to go with you?" he offered, his hand leaving the marble counter to rest on top of hers. Briefly. Because if he touched her any longer, it would be damn near impossible to keep his head on straight. "Spending hours at the cop shop is no one's idea of fun."

A hint of a smile curved her lips. "I'll be fine," she insisted.

Refusing his offer, but not moving her fingers out from under his. He shifted fractionally closer.

Her head came up, her gaze wary. Still, he thought there might have been a flash of hot awareness in those beautiful eyes.

"What about the date you promised me?" He tipped up her chin to better see her face, read her expression.

She sucked in a quick breath. Then, as if to hide the reaction, she bit her lip.

He imagined the soft nip of those white teeth on his own flesh, a phantom touch.

"Name the day," he coaxed her as the moment drew out, the desire to taste her getting stronger with each passing breath.

"I told you that it's a bad idea for us to spend more time together," she said finally, not sounding the least bit sure of herself. "Considering how things spiraled out of control after the party at your house."

He skimmed a touch along her jaw, thinking about all the ways he hadn't touched her yet. All the ways he wanted to.

"I've spent so much time thinking about that night, I'm not sure I can regret it." His gaze dipped to the lush softness of her mouth. He trailed his thumb along the seam. "Can you?"

Her lips parted, a soft huff of her breath grazing his knuckle.

"Maybe not." She blinked fast. "But just because you successfully run into and escape from a burning building once doesn't mean you should keep tempting fate with return trips."

"Is that what this is?" He released her, knowing he needed to make his case with his words and not their combustible connection. "A burning building?"

"You know what I mean. We seem destined to be at odds while I search for answers about Zach. There's no point blurring the battle lines." She spoke quickly, as if eager to brush the whole notion aside so she could move on.

He hoped the hectic color in her cheeks was evidence that he affected her even a fraction of how much she tempted him. But he didn't want to press her more tonight for fear she'd run again. For now, he would have to content himself that she'd agreed to speak to the police tomorrow.

"Then we'll have to disagree on that point." He shoved his hands in the pockets of the leather jacket he'd never removed. "The fact is, you owe me a date, and I'm not letting you off the hook."

Still, he backed up a step, wanting to give her space to think it over.

"You're leaving?" She twisted a dark strand of hair around one finger.

He would not think about how that silky hair had felt wrapped around his hand the night they'd been together. "You deserve an evening to yourself. And while I hope you'll change your mind about a date, I'm not going to twist your arm. I have the feeling we'll run across each other again this week since we have a common interest in Zach's story."

"Maybe we will." Her bottle-green eyes slid over him before she squared her shoulders and picked up her bowl of popcorn. "Good night, Miles."

He would have liked to end the night very differently, but he would settle for her roaming gaze and the memory of her biting her lip when they touched. Those things might not keep him warm tonight, but they suggested the odds were good of her landing in his bed again.

For now, that was enough.

* * *

So much for her relaxing evening in front of the fire with popcorn and a book.

Chiara couldn't sit still after Miles left. Unsatisfied desires made her twitchy and restless. After half an hour of reading the same page over and over again in her book, never once making sense of it, she gave up. She replaced the throw blanket and pillows on the sofa, then took her wine and empty popcorn bowl into the kitchen.

Even now, as she opened her laptop and took a seat at the island countertop, she swore she could feel the place where Miles's thumb had grazed her lip. That, in turn, had her reliving his kisses and the way their bodies had sought one another's that night in Mesa Falls.

Could that kind of electrifying chemistry be wrong? She guessed *yes*, because she and Miles were going to be at odds over Zach. All the sizzling attraction in the world was only going to confuse her real goal—to honor Zach's memory by clearing away the mystery of his death.

But denying that she felt it in the first place, when she wasn't deceiving anyone with her protests, seemed foolish. Miles had surely recognized the attraction she felt for him. And yet he'd walked away tonight, letting her make the next move.

Instead of losing herself in his arms, she opted to search her files on Zach one more time. Checking her inbox, she noticed a retired administrator from Dowdon School had gotten back to her on an email inquiry she'd made long ago. Or, more accurately, the administrator's former assistant had responded to Chiara. She hadn't asked directly about Zach; instead, she'd asked for information about the school year when he'd died under the guise of writing a general retrospective for a class reunion.

Apparently, the assistant hadn't cared that she wasn't a former student. She had simply attached a few files, including some flyers for events around campus, including one for the art fair where Chiara had last seen Zach. There was also a digital version of the small Dowdon yearbook.

After saving all the files, she opened them one by one. The art fair poster brought a sad, nostalgic smile to her face but yielded no clues. Seeing it reminded her how much of an influence Zach had on her life, though, his eye for artistic composition inspiring her long afterward. Other pamphlets advertised an author visit, a homecoming dance in conjunction with Brookfield and a football game. She wrote down the email contact information for the dance and sent a message to the address, using the same pretext as before.

Pausing to sip her wine, Chiara swiped through the yearbook even though she'd seen it twice before. Once, as soon as it came out; she'd made an excuse to visit the Brookfield library to examine a copy since the school kept all the Dowdon yearbooks in a special collection. She only paged through it enough to know Zach hadn't been in there. No photo. No mention.

Like he'd never existed.

Then, a year ago, she'd seen Jonah's copy at Astrid's house and had flipped through. Now, she examined the content more carefully in the hope of finding anything she'd overlooked.

First, however, she searched for Miles's photo. He was there, alphabetized in his class year next to his brother, Weston Rivera. They weren't twins, but they were as close in age as nontwin siblings could be.

The Rivera men had been swoonworthy even then. Wes's hair had been longer and unruly, his hazel eyes mischievous, and his look more surfer than rancher. Miles appeared little changed since the photo was taken, beyond the obvious maturing of his face and the filling out of the very male body she remembered from their night together. But his serious aspect and set jaw were the same even then, his blue eyes hinting at the old soul inside.

Before she could stop herself, her finger ran over his image on the screen.

Catching herself in the midst of fanciful thinking, she dismissed the unfamiliar romantic notions that had somehow attached themselves to Miles. She navigated away from the student photos section to browse the rest of the yearbook while she nibbled a few pieces of cold popcorn.

Half an hour later, a figure caught her eye in the background of one of the candid group shots taken outdoors on the Dowdon soccer field. It was a young woman in a knee-length navy blue skirt and sensible flats, her blond hair in a side part and low ponytail.

An old memory bubbled to the surface of seeing the woman. And she was a woman, not a girl, among the students, looking more mature than those around her.

Chiara had seen her before. Just once. Long ago.

With Zach.

The thrill of discovery buoyed her, sending her mind twirling in twenty directions about what to do with the new information. Funny that the first person who came to mind to share it with was Miles.

Would he know the woman? She picked up her phone, seeing his contact information still on the screen since the last message she'd received had been from him, letting her know he was at her door. The desire to share this with him was strong. Or was it only her desire to see him again? The ache of seeing him walk out her door was still fresh.

With an effort, she set the phone aside.

As much as she wanted to see if Miles recognized the mystery woman, she acknowledged that he might not answer her truthfully. He'd made it clear he planned to keep Zach's secrets. That she couldn't trust someone who could turn her inside out with a look was unsettling.

Tonight, she would research all she could on her own. Tomorrow, she would meet Astrid for lunch and—with a little good luck in the timing department—maybe she could waylay Astrid's husband before he went into his meeting with the Mesa Falls partners.

All she wanted was a real, unfiltered reaction to the image of the woman she'd seen with Zach. Miles was too guarded, and he knew her motives too well. Perhaps Jonah wouldn't be as careful.

Intercepting one of the Mesa Falls partners before the meeting Astrid had mentioned proved challenging. Chiara arrived at the Excelsior early, but with multiple parking areas and valet service, the casino resort didn't have a central location where she could monitor everyone who entered the building. For that matter, having her bodyguard with her made it difficult to blend in, so she'd asked Stefan to remain well behind her while she scoped out the scene.

Chiara decided to surveil the floor with the prominent high-roller suite the group had used for a meeting a month ago when she had first started keeping tabs on them. She hurried up the escalator near a courtyard fountain among the high-end shops. Water bubbled and splashed from the mouth of a sea dragon into a marble pool at the base of the fountain, the sound a soothing murmur when her nerves were wound tight. The resort was already busy with tourists window-shopping and taking photos.

As she reached the second-floor gallery, she spotted Gage Striker entering the suite. The huge, tattooed New Zealander was too far ahead for her to flag his attention, but at least she knew she was in the right place. Maybe Jonah and Astrid would come this way soon. As she darted around a pair of older ladies wearing matching red hats, Chiara pulled her phone from her handbag shaped like a rose, wanting the device ready with the right screen to show Jonah the photo of the mystery woman.

A voice from over her right shoulder startled her.

"Looking for someone?"

The deep rasp that could only belong to Miles skittered along her nerve endings.

Her body responded instantly, thrilled at the prospect of this man's nearness. But she battled back those feelings to turn toward him coolly.

"You're not much for traditional greetings, are you?" She eyed his perfectly tailored blue suit, the jacket unbuttoned over a subtly pinstriped gray shirt with the collar undone. Her attention snagged on the hint of skin visible at the base of his neck before she remembered what she was saying. “Most people open with something like *hello*. Or *nice to see you, Chiara*.”

A hint of a smile lifted his lips on one side as he stopped just inches from her. With any other man getting this close, Stefan might have come to her side, but her security guard had been at the party in Mesa Falls the night Chiara stayed with Miles. Stefan didn’t intervene now.

“Maybe other people can’t appreciate the pleasure I find in catching you off guard.” Miles lingered on the word *pleasure*.

Or else she did. She couldn’t be certain. She was too distracted by the hint of his aftershave hovering between them.

“I’m joining Astrid for lunch while Jonah attends another super-secret Mesa Falls meeting.” She glanced at her nails and pretended to inspect her manicure. She’d far rather he think her superficial than affected by his nearness.

Miles studied her. Keeping her focus on her hands, she felt his gaze more than saw it. She wouldn’t have a chance to speak to Jonah now. Not without Miles being present, anyway. While she considered her plan B, a group of women in tiaras and feather boas strolled past, with the one in the center wearing a pink sash that said, “Birthday Girl.”

“How did it go at the police station?” Miles asked, his fingers alighting on her forearm to draw her farther from the thoroughfare that led to the second-floor shops.

There were two couches in front of the high-roller suite and a low, clear cocktail table between them. Miles guided her to the area between the couches and the door to the suite, affording them a little more privacy.

"I had some other things to take care of this morning, but I'll call after lunch." She'd been so consumed with finding out the identity of the woman in the yearbook photo, she'd forgotten all about reporting the harassment.

Miles frowned. "I can't in good conscience let you put it off. After the meeting, I'll take you myself."

She bristled at his air of command. "I don't need an escort. I'll take care of it."

He pressed his lips together, as if reining in his emotions for a moment before he spoke. "Remember when you told me you had to be a one-woman content creator, marketing manager and finance director?" He clearly recalled how she'd defended her hard work when he'd been dismissive of her job. "Why don't you let someone else give you a hand?"

His thoughtfulness, underscored by how well he'd listened to her, made her relax a little. "It does sound better when you say it like that," she admitted.

"Good. And this way, you can ask me all the questions you want about the meeting." He nodded as if the matter was settled.

"Any chance you'll actually answer them?" She wasn't sure it was wise for them to spend more time alone together, but maybe she could find a way to ask him about the photo of the unidentified woman without putting his guard up.

"I've said all along we should be working together." He took her hand in his, holding it between them while he stroked her palm with his thumb. "Where should I look for you after I finish up here?"

Her breath caught from just that smallest of touches. Her heart pounded harder.

"Spice Pavilion," she answered, seeing Astrid and Jonah heading toward them out of the corner of her eye.

"I'll look forward to it." Miles lifted the back of her hand to his lips and kissed it before releasing her.

Skin tingling pleasantly, she watched him disappear into the high-roller suite and wondered what she'd just gotten herself into. She noticed his brother followed him a moment later, while Astrid and Jonah gave each other a lingering goodbye kiss nearby. The blatant public display of affection seemed all the more romantic considering the couple were new parents.

What would it be like to have that kind of closeness with someone day in and day out?

Not that she would be finding out. Although her recent night with Miles reminded her how rewarding it was to share passion, she owed it to Zach not to let the connection distract her from her goal. She would spend time with Miles because he was still her most promising resource for information. And despite the coincidental timing of the threats against her, she'd had time to realize Miles was too honorable a man to resort to those tactics. She was safe with him.

She just had to find a way to get him talking.

Seven

Restless as hell, Miles prowled the perimeter of the high-roller suite, waiting for the meeting to get underway. Weston and Desmond were deep in conversation on a curved leather sofa in the center of the room, while a server passed through the living area with a tray of top-shelf bottles. Gage stared down into the fire burning in a sleek, modern hearth, a glass of his preferred bourbon already in hand. A massive flat-screen television was mounted over the fireplace, but the display was dark. In the past, the group had used the screens to teleconference in the missing Mesa Falls owners, but today all were present in person. Even Jonah, the new father, and Alec Jacobsen, the game developer who spent most of his time globe-hopping to get inspiration for the complex world-building required for his games. The two of them lounged near the pool table.

On either side of the fireplace, windows overlooked Lake Tahoe, the clear sky making the water look impossibly blue. Miles paused by one of them, waving off the offer of a beverage from the bow-tied server. He'd need his wits sharp for his meeting with Chiara afterward.

Hell, maybe he needed to worry more about having his instincts honed for the meeting with his friends. The possibility of a traitor to their shared cause had kept him up at night ever since Chiara had been threatened. He'd never doubted the men in this room before. But who else even knew about Zach to make a threat like the one Chiara had received?

"Are we ready?" Miles stopped pacing to ask the question, his back to a mahogany bookcase. He wasn't usually the one to spearhead discussions like this, but today the need for answers burned hot. "I know you're all busy. The sooner we figure out a plan, the sooner we can all go home."

Desmond gave a nod to the server, who left the room quickly, closing the door to the multilevel suite behind her. As the owner of Excelsior, Desmond commanded the operations of the resort and served as their host when they met on the property.

Weston cleared his throat. "Can you bring us up to speed on what's happening?"

The fact that his brother was the first to respond to him surprised Miles given the enmity between him and Wes that had started when they'd been pitted against one another at an early age by their parents. The tension had escalated years ago when they'd briefly dated the same woman. But they'd made strides to put that behind them over the last year. Miles suspected Wes had mellowed since finding love with April Stephens, the financial investigator who'd discovered where the profits of Alonzo's book were going.

"Chiara Campagna has been digging around to find out how Zach died. She knew him in school," he told them bluntly, fisting his hands in the pockets of his pants as he tried to gauge the reactions of his friends. "She attended Brookfield before she became an internet sensation, and she met Zach through the school's art program."

There were no murmurs of reaction. The only sound in the room was the clink of ice cubes in a glass as a drink shifted. But then, they'd known the meeting was called to discuss this issue before walking in the door. So Miles continued.

"She wants to know the circumstances of Zach's death, suspecting some kind of cover-up since there was no news released about it." As he explained it, he understood her frustration. And yes, pain.

Just because she'd been a fifteen-year-old with a crush on a friend didn't diminish their connection. He recognized the power and influence those early relationships could hold over someone.

Near the fireplace, Gage swore and finished his drink. His influential father had been the one to insist the story of Zach's accident remain private. The gag order surrounding the trauma had been one more complication in an already thorny situation.

"But why now?" Alec asked, spinning a cue ball like a top under one finger while he slouched against the billiard table. He wore a T-shirt printed with shaded outlines of his most iconic game characters, layered under a custom suit jacket. "Zach's been dead for fourteen years. Doesn't it seem strange that she's taken a renewed interest now?"

"No." Gage stalked over to the tray the server had left on the glass-topped cocktail table and helped himself to another shot of bourbon, tattoos flashing from the cuffs of his shirtsleeves as he poured the drink. "Chiara told Elena that she'd given up searching for answers about Zach until the Alonzo Salazar story broke at Christmas. With Mesa Falls and all of us in the spotlight, Chiara saw an opportunity to press harder for the truth."

Miles mulled over the new information about Chiara, interested in anything he could gather about the woman who dominated his thoughts. Elena Rollins was a lifestyle blogger who'd visited Mesa Falls to chase a story on Alonzo, but she'd ended up falling for Gage and had backed off. The two women had developed a friendship when Chiara had lent the power of her social media platform to bolster Elena's following.

"But that opportunity is going away now that we've given the public a story about where the profits from Alonzo's book went," Alec chimed in again, using his fingers to shoot the eight ball into a side pocket with a backspin. "Media interest will die out, and we'll go back to living in peace. No one needs to find out anything about Zach."

Even now, it was difficult to talk about the weekend that Zachary Eldridge had jumped to his death off a cliff into the Arroyo Seco River. The men in this room had once argued to the point of violence over whether Zach had planned to take his own life or it had truly been an accident. Eventually, they'd agreed to disagree about that, but they'd made a pact to keep their friend's memory away from public speculation. It had been tough enough for them to deal with the possibility that Zach had jumped to his death on purpose. The thought of dredging all that up again was…unbearable.

"Maybe. Maybe not," Miles returned slowly, turning it over in his head, trying to see what they knew from another angle. "But just because the public doesn't know about the mystery benefactor of the book profits doesn't mean we should just forget about him. We know the boy is thirteen years old puts his conception around the time of the accident. The last time we met, we were going to have a detective track the boy and his guardian."

He didn't remind them of the rest of what they needed to know—if there was a chance any of them had fathered the child.

Around the holidays, a woman had worked briefly at the ranch under the alias Nicole Smith and had claimed that Alonzo's book profits were supporting her dead sister's son—a boy born in a hospital close to Dowdon School seven and a half months after Zach's death. But before any of the ranch owners could speak to her directly, Nicole was abruptly fired. When they'd tried to track down the supervisor responsible for dismissing her, they learned the guy had quit the next day and didn't leave a forwarding address.

All of which raised uncomfortable questions about the integrity of the group in this room. Had one of them ordered the woman's dismissal? Had Nicole been too close to the truth—that Alonzo Salazar had been helping to support Nicole's nephew because he knew who'd fathered the boy? They'd learned that the woman's real name was Nicole Cruz, and they'd obtained some basic information about the boy, Matthew. But they were trying to find her to meet with her in person.

"I'm handling that." Weston sat forward on the couch to flick on the huge wall-mounted television screen controlled by a tablet in front of him. "A detective is following a lead to Nicole and Matthew Cruz in Prince Edward Island. He's supposed to land tonight to check out the address."

Wes flicked through a series of photos on his tablet that then appeared on the TV screen, images of Nicole and Matthew—neither of whom they recognized—followed by grainy security system footage from when Nicole had worked at the ranch, as well as some shots of the boy from his former school. The different angles didn't do anything to help Miles recognize the boy.

"With any luck, the detective finds them." Miles turned his attention back to his colleagues. "And brings them to Mesa Falls so we can speak to the guardian at length and request permission to run a DNA test on the boy."

"Right." Wes clicked to another slide labeled "instructions for obtaining DNA."

"In the meantime, I've sent you all the file and collection kits by courier service. Most of you have already submitted yours, but we still need samples from Gage and Jonah. I've got a shipper ready to take them before you leave the meeting today. Alonzo's sons have already provided samples."

The silence in the room was thick. Did Jonah or Gage have reasons for dragging their feet? It had taken Miles two seconds to put a hair in a vial and ship the thing out.

Jonah blew out a sigh as he shoved away from the pool table and wandered over to a piano in the far corner of the room. He plunked out a few chords while he spoke. "That's fine. But none of us is going to be the father. Alonzo would have never stood by idly and paid for the boy's education if any of us were the dad. He would have demanded we own up to our responsibility once we were old enough to assume that duty."

"Maybe he was a mentor to the boy's mother, and not the father," Gage mused aloud, not sounding convinced. "This kid might not have anything to do with us."

"Possibly," Wes agreed. "But the kid was important to Alonzo, and that makes him important to us. Let's rule out the more obvious connection first."

"Agreed." Miles met his brother's hazel eyes, trying to remember the last time they'd been on the same page about anything. "But the more pressing issue today is that Chiara's social media accounts were hacked and she received an anonymous text threatening more attacks if she kept pursuing answers about Zach's death."

Recalling that morning at his house, Miles felt anger return and redouble that someone had threatened her, a woman who'd gotten under his skin so fast he hasn't seen it coming. That it had happened while she was in his home, as his guest, only added to his sense of responsibility. That it could be one of his friends, or someone close to them, chilled him.

"Anyone remember her from when she attended Brookfield?" Gage asked as Wes switched the image on the screen to show a school yearbook photo of Chiara. "When she was known as Kara Marsh?"

Wariness mingled with suspicion as Miles swung around to face Gage. "You knew?"

He'd texted Gage that night to ask him what he knew about Chiara, and he'd never mentioned it.

"Not until two days ago." Gage held both hands up in a sign of his innocence. "Elena told me. She and Chiara have gotten close in the last month. Apparently Chiara mentioned she used to go by a different name and that none of us remembered her even though she attended a school near Dowdon. If she confided in Elena, she obviously wasn't trying to hide it. And Astrid must be aware."

Miles studied Gage's face but couldn't see any hint of falseness there. Of all of them, Gage was the most plainspoken and direct. The least guarded. So it was tough to envision the big, bluff New Zealander keeping secrets.

From across the room, Alec's voice sliced through his thoughts.

"I remember Kara Marsh." Alec's eyes were on the television screen. "She came to Dowdon that Christmas asking questions about Zach."

Of all the friends, Alec had been closest to Zach. After the accident, he had retreated the most. To the point that Miles had sometimes feared the guy would follow in Zach's footsteps. He'd wondered if they'd wake up one morning to find out Alec had stepped off a cliff's edge in the middle of the night. Alonzo Salazar had shared the concern, speaking privately to all of them about signs to look for when people contemplated suicide. Alec came through it, as they all had. They were good now. Solid. But it had been a rough year.

"Did you talk to her?" Miles asked, needing to learn everything he could about Chiara.

He'd called this meeting out of a need to protect Zach's memory. And yet he felt a need to protect Chiara, too. To find out if any of his partners were the source of the leak that led to Chiara's getting hacked. He'd been watching them all carefully, studying their faces, but he hadn't seen any hint of uneasiness in any one of them.

"No." Alec shook his head as he stroked his jaw, looking lost in thought before his gaze came up to fix on Miles. "But you did. She spoke to you, and then she went to Gage. I was hanging out under the bleachers near the football field with—" he hesitated, a small smile flashing before it disappeared again "—with a girl I knew. Anyway, I was there when I saw Kara sneak onto the campus through the back fence."

"You followed her?" Jonah asked, dropping onto the bench in front of the piano.

Alec shrugged, flicking a white cue ball away from him where he still leaned against the pool table. "I did. The girl I was with was in a snit about it, but I wanted to see what Kara was up to. Besides, in those days, I was more than happy to look for diversions wherever I could find them."

They had all been emotionally wrecked during those weeks, not sleeping, barely eating, unable to even talk to each other since being together stirred up painful memories. Miles had thrown himself into work, taking a part-time job in the nearest town to get away from school as much as possible.

"Did Chiara see you?" Miles wished like hell he remembered that day more clearly.

"I don't think so." He spun the ball under one fingertip, seeming more engaged in the activity than the conversation. But that had always been his way. He had frequently disappeared for days in online realms as a kid and had used that skill as a successful game developer. "She looked nervous. Upset. I had the impression she was afraid of getting caught, because she kept glancing over her shoulder."

Miles tried to conjure up a better picture of her from that day when she'd cornered him outside the library. Mostly he remembered that her voice had startled him because it was a girl's, forcing him to look at her more closely since she'd been dressed the same as any of his classmates—jeans, loafers, dark jacket. The clothes must have been borrowed, because they were big on her. Shapeless. Which was probably the point if she wanted to roam freely among them.

Even her hair had been tucked half under a ball cap and half under her coat.

The memory of Chiara's pale face the morning she'd received the threat returned to his brain, reminding him he needed to figure out who would threaten her. Clenching his fist, he pounded it lightly against the window sash before he spoke.

"Who else even knows about Zach?" he asked the group around him, the friends he thought he knew so well. "Let alone would feel threatened if his story came to light?"

For a long moment, the only sounds were the billiard balls Alec knocked against the rails and the sound of ice rattling in Gage's glass. The silence grated Miles's nerves, so he shared his last piece of important news to see if it got his friends talking.

"I'm taking Chiara to the police station after this to let them know about the threats she's receiving, so there's a chance we'll have to answer questions from the authorities about Zach." He knew it went against their longtime promise to protect their friend's memory. But her safety had to come first.

"You would do that?" Alec shook his head and pushed away from the pool table.

Desmond spoke at the same time. "The negative publicity around Mesa Falls is going to have consequences."

From his seat on the leather sofa, Wes shut down the television screen on the wall before he spoke.

"In answer to your question about who else would remember Zach, he was well-known at Dowdon. Teachers and other students all liked him. As for why someone wouldn't want his story to come out..." Wes hesitated, his hazel eyes flicking from one face to the next. "He had a past. And secrets of his own. Maybe we didn't know Zach as well as we thought we did."

That left the suite even quieter than before. Desmond broke the silence with a soft oath before he leaned over and poured himself a drink from the tray in front of the couch.

The meeting ended with a resolution to convene the next day in the hope they got word from their investigator about Matthew and Nicole Cruz by then. As they began filing out of the suite, Alec and Jonah were still arguing about the idea that they didn't know Zach after all. Miles didn't stick around, not sure what he thought about the possibility.

For now, he needed to see Chiara.

Stalking out of the meeting room, he ran into a young woman hovering around the door. Dressed in leggings and high-top sneakers paired with a blazer, she didn't have the look of a typical casino guest. A red curl fell in her face as she flushed.

"Sorry. Is the meeting over?" she asked, pushing the curl away from her lightly freckled face. As she shifted, her blazer opened to reveal a T-shirt with the characters from Alec's video game. "I'm waiting for Alec—" She glanced over Miles's shoulder. "Is he here?"

Miles nodded but didn't open the door for her since his partners were still discussing Zach. "Just finishing up. He should be out in a minute. Do you work with Alec?"

She hesitated for the briefest moment, a scowl darkening her features, before she thrust out her hand. "I'm his assistant, Vivian Fraser."

Miles shook it, surprised they hadn't met before. "Miles Rivera. Nice to meet you, Vivian."

Politely, he moved past her, writing off the awkward encounter as his thoughts turned to Chiara.

He'd promised her a date, yes. And the drive to see her was stronger than ever after a meeting that had shaken his foundations. But more importantly, he had questions for her. Questions that couldn't afford to get sidelined by their attraction, no matter how much he wanted to touch her again.

Chiara sent her bodyguard home for the day when she saw Miles approaching the restaurant. Astrid had departed five minutes before, after seeing Jonah's text to meet him in a private suite he'd taken for the rest of their afternoon together.

The new mother had seemed surprised, flustered and adorably excited to have her husband all to herself for a few hours. Chiara had felt a sharp pang of loneliness once she'd left, recognizing that she'd never felt that way about a man. The lack had never bothered her much. Yet between the incredible night she'd spent with Miles and seeing Astrid's happiness transform her, the universe seemed to be conspiring to make her crave romance.

So when Miles slowed his step near the hostess stand of Spice Pavilion, Chiara bristled with defensiveness before he'd even spoken. It didn't help that he was absurdly handsome, impeccably dressed and only had eyes for her, even though he attracted plenty of feminine attention.

"Hello, Chiara." He spoke the greeting with careful deliberation, no doubt emphasizing his good manners after she'd mentioned his habit of skipping the social niceties. "Did you enjoy your lunch?"

She'd been too preoccupied—and maybe a little nervous—about spending more time with him to eat much of anything, but she didn't share that. She rose from the bench where she'd been waiting, restless and needing to move.

"It's always a treat to see Astrid," she told him instead, her slim-cut skirt hugging her thighs as she moved, her body more keenly aware whenever he was near her. "But what about you? Have you eaten?"

She didn't know what went on behind closed doors during a Mesa Falls owners' meeting, but she couldn't envision some of the country's wealthiest men ordering takeout over a conference table. As they walked through the wide corridor that connected the shops to the casino, Chiara dug in her handbag for a pair of sunglasses and slid them into place, hoping to remain unrecognized. The casino crowd was a bit older than her traditional fan base, but she didn't want to risk getting sidetracked from her goal.

"I'm too keyed up to be hungry." Miles took her hand in his, the warmth of his touch encircling her fingers. "Let's take care of reporting the threats against you, and then we need to talk."

She glanced over at him, but his face revealed nothing of his thoughts.

"We're on the same page then." She kept close to him as he increased his pace, cutting through the crowd of tourists, gamblers and locals who visited the Excelsior for a day of entertainment. "Because I hardly touched my lunch for thinking about how much we needed to speak."

He slowed his step just long enough to slant her a sideways glance. "Good. After we take care of the errand at the police station, we can go to your house or my suite. Whichever you prefer for privacy's sake."

The mention of that kind of privacy made her remember what happened when they'd been alone behind closed doors at his home in Mesa Falls. But she agreed. They needed that kind of security for this conversation.

"You have a suite here?" she asked, her heartbeat picking up speed even though they were already heading toward the parking lot, where she guessed Miles had a car waiting.

She suddenly remembered Astrid's face when Jonah had texted her to meet him in a suite for the afternoon. Her friend had lit up from the inside. Chiara had the feeling she looked the exact same way even though her meeting behind closed doors with Miles had a very different purpose.

"I do." His blue gaze was steady as he stopped in the middle of the corridor to let a small troop of feather-clad dancers in matching costumes and sky-high heels glide past them. "Should we go there afterward?"

A whirlwind of questions circled beneath that deceptively simple one. Would she end up in his bed again? Did he want her there? But first and foremost, she needed to know what had happened at the meeting and if Miles had any ideas about who was threatening her.

So she hoped for the best and gave him the only possible response.

“Yes, please.”

Eight

Filing a formal complaint with the proper authorities took more time than Chiara would have guessed, which left her more than a little frustrated and exhausted. She hitched her purse up on her shoulder as she charged through the sliding door of the local police station and into a swirl of late-afternoon snow flurries. The whole process had stretched out as Miles spoke to multiple officers at length, eliciting information on possible precautions to take to protect her.

Each cop they'd spoken to had been courteous and professional but not very encouraging that they would be able to help. With the rise of cybercrime, law enforcement was tapped more and more often for infractions committed online, but most local agencies weren't equipped to provide the necessary investigative work. The FBI handled major cases, but at the local level, the best they could do was point her in the direction of the appropriate federal agency, especially considering the threat had targeted Chiara's livelihood and not her person. Still, the importance of the case was increased by the fact that she was a public figure. She'd worked with the local police to file the complaints with the proper federal agencies, and they'd suggested she keep careful records of any problems in the future.

Bottom line, someone would look into it, but chances were good nothing more would come of it unless the threats against her escalated. And thanks to Miles, she wasn't handling this alone.

Chiara glanced back over her shoulder at him as he rebuttoned his suit jacket on their way out the door.

"Thank you for going with me." Chiara held the handrail as she descended the steps outside the municipal building almost three hours after they'd arrived. Her breath huffed visibly in the chilly mountain air as flurries circled them on a gust of wind. "I know it wasn't as satisfying as we might have hoped, but at least we've laid the groundwork if the hacker follows through on his threats."

"Or *her* threats," Miles added, sliding a hand under her elbow and steering her around a patch of ice as they reached the parking lot. "We haven't ruled out a woman's hand in this."

She pulled her coat tighter around her, glad for Miles's support on the slick pavement. The temperature had dropped while they were inside. Then again, thinking about someone threatening her business empire might have been part of the chill she felt. She'd given up her dream of becoming an artist to build the social media presence that had become a formidable brand. That brand was worth all the more to her considering the sacrifices she'd made for it along the way.

"Did you speculate about who might be behind the threats in your meeting today?" she asked, unwilling to delay her questions any longer as they reached his big black Land Rover with snow dusting the hood. "You said you'd share with me what you discussed. And I know Zach's legacy is a concern for you and your friends."

Miles opened the passenger door for her, but before he could reply, a woman's voice called from the next row over in the parking lot.

"Chiara Campagna?"

Distracted, Chiara looked up before thinking the better of it. A young woman dressed in black leggings and a bright pink puffer jacket rushed toward them, her phone lifted as if she was taking a video or a picture.

Miles urged Chiara into the SUV with a nudge, his body blocking anyone from reaching her.

"We should have kept your bodyguard with us," he muttered under his breath as other people on the street outside the municipal building turned toward them.

"Can I get a picture with you?" the woman asked her, already stepping into Miles's personal space and thrusting her phone toward him as she levered between the vehicle and the open door. "I'm such a huge fan."

Chiara put a hand on Miles's arm to let him know it was okay, and he took the phone from the stranger. Chiara knew it might be wiser to leave now before the crowd around them grew, but she'd never been good at disappointing fans. She owed them too much. Yet, in her peripheral vision, she could see a few other people heading toward the vehicle. Impromptu interactions like this could be fun, but they could quickly turn uncomfortable and borderline dangerous.

"Sure," Chiara replied, hoping for the best as she tilted her head toward the other woman's, posing with her and looking into the lens of the camera phone. "But I can only do one," she added, as much for Miles's benefit as the fan's.

Miles took the shot and lowered the phone, appearing to understand her meaning as he met her gaze with those steady blue eyes of his. Without ever looking away from her, he passed the woman in the puffer jacket her phone.

"Ms. Campagna is late for a meeting," he explained, inserting himself between Chiara and the fan before shifting his focus to the other woman. "She appreciates your support, but I need to deliver her to her next appointment now."

He backed the other woman away, closing and locking the SUV's passenger door just in time, as two teenaged boys clambered over to bang on the vehicle's hood and shout her name, their phones raised.

The noise made her tense, but Chiara slid her sunglasses onto her nose and kept her head down. She dug in her bag for her own phone, hoping she wouldn't need to call Stefan for assistance. She'd been in situations with crowds that had turned aggressive before, and the experiences had terrified her. She knew all too well how fast things could escalate.

But a moment later, the clamor outside the SUV eased enough for Miles to open the driver's door and slide into his own seat. She peered through the windshield then, spotting a uniformed police officer disbanding the gathering onlookers who had quickly multiplied in number. The teenaged boys were legging it down the street. The woman in the puffer jacket was showing her phone to a group of other ladies, gesturing excitedly with her other hand. People had gathered to see what was happening, stepping out of businesses in a strip mall across the parking lot.

"I'm sorry about that." Miles turned on the engine and backed out of the parking space. He gave a wave to the officer through the windshield. "Does that happen often?"

"Not lately," she admitted, shaken at the close call. "I've gotten better in the last year about wearing hats and sunglasses, keeping security near me, and having my outings really scripted so that I'm never in public for long."

She'd been so distracted ever since spending the night with Miles that she was forgetting to take precautions. She pressed farther back in her seat, ready to retreat from the world.

"That doesn't sound like a fun way to live." He steered the vehicle out of the parking lot and started driving away from town. "And now that news of your presence here has no doubt been plastered all over the web, I'd like to take you to the villa you rented instead of the resort. It will be quieter there."

"That's fine." She appreciated the suggestion as the snow began falling faster. "I'll message Stefan—he's my head of security—and ask him to bring in some more help for the rest of my stay."

"Good." Miles nodded his approval of the plan, his square jaw flexing. "Until we find out who's been threatening you, it pays to take extra safety measures."

She drew a deep breath, needing to find a way to

reroute this conversation. To return to her goal for this time with Miles, which was to learn more about what happened to Zach. But she hadn't quite recovered from the near miss with fans who could turn from warm-hearted supporters to angry detractors with little to no warning. It only took a few people in a crowd to change the mood or to start shoving.

"Or..." Miles seemed to muse aloud as he drove, the quiet in the car all the more pronounced as they left the more populated part of the lakeshore behind them.

When he didn't seem inclined to finish his thought, Chiara turned to look at him again, but she couldn't read his expression, which veered between a frown and thoughtful contemplation.

"Or what?" she prodded him, curious what was on his mind.

"I was just going to say that if you decide at any time you would prefer more seclusion, my ranch in the Sierra Nevada foothills is open to you." He glanced her way as he said it.

"Rivera Ranch?" She knew it was his family seat, the property he invested the majority of his time in running.

The invitation surprised her. First of all, because Miles seemed like an intensely private man, the most reserved of the Mesa Falls owners. He didn't strike her as the kind of person to open his home to many people. Secondly, she wouldn't have guessed that she would rank on the short list of people he would welcome.

"Yes." His thumbs drummed softly against the steering wheel. "It's remote. The property is gated and secure. You'd be safe there."

"Alone?" The word slipped out before she could catch it.

"Only if you chose to be. I'm happy to escort you. At least until you got settled in."

The offer was thoughtful, if completely unexpected. Still, it bore consideration if the threats against her kept escalating.

"I hope it doesn't come to that," she told him truthfully. "But thank you."

"Just remember you have options." He turned on the long private drive that led to her villa on the lake. "You're not in this alone."

She was tempted to argue that point. To tell him she felt very much alone in her quest to learn more about Zach since Miles refused to talk about their mutual friend. But he was here with her now. And he'd said they needed to help each other. Maybe he was ready to break his long silence at last.

Yet somehow that seemed less important than the prospect of spending time alone with this man who tempted her far too much.

Miles recognized the couple waiting in front of Chiara's villa as he parked the vehicle. The tall, athletic-looking brunette was Chiara's assistant, and the burly dude dressed all in black had been Chiara's bodyguard the night of the party at Mesa Falls Ranch. The two held hands, wearing matching tense expressions. They broke apart when Miles halted the vehicle but still approached the passenger door as a team.

"They must have seen photos from the police department parking lot online." Chiara sighed in frustration as she unbuckled her seat belt and clutched her handbag. "I'll just need a minute to bring them up to speed."

"Of course." Miles nodded at the muscle-bound man

who opened Chiara's door for her. "Take your time. I'll check out your lake view to give you some privacy."

"That's not necessary," she protested, allowing her bodyguard to help her down from the vehicle.

Opening his own door, Miles discovered the tall assistant was waiting on his side of the Land Rover. Meeting her brown eyes, he remembered her name from the party at Mesa Falls.

"Hi, Jules," he greeted the woman, who had to be six feet tall even in her flat-soled running shoes. She wore a sweater and track pants, seemingly unconcerned with the cold. "Nice to see you again."

"You, too." She gave him a quick smile, but it was plain she had other things on her mind. A furrow between her brows deepened before she lowered her voice to speak to him quietly. "I wanted to warn you that while you were out with Chiara today, you attracted the interest of some of her fans."

"Should I be concerned?" He stepped down to the pavement beside her while, near the rear of the SUV, Chiara related the story of what happened at the police department to her security guard.

"Not necessarily." Jules hugged her arms around her waist, breathing a white cloud into the cold air. "But since Chiara's fan base can be vocal and occasionally unpredictable, you should probably alert your PR team to keep an eye on the situation."

"I'm a rancher," he clarified, amused. He stuffed his hands in his pockets to ward off the chill of the day. "I don't have a PR team."

"Mesa Falls has a dedicated staffer," she reminded him, switching on the tablet she was holding. A gust of wind caught her long ponytail and blew it all around her. "I remember because I dealt with her directly about the party at your place. Would you like me to contact her about this instead?"

Puzzled, Miles watched the woman swipe through several screens before pausing on an avatar of the Montana ranch.

"Just what do you think could happen?" he asked her, curious about the potential risks of dating someone famous.

If, in fact, what they were doing together could even be called dating. His gaze slanted over to Chiara, who was heading toward the front door of the villa, flashes of her long legs visible from the opening of her coat. He realized he wanted more with her. At very least, he wanted a repeat of their incredible night together. Preferably, he wanted many repeats of that night.

Beside him, Chiara's assistant huffed out a sigh that pulled him back to their conversation.

"Anything could happen," Jules told him flatly as she frowned. "You could become a target for harassment or worse. Your home address could be made public, and you could find yourself or your family surrounded in your own home. Your business could be boycotted if Chiara's fans decide they don't like you. People have no idea how brutal it can be in the public eye."

She sounded upset. Miles wondered what kinds of things Chiara had weathered in the past because of her fame.

He felt his eyebrows rise even as the idea worried him more for Chiara's sake than his own. "I appreciate the warning. If you don't mind sending a message to the Mesa Falls publicity person, I'd appreciate it."

"Of course." She nodded, tapping out some notes

on her tablet even as snowflakes fell and melted on the screen. "And you should consider security for yourself once you leave the villa. At least for the next week or so until we know how the story plays out."

"I'll consider it," he assured her, sensing it would be better to placate her for now, or until he had a better handle on the situation for himself. He didn't want to rile Chiara's assistant when the woman already seemed upset. "Did today's incident cause problems for you?"

Jules shoved her tablet under her arm again. "For me personally? Not yet. But having her photographed in front of a police station is already causing speculation that we'll have to figure out how to address."

He nodded, beginning to understand how small missteps like today could have a big impact on Chiara's carefully planned public image. "I should have taken steps to ensure she wasn't recognized."

A wry smile curved the woman's lips. "Bingo."

"I can't fix what already happened today, but I can promise I'll take better care of her in the future," he assured the woman, gesturing her toward the house.

Jules pivoted on the heel of her tennis shoe and walked with him toward the stone steps at the side entrance. "If she keeps you around, I would appreciate that."

Miles chucked softly as he opened the front door for her. "Do you think my days are numbered with her after this?"

"No. Well, not because of today. But Chiara is notoriously choosy when it comes to the men in her life." She lowered her voice as they crossed the threshold of the huge lakefront house.

From the foyer, Miles could see Chiara standing with

her bodyguard in the kitchen. Behind her, the setting sun glittered on the lake outside the floor-to-ceiling windows.

"That's a good thing." Miles was damned choosy himself. Until Chiara, he hadn't let any woman close to him for more than a night ever since he'd accidentally ended up dating the same woman as his brother. "I admire a woman with discriminating taste."

Jules laughed. "Then maybe you two have more in common than I would have guessed. I've worked with Chiara for three years, and you're the first man she's ever changed her schedule for."

He wanted to ask her what she meant by that, but as soon as the words were out, Chiara entered the foyer alone. Something about the way she carried herself told him she was upset. Or maybe it was the expression on her face, the worry in her eyes. And damned if he hadn't spent enough time studying her to recognize the subtle shift of her moods.

"Jules." Chiara still wore her long coat, her arms wrapped around herself as if she was chilled. "Stefan went out the back to the guesthouse, but he said he'll meet you out front if you still want to head into town."

Jules looked back and forth between them, but then her attention locked in on Chiara, perhaps seeing the same stress that Miles had noted. Jules stroked her friend's hair where it rested on her shoulder. "I don't want to go anywhere if you need me."

Miles wondered if he'd missed something. If the photos online were a bigger deal than he was understanding. Or was it his presence causing the added stress?

"I can take off if this is a bad time," he offered,

unwilling to stay if they needed to take care of other things. He'd come a long way from the guy who'd written off Chiara's job as glorified partying, but no doubt he still didn't understand the nuances of her work, let alone the ramifications of the day's unexpected encounter with her fans.

Chiara's green eyes lifted to his. "No. I'd like to talk." Then she turned to her assistant and squeezed Jules's hand. "I'm fine. But thank you. I want you to have fun tonight. You work too hard."

"It never feels like work for me when we're hanging out," the other woman insisted before she gave a nod. "But if you're sure you don't mind—"

"I insist." Chiara walked toward the oversize door with her. "Stefan already has two guards watching the house tonight, and Miles will be here with me for a few more hours."

He couldn't help but hope that boded well for their evening together. Although maybe Chiara was just trying to soothe her friend's anxiety about leaving her.

In another moment, Jules departed, and the house was vacant except for the two of them. The sound of the door shutting echoed from the cathedral ceiling in the foyer. Chiara took a moment to check that the alarm reset before she turned toward him again.

"May I take your coat?" he asked, moving closer to her.

Wanting to touch her, yes. But wanting to comfort her, too.

She looked down at what she was wearing and shook her head, clearly having forgotten that she'd left her coat on.

"Oh. Thank you." She sucked in a breath as he

stepped behind her and rested his hands on her shoulders for a moment. "I think I got a chill while we were out."

"Or maybe it's the combination of dealing with the threats, the police and the work crisis that seems to have snowballed from having our photo taken today." He took hold of the soft wool and cashmere cloak and helped her slide it from her arms.

The movement shifted her dark waves of hair and stirred her citrusy scent. He breathed it in, everything about her affecting him. As much as he wanted to turn her toward him and kiss her, he realized he wanted to ease her worries even more. So after hanging the coat on a wooden peg just inside the mudroom off the foyer, he returned to her side, resting his hand lightly on her spine to steer her toward the living room.

"You're probably right. The police station visit would have been daunting enough without the drama afterward." She shivered and hugged her arms tighter around herself.

Miles led her to the sofa, moving aside a throw pillow to give her the comfortable corner seat. Then he pulled a plush blanket off the sofa back and draped it around her before finding the fireplace remote and switching on the flames. The blinds in the front room were already drawn, but he pulled the heavy curtains over them, too.

Then he took a seat on the wide ottoman, shoving aside a tray full of design books and coasters to make more room.

"May I take these off for you?" He gestured toward the high leather boots she was still wearing.

Her lips lifted on one side. "Really?" A sparkle returned to her green eyes, a flare of interest or anticipation. At least, he hoped that's what it was. "If you don't mind."

"I want to make you comfortable. And I don't want you to regret sending away your friends tonight." He lowered the zipper on the first boot, reminding himself he was only doing this to help her relax. Not to seduce her.

Although skimming his hand lightly over the back of her calf as he removed the boot was doing a hell of a job of seducing *him*.

"I won't." Her gaze locked on his hands where he touched her. "I've been anxious to talk to you all day."

The reminder that this wasn't a real date came just in time as Miles eased off the second boot. Because he'd been tempted to stroke back up her leg to her knee.

And linger there.

Even now, the hem of her skirt just above her knee was calling to him. But first, they needed to address the topic he'd avoided for fourteen years.

Damn it.

With an effort, he set aside her footwear and released her leg. Then he took the seat next to her on the couch.

"Okay." He braced himself, remembering that his friends hadn't been any help today. It was time to break the silence. "Let's talk."

"I have a question I've been wanting to ask you." Reaching beneath the blanket, Chiara shifted to gain access to a pocket on the front of her houndstooth skirt. She withdrew a piece of paper and smoothed it out to show him a grainy photo. "Do you know who this is, Miles?"

He glanced down at the photo, and passion faded

as suspicion iced everything he'd been feeling. Apparently Chiara wasn't stopping her quest for answers about Zach. Because the face staring back at Miles from the image was someone he and Zach had both known well. And he couldn't begin to guess why Chiara wanted to know about her.

Nine

Chiara didn't miss the flare of recognition in Miles's eyes as he looked at the yearbook photo.

"You're pointing at this woman in the background?" he asked, stabbing the paper with his index finger.

"The one with the side part and the navy blue skirt," she clarified. "She doesn't look like a student."

"She wasn't. That's Miss Allen, one of the student teachers at Dowdon." He met her gaze as he smiled. "Lana Allen. We were all a little in love with her."

"A teacher?" Shock rippled through her, followed by cold, hard dread. "Are you sure? She's not in the yearbook anywhere else. How old do you think she was?"

Miles must have read some of her dismay, because his expression went wary. He tensed beside her on the sofa.

"There was major backlash about her being at our

school since she was just nineteen herself. She didn't stay the full year at Dowdon after one of the administrators complained she was a distraction. She worked with Alonzo Salazar briefly during the fall semester and then she was gone—" His jaw flexed as if mulling over how much to say. "Before Christmas break. Why?"

Her stomach knotted at the implications of what this new revelation meant. She hoped it wasn't a mistake to confide in him. But if one of them didn't take the leap and start sharing information, they'd never figure out who was harassing her or what it had to do with Zach.

Taking a deep breath, she sat up straighter and told him. "I saw Zach kissing her. As in a real, no-holds-barred, passionate kiss."

Miles shook his head then gripped his temples between his thumb and forefinger, squeezing. "Impossible. It must have been someone else."

"No." She was certain. How many times had she relived that moment in her mind over the years? "Miles, I had the biggest crush on him. I followed him around like the lovesick teenager I was, just hoping for the chance to talk to him alone. I never would have mistaken him for someone else."

"Then you're confused about her," he insisted. "It was a long time ago, Chiara, how can you be sure—"

"I picked her face out of the background crowd in this photo just like that." She snapped her fingers. "The memory has been burned into my brain for fourteen years, because it broke my heart to see that Zach already had a girlfriend."

"She couldn't have been his girlfriend—"

"His romantic interest, then," she amended, staring into the flames flickering in the fireplace as she tucked her feet beneath her and pulled the plush throw blanket tighter around her legs. "Or hers, I guess, since she was a legal adult by then and he was still technically a kid." The woman had no business touching a student, damn it. The idea made her ill.

"Zach was older than us—seventeen when he died. But obviously that doesn't excuse her. If anything, the relationship gives a probable cause for Zach's unhappiness before he died." His scowl deepened.

A fresh wave of regret wrenched her insides at the thought of Zach hurting that much. "I saw them together at the art show where Zach and I were both exhibiting work. I couldn't find him anywhere, so I finally went outside looking for them, and they were hidden in one of the gardens, arms wound around each other—"

She broke off, the memory still stinging. Not because of the romantic heartbreak—she'd gotten over that in time. But she'd left the art show after that, turning her back on Zach when he'd called after her. Little did she know she'd never see him again. Remembering that part still filled her with guilt.

Miles studied her face, seeming content to wait for her to finish, even as he saw too much. When she didn't speak, he reached between them to thread his fingers through hers. The warmth of his touch—the kindness of it—stole her breath. He'd been an anchor for her on a hard day, and she didn't have a chance of refusing the steadiness he offered.

"Okay. Assuming you're correct, why would Zach tell us he was gay if he wasn't?"

"He might have been confused. Fourteen years ago there wasn't as much discussion about sexuality, so he could have misidentified himself." Although he'd always seemed so sure of himself in other ways… She remembered how mature Zach had been. "Or maybe he thought he was protecting her—misdirecting people so no one suspected their relationship."

Miles seemed to consider this for a moment.

"But he told us over the summer," Miles argued. "We had a group video call before the semester even started, and he told us then."

"Zach and I were both at school all summer," she reminded him. "For our art program. Lana Allen could have been around Dowdon during the summer months, too."

Miles swore softly under his breath, and she wondered if that meant he was conceding her point. He dragged a hand over his face and exhaled as he turned to look her in the eye. His thigh grazed her knee where her legs were folded beneath her, the contact sizzling its way up her hip.

"This is huge." He squeezed her palm, his thumb rubbing lightly over the back of her hand. "It changes everything."

"How so?" She went still, hoping he was finally going to trust her enough to share the truth about Zach's death.

He looked uneasy. Then, taking a deep breath, he said, "For starters, I think Zach might have a son."

The news was so unexpected it took her a moment to absorb what he was saying.

"By this woman?" she wondered aloud, doing the math in her head. Zach had been seventeen at the time, and he'd died fourteen years ago. His son would be at least thirteen by now. "Why? Have you seen her?"

"No." Releasing her hand, Miles rose to his feet as

if seized by a new restless energy. He massaged the back of his neck while he paced the great room. When he reached the windows overlooking the mountains, he pivoted hard on the rug and stalked toward her again. "A woman came to Mesa Falls a few months ago claiming to have custody of her sister's child—a thirteen-year-old boy of unknown paternity. The mother died suddenly of an aneurysm and had never told anyone who the father was."

Chiara hugged herself as she focused on his words. "And that's the child you think could be Zach's son?"

He nodded. "The woman claimed the kid's upbringing was being funded by profits from *Hollywood Newlyweds*. At the time, we wondered if the child could have been one of ours, since Alonzo had helped us all through the aftermath of Zach's death. He was a mentor for all of us."

She covered her lips to smother a gasp of surprise as new pieces fell into place. The news that a private school English teacher had been the pseudonymous author behind *Hollywood Newlyweds* had been splashed everywhere over Christmas, sending tabloid journalists scrambling to piece together why the author had never taken credit for the book before his death. It made sense to her that he would keep it a secret if he was using the profits to help Zach's son.

Aloud, she mused, "You think Salazar knew about Zach's son and was trying to funnel some funds to the mother to help raise the baby?"

"Since Lana Allen was his student teacher, maybe he discovered the affair at some point. Although if he knew and didn't report her to the authorities—*hell*. Maybe he felt guilty for not intervening sooner." Miles stopped at the other end of the great room, where Chiara had left her sketchbook. He traced a finger over the open page. "It's all speculation, but you can see where I'm going with this."

Her mind was spinning with the repercussions of the news, and she wasn't sure what it meant for the friends Zach had left behind. For her. For Miles. And all the other owners of Mesa Falls Ranch. Was this the secret her hacker was trying to steer her away from finding? And if so, why?

Needing a break from the revelations coming too fast to process, she slid off her throw blanket and rose to join Miles near the table that held her sketchbook. For the moment, it felt easier to think about something else than to wade through what she'd just learned.

So instead, she wondered what he thought of her drawings. She couldn't seem to give up her love of art even though she'd ended up working in a field that didn't call for many of the skills she wished she was using.

Yet another question about Zach's son bubbled to the surface, and she found herself asking, "Where is the boy now? And the woman who is guarding him—his aunt? She might have the answers we need."

Miles spoke absently as he continued to peruse the sketches. "We have a private detective following a lead on them now. We discussed this at yesterday's meeting, but I don't know if the lead panned out yet." He pulled his attention away from her drawings to meet her gaze. "These are yours?"

She suspected he needed a break from the thoughts about Zach as much as she did.

"Yes." Her gaze followed the familiar lines of pencil

drawings from long ago. She'd been carrying around the sketchbook ever since her days at Brookfield, hoping that seeing the drawings now and then would keep her focused on her quest to find out what happened to Zach. Seeing them now helped her to say to Miles, "You're welcome to look at them, but I wish you'd tell me about the day Zach died. I know you were with him."

She'd learned long ago that the Mesa Falls Ranch owners had all been on a horseback riding trip that weekend. She knew seven riders had left Dowdon but only six had returned.

The firelight cast flickering shadows on Miles's face as he flipped a page in the sketchbook, revealing a cartoonish horse in muted charcoals. He must have recognized the image, because his expression changed when he saw it.

"This horse looks like the one in Alec's video game," he noted, the comment so off-topic from what she'd asked that she could only think Miles wasn't ready to talk about it.

Frustrated, she shook her head but let him lead her back to the discussion of the drawings.

"No." She pointed at the image over his shoulder, the warmth of his body making her wish she could lean into him. "That's a favorite image of Zach's. The horse motif was really prevalent in his work over the four months before he died." She thought she'd done a faithful job of copying the sort of figure Zach had sketched so often. He'd inspired her in so many ways. "Why? What does it have to do with a video game?"

Miles's brow furrowed. "Alec Jacobsen—one of my partners—is a game developer. The series he created using this horse as a character is his most popular."

How had she missed that? She made a mental note to look for the game.

"Then Zach's work must have inspired him," she said firmly, knowing that her friend had worked similar images into most of his dreamlike paintings.

"No doubt. Those two were close friends. I think Alec credited Zach somewhere on his debut game." He flipped another page in the book while a grandfather clock in the foyer struck the hour with resonant chimes. "As for how Zach died, it's still disputed among us."

Her nerve endings tingled to hear the words. To realize she was close to finally learning the truth after all this time. She held her breath. Waiting. Hoping he would confide in her.

Miles never took his gaze from the sketchbook as he spoke again. Quietly.

"He jumped off one of the cliffs into the Arroyo Seco River on a day after heavy rainstorms that raised the water level significantly." He dragged in a slow breath for a moment before he continued. "But we were never sure if he jumped for fun, because he was a daredevil who lived on the edge, or if he made that leap with the intent to end his life."

Chiara closed her eyes, picturing the scene. Zach has been a boy of boundless energy. Big dreams. Big emotions. She could see him doing something so reckless, and she hurt all over again to imagine him throwing everything away in one poor decision.

"He drowned?" Her words were so soft, they felt like they'd been spoken by someone else.

"He never surfaced. They found the body later downstream." Miles paused a moment, setting down the sketchbook and dragging in a breath. "Since there were no suspicious circumstances, they didn't do an autopsy. His death certificate lists drowning as the cause of death."

"How could it not be suspicious?" she asked, her heart rate kicking up. She felt incensed that no one had investigated further. "Even now, you don't know what happened for sure."

"The accident was kept quiet since suicide was a possibility. And Zach had no family."

"Meaning there was no one to fight for justice for him," she remarked bitterly, knowing from personal experience how difficult it had been to find out anything. "So the school ensured no one found out that a fatal incident occurred involving Dowdon students."

The bleakness in his eyes was impossible to miss. "That's right." His nod was stiff. Unhappy. "On the flip side, there was concern about the rest of us. We were all shell-shocked."

Something in his voice, the smallest hesitation from a man normally so confident, forced her to step back. To really listen to what he was saying and remember that this wasn't just about Zach. What happened on that trip had left its mark on Miles and all of his friends.

"I'm sorry," she offered quietly, threading her fingers through his the way he had earlier. "It must have been awful for you."

"We all went in the water to look for him," he continued, his blue gaze fixed on a moment in the past she couldn't see. "Wes could have died—he jumped right in after him. The rest of us climbed down to the rocks below to see if we could find him."

For a long moment, they didn't speak. She stepped

closer, tipping her head to his shoulder in wordless comfort.

"Time gets fuzzy after that. I don't know how we decided to quit looking, but it took a long time. We were all frozen—inside and out. Eventually, we rode back to get help, but by then we knew no one was going to find him. At least—" his chin dropped to rest on the top of her head "—not alive."

Her chest ached at the thought of sixteen-year-old Miles searching a dangerously churning river for his friend and not finding him. She couldn't imagine how harrowing the aftermath had been. She'd grappled with Zach's loss on her own, not knowing the circumstances of his death. But for Miles to witness his friend's last moments like that, feeling guilt about it no matter how misplaced, had to be an unbearable burden. A lifelong sorrow.

Helpless to know what to say, she stepped into him, wrapping her arms around his waist. She tucked her forehead against his chest, feeling the rhythmic beat of his heart against her ear. She breathed in the scent of him—clean laundry and a hint of spice from his aftershave. Her hands traced the contours of his strong arms, the hard plane of his chest and ridged abs.

At his quick intake of breath, she glanced up in time to see his eyes darken. Her heart rate sped faster.

Miles cupped her chin, bringing her mouth closer to his.

"I never talk about this because it hurts too damned much." His words sounded torn out of him.

"Thank you for trusting me enough to tell me." She'd waited half her life to hear what had happened to her friend. "At least he wasn't alone."

"No. He wasn't." Miles stroked his fingers through her hair, sifting through the strands to cup the back of her head and draw her closer still. "Any one of us would have died to save him. That's how close we were."

She'd never had friendships like that when she was a teen. Only later, once she met Astrid and then Jules, did she feel like she had people in her life who would have her back no matter what. Could she trust what Miles said about his love for Zach? She still wondered at his motives for keeping the details of Zach's death private. But as she drew a breath to ask about that, Miles gently pressed his finger against her mouth.

"I promise we can talk about this more," he told her, dragging the digit along her lower lip. "But first, I need a minute." He wrapped his other arm around her waist, his palm settling into the small of her back to seal their bodies together. "Or maybe I just need you."

Miles tipped his forehead to Chiara's, letting the sensation of having her in his arms override the dark churn of emotions that came from talking about the most traumatic day of his life. He felt on edge. Guilt-ridden. Defensive as hell.

He should have been at Zach's side when he jumped. He knew the guy was on edge that weekend. They'd stayed up half the night talking, and he'd known that something was off. Of course, they'd *all* known something was off since Zach had initiated the unsanctioned horseback riding trip precisely because he was pissed off and wanted to get away from school.

But he'd hinted at something bigger than the usual problems while they'd talked and drank late into the night. Miles had never been able to remember the conversation clearly, since they'd been drinking. The night only came back to him in jumbled bits that left him feeling even guiltier that he hadn't realized Zach was battling big demons.

Miles had still been hungover the morning of the cliff-jumping accident. He hadn't wanted to go in the first place because of that, and he sure as hell hadn't been as clearheaded as he should have been while they'd trekked up the trail. He'd lagged behind the whole way, and by the time he realized that Zach had jumped despite the dangerous conditions, Miles's brother was already throwing himself off the precipice to find him.

His brain stuttered on that image—the very real fear his brother wouldn't surface, either. And it stuck there.

Until Chiara shifted in his arms, her hips swaying against him in a way that recalibrated everything. His thoughts. His mood. His body. All of his focus narrowed to her. This sexy siren of a woman who fascinated him on every level.

Possessiveness surged through him along with hunger. Need.

A need for her. A need to forget.

He edged back to see her, taking in the spill of dark hair and mossy-green eyes full of empathy and fire, too. When her gaze dipped to his mouth, it was all he could do not to taste her. Lose himself in her.

But damn it, he needed her to acknowledge that she wanted this, too.

"I could kiss you all night long." He stroked along her jaw, fingers straying to the delicate underside of her chin where her skin was impossibly soft.

He trailed a touch down the long column of her throat and felt the gratifying thrum of her pulse racing there.

He circled the spot with his thumb and then traced it with his tongue.

"Then why don't you?" she asked, her breathless words sounding dry and choked.

"I can't even talk you into the date you owe me." He angled her head so he could read her expression better in the light of the fire. Her silky hair brushed the back of his hand. "It seems presumptuous of me to seduce you."

"Not really." She tilted her face so that her cheek rubbed against the inside of his wrist, her eyelids falling to half-mast as she did it, as if just that innocent touch brought her pleasure.

Hell, it brought him pleasure, too. But then his brain caught up to her words.

"It wouldn't be presumptuous?" he asked, wanting her to take ownership of this attraction flaring so hot between them he could feel the flames licking up his legs.

"No." Her breath tickled against his forearm before she kissed him there then nipped his skin lightly between her teeth. "Not when being with you is all I think about every night."

The admission slayed him, torching his reservations, because *damn*. He thought about her that much, too. More.

"Good." He arched her neck back even farther, ready to claim her mouth. "That's…good."

His lips covered hers, and she was even softer than he remembered, sweetly yielding. Her arms slid around him, her body melting into his, breasts molding to his chest. He could feel the tight points of her nipples right through her blouse and the thin fabric of her bra. It felt like forever since he'd seen her. Held her. Stripped off her clothes and buried himself inside her.

He couldn't wait to do all those things, but he wouldn't do them here in the middle of the living room. With someone tracking her activities, he wanted as many locked doors between them and the rest of the world as possible. He needed her safe. Naked and sighing his name as he pleasured her, yes.

But above all, safe.

Breaking the kiss, he spoke into her ear. "Take me to your bedroom. Our night is about to get a whole lot better."

Ten

Chiara didn't hesitate.

She wanted Miles with a fierceness she didn't begin to understand, but ever since their one incredible night together, she'd been longing for a repeat. Maybe a part of her hoped that she'd embellished it in her mind, and that the sizzling passion had been a result of other factors at work that night. That it was a result of her nervousness at being caught in his office. Or her fascination with meeting one of Zach's closest friends.

But based on the way she was already trembling for want of Miles, she knew her memory of their night together was as amazing as she remembered. Wordlessly, she pulled him by the hand through the sprawling villa. At the top of the split staircase, she veered to the right, where the master suite dominated the back of the house.

She drew him into the spacious room, where he paused to close the door and lock it, a gesture that felt symbolic more than anything, since they were the only ones home. The soft *snick* of the lock sent a shiver through her as she flipped on the light switch and dimmed the overhead fixture. A gas fire burned in the stone hearth in the wall opposite the bed, and even though the flames lit the room, she liked to have the overhead light on to see Miles better. She watched him wander deeper into the room to the doors overlooking the lake. He shrugged off his blue suit jacket and laid it over the back of a leather wingback by the French doors. Picking up the control for the blinds, he closed them all and turned to look at her.

With his fitted shirt skimming his shoulders, it was easy to appreciate his very male physique. Her gaze dropped lower, sidetracked by the sight of still *more* maleness. All for her.

She wanted him, but it felt good to know he wanted her every bit as much. She dragged in breath like she'd just run a race. Heat crawled up her spine while desire pooled in her belly.

After a moment, Miles beckoned to her. "You're too far away for us to have as much fun as I was hoping."

The rasp of his voice smoked through her. Anticipation spiked, making her aware of her heartbeat pulsing in unexpected erogenous zones. But she didn't move closer. She lifted her gaze, though, meeting his blue eyes over the king-size bed.

"Give me a moment to take it all in. The first time we were together, I didn't get to appreciate all the details." In her dreams, she'd feverishly recreated every second with him, but there were too many gaps in her memories. How his hair felt in her fingers, for example. Or the texture of his very capable hands. "Tonight, I'm savoring everything."

As soon as she said it, she realized it made her sound like she was falling for him. She wanted to recant the words. To say what she meant another way. But if Miles noticed, he didn't comment. Instead he turned his attention to unbuttoning his shirt.

"I like the way you think." His lips curved in a half smile. "But if I'm going to show you all my *details* to savor, I hope you plan to do the same."

She knew she should just be grateful for the out—he hadn't taken her words to mean anything serious. And she hadn't meant them that way. But now that the idea was out there in the ether, she had to acknowledge that it rattled her. Worried her. She couldn't fall for Miles.

Could she?

A swish of material jolted her attention back to Miles's shirt falling to the floor. His chest and abs were burnished gold by the firelight, the ripples of muscle highlighted by the shadowed ridges in between them. She wanted to focus on him. On them.

"Chiara." He said her name as he charged toward her. "What's wrong?"

His hands slid around her waist. Bracketed her hips. The warmth of his body rekindled her heat despite her spiraling thoughts.

"Is it crazy for us to indulge this?" She steadied herself by gripping his upper arms, and he felt so good. Solid. Warm.

Like he was hers.

For tonight, at least.

"Why would it be?" He frowned as he planted his feet wider to bring himself closer to her eye level. "What could possibly be wrong with finding pleasure together after the day you've had? Your business has been threatened, but the cops won't help. I'm scared as hell that you could be vulnerable, and yet you don't want to let me get too close to you or take care of you."

The urge to lean into him, to let him do just that, was almost overwhelming. But she had to be honest, even if it doused the flame for him. "Trust comes hard for me."

Her parents hadn't bothered to tell her when they lost their fortune. Zach had kept secrets from her. Miles kept secrets, too. Although he *had* confided more to her tonight.

"Which is why I haven't pushed you to stay with me so I can protect you. But you told me yourself that you thought about being with me every night." His hands flexed against her where he held her hips, a subtle pressure that stirred sweet sensations. "So maybe you could at least trust me to make you feel good."

"I do." She swayed closer, telling herself she could have one more night with him without losing her heart. "I have absolute faith in that."

He gripped the silk of her blouse at her waist and slowly gathered the fabric, untucking the shirttail from her skirt.

"I'm glad. Remember when you told me you chose work over fun for a long time?" he asked, leaning closer to speak into her ear. And to nip her ear with his teeth.

A shiver coursed through her along with surprise that he recalled her words. "Y-yes."

"That ends now."

* * *

Miles kissed his way down her neck, smoothing aside her thick, dark hair to taste more of her. She needed this as much as he did. Maybe even more.

It stunned him to think he read her so clearly when they'd spent so little time together, but he recognized how hard she pushed herself. How much she demanded of herself even when her world was caving in around her. The devotion of her staff—all personal friends, apparently—spoke volumes about who she was, and it made him want to take care of her, if only for tonight. He was going to help her forget all about her burdens until she lost herself in this.

In him.

Not that he was being unselfish. Far from it. He craved this woman.

Flicking open the buttons on her blouse, he nudged the thin fabric off her shoulders and let it flutter to the floor before he lifted his head to study her in the glow of the firelight.

"Are you still with me?" He followed the strap of her ivory lace bra with his fingertip.

The dark fringe of her eyelashes wavered before she glanced up at him, green eyes filled with heat. "Definitely."

The answer cranked him higher. He raked the straps from her shoulders and unhooked the lace to free her. The soft swells of her breasts spilled into his waiting hands, stirring the citrus fragrance he'd come to associate with her.

Hauling her into his arms, he lifted her, taking his time so that her body inched slowly up the length of his. He walked her to the bed and settled her in the space between the rows of pillows at the head and the down comforter folded at the foot, her hair spread out behind her like a silky halo. She followed his movements with watchful green eyes as he unfastened the side zipper of her skirt and eased it down her hips, leaving her in nothing but a scrap of ivory lace.

She made an enticing picture on the bed while he removed the rest of his own clothes. When he paused in undressing to find a condom and place it on the bed near her, she kinked a finger into the waistband of his boxers and tugged lightly.

"You're not naked enough." She grazed a touch along his abs, making his muscles jump with the featherlight caress.

"I'm working on it," he assured her, stilling her questing hand before she distracted him from his goal. "But we're taking care of you first."

"We are?" Her breath caught as he leaned over her and kneed her thighs apart to make room for himself.

The mattress dipped beneath them, their bodies swaying together.

"Ladies first." He kissed her hip, and she arched beneath him. "Call me old-fashioned."

He slid his hand beneath the ivory lace and stroked the slick heat waiting for him there. Her only reply was a soft gasp, followed by a needy whimper that told him she was already close.

She sifted her fingers through his hair, wriggling beneath him as he kissed and teased her, taking her higher and then easing back until they were both hot and edgy. The third time he felt her breathing shift, her thighs tensing, he didn't stop. He fastened his lips to her as she arched against him, and with a hard shudder, she flew apart.

He helped her ride out the sensations, relishing every buck of her hips, every soft shiver of her damp flesh. When he kissed his way back up her torso, he stopped at her breasts to pay homage to each in turn. Chiara patted around the bed for the condom and, finding it, rolled it into place. The feel of her hands on him, that efficient stroke of her fingers, nearly cost him his restraint. He closed his eyes against the heat jolting through him.

"Your turn," she whispered huskily in his ear before she gently bit his shoulder. "I'm in charge."

She pushed against his shoulder until he flipped onto his back. When she straddled him, her dark hair trailed along his chest while she made herself comfortable. Her green eyes seemed to dare him to argue as she arched an eyebrow at him.

But Miles couldn't have denied her a damn thing she wanted. Not now, when her cheeks were flushed with color, her nipples dark and thrusting from his touch. The glow of the chandelier brought out the copper highlights in her raven-colored hair. He caught her hips in his hands, steadying her as she poised herself above him.

Their eyes met, held, as he lowered her onto him. Everything inside him stilled, the sensation of being inside her better than any feeling he'd ever known.

Damn.

He cranked his eyes closed long enough to get command of himself. To grind his teeth against the way this woman was stealing into his life and rewiring his brain. When he opened his eyes again, he sat up, wrapping his arms around her waist to take her to the edge of the bed so she was seated on his lap.

They were even this way. Face-to-face. They had equal amounts of control.

He told himself that with every thrust. Every breath. Every heartbeat. They moved together in sweet, sensual harmony. Their bodies anticipating one another, pushing each other higher. She held on to his shoulders. He gripped her gorgeous round hips.

By the time he saw her head tilt back, her lips part and felt her fingernails dig into his skin, he knew he couldn't hold back when she came this time. He let the force of her orgasm pull him over the edge. They held on to each other tight while the waves of pleasure crashed over them, leaving them wrung out and panting.

Breathless.

Miles found a corner of the folded duvet at the foot of the bed and hauled it around them as he laid them both back down. They were still sideways on the mattress, but it didn't matter. He couldn't move until the world righted. For now, he tucked her close to him, kissing the top of her head, needing her next to him.

He breathed in the scent of her skin and sex, the passion haze behind his eyelids slowly clearing. He'd wanted to make her feel good, and he was pretty sure he'd accomplished that much. What he hadn't counted on was the way being with her had called forth more than a heady release. He'd damned near forgotten his name.

And even worse? After today, he was pretty sure he'd never be able to dig this woman out of his system.

Chiara awoke some hours later, when moonlight filtered through a high transom window over the French doors in the master suite. Even now, Miles's hand rested on her hip as he slept beside her, in just the same position as they'd fallen asleep, her back to his front.

For a moment, she debated making them something to eat since they'd never had dinner, but her body was still too sated sexually to demand any other sustenance. What a decadent pleasure to awake next to this man in her bed.

And yet, no matter how fulfilled her body, her brain already stirred restlessly. After fourteen years, she now knew what had happened to Zach Eldridge. Or at least, she seemed to know as much as Miles did. Miles had insisted he wasn't sure—that none of his friends were sure—whether or not Zach had jumped to end his life or if he'd jumped in a moment of reckless thrill seeking.

Maybe it didn't matter.

But what if it did? What if one of the Mesa Falls Ranch owners knew more about Zach's motives or mindset than they let on? Was one of them more morally responsible than the others for not stopping Zach's trek up to the top of those cliffs in the first place? Was one of them responsible for Zach's death?

She burrowed deeper into her down pillow, trying to shut out the thoughts. If she didn't get some sleep, she wouldn't be able to solve the mystery. Yet her brain kept reminding her that someone knew she was looking into Zach's death, and whoever it was felt threatened enough by her search that he—or she—had tried blackmailing her into giving up.

"Everything okay?" the warm, sleep-roughened voice behind her asked.

A shiver went through her as Miles stroked his palm along her bare hip under the covers. What might it have been like to meet him under different circumstances?

Would she have been able to simply relax and enjoy the incredible chemistry?

"Just thinking about Zach. Trying to reconcile the things you told me with my own understanding of him." That was true enough, even if she had bigger concerns, too. Absently, she traced the piping on the white cotton pillowcase.

Propping himself on his elbow, he said, "If he had an affair with a teacher and she ended up pregnant, it definitely accounts for why he was stressed that weekend. She could have gone to prison for being with him, too, which would have provided another level of stress."

His other hand remained on her hip, his fingers tracing idle patterns that gave her goose bumps.

"She put him in a position no seventeen-year-old should ever be in. Who's to say how he felt about her that weekend? He could have been stressed because she ended things with him. Or because someone found out their secret." She tried to envision what would drive Zach to total despair or to feel reckless enough to make that unwise jump. "Then again, maybe he was stressed because she wanted him to commit to her."

Miles's hand stilled. "What nineteen-year-old woman would want to play house with a seventeen-year-old kid?"

"The same woman who would have had an affair with a student in the first place." Even fourteen years later, she felt angry at the woman for taking advantage of someone she should have been protecting. No matter how much more mature Zach seemed than the other students around him, he was still a kid.

"I should check my phone." Rolling away from her, Miles withdrew his hand from under her body to reach for his device on the nightstand. "I might have heard back from the PI about the stakeout around Nicole Cruz's house."

Instantly alert, Chiara sat up in the bed, dragging a sheet with her. The room was still dark except for the moonlight in the transom window, so Chiara flicked the remote button to turn on the gas fireplace. Flames appeared with a soft whoosh while Miles turned on his phone then scrolled through various screens, his muscles lit by the orange glow.

When his finger stopped swiping, she watched his expression as his blue eyes moved back and forth. Tension threaded through his body. She could see it in his jaw and compressed lips.

"What is it? Did they find her?"

For a moment, when he looked up at her blankly, she wondered if he would go back to shutting her out of news about Zach. Or news about this woman—whether or not she had a direct tie to Zach.

But then his expression cleared, and he nodded.

"According to Desmond's note, Nicole Cruz won't return to Mesa Falls with our private investigator until all the ranch owners submit DNA for paternity testing." His voice was flat. His expression inscrutable. "She's agreed to submit a sample from her sister's son."

"That's good news, right?" she asked, feeling a hunch the child wouldn't be linked to any of them. Her gut told her the mystery boy was Zach's son. "And in the meantime, maybe your detective can see if there's a link between Nicole Cruz and the teacher—Lana Allen. Were they really sisters?"

Miles's fingers hovered over his phone screen. "It would be good to have a concrete lead to give him."

He hesitated. “Are you comfortable with me sharing what you told me?”

The fact that he would ask her first said a lot about his ability to be loyal. To keep a confidence. He’d certainly maintained secrecy for Zach’s sake for a long, long time. The realization comforted her now that she more clearly understood his reluctance to reveal the truth.

“Would you be sharing the information directly with the investigator, or are you asking for permission to communicate it with all your partners?” She understood that Miles trusted his friends, but her first loyalty had to be to Zach.

A veil of coolness dropped over Miles’s features as a chill crept into his voice. “Until now, my partners and I have pooled our knowledge.”

She waited for him to elaborate, but he didn’t.

She needed to tread carefully, not wanting to alienate him now that he’d finally brought her into his confidence. And yet her feelings for him—her fear of losing him—threatened her objectivity. Hugging the sheet tighter to her chest, she felt goose bumps along her arms. If only it was the room getting cooler and not Miles’s mood casting a chill. She weighed how to respond.

“I know you trust your friends.” She couldn’t help it if she didn’t. “But you have to admit that the last time you communicated my interest in Zach to that group, the threats against me came very quickly afterward.”

If she’d thought his face was cool before, his blue gaze went glacial now.

“Coincidence,” he returned sharply. “I’m not in the habit of keeping secrets from the men I trust most.”

A pain shot through her as she realized that the last few hours with Miles hadn't shifted his opinion of her or brought them closer together. If anything, she felt further apart from him than ever. The hurt made her lash out, a safer reaction than revealing vulnerability.

"You realize my entire livelihood rests in the balance?" She couldn't help but draw a second blanket over her shoulders like armor, a barrier, feeling the need to shore up her defenses that had dissolved too fast where he was concerned. "And possibly my safety?"

She thought she spied a thaw in his frosty gaze. He set his phone aside and palmed her shoulder, his fingers a warm, welcome weight.

"I've already told you that I will do everything in my power to keep you safe." The rasp in his voice reminded her of other conversations, other confidences he'd shared with her. She wanted to believe in him.

"I want to find out what drove Zach over that cliff as much as anyone." She swallowed back her anxiety and hoped she wasn't making a huge mistake. "If you think it's best to share what I told you with his other friends in addition to the PI, then you're welcome to tell them what I knew about Zach and the teacher—Miss Allen."

Miles's gaze held hers for a moment before he gave a nod and picked up his phone again to type a text. For a long time afterward, Chiara couldn't help but think his expression showed the same uneasiness she felt inside. But once Miles hit the send button, she knew it was too late to turn back from the course they'd already set.

Eleven

Snow blanketed the Tahoe vacation villa, the world of white momentarily distracting Miles from the tension hanging over his head ever since he'd shared Chiara's insights about Zach with his friends two days ago. A storm had taken the power out the day before, giving them a grace period to watch the weather blow in, make love in every room of that huge villa and not think about their time together coming to an end as they got closer to learning the truth about Zach's death.

Miles had continued to shove his concerns to the back burner this morning, managing to talk Chiara into taking a walk through the woods with him after breakfast. They'd ridden a snowmobile to the casino the day before to retrieve some clothes from his suite.

Now, he held her gloved hand in his as they trudged between sugar pines and white fir trees, the accumulation up to their knees in most places. A dusting clung to her jeans and the fringe of her long red wool jacket. Her cheeks were flushed from the cold and the effort of forging a path through the drifts. Her dark hair was braided in a long tail over one shoulder, a white knitted beanie framing her face as she smiled up at a red-tailed hawk who screeched down at them with its distinctive cry.

For a moment, he saw a different side of her. With no makeup and no fans surrounding her, no couture gown or A-list celebrities clamoring for a photo with her, Chiara looked like a woman who might enjoy the same kind of quiet life he did.

But he knew that was only an illusion. She circulated in a glamorous world of nightlife and parties, far from the ranch where he spent his time.

"I'm glad we got out of the house." She leaned against the rough bark of a Jeffrey pine as they reached an overlook of the lake, where the water reflected the dull gray of the snow clouds. "While having a snow day was fun yesterday, it only delayed the stress fallout from visiting the police station and having it posted online. I feel like I'm still waiting for the other shoe to drop."

Miles leaned back against the trunk near her, still holding her hand. The reminder of those things hanging over them still made him uneasy, and he wished he could distract her. How she felt mattered to him more than it should, considering the very lives they led. And how fast she'd be out of his life again.

He knew her time in Tahoe was bound to her search for answers about Zach, which was why Miles hadn't found a way to tell her yet about the DNA test results he'd received from Desmond earlier that morning. All the Mesa Falls owners had been ruled out, as had Alonzo Salazar through DNA provided by his sons.

Which meant there was a strong chance Zach was the father. But Miles hadn't shared that yet, knowing damn well Chiara might leave once she knew. The possibility of her going weighed him down like lead, but he was also still worried about her safety after the anonymous threats. But he ignored his own feelings to try to reassure her.

"It's been two days since the photos of us at the police station started appearing online." He'd checked his phone before driving over to the casino for his clothes, wanting to make sure there'd been no backlash from her fans. "Maybe it won't be a big deal."

Below them on the snowy hill, a few kids dragged snow tubes partway up the incline to sled down to the water, even though the conditions seemed too powdery for a good run. A few vacation cabins dotted the coastline, and he guessed they were staying in one of them. Chiara's gaze followed the kids, too, before she looked up at him.

"Maybe not." She didn't sound convinced. "And my social media accounts are still working." She held up her phone with the other hand. "I successfully posted a photo of the snow-covered trees a moment ago."

While he was glad to hear her accounts hadn't been hacked, he was caught off guard by the idea of her posting nature photos to her profile that was full of fashion. And he was grateful to think about something besides the guilt gnawing at him for not confiding in her about the DNA news.

"Just trees?" He gave her a sideways glance, studying her lovely profile.

Her lips pursed in thought. "I've been posting more artistic images." She shifted against the tree trunk so she faced him, her breath huffing between them in a drift of white in the cold air. "Thinking more about Zach this week has made me question how I could have gotten so far afield from the mixed media art that I used to love making."

Regret rose as he remembered how he'd dismissed her work when they'd first met. "I hope it didn't have anything to do with what I said that night about your job. I had no right—"

She shook her head, laying a hand on his arm. "Absolutely not. I know why I launched my brand and created the blog since I couldn't afford art school. But there's nothing stopping me from doing something different now. From reimagining my future."

While the kids on the hill below them laughed and shouted over their next sled run, Miles shifted toward Chiara, the tree bark scraping his sheepskin jacket as he wondered if she could reimagine a future with him in it. Did he want that? Gazing into her green eyes, he still wrestled with how much they could trust each other. He felt her wariness about his friends. And for his part, he knew she was only here now because of her loyalty to Zach.

So he kept his response carefully focused on her even when he was tempted as hell to ask for more.

"No doubt, you could do anything you wanted now." He brushed a snowflake from her cheek, the feel of her reminding him of all the best highlights from their past two nights together.

Funny that despite seeing stars many times thanks to her, the moments he remembered best were how she'd felt wrapped around him as he fell asleep the last two nights, resulting in the best slumber he'd had in a long time. He'd been totally relaxed, like she was supposed to be right there with him.

She closed her eyes for a moment as he touched her. He'd like to think she relished the feel of him as much he did her. Her long lashes fluttered against her cheeks for a moment before she raised her gaze to meet his again.

"For a long time, I worried that any artistic talent I once had was only because of the inspiration from the year I knew Zach," she confided quietly. "Like I was somehow a fraud without him."

The statement stunned him, coming from someone so obviously talented. "You built your success because of your artistic eye. And hell yes, I know that because I read up on you after we met."

He wasn't about to hide that from her if he could leverage what he'd learned to reassure her. He lifted her chin so she could see his sincerity.

"Thank you." Her gloved fingers wrapped around his wrist where he touched her, the leather creaking softly with the cold. "Oddly, I've been more reassured as I've reconnected with my old sketchbooks. There is a lot more original work in there than I remembered. I think I let Zach's influence magnify in my mind over the years because of the huge hole he left in my life in other ways. I spent at least a year just redrawing old works of his from memory, trying to keep him in my heart."

Tenderness for her loss swamped him. He recognized it. He'd lived it. "I know what you mean. All of us tried to fill the void he left in different ways. Weston took up search and rescue work. Gage disappeared into numbers and investing."

He mused over the way his friends had grown an unbreakable bond, while at the same time venturing decidedly away from the experience they'd shared. Zach's death had brought them together and kept them all isolated at the same time.

"What about you?" Chiara asked as his hand fell from her chin. "What did you do afterward?"

He couldn't help a bitter smile. "I became the model son. I threw myself into ranching work to help my father and prepare for taking over Rivera Ranch."

"That sounds like a good thing, right?" She tipped her head sideways as if not sure what she was hearing. "Very practical."

"Maybe it was. But it only increased the divide between my brother and me." He hated that time in his life for so many reasons. The fact that it had alienated him from the person who knew him best had been a pain that lasted long after. "I could do no wrong in my parents' eyes after that, and it was the beginning of the end for my relationship with Wes."

Her brows knit in confusion as the snow started falling faster. A flake clung briefly to her eyelash before melting.

"Why would your brother resent your efforts to help your family?" she asked with a clarity he could never muster for the situation.

The fact that she saw his life—him—so clearly had him struggling to maintain his distance. The intimacy of the last two days was threatening to pull him under. Needing a breather, he stirred from where he stood.

"He didn't." Miles shrugged as he straightened, gesturing toward the path back to her villa. "But our parents treated us so differently it got uncomfortable for Wes to even come home for holidays. I hated how they treated him, too, but since I spent every second away from school working on Rivera Ranch, I let that take over my life."

For a few minutes, they shuffled back along the paths they'd made through the deep snow on their way out. He, for one, was grateful for the reprieve from a painful topic. But then again, if there was a chance he would be spending more time with Chiara in the future, he owed her an explanation of his family dynamics.

He held his hand out for her to help her over an icy log in the path.

"It seems like the blame rests on your parents' shoulders. Not yours or Weston's," she observed, jumping down from the log to land beside him with a soft thud of her heavy boots.

The sounds from the sledders retreated as they continued through the woods.

"Maybe so. But then, on one of Wes's rare trips home, we ended up dating the same woman without knowing. That didn't help things." It had been a misguided idea to date Brianna in the first place, but Miles had been on the ranch and isolated for too long. So even though Brianna was a rebel and a risk taker, he'd told himself his life needed more adventure.

He'd gotten far more than he'd bargained for when he'd seen Wes in a lip lock with her at a local bar a few weeks later. That betrayal had burned deep.

"That sounds like her fault. Because you may not have known, but she must have." She scowled as she spoke.

Miles couldn't help a laugh. "I appreciate your defense of me. Thank you."

He could see Chiara's villa ahead through the trees

and the snow, and his steps slowed. He wasn't ready to return to the real world yet. Didn't want to know what had happened with Nicole Cruz, or with Chiara's anonymous hacker. He wanted more time with her before he lost her to her work and her world where he didn't belong.

Chiara slowed, too, coming to a halt beside him. They still held hands. And for some reason stepping out of the trees felt like it was bringing them that much closer to the end of their time together.

"I like you, Miles," she admitted, dropping her forehead to rest on his shoulder as if she didn't want to return to the real world yet, either. "In case you haven't guessed."

Her simple words plucked at something inside him. Made him want to take a chance again for the first time in a long time. Or confide in her, at the very least. But long-ingrained habit kept him silent about the deeper things he was feeling. Instead, he focused on the way they connected best.

"I like you a whole lot, too," he growled, winding an arm around her waist to press her more tightly to him. "I'll remind you how much if you take me home with you."

She lifted her eyes to his, and for the briefest of seconds, he thought he saw her hesitate. But then her lids fell shut and she grazed her lips over his, meeting his kiss with a sexy sigh and more than a little heat.

Chiara was half dazed by the time Miles broke the kiss. Heat rose inside her despite the snow, her body responding to everything about him. His scent. His touch. His wicked, wonderful tongue.

Heartbeat skipping, she gladly followed him as he led her back toward the huge stone-and-wood structure, her thoughts racing ahead to where they'd take the next kiss. Her bed? The sauna? In front of the massive fireplace? Sensual thoughts helped keep her worries at bay after the way Miles seemed to pull back from her earlier. Or had that been her imagination?

Sometimes she sensed that he avoided real conversation in favor of touching and kissing. But when his every touch and kiss set her aflame, could she really argue? She'd let her guard down around him in a big way, showing him a side of herself that felt new. Vulnerable. Raw.

Breathless with anticipation, she tripped into the side door behind him, peeling off her snowy boots on the mat. Her hat and gloves followed. He shook off his coat and boots before stripping off her jacket and hanging it on an antique rack for her. He didn't wait to fold her in his arms and kiss her again. He gripped her hips, steadying her as he sealed their bodies together. Heat scrambled her thoughts again, her fingers tunneling impatiently under his cashmere sweater where she warmed them against his back before walking them around to his front, tucking them in the waistband of his jeans.

The ragged sound in his throat expressed the same need she felt, and he pulled away long enough to grip her by the hand and guide her across the polished planked floor toward the stairs.

Her feet were on the first wide step of the formal divided staircase when a knock sounded on the back door.

Miles stopped. His blue gaze swung around to look at her.

Her belly tightened.

"Maybe it's just Jules checking to see how we're faring after the storm." At least, she hoped that was all it was.

Still, her feet didn't move until the knock sounded again. More urgently.

"We'd better check," Miles muttered, frustration punctuating every word. He kept holding her hand as he walked with her through the kitchen.

She sensed the tension in him—something about the way he held himself. Or maybe the way he looked like he was grinding his teeth. But she guessed that was the same sexual frustration she was feeling right now.

Still, her nerves wound tight as she padded through the room in her socks. Through a side window, she could see Jules and Stefan—together—on the back step. Vaguely, she felt Miles give her hand a reassuring squeeze before she pulled open the door.

"What's up?" she started to ask, only to have Jules thrust her phone under Chiara's nose as she stepped into the kitchen, Stefan right behind her.

Miles closed the door.

"Your page is down." Jules's face was white, her expression grim as she waggled the phone in front of Chiara with more emphasis. "We've been hacked."

She could have sworn the floor dropped out from under her feet. Miles's arm wrapped around her. Steadying her.

Chiara stared at Jules's device, afraid to look. Closing her eyes for a moment, she took a deep breath before she accepted the phone. Then, sinking onto the closest counter stool, she tapped the screen back to life.

Miles peered over her shoulder, his warmth not giving her the usual comfort as a shiver racked her. His hand rubbed over her back while her eyes focused on what she was seeing.

Oddly, the image at the top of her profile page—her home screen—was of Miles. Only he wasn't alone. It was a shot of him with his face pressed cheek to cheek with a gorgeous woman—a brown-eyed beauty with dark curling hair and a mischievous smile. A banner inserted across the image read, "Kara Marsh, you'll always be second best."

Miles might have said something in her ear, but she couldn't focus on his words. If she'd thought the floor had shifted out from under her feet before, now her stomach joined the free fall. As images went, it wasn't particularly damaging to her career.

Simply to her heart.

Because the look on Miles's face in that photo was one she'd never seen before. Pressed against that ethereally gorgeous creature, Miles appeared happier than he'd ever been with Chiara. In this image, his blue eyes were unguarded. Joyous. In love.

And that hurt more than anything. In the woods this morning, when she'd tentatively tested out his feelings with a confession that she liked him—not that it was a huge overture, but still, she'd tried—he'd responded with sizzle. Not emotions.

Jules crouched down into her line of vision, making Chiara realize she'd been silent too long. With an effort, she tried to recover herself, knowing full well her hurt must have been etched all over her face in those first moments when she'd seen the picture.

"It could be worse," she managed to say, sliding the phone across the granite countertop to Jules, avoiding pieces from a jigsaw puzzle she'd worked on for a little while with Miles during the snowstorm. "That's hardly a damning shot."

"I agree," Jules said softly, her tone a careful blend of professionalism and caution. "But the banner—coupled with the fact that you were recently photographed with Miles—creates the impression that either Miles or his—" she hesitated, shooting a quick glance at Miles "—um, former girlfriend were the ones to hijack your social media properties. This same image is on your personal blog, too. I'm worried your fans will be defensive of you—"

"I'm sure we'll get it cleared up soon." She wasn't sure of any such thing as she picked up one of the puzzle pieces and traced the tabs and slots. But the need to confront Miles privately was too strong for her to think about her career. Or whatever else Jules was saying. "Could you give us a minute, Jules? And I'll come over to help you figure out our next steps in a little while?"

Her heartbeat pounded too loudly for her to even be sure what Jules said on her way out. But her friend took Stefan by the arm—even though her bodyguard looked doubtfully from Miles to Chiara and back again—and tugged him out the villa's back door.

Leaving her and Miles alone.

He put his hands on her shoulders, gently swiveling her on the counter stool so that she faced him.

"Are you all right?" He lowered himself into the seat next to her, perching on the edge of the leather cushion. "Would you like me to get you something to drink? You don't look well."

"I'm fine." That wasn't true, but a drink wouldn't help the tumultuous feelings inside her. The hurt deeper than she had a right to feel over a man she'd vowed could only be a fling.

"You don't look fine." His blue eyes were full of concern. Though, she reminded herself, not love. "You can't think for a second I had anything to do with posting that."

"Of course not." That hadn't even occurred to her. She hadn't roused the energy to think about who was behind the post because she was too busy having her heart stepped on. Too consumed with feelings she'd assured herself she wasn't going to develop for this man. But judging by the jealousy and hurt gnawing away at her insides, she couldn't deny she'd been harboring plenty of emotions for this man.

Still, she needed to pull herself together.

"For what it's worth, that's obviously not a recent photo," Miles offered, his hands trailing down her arms to her hands where he found the puzzle piece she was still holding. He set it back on the counter. "I'm not sure where someone would have gotten ahold of it, but—"

"Social media," she supplied, thinking she really needed to get back online and start scouring her pages to see what was happening. Jules had to be wondering why Chiara had only wanted to talk to Miles. "It looks like a selfie. My guess is your old girlfriend has it stored on one of her profiles."

"Makes sense." He nodded, straightening, his touch falling away from her. "But I was going to say that I haven't seen Brianna Billings in years, so I'm sure she wouldn't be sending you anonymous threats."

Not wanting to discuss the woman in the photo, or the feelings it stirred, Chiara stared out the window behind Miles's head and watched the snowfall as she turned the conversation in another direction.

"So if we rule out you and your ex for suspects in hacking the page," she continued, knowing she sounded stiff. Brusque. "Who else should we look at? I'll call the police again, of course, but they'll ask us who we think might be responsible. And personally, I think it's got to be one of your partners at Mesa Falls. One of Zach's former friends."

"No." He shook his head resolutely and stood, then walked over to the double refrigerator doors and pulled out a bottle of water. He set it on the island before retrieving two glasses. "It can't be."

She didn't appreciate how quickly he wrote off her idea. Especially when her feelings were already stirred up disproportionately at seeing a different side of Miles in that photo. She felt Miles pulling away. Sensed it was all plummeting downhill between them, but she didn't have a clue how to stop things from going off the rails.

"Who else would be tracking my efforts to find out what happened to Zach, and would know about your past, too?" she asked him sharply. "I'm not the common denominator in that equation. It's the Mesa Falls group."

"It's someone trying to scare you away from looking into Zach's past. Maybe Nicole Cruz?" he mused aloud as he filled the two glasses of water. Although as soon as he said it, he glanced up at her, and she could have sworn she saw a shadow cross through his eyes.

Then again, she was feeling prickly. She tried to let go of the hurt feelings while he returned the water bottle to the stainless steel refrigerator. Frustration and hurt were going to help her get to the bottom of this.

"It could be whoever fathered the mystery child," she pressed, wondering about the DNA evidence. "Once we know who the father is—"

"It's none of us," Miles answered with a slow shake of his head. He set a glass of water in front of her as he returned to the seat beside her.

His answer sounded certain. As if he knew it for a fact. But she guessed that was just his way of willing it to be the truth.

"We'll only know that for sure once the test results come in," she reminded him before taking a sip of her drink.

"They already have. All of the Mesa Falls partners have been cleared of paternity, along with Alonzo Salazar, courtesy of DNA provided by his sons." Miles's fingers tightened around his glass.

Surprised, Chiara set hers back down with a thud, sloshing some over the rim.

"How long have you known?" she asked, her nerve endings tingling belatedly with uneasiness.

"Desmond texted me early this morning."

"And just when were you going to tell me?" She knew logically that not much time had passed. But she'd been waiting half of a lifetime for answers about Zach. And damn it, she'd spent her whole life being in the dark because of other people's secrets. Her family's. Zach's friends'. Even, she had to admit, Zach's.

Indignation burned. Her heart pounded faster, her body recognizing the physical symptoms of betrayal. Of secrets hidden.

"Soon," Miles started vaguely, not meeting her eyes. "I just didn't want—"

"You know what? It doesn't matter what you did or

didn't want." She stood up in a hurry, needing to put distance between herself and this man who'd slid past her defenses without her knowing. She didn't have the resources to argue with him when her heart hurt, and she'd be damned if she'd let him crush more of the feelings she'd never meant to have for him.

She needed to get her coat so she could go talk to Jules and focus on her career instead of a man who would never trust her. More than that, she needed to get out of the same town as him. Out of the same state.

There was no reason to linger here any longer. The time had come to return home, back to her own life in Los Angeles.

"Chiara, wait." Miles cut her off, inserting himself in her path, though he didn't touch her.

"I can't do secrets, Miles," she said tightly, betrayal stinging. And disillusionment. And anger at herself. "I'm sure that sounds hypocritical after the way I searched your computer that night—"

"It doesn't." He looked so damned good in his jeans and soft gray sweater, his jaw bristly and unshaven. "I know trust comes hard for you."

"For you, too, it seems." She folded her arms to keep herself from touching him. If only the want could be so easily held at bay.

"Yes. For me, too," he acknowledged.

She waited for a long moment. Waited. And heaven help her, even hoped. Just a little. But he said nothing more.

Tears burning her eyes, she sidestepped him to reach for her coat.

"I'm going to be working the rest of the day," she informed him, holding herself very straight in an effort to keep herself together. Her heart ached. "I'll head back to LA tomorrow. But for tonight, I think it would be best if you weren't here when I return."

Miles didn't argue. He only nodded. He didn't even bother to fight for her.

Once she had her boots and coat on, she shoved through the door and stepped out into the snow. Some wistful part of her thought she heard a softly spoken, "Don't go" from behind her. But she knew it was just the foolish wish of a heart broken before she'd even realized she'd fallen in love.

Twelve

Three days later, gritty-eyed despite rising late, Miles prowled Desmond's casino floor at noon. Navigating the path to Desmond's office through a maze of roulette wheels, blackjack tables and slot machines, he cursed the marketing wisdom that demanded casino guests walk through the games every time they wanted to access hotel amenities.

No doubt the setup netted Desmond big profits, but the last thing Miles wanted to see after Chiara's defection was a tower of lights blinking "jackpot!" accompanied by a chorus of electronic enthusiasm. A herd of touristy-looking players gathered around the machine to celebrate their good fortune, while Miles suspected he'd never feel lucky again.

Not after losing the most incredible woman he'd ever met just two weeks after finding her. He'd surely set a record for squandering everything in so little time.

He hadn't been able to sleep for thinking about the expression on her face when she'd discovered he hadn't told her about the DNA test results. He'd known—absolutely known—that she would be hurt by that given the trust issues she'd freely admitted. And yet he'd withheld it anyhow, unwilling to share the news that would send her out of his life.

So instead of letting her choose when she should return to her California home once she'd found out all she could about Zach, he'd selfishly clung to the information in the hope of stretching out their time together. And for his selfishness, he'd hurt her. Sure, he'd like to think he would have told her that afternoon. He couldn't possibly have gone to bed by her side that night without sharing the news. But it didn't matter how long he'd kept that secret.

What mattered was that she'd told him how hard it was for her to trust. Something he—of all people—understood only too well. Yeah, he recognized the pain he'd caused when he'd crossed the one line she'd drawn with him about keeping secrets.

When he finally reached the locked door of the back room, a uniformed casino employee entered a code and admitted him. At least the maze of halls here was quiet. The corridors with their unadorned light gray walls led to a variety of offices and maintenance rooms. Miles bypassed all of them until he reached stately double doors in the back.

Another uniformed guard stood outside them. This one rapped his knuckles twice on the oak barrier before admitting Miles.

A stunning view of Lake Tahoe dominated one side of the owner's work suite, with glass walls separating a private office, small conference room and a more intimate meeting space. All were spare and modern in shades of gray and white, with industrial touches like stainless steel work lamps and hammered metal artwork. Desmond sat on a low sofa in front of the windows overlooking Lake Tahoe in the more casual meeting space.

Sunlight reflecting off the water burned right into Miles's eyes until he moved closer to the window, the angle of built-in blinds effectively shading the glare as he reached his friend. Dressed in a sharp gray suit and white collared shirt with no tie, Desmond drank a cup of espresso as he read an honest-to-God newspaper—no electronic devices in sight. The guy had an easy luxury about him that belied a packed professional life.

As far as Miles knew, he did nothing but work 24/7, the same way Gage Striker had when he'd been an investment banker. Gage's wealth had convinced him to start taking it easier as an angel investor the last couple of years, but Desmond still burned the candle at both ends, working constantly.

"Look what the cat dragged in," Desmond greeted him, folding his paper and setting it on a low glass table in front of him. With his posh manners and charm, Desmond looked every inch the worldly sophisticate. And it wasn't just an act, either, as he held dual citizenship in the United States and the UK thanks to a Brit mother.

But Miles remembered him from darker days, when Desmond's father had been a ham-fisted brute, teaching his son to be quick with a punch out of necessity, to protect himself and his mother. It was a skill set Desmond hid well, but Miles knew that a lot of his work efforts still benefited battered women and kids. And he'd channeled his own grief about Zach into something positive, whereas Miles still felt like the old wounds just ate away at his insides. What did he have to show for the past beyond Rivera Ranch? All his toil had gone into the family property. And he hadn't really done anything altruistic.

"I only came to let you know I'm returning to Mesa Falls." Miles dropped onto a leather chair near the sofa, eager to leave the place where his brief relationship with Chiara had imploded. "I'm meeting the pilot this afternoon."

"Coffee?" Desmond offered as he picked up a black espresso cup.

Miles shook his head, knowing caffeine wouldn't make a dent in the wrung-out feeling plaguing his head. He'd barely slept last night for thinking about Chiara's parting words that had been so polite and still so damned cutting.

I think it would be best if you weren't here when I return.

"It's just as well you came in." Desmond set aside his empty cup and leaned back into the sofa cushions. "I was going to message you anyhow to let you know you don't need to return to Mesa Falls."

Miles frowned as he rubbed his eyes to take away some of the gritty feeling. "What do you mean? Someone's got to oversee things."

"Nicole Cruz is flying to Montana tonight," Desmond informed him, brushing some invisible item from the perfectly clean cushion by his thigh. "I assured her I would be there to meet her. Them."

Miles edged forward in his seat, trying to follow.

"You want to be there to meet the guardian of the kid who's most likely Zach's son?" he clarified, knowing something was off about the way Desmond was talking about her.

Was it suspicion?

He'd like to think they were all suspicious of her, though. This seemed like something different.

"I've been her only point of contact so far," Desmond explained, giving up on the invisible dust. He gave Miles a level gaze. "The only one of us she's communicated with. We can't afford to scare her off when it took us this long to find her."

"Right. Agreed." Miles nodded, needing to rouse himself out of his own misery to focus on their latest discovery about Zach. "If Matthew is Zach's son, we don't want to lose our chance of being a part of his life."

Regret stung as he considered how much Chiara would want to meet the boy. He didn't want to stand in her way, especially when they might not have come this far figuring out Zach's secrets without her help.

Desmond's phone vibrated, and he picked it up briefly.

"I've asked the PI to back off investigating Nicole and Matthew," Desmond continued as he read something and then set the device back on the table. Sun glinted off the sleek black case.

"Why?" Miles picked up his own phone, checking for the thousandth time if there were any developments on who had targeted Chiara's sites. Or, if he was honest, to see if she had messaged him. Disappointment to find nothing stung all over again.

He missed her more than if she'd been out of his life for years and not days. He'd only stuck around Lake Tahoe this long in hopes he'd be able to help the local police, or maybe in the hope she'd return to town to see Astrid. Or him.

But there was only a group message from Alec telling any of the Mesa Falls partners still on site at the casino to meet him at Desmond's office as soon as possible. Miles wondered what that was about.

"Nicole has been dodging our investigators to protect Matthew for weeks. She's exhausted and mistrustful. She asked me to 'call off the dogs' if she agreed to return to Montana, and I have given her my word that I would." Desmond straightened in his seat, appearing ready to move on as he checked his watch. "And, actually, I have a lot to do today to prepare my staff for my absence. Alec agreed to watch over things here, but he's late."

As he spoke, however, a knock sounded at the outer double doors before they opened, and Alec appeared.

Miles only had a second to take in his friend's disheveled clothes that looked slept in—a wrinkled jacket and T-shirt and rumpled jeans. His hair stood up in a few directions, and his face had a look of grim determination as he wound through the office suite to the glassed-in room where Desmond and Miles sat.

"Sorry I'm late." Alec juggled a foam coffee cup in his hand as he plowed through the last door. "I've been at the police station giving my statement. They arrested my personal assistant, Vivian, for threatening Chiara Campagna."

"You're kidding." Miles tensed, half rising to his feet. Then, realizing the woman in question was already in custody, he lowered himself into the chair again. "How did they find out?"

Miles had checked with the local police just the night

before but hadn't learned anything other than that they were still looking into the complaint Chiara filed after the second incident.

Alec lowered himself into the chair opposite Miles at the other end of the coffee table. He set his coffee cup on a marble coaster.

"Apparently it wasn't tough to track her once they got a cybercrimes expert to look into it. Vivian and I were working late last night when she got a call from the police asking her to come in so they could ask her some questions." Alec shrugged and then swiped his hand through the hair that was already standing straight up. "I drove her over there, never thinking they already had evidence on her. They arrested her shortly afterward."

"Does Chiara know?" Miles wanted to call her. Check on her. Let her know that the police had done their job.

Hell. What he really wanted was to fold her into his arms.

But holding her wasn't his right anymore.

"I'm not sure if they've contacted her yet." Alec retrieved his coffee cup, a thick silver band around his middle finger catching the light and refracting it all over the room. "I'm still trying to process the news myself."

Before Miles could ask more about it, a knock sounded again on the outer door, and his brother, Weston, ambled in wearing jeans and a T-shirt. With his too-long hair and hazel eyes, he and Miles couldn't be less alike.

"What's up? April and I were going to hit the slopes today. Conditions are incredible." He stopped himself as he looked around at his friends. "What happened?"

As he sank to a seat on the other end of the couch

from Desmond, Alec repeated the news about Vivian before adding, "I had no idea Vivian was imagining we had a much deeper relationship than we do, but sometime in the last few years she started crossing the line as my assistant to make sure things went my way—bribing contacts into taking meetings with me, padding the numbers on our financial statements to make the gaming company look stronger for investors, a whole bunch of stuff unrelated to what happened with Chiara."

Miles recalled meeting Vivian lurking outside the high-roller suite that day after the meeting of the Mesa Falls partners. "So why would she hassle Chiara?"

"I guess she intercepted a text on my phone about Chiara's interest in Zach." Alec glanced upward, as if trying to gather his thoughts, or maybe to remember something. "Vivian never liked her. She was a student at Brookfield, too, and I was with her that day at Dowdon that Kara—Chiara—came to school to talk to Miles and Gage."

Miles remembered Alec saying he'd been with a girl under the bleachers that day. Still, fourteen years seemed like a long time to hold a grudge against Chiara. Once again his protective instincts kicked into gear. If he couldn't be with Chiara or make her happy, he owed it to her to at least keep her safe. Which meant getting full disclosure on everything related to Zach's death.

Desmond spoke before Miles had a chance to ask about that.

"So Vivian must have known about Zach if you've been friends that long." Desmond seemed to put the pieces together faster, but maybe it was easier to have more clarity on the situation than Miles, who'd lost objectivity where Chiara was concerned a long time ago.

"Maybe she figured it was somehow helping you to keep Chiara from asking too many questions."

Weston whistled softly under his breath. "She sounds like a piece of work."

Alec bristled. "She's smart as hell, actually. Just highly unethical."

The conversation continued, but Miles couldn't focus on it with the urge to see Chiara, to make sure she knew that her hacker was in custody, so strong. He wanted to share the news with her, to give her this much even though he'd failed their fledgling relationship.

"Why did she feel the need to post a picture of me with an old girlfriend on Chiara's page?" he found himself asking, curious not so much for himself, but for Chiara's sake. He'd known that image had bothered her.

And if he was able to see her again—or even just speak to her—he wanted to share answers with her. Answers he owed her after the way he'd withheld information from her before.

Alec took another drink of his coffee before responding. "I wondered about that, too. I guess Vivian was upset about a photo of me with Chiara from that night at your party, Miles. Then, when she saw the pictures of you at the police station with Chiara—looking like a couple—she figured the best way to hurt Chiara would be with an image of you and someone else."

Miles remembered the jealousy that had gone through him when he saw Alec's hand on the small of Chiara's back that night, touching her bare skin through the cutout of her silver gown.

Weston spoke up. "For a smart woman, she definitely made some stupid mistakes. But lucky for us, right? Because now she's behind bars." He stood as if to leave. "I've got to get back to April to meet the car taking us to the mountain."

Miles rose as well, edgy to be out of Tahoe. Now that he'd been relieved of his duties at Mesa Falls, he was free to use the afternoon's flight to see Chiara. To share what he'd learned, at least. "Desmond, if you've got things covered at Mesa Falls, I'm going to head back home."

"You're returning to Rivera Ranch?" Desmond stood and walked to the door with them, though his question was for Miles.

"Eventually." Miles could only think about one destination today, however. "I need to make a stop in Los Angeles first."

After a quick exchange of pleasantries, Miles and Weston left the owner's suite together.

"Los Angeles?" Weston wasted no time in posing the question.

Slowing his step in the long, empty corridor between the casino floor and the offices, Miles couldn't deny the rare impulse to unburden himself. His brother, after all, owed him a listening ear after the way Miles had helped him patch up his relationship with April Stephens, the woman Wes loved beyond reason.

"I messed up with Chiara," he admitted, done with trying to label what happened as anything other than his fault. "I was selfish. Stupid. Shortsighted—"

Weston halted in the middle of the echoing hall, clamping a hand on Miles's shoulder. "What happened?"

Miles explained the way he'd withheld the news about the DNA evidence to give himself more time with her, to try to think of a way to make her stay, even though he'd known about her past and the way her own family had kept secrets from her. Even though she'd told him how hard it was for her to trust. When he finished, Weston looked thoughtful.

"You remember when I screwed up with April, you told me that I needed to be the one to take a risk. To put myself on the line?"

"Yes." Miles remembered that conversation. Of course, taking chances was like breathing to his brother, so it hadn't seemed like too much to ask of him to be the one to tell April he loved her. "I also told you that not everyone can be such a romantic."

Miles knew himself too well. He had two feet on the ground at all times. He was a practical man. Salt of the earth. A rancher. He didn't jump first and ask questions later. That had always been Wes's role. But maybe it was time to take a page from his brother's book, to step up and take a risk when the moment called for it. His gut burned to think he hadn't already done so.

"News flash. What you're feeling doesn't have a thing to do with romance. It has everything to do with love, and you're going to lose it, without question, if you can't get your head on straight and see that." Weston's expression was dire.

Grave.

And Miles wasn't too proud to admit it scared the hell of out of him. Especially if what he'd walked away from was love. But by the way the word encapsulated every single aspect of his feelings for Chiara, he knew Weston was right.

"You think I already blew it for good?" He wondered how fast his plane could get to LA.

"It's been three days and you haven't even called?

Haven't gone there to tell her how wrong you were?" Weston shook his head. "Why didn't you call me sooner to help you figure this out? I owed you, man. Maybe, with more time, I could have—"

Miles cut his brother off, panic welling up in his chest.

"I've got a plane to catch." He didn't wait to hear any more about how much he'd screwed up. If time was of the essence, he wasn't wasting another second of it to see Chiara and tell her how he felt about her.

That he loved her.

Thirteen

Seated in a low, rolled-arm chair close to her balcony, Chiara sniffed a small vial of fragrance, knowing she'd have a headache soon if she kept testing the samples from her perfumer. Although maybe the impending headache had more to do with all the tears she'd shed for Miles this week. Still, she needed the distraction from her hurt, so she sniffed the floral fumes again, trying to pinpoint what she didn't like about the scent.

The setting sun smudged the western sky with lavender and pink as lights glowed in the valley below her Hollywood Hills home. The glass wall was retracted between her living room and the balcony so that the night air circulated around the seating area where she tested the samples. She'd adored this property once, so modern and elegant, but it felt incredibly lonely to her since she'd returned to it earlier in the week. As for the fragrance vial in her hand, the hint of honeysuckle—so pleasing in nature—was too heavy in the mixture. She handed it back to Mrs. Santor, her housekeeper. In addition to her regular duties, she was giving her input on developing a signature fragrance for Chiara's brand.

"I didn't like that one, either," Mrs. Santor said from the seat beside her, packing away the vial in a kit Chiara had received from a perfumer. "You should call it a night, honey. You look spent."

Amy Santor was Jules's mother and a former next-door neighbor in Chiara's old life. Mrs. Santor had cleaned houses all her life, and when Chiara's business had taken off, she would have gladly given Mrs. Santor any job she wanted in her company to repay her for kindnesses she'd shown Chiara in her youth. But Jules's mom insisted that she enjoyed keeping house, and Chiara felt fortunate to have a maternal figure in her home a few times a week.

"I shouldn't be. It's still early." She checked her watch, irritated with herself for not being more focused.

She'd given Jules a much-needed night off but hadn't taken one herself, preferring to lose herself in work ever since the heartbreak of leaving Lake Tahoe.

She'd heard from a detective today about arresting the woman who'd hijacked her social media, so it should have felt like she had closure. But that conversation had only made her realize how much more losing Miles had hurt her than any damage a hacker could wreak.

At any rate, she'd *tried* to lose herself in work since that had always been her escape. Her purpose. Her calling. She'd built it up in spite of the grief she'd had for Zach, trusting the job to keep her grounded. But it didn't provide a refuge for her now.

"I'll make you some tea before I go," Mrs. Santor continued, putting away the paperwork from the fragrance kit. "I know you don't want to talk about whatever happened on your travels, but trust me when I tell you that you need to take care of yourself."

And with a gentle squeeze to Chiara's shoulder, Mrs. Santor started the kettle to boil in the kitchen while Chiara tried to pull herself together. Maybe she should have confided in her longtime friend. She hadn't talked to Jules, either, refusing to give the people she loved the chance to comfort her.

For so many years she'd been an island—isolated, independent, and no doubt taking too much pride in the fact. But what good was pride when she felt so empty inside now?

Walking away from Miles was the hardest thing she'd ever done. Second only to the restraint it took every day—every hour—not to call or text him. She wondered if he'd returned to Mesa Falls by now or if he'd gone back to Rivera Ranch. Mostly, she wondered if he ever missed her or regretted the way they'd parted.

A moment later, Mrs. Santor returned with a steaming cup and set it before her. "I'm heading out now, hon. I'll see you Saturday, okay?"

Grateful for the woman's thoughtfulness, Chiara rose and hugged her. "Thank you."

Jules's mother hugged her back with the same warmth she gave her own daughter. "Of course. And don't work too hard."

When Mrs. Santor left, Chiara settled in for the evening. But just as she took a sip of her tea to ward off the loneliness of her empty house, the guard buzzed her phone from the gate downstairs. She picked up her device.

"Ms. Campagna, there's a Miles Rivera to see you."

Everything inside her stilled.

There'd been a time he could have had security toss her out of his home for invading his privacy, but instead, he'd listened to her explanation. For that alone, he deserved an audience now. But more than that, she couldn't resist the chance to see him again. She'd missed him so much.

"You can let him in," she answered, feelings tumbling over each other too fast for her to pick through them.

She'd been thinking about him and wishing she could see him. Now that he was here, was she brave enough to take a chance with him? She didn't want to let Miles go, either. What good did her pride do her if it left her feeling heartbroken and lonely?

Chiara resisted the urge to peek in a mirror, although she may have fluffed her hair a little and smoothed her dress. Who didn't want to look their best in front of the one who got away?

She rose from the seat to stand out on the balcony. Even though she was staring out at the spectacular view with her back to the house, Chiara could tell when Miles was close. The hairs on the back of her neck stood, a shiver of awareness passing over her. She pressed her lips together to ward off the feelings, reminding herself of what had happened to drive them apart.

"I've never seen such a beautiful view." The familiar rasp in his voice warmed her. Stirred her.

Turning on her heel, she faced him as he paced through the living area and out onto the balcony. With his chiseled features and deep blue eyes, his black custom suit that hinted at sculpted muscles and the lightly tanned skin visible at the open collar of his white shirt, he was handsome to behold.

But she remembered so many other things about him that were even more appealing. His thoughtfulness in watching out for her. His insistence she go to the police. His touch.

"Hello to you, too," she greeted him, remembering his fondness for launching right into conversation. "I'm surprised to see you here."

"I wanted to be sure you heard the news." He stepped closer until he leaned against the balcony rail with her. "That your harasser is behind bars."

She shouldn't be disappointed that this practical man would be here for such a pragmatic purpose, yet she couldn't deny she'd hoped for more than that. Should she tell him how much she'd missed him? How many times she'd thought about calling?

Absently, she drummed her fingernails against the polished railing, trying not to notice how close Miles's hands were to hers. "Yes. A detective called me this morning with some questions about Vivian Fraser from our time together at Brookfield. I didn't realize she worked for Alec now."

"Were you aware she was jealous of you?"

"No. I don't remember her well from Brookfield other than recalling she was a popular girl with a lot of friends. Our paths never crossed much, as she favored chess club and science over the art activities that I liked." She'd been stunned to hear that Alec's personal assistant had intercepted his messages and decided to "protect" Zach's memory for him by attempting to scare Chiara away from her search for answers.

But apparently there was a clear digital trail that led

to Vivian's personal computer, and she'd admitted as much to the police. The woman was in love with Alec and would do anything to protect him. She'd also done her best to keep other women away from him since they'd had an on-again, off-again relationship dating all the way back to high school. It was sad to think a promising young woman had gotten so caught up in wanting attention from a man that she'd given up her own dreams and identity in an effort to capture his notice.

"I breathed a whole lot easier once I heard the news," Miles said as he looked over the lights spread out below them now that the pink hues of sunset had faded. "I'm sure you did, too."

She couldn't help but glance over at his profile. The strong jaw and chin. The slash of his cheekbone. His lips that could kiss her with infinite tenderness.

"I guess." She spoke quickly once she realized she'd stared too long. "But the whole business with my blog and Vivian were distractions from my real purpose. I really went there to find out about Zach's final days."

She felt more than saw Miles turn toward her now. His eyes looking over her the way she'd studied him just a moment ago. Her heat beat faster as a soft breeze blew her white dress's hem against her legs, the silk teasing her already too-aware skin.

"I know you did, Chiara. And I'm sorry that I got in the way of what you were doing by not sharing what I knew as soon as I knew it." The regret and sincerity in his voice were unmistakable. "You deserved my full help and attention. And so did Zach."

Drawn by his words, she turned toward him now, and they faced one another eye to eye for the first time tonight. He seemed even closer to her now. Near enough to touch.

"I recognize that I probably should have been more understanding. Especially after the way you overlooked me trying to get into your personal files. I crossed a line more than you did." She hadn't forgotten that, and the unfairness of her response compared to his seemed disproportionate. "But I didn't know you when I sneaked into your office. Whereas—"

"The situations were completely different." He shook his head, not letting her finish her sentence. "You had every right to think I might have been a bad friend to Zach or even an enemy. But I knew you had his best interests at heart that day I kept quiet about the DNA. My only defense was that I wanted one more day with you."

Startled, she rewound the words in her mind, barely daring to hope she'd heard him right. "You—what?"

"I knew that once I told you the DNA results you'd have no reason to stay in Tahoe any longer." He touched her forearm. "And our time together had been so incredible, Chiara, I couldn't bear for it to end. I told myself that keeping quiet about it for a few more hours wouldn't hurt. I just wanted—" He shook his head. "It was selfish of me. And I'm sorry."

The admission wasn't at all what she'd expected. "I thought you were keeping secrets to hold me at arm's length. It felt like you didn't want to confide in me."

But this? His reason was far more compelling. And it shot right into the tender recesses of her heart.

"Far from it." A breeze ruffled Miles's hair the way she longed to with her fingers. His hand stroked up her arm to her shoulder. "Talking to you was the highlight of my week. And considering everything else that happened, you have to know how much it meant to me."

She melted inside. Absolutely, positively melted.

"Really?" She'd hoped so, until he'd walked away. But she could see the regret in his eyes now, and it gave her renewed hope.

"Yes, really." He stepped closer to her, one hand sliding around her waist while the other skimmed a few wind-tossed strands of hair from her eyes. "Chiara, I got burned so badly the last time I cared about someone that I planned to be a lot more cautious in the future. I figured if I took my time to build a safe, smart relationship, maybe then I could fall in love."

Her pulse skipped a couple of beats. She blinked up at him, hanging on his words. Trying not to sink into the feeling of his hands on her after so many days of missing him. Missing what they'd shared. Aching for more. For a future.

"I don't understand. Are you suggesting we didn't build a safe relationship?"

"I'm suggesting that whatever my intentions were, they didn't matter at all, because you showed up and we had the most amazing connection I've ever felt with anyone." His hold on her tightened, and she might have stepped a tiny bit closer because the hint of his aftershave lured her.

"I felt that, too," she admitted, remembering how that first night she'd felt like the whole world disappeared except for them. "The amazing connection."

"Right. Good." His lips curved upward just a hint at her words. "Because I came here tonight—why I *really* came here tonight—to tell you that I fell in love with you, Chiara. And if there's any way you can give me another chance, I'm going to do everything in my power to make you fall in love with me, too."

Her heart hitched at his words, which were so much more than she'd dared hope for—but everything she wanted. Touched beyond measure, she couldn't find her voice for a moment. And then, even when she did, she bit her lip, wanting to say the right thing.

"Miles, I knew when we were in the woods that day that I loved you." She laid her hand on his chest beside his jacket lapel, just over his heart. She remembered every minute of their time together. "I didn't even want to go back to the house afterward because it felt like our time together was ending, and I didn't want to lose you."

He wrapped her tight in his arms and kissed her. Slowly. Thoroughly. Until she felt a little weak-kneed from it and the promise it held of even more. When he eased back, she was breathing fast and clinging to him.

"You're not going to lose me. Not now. Not ever." His blue eyes were dark as midnight, the promise one she'd never forget.

It filled her with certainty about the future. Their future.

"You won't lose me, either," she vowed before freeing a hand to gesture to the view. "Not even if I have to leave all this behind to live on Rivera Ranch with you."

"You don't have to do that." He tipped his forehead to hers. "We can take all the time you want to talk about what makes most sense. Or hell, just what we want. I know you want to go back to art school one day, so we can always look at living close to a good program for you."

No one had ever put her first before, and it felt incredibly special to have Miles do just that. The possibilities expanded.

"You don't need to be at the ranch?" she asked, curious about his life beyond Mesa Falls. She wanted to learn everything about him.

"I've worked hard to make it a successful operation that runs smoothly. I've hired good people to maintain that, so even if I'm not there, the ranch will continue to prosper." He traced her cheek with his fingers, then followed the line of her mouth.

She sucked in a breath, wanting to seal the promise of their future with a kiss, and much, much more. Lifting her eyes to his, she read the same steamy thoughts in his expression.

"I'll be able to weigh the possibilities more after I show you how much I've missed you," she told him, capturing his thumb between her teeth.

With a growl that thrilled her, he lifted her in his arms and walked her inside the house.

She had a last glimpse of the glittering lights of the Hollywood Hills, but the best view of all was wherever this man was. Miles Rivera, her rancher hero, right here in her arms.

* * * * *

RUNNING AWAY WITH THE BRIDE

SOPHIA SINGH SASSON

To all those who have been afraid to go for
what they really want.

This book, and the entire Nights at the Mahal series, would not have happened without my awesome editor, Charles Griemsman, and my agent, Barbara Rosenberg.

Most of all, thank you to my readers.
Your reviews, emails and letters keep me writing.

One

"Stop this wedding!"

Ethan Connors searched the stage on the back lawn of the Mahal Hotel where a *mandap* had been set up. The couple was seated on floor-level settees under a pergola-like structure in front of a small fire. A priest dressed in loose orange clothing chanted and threw things into the fire, making it crackle and smoke.

Ethan wished he'd paid more attention to the wedding sequence the one time he'd been to an Indian wedding with Pooja. He had no idea if he'd made it in time to stop hers.

At his outcry, the bride, groom and the dozen or so people surrounding them looked at him with surprise. The priest froze and the chatter of the crowd behind Ethan died. He could feel the stares of hundreds of guests on him. He tried to catch Pooja's eyes but the heavy bridal veil covered her head and fell halfway across her face. The smoke from the fire swirled around her. He looked at the older Indian couple seated next to her. *Were they Pooja's parents?* If the glare they were shooting him was any indication, they were.

A knot twisted in his stomach. After six months of dating, including three months of living together, she'd never introduced him to her parents, and he couldn't pick them out based on the pictures he'd seen on her bookshelf.

A younger man seated next to the bride stood and made his way to Ethan. "I don't know who you are but you're interrupting my sister's wedding. You best leave quietly before I call security." The man's voice was low and icy.

But Ethan was determined he wasn't going to lose her again. He may have come to his senses in the eleventh hour, but he was going to save himself, and Pooja. She'd known the guy sitting next to her for three months. How could she marry him? *I want to know my husband and be sure that we're compatible*, she'd said to Ethan. He and Pooja were compatible. Why hadn't he seen that sooner? When she'd first brought up marriage—and how her family wouldn't approve of her relationship with a white Midwesterner unless he put a ring on her finger—he'd thought he needed more time to figure things out. But what was left to think about? He was pushing forty. His brother was ten years younger and had been married for nine years and had two kids. Pooja was the only woman who had deemed him worthy enough to even discuss marriage. He wasn't going to let her get away a second time.

Pooja was now standing, but Ethan still couldn't get a clear line of sight through the crowd that was gathering around him. He hadn't spoken to her since she walked out three months ago, but she'd sent him an email telling him she was getting married today. Why would she do that if she didn't want him to make a grand gesture? It would've been helpful if she'd sent him some details other than that her groom was planning "a grand *baarat* down the Vegas strip." He'd spent the entire morning driving up and down the strip, looking for a groom on a horse surrounded by a bunch of people dancing. The traditional Indian *baarat,* the arrival of the groom's party, would be hard to miss, or so he thought. He'd been on the other side of the strip when he'd heard on the radio that traffic was snarled because of an Indian wedding, and he'd driven like a madman to get there.

He had charged in ready to take on the world, or at least a bunch of angry relatives, but now doubt snaked its way through him. Did Pooja really want him to rescue her? And how the hell was he going to get out of the hotel without hundreds of guests and hotel security guards stopping him?

Take off your veil and look at me, Pooja. He wanted to tell her that she didn't have to succumb to her parents' pressure and marry whichever Tom, Dick or *Hari* they had found for her. He was ready to step up and make a commitment.

Another man who bore a family resemblance to the one who'd identified himself as Pooja's brother broke through the crowd and strode toward him. Who knew how many family members there were, and Ethan had zero backup. *When will you stop being so impulsive?* His mother's familiar recrimination blared in his head.

He focused on Pooja, who was clearly looking in his direction, despite the veil on her face. "I'm sorry I was such an ass and didn't realize how much you meant to me. I want to marry you. Run away with me." Brother One whispered something into a phone, no doubt calling security. "We must go now!"

"Yo dude, this isn't some Hollywood film. What do you think you're doing?" Brother Number Two was now within punching distance and didn't seem quite as reserved as Brother One. "My sister doesn't know who you are. Get out before I…" He pulled his arm back, clearly preparing to punch Ethan in the face.

"Wait!" Pooja's voice sounded strange.

All eyes turned toward her. As she stepped down from the stage with an easy grace, she fisted some of the long burgundy skirt that flowed to her heels. It was covered with shiny gold thread and shimmering diamond jewels. The gold-colored top was cropped a few inches above her navel, showing a tantalizing strip of her stomach and back. Visions of running an ice cube across that navel, then licking up the droplets of water flashed through his mind. Why hadn't he actually done that with Pooja when they were together?

Her hands had intricate henna patterns from her fingers to her elbow, and her wrists were covered in red-and-white bangles. The crowd dispersed to let her through to him. She lifted her veil as she made her way toward him, and his heart slammed into his chest.

It wasn't Pooja.

"I love you! I cannot go through with this wedding." She leaped into his arms and crushed all the air out of his lungs. He instinctively placed his hands on her waist as she clung to him. Her skin was cool and soft beneath his fingers. She smelled like vanilla and cinnamon.

"What the…?" But he didn't finish what he was going to say because she pressed her lips to his and all rational thought left his brain. His arms tightened around her, and the silence of the stunned crowd matched his stopped heartbeat.

She broke the kiss a bare second after it had begun, leaving him feeling shorted.

"Do not say a word." Her warm breath teased his ear, rousing a fire in his belly. "If you tell them you have the wrong wedding, my brothers will beat you to a pulp for kissing me. I suggest we take advantage of the surprise and run."

She had a slightly Indian, slightly musical and entirely arousing accent. He reluctantly moved his eyes from her mouth and looked at her brothers, whose murderous expressions got him to haul ass.

"Out of our way!" He grabbed her hand. Given that there had to be hundreds of guests milling about, they had surprisingly little trouble getting moving. The guests eagerly parted so they could get a better angle for cell phone pictures and videos and then helpfully got in the way of their pursuers. It made for better social media posts if the bride actually got away.

Just wait until they find out who I am.

She matched his fast pace, despite the fact that they were on grass and she was wearing two-inch-high heels and a skirt that probably weighed more than she did. Once they got past the guests, she yanked his arm and he let her take the lead. People were shouting in various languages behind him, and he was glad he had no idea what they were saying.

Instead of running into the main building, where four men in black were making their way toward them, the bride banked a hard left. "There's a gate through the serenity garden that isn't guarded." She led them to a wooden gate embedded in a perimeter wall.

I don't think this is what they had in mind when they made this emergency exit.

It had one of those childproof locks, but she expertly handled it. Had she planned the escape route? Ethan hoped so; her brothers had recovered from their shock and were almost upon them.

They went through the gate and he pulled it shut behind him just as a hand snaked out. By the yelp he heard on the other side of the door, he'd succeeded in slamming the door shut. They exited onto a side street and he looked around to get his bearings. The front of the hotel faced the famous Vegas strip.

"Where's your car parked?" she asked urgently.

"Not far," he said and led her down the street. He had illegally parked nearby, and they had miraculously exited on the right side of the hotel, so the car was just down the block. As they approached it, he saw a ticket on the windshield. He ignored the piece of paper and went to the passenger side and touched the handle. The Tesla roadster recognized his fingerprint and unlocked. He opened the door and the bride gracefully lowered herself into the deep bucket seat. Just as he started the car, a hand smacked the passenger-side window, and he looked to see Brothers One and Two at her door. He floored the accelerator. Vegas traffic didn't really allow for a high-speed chase, so he made a series of turns, hoping to lose whoever pursued them.

"We *need* to get out of Vegas," the bride said, her voice frantic.

He drove aggressively until they were at least a mile from the hotel, then pulled into a public parking garage and stopped the car. He turned to her. Her beautiful dark eyes gazed back at him with such lustrous excitement that he momentarily lost his train of thought.

"We aren't going anywhere until you tell me who you are."

She stuck out her hand. "Divya Singh. Very nice to meet you. Now we have to get moving."

He shook his head. "*You* have to get moving. I have a wedding to crash. The right one this time."

Two

Divya resisted the urge to scream at the man sitting next to her. He didn't owe her anything, but she needed him if she was going to get away from her family. "How about I help you find the right wedding? I assume you're after an Indian bride. You'll have an easier time getting in with me by your side." The last place her brothers would look for her was at another wedding. They had no way of knowing that the man sitting next to her was a perfect stranger, and she needed his help if she was going to get to New York City. Now that she'd done the unthinkable, this was her only chance to do the one thing she needed to do.

He narrowed his eyes, and she tried not to focus on how crystal blue they were or the way that the little crinkles in the corners of his mouth sent a little tingle down her spine. He wasn't even her type. Though it was hard not to notice his sandy-brown hair, which glinted when it caught the sunlight streaming through the windows, or the angular cheekbones, sharp nose and broad shoulders. He looked effortlessly athletic and chic in a black tuxedo that looked tailor-made for him.

"Let's start with your name," she said.

He gave her a half smile and her heart gave a little kick. "Ethan Connors."

Somewhere in the recesses of her brain, the name sounded familiar, but she was sure she'd never met him before. *I wouldn't ever forget him.* She produced her best smile. "It's nice to meet you. Now, about that wedding you want to crash. What's the bride's name?"

"Pooja Chaudhry."

Divya pointed to his phone.

"I already tried googling her name and today's date and every other key word I could think of."

"Look at her social media."

"I already did."

Divya just held out her hand and raised one perfectly shaped eyebrow. He sighed, then tapped on the phone several times and finally handed it to her. Pooja's Facebook page was on the screen. She was an attractive Indian woman with straight black hair, brown eyes, a sharp nose, cheekbones to die for, skin the color of white sand and a wide mouth. Dressed in a sundress with a field of sunflowers behind her, she looked gorgeous. No wonder Ethan had fallen hard for her. Divya felt an unfamiliar twinge deep in her chest. She had no complaints about winning the genetic lottery in the looks department, so why did this woman's beauty bother her?

She clicked on Pooja's friends and began looking through their recent posts. In a few minutes, she found what she was looking for and turned the phone so Ethan could see. There was a shot of a smiling Pooja in a stunning bridal *lehnga* with the MGM Grand logo behind her.

He reversed the car and punched the accelerator. They tore through the streets of Vegas, though as much as he changed lanes, Ethan couldn't escape the slow-moving traffic on the strip. The one-mile journey took them almost twenty minutes. He finally screeched to a stop at the front of the hotel, handed the valet a key and a hundred-dollar bill. "Keep it right here, ready to go, and I'll give you a real tip when I leave."

They asked where the wedding was and were directed to one of the large ballrooms. They went inside, and as soon as she caught sight of the bride, Divya grabbed Ethan's arm. But he kept walking.

"You're too late," she said a little too loudly and cringed as a few of the guests looked in their direction. He stopped. "I'm sorry, Ethan. See how she's throwing rice onto the cloth behind her? This is done after the wedding ceremony as the bride says goodbye to her family."

Divya looked at Ethan's face, expecting it to crumple, but he sighed, and she had a feeling it was in relief and not frustration.

"I should talk to her." The way he said it, Divya wasn't sure if he'd meant it as a question.

"I believe Vegas is very liberal with their marriage annulments. If you are serious about marrying her, you should make your case."

They both studied Pooja. Like Divya, she was wearing the traditional red-and-white *choora* bangles worn by brides on their wedding day and for months to a year after, depending on the family's traditions, to signify her newlywed status. Her *lehnga* was a pink bejeweled skirt with a royal blue border and a matching top that showed off a small section of her midriff. The groom whispered something in her ear, and she smiled stunningly. She whispered something back and he laughed, then leaned over and kissed her on the cheek to the general merriment of the gathered crowd.

"It doesn't look like she wants me to save her," Ethan muttered.

Divya had to agree. The bride looked excited and happy, not teary-eyed or forlorn in any way. Not the way she herself had looked earlier this morning. A pang of jealously hit Divya. She didn't want to get married, but if she had to, she wanted to be as happy as Pooja looked with her groom.

Ethan stared at Pooja and Divya realized they were attracting a few looks. Pooja looked in their direction and Divya stepped away from Ethan.

Pooja's eyes widened. She whispered to her groom, then stepped toward them. The eyes of two hundred people followed her. "What are you doing here?" she said in a low voice once she came closer. Her eyes flicked to Divya, then back to Ethan. He stood silent.

Divya stepped up to Pooja and hugged her, then whispered in her ear, "He crashed my wedding, looking for you." She released Pooja and said in a loud voice, "We had to come congratulate you, even though it's also my wedding day."

Pooja caught on quick. She turned around. "I need just one minute with my friend, then I'll be back."

An older lady stepped forward. "Hurry up, Pooja. The car is ready."

Pooja led the way and Divya took Ethan's hand. He frowned, and she leaned over and stood on tiptoe to whisper, "She's a married woman. Appearances are important."

He didn't argue but his lips thinned. Pooja led them through a set of doors and into a food-prep area. A waiter came toward them. "Please, just one minute," Pooja said, and he nodded.

"I'll wait outside," Divya started, but Pooja shook her head. "I need you to stay here."

Ethan shook his head. "I came here to break up your wedding and you're still worried about appearances."

Pooja glared at him. "How dare you show up here to ruin things for me? You had me, Ethan, and you let me go. If I wanted you here, I would've sent you an invitation. You're doing what you always do, going for what you want without considering how it affects everyone around you."

"If you didn't want me here, why did you send me that email saying you loved me and would've married me?"

She sighed. "Past tense, Ethan. I sent you that email for closure. It was a goodbye, not an invitation." She stepped closer and put her hand on his arm. "I said some really harsh things the last time we saw each other. I didn't want to start my new life by leaving things like that with us. I wanted you to know that you were special to me."

Ethan was silent and Divya resisted the urge to stand up for him. She looked at him, and though his eyes were focused on Pooja, he seemed to be a million miles away.

Finally he asked, "Do you want to be married to that guy?"

Pooja's eyes softened. "Yes," she said. "My parents set us up, but Anil and I fell in love."

"So quickly?" he said skeptically.

"I know you think arranged marriages are forced, but that's not the case. I was ready to settle down and so was he. We already got along with each other's families. There was no bullshit between us, so Anil and I could focus on whether we wanted to be together. It doesn't take long to fall in love once you're ready."

Pooja's eyes flicked to the door. "I'm sorry, Ethan. What you and I had was something special, but you know as well as I do that you were never going to marry me."

She gave him a chaste kiss on the cheek. "I've got to go. Try not to get in the way of your own happiness."

Ethan stood rigid with his back to the door as she left.

Divya touched his arm. "Are you okay?"

He shrugged. "Guess that's that. Where do you want me to take you?"

Divya stared at him. *How could he be so nonchalant about the woman he loved getting married to someone else?* Divya had a ton of questions for him, but he turned away from her, and she sensed that he didn't want to talk about it. Maybe he was embarrassed.

"What do you want to do next?" he asked.

Divya chewed on her lip. *Do I dare?* She'd come this far, might as well go all the way.

"There is someplace I'd like to go but..." As she said the words, the weight of what she'd done began to descend on her. She had wrestled with the decision for weeks, ever since her parents had announced her wedding to Vivek. She had protested and threatened and planned her escape, but ultimately, she'd lacked the courage to stand up to them. It wasn't until she was sitting next to Vivek by the holy marital fire that the realization hit her that she would never get a chance to love a man or be free to chart the course of her life. Nor would she get a chance to do the one thing she had dreamed of. She wasn't that religious, but in that moment, she'd prayed for an escape. And then Ethan had shown up.

"I don't have any money with me."

"You have enough jewelry on you to buy a house."

Divya's hand flew to the diamond choker around her neck. "This is my mother's. You can't sell family jewelry."

Ethan smirked. "Spoken like someone who comes from money."

Divya bristled. "You don't seem hard up. A Tesla isn't a poor man's car."

"I earn my money," Ethan said wryly.

"Well, I work, too, and if I could, I would happily live on what I earn," she said hotly, but his words burned into her. She'd been handed everything in life. While she knew how lucky and privileged she was, she had no sense of whether she was worth anything beyond her family's wealth.

She took a breath. "We don't have time to waste. I need to lay low for a few days. I don't want to face my family when they're so angry with me and while there's still a chance for them to resume the wedding. I have a bag packed with some essentials. I could call my sister and see if she could deliver it somewhere." Even as Divya said it, she knew her sister's phones and movements would be monitored by her family.

"It's probably not a good idea to contact your sister if you're trying to avoid the rest of your family. Do you have your driver's license?" He scanned her body slowly and deliberately as though he were examining her with X-ray vision.

"Hey, eyes up here." She glared at him, though little sparks of excitement coursed through her at the obvious interest in his eyes. She reached into her tight-fitting blouse and pulled out a well-worn dark blue passport with Republic of India stamped on the front.

"You're not American."

She raised an eyebrow. "Do I sound like an American?"

"Why get married in Vegas?"

"Because my fiancé—*ex-fiancé*—is American." She didn't have time for small talk, though; it wouldn't be long before her eldest brother Arjun mobilized his considerable influence to find her. "Listen, I really need to get out of Vegas. I was only able to fit this passport in my blouse. I don't have any money, but I promise you that if you can pay for a bus ticket to New York, I'll—"

He waved her off. "I'll give you whatever money you need."

"Thank you. I'll pay you back as soon as I—"

"I have more money than I can spend in my lifetime. It's meaningless to me." The catch in his voice hit her in the chest.

"Is there anything I can do for you? Talk to Pooja?"

He looked at her, and she saw frustration and also a shadow of something darker in his eyes. "I think you and I both know that I've lost Pooja. Don't worry. I'm used to it. How about we focus on getting you out of town."

She wanted to know more. How could he let go of the love of his life as if he'd lost nothing more than money at a casino? *He is not my problem.* Right now she had a very short window to get away. She hadn't come to America to get married. She'd come for a taste of freedom, to do the one thing she'd never be allowed to do: to take a chance on a dream and see if she could make it come true.

"Why New York City?"

"There is something I need to do there. I'll explain later. Can you drop me at a bus stop?"

He smiled. "I have a better way to get you there. Let's go. I'll explain on the way."

Excitement exploded through her. *Can this really be happening? Am I really going to get to New York?* The idea of being able to go without the shackles of her family was incredible. She began running through the list of things she needed to do as Ethan led her out of the hotel.

They retrieved the car, which the valet had kept front and center. He handed the key card back to Ethan, who peeled off several hundred-dollar bills and handed them to the wide-eyed man.

As Divya took her seat, it hit her. *I must be mad.* Ethan was a complete stranger and she was getting in a car with him not knowing where he was taking her. What if he was a psycho or axe murderer? Why was she so at ease around him? She knew nothing about the man.

"Can I borrow your phone to check my email?"

He held the phone to his face so the facial recognition program unlocked it and gave it to her. He motored the car out of the hotel's drive-through and back into Vegas traffic. She opened up a web browser and typed his name. *Ethan Connors.* She gasped audibly as the search results displayed.

"I guess you googled me."

She looked at him guiltily. His eyes were focused on the traffic ahead, but his lips twitched.

"I'm sorry. I was curious and I just—"

"—wanted to make sure I wasn't some serial killer?"

She smiled sheepishly. "Your name sounded familiar. My family business is hotels, so I don't regularly follow the tech world, but I remember reading the headlines when your app hit one billion users and you branched into India."

He smiled. "We're at three billion globally now."

"I can't believe I didn't recognize your name. You're almost as famous as Mark Zuckerberg. Why didn't you say something?"

Ethan shrugged; his smile was shy as he focused on the road ahead. His expression sent a ping right to her heart. "Mark gets better publicity. Mine isn't so flattering."

"And why is that?"

"I'm known to be a bit of a troublemaker."

"Is that why you're helping me?"

He was silent for several seconds. "Maybe. Maybe it's because you're a nice distraction from losing my future wife."

"You hardly seem heartbroken about Pooja."

He put a hand to his chest. “And how would you know what I’m feeling?”

Had she imagined the fleeting look of relief on his face when Pooja had told him she loved her husband? *What do I know?* Divya was a basket case of emotions. Her family would be worried about her. And they didn’t deserve the embarrassment and shame that would ensue in the Indian community from her running away so publicly. She should have done it before the invitations went out, or before the guests arrived, or even last night when her family could’ve claimed she was sick and saved face. She’d been so anxious about what it would do to them, that in the end, she’d forced herself into the worst of possible options.

She clicked through various friends’ social media pages and gasped when she saw a picture of her and Ethan escaping from the wedding. As she scrolled through the feed, her heart sank even further. “There are social media hashtags about us. The one that’s trending is #BrideSnatcher.”

“Ha, that’s clever since my company is called Deal Catcher.”

Divya turned the phone off. If she read any more, her already weakening resolve would crumble further. “My parents are going to be furious. They are so careful about their media image. They’re never going to forgive me.”

Ethan flipped his hand dismissively. “It’ll blow over in a day or two, as soon as a Hollywood celebrity announces a baby on the way or there’s a new royal scandal.”

It wouldn’t ever blow over with her family. *What have I done?* So what if she had to marry boring Vivek? Would it be worse than being disowned by her family? He wasn’t a bad guy. So what if he didn’t make her heart go pitter-patter? Yes he’d laughed at her dream career, but she could’ve worked on him. He wasn’t as traditional as her parents; she could’ve convinced him eventually. That was the conclusion that had driven her to step into the wedding *mandap* that morning. She mentally shook her head. *The damage was done.* There would be no point running away if she didn't do the one thing she needed to do. After that, she could return and face the music with her family. Like she always did.

Divya was so lost in her thoughts that she hadn't noticed where Ethan was driving. When he stopped the car, she realized they were at the airport. More specifically, at the private-aviation gate.

"You have your own plane?"

Of course he did. He was Ethan Connors. From the little she remembered and her quick read of his Wikipedia page, he'd started his company with an app that helped people search multiple websites for the best price on products and set an alert when items they were looking for went on sale. During the coronavirus pandemic, the app had helped people find toilet paper and other necessities and report price gouging. Since then, the app had grown into an enterprise that included an online store for exclusive products and was expanding into other areas such as real estate bargains. He'd become an overnight billionaire. Lucky for her, he wasn't an axe murderer. An adventure junkie and playboy, yes, but that she could handle.

"It's a business expense," he replied flippantly.

"And you just happened to have it ready to go?"

He smiled wistfully. "I was planning to whisk a bride away."

Her pulse jumped. *What am I doing?* Ethan had to be emotionally messed up, and here she was, taking advantage of him.

He parked the car next to a plane that looked bigger than the medium-sized Gulfstream her parents had. He exited the car, and before she had a chance to gather her skirt, he opened her door and held out his hand. *A man with manners.* She placed her hand in his and immediately felt his strength as he pulled her up. She came face-to-face with him as she stood. A warmth spread in her chest as she thought about the brief kiss she'd given him at her wedding to convince everyone that she knew him. It had been the lightest touch, but it'd felt so electric, she had pulled away fast. Now, with their faces so close, she wondered what it would be like to kiss him properly.

They stood there for several seconds, until he let go of her hand. He pointed toward the stairs leading up into the airplane.

She paused at the bottom step, the handrail hot under her hand. *This is a bad idea.* There was still time to make it right with her family. An hour had passed since she'd left her wedding. All the guests would still be there, enjoying the food and drinks her brother had likely served up in the hope that they'd find her or she'd return. If she went back, she could play it off as nerves. Her parents would be angry, but at the end of the day, the marriage to Vivek would be all that mattered. The media storm would die down. Everything would go back to normal.

But the more time passed, the more unforgiveable her actions became. There was no turning back if she stepped onto the plane.

She eyed the jet. Her entire life had been carefully mapped out. She never made a move without a plan; even an evening out required meticulous preparation. Getting on a plane with a stranger was a recipe for disaster.

"Are you ready?" Ethan's mouth curved into a smile. Her heart stuttered. She knew what she had to do.

Three

What am I thinking? He had spent most of yesterday rehashing all the poor choices he'd made in life, and today he'd made two more spectacularly bad decisions: the first to crash Pooja's wedding, and the second to get involved with Divya's escape.

Last night he'd been at his condo in Los Angeles, unable to sleep. He barely recognized the furniture in the place, let alone remembered how to operate the overly complicated coffee machine. He owned a condo in every major city where he had to spend time for his business. He was tired of hotel rooms, yet none of these condos was home. The closest he'd come to feeling grounded was living with Pooja for three months. But when he'd been with Pooja, all he'd been able to think about was all the things that didn't work in their relationship. After she'd left, he'd been unable to stop thinking about how great things could've been between them.

He'd woken up in a cold sweat this morning, wondering whether he'd die alone in one of his ubiquitous condos. Living on his airplane, jetting from city to city was getting old. He wanted a place where he belonged; he wanted what his brother and his parents had—a soul mate. In her email, Pooja had accused him of setting an impossible standard that no woman could ever meet. Maybe she was right. He had a black book full of failed relationships. So he'd put his jet on standby and charged into Vegas, intent on getting Pooja back.

But here he was, with another woman, thinking about how her luscious pink lips had tasted of vanilla when she'd kissed him earlier. Was his mother right? Was he afraid of commitment? As he watched Divya negotiate the narrow steps of the plane in her heavy skirt, he knew it was a bad idea to spend time with her. He was attracted to her and felt the familiar urge to throw caution to the wind and pursue her like he did any endeavor that caught his attention.

"Welcome back, Mr. Connors." Kathy was one of the regular cabin attendants who worked the plane. While the jet was his, he used a contract service to provide pilots and staff. She greeted them as they entered, dressed in her regular black pantsuit, white-collared shirt and red scarf around her neck. Her graying dark hair was knotted stylishly at the nape of her neck.

"Long time no see, Kathy," he quipped.

She looked at her watch. "This isn't our fastest turnaround. I believe your record is fifteen minutes. We did get new pilots, though."

Kathy had flown with him from LA earlier in the day. If she was surprised to see Divya instead of Pooja, she kept it to herself.

He turned to Divya. "There's a bedroom in the back that has some of my clothes. Feel free to borrow something if you want to change."

Divya looked like she was going to say something, then thought better of it. While Divya was changing, Ethan discussed the flight plan with the pilots.

Divya emerged wearing one of his black T-shirts and a pair of shorts. She looked like a kid wearing a grown-up's clothes. The T-shirt swelled over her breasts, then hung down to her thighs, and his basketball shorts looked like cropped pants. She looked impossibly sexy. Her feet were bare, revealing pink-tipped toes and intricate henna patterns like she had on her hands and arms. Her black hair fell in waves over her shoulders. She'd taken off the heavy jewelry and scrubbed her face, making her look incredibly young.

Kathy closed the outside cabin door. They were in the main seating area, which consisted of several tan-leather recliner chairs, a couch with a coffee table and a mahogany-finished bar. Another door separated them from the cockpit and service area, where Kathy now disappeared.

"Are we really going to New York City?"

Her voice held such longing that it wrenched his heart.

"What's so important in New York?"

A mischievous smile played on her lips. "Can I have your phone again?"

She took it, quickly typed in an address and handed it back to him, open to a webpage for Café Underground.

"It's a club that does open mic for new singers."

"You sing?"

She shrugged. "I like to sing. But I don't know if I have any talent. I sing at family events and my relatives and friends pump me with praise. I love singing. If I could do anything in life, that's what I'd want to do. But I need to know whether or not I have real talent. Just once, I want to stand in front of a real audience and see what it's like to perform live."

Her face held so much hope that all he wanted to do was

make it happen for her. "You can probably find an open mic right here in Vegas. Why go all the way to New York?"

"This place is special to me." She took a breath. "When the entire world was under lockdown, Café Underground started doing these video open mics. They gave me a chance to perform, and it's the only time I've sung for someone other than my family. It went well, but it was different sitting in my bedroom, singing to a computer screen. They made me promise I'd come to do my first live performance at their club. I know it's superstitious, but I believe the place is my good luck charm. I would never have thought about a singing career if I hadn't accidently found out about their virtual open mic."

"It's a done deal. Tonight, you'll be singing at Café Underground."

She launched herself at him and gave him a hug. His arms automatically went around her waist and the feel of her took his breath away. His body went hot at the way her breasts crushed against his chest and her breath warmed his neck. "Thank you, thank you. You have no idea what this means to me."

He gently disentangled himself before his body gave him away. *What's wrong with me?* How could he go from wanting to marry Pooja to being insanely attracted to Divya? This was what he was always afraid of: that he'd turn out like his father. *Connors men have a hard time holdin' on to good.* The pattern was always the same. His father, Wade, would lose a job, his mother would work longer hours to make money for the household, and his dad would go day drinking. His mother would come home and make dinner, while his father sat in front of the TV, drinking Jim Beam until he passed out. To this day, Ethan couldn't stand the smell of whiskey. His mother had eventually left his father and married Bill. That's when Ethan had learned what an ideal marriage looked like. Bill had adopted Ethan, and his father hadn't thought twice about signing away his parental rights in exchange for never having to pay child support. Ethan wanted what his mother and Bill had, but he lived in fear of ending up like Wade.

There was a knock from the service door and the pilot stepped in, followed by Kathy.

"Sir, the operations control center is asking if we have a Miss Divya Singh on board. Apparently her family is looking for her." The pilot looked from Ethan to Divya.

Divya's eyes widened.

"No one here by that name. This is Pooja Chaudhry, my longtime girlfriend," Ethan said firmly.

The pilot looked at Kathy, who nodded, and then he left.

Ethan mouthed a thank-you to Kathy, who smiled serenely and asked for their drink orders. He ordered a coffee and Divya asked for a glass of white wine.

Divya sank into a recliner as the jet began to taxi, and Ethan took a seat opposite her. She looked out of the window while chewing on her lip.

"Are you expecting your family to show up with guns blazing?"

She nodded. "I've snuck out of the house before, but this is a whole new level of rebellion."

"You're a grown woman. Why do you need to sneak out of the house?"

She sighed. "My family is very old-fashioned, even by Indian standards. They believe there is an etiquette that the women, the *girls* of the house as they call us, must follow."

"Pooja's family had some very strict rules on who she was allowed to date."

"If her family was even half as traditional as mine, I'm guessing a white man was at the top of the list of unsuitable boys."

He smiled. It had taken Pooja two months to tell him in polite terms that he was not what her family had in mind for her. Divya had bluntly stated it two hours after meeting him. "I was definitely not on her parents' list of eligible bachelors, that's for sure. How did you meet your fiancé?"

She rolled her eyes. "My brother set us up. *Girls* in our family don't date random men. We're set up with eligible bachelors who promise to behave themselves but, in reality, are just as wretched as a bar sleaze from the worst part of town."

"Pooja called it a global dating service." Despite the fact that they were living together, Pooja had still endured the occasional setup from her parents.

Divya nodded. "It's great for people who actually want to settle down."

"Who was the guy you were supposed to marry?"

Divya looked out the window as the jet shuddered, gathering speed in preparation for takeoff.

"Vivek. He's an NRI, a nonresident Indian as we say in India. He's a very nice guy..." She trailed off and bit her lip. "But I'm not ready to get married. To anyone. I came to Vegas two months ago to visit my brother. He set me up with Vivek and we started dating. When I went back to India, I thought our affair would fizzle out, but he proposed marriage to my family, which is the proper way of doing things. No one bothered to ask me if I really wanted it. They assumed that I was ready to get on the marriage-and-baby-making train. Arjun and Vivek planned this big Vegas wedding, and my family packed my bags so I could start my married life in America."

"What's wrong with marriage and babies?"

"Nothing. If that's what you want. But I am thirty-two years old and I haven't done anything with my life. I've traveled the world but haven't really experienced it. I'm a lawyer but I work for my family business doing paperwork. I've never lived on my own or done things for myself. I've taken singing classes but never really sung to a real audience. I've done nothing in my life. There are things I want to do, and if I get married, I'll never get a chance to do them."

"Why not? Marriage isn't a prison."

"It comes with responsibility and a sense of obligation. Everything becomes about the family," she said bitterly.

And what's wrong with that? He had the freedom, money and time to do anything he wanted; it got lonely after a while. All his friends had long since married and he envied their complaints about soccer games, homework and birthday parties. They all had their own families and he didn't.

The jet nosed into the sky, and Ethan followed Divya's gaze outside the window as they left Las Vegas and headed into the clouds. Then she turned to him. "I've told you my poor-little-rich-girl story. What's yours?"

He smiled. "Well, this poor little successful billionaire started out with a wonderful family that didn't have much money but always had love." Bill had adopted him when he was ten. They'd moved to a new neighborhood and he'd started middle school without anyone knowing that Bill wasn't his real father. In all the interviews he gave—and answering Divya now—his life story began at age ten. He didn't miss Wade. Once his mother had married Bill, Ethan had realized what a real father was supposed to be. But he'd always felt like the third wheel in his parents' marriage. And then his brother had been born.

"I have a younger brother who's married and has two awesome kids. They live down the street from my parents in Stillwater. It's a suburb of Minneapolis." He leaned forward. "I want what they have, but it seems no woman deems me worthy of lifelong commitment."

Divya raised her brows. "Oh come on! What is it women don't like? The fact that you're rich or that you're handsome?"

"You think I'm handsome?"

A smile played on her lips, and he itched to lean over and kiss her luscious mouth. "You're not my type, but most women would find you okay-looking."

"What is your type then? Tall and dark?"

"Maybe," she said coyly, and a fire licked in his belly at the way her mouth curved. "So what's wrong with you? Women think you're a spoilt rich kid?"

He shrugged. "I've only been rich for the last few years. Before my company took off, I was an average Joe with a nine-to-five job. Women loved dating me but said I wasn't the type of guy they'd marry."

Divya frowned. "Do you have strange habits or crazy fetishes?"

He shrugged. "Not that I know of. Although I do like a bit of adventure in bed."

She met his gaze. "Most women like a little fun in bed." Heat rose deep in his core and he had the insane urge to pull her by the loose T-shirt she was wearing and kiss her senseless.

She broke eye contact first. "I'll figure it out. I'm good at finding out what's wrong with men."

"Gee, thanks. There's nothing wrong with me. I think women don't know what they want."

"Or you only go out with women who are unavailable, so you don't have to commit."

The comment pulsed through him. "That's not true. I knew Pooja wanted to settle down and that's part of what attracted me to her. I asked her to move in after just three months of us being together because I was serious about her."

"Then, why did she marry someone else?"

"Because I took too long to propose."

"And why did you do that?"

Why indeed? "I needed a little more time. We'd only been living together for three months and had been dating for a total of six. That's not enough time to know that you want to spend the rest of your life with someone."

"Vivek knew in three weeks that he wanted to marry me. He didn't need more time."

"But you did."

"Because I don't want to get married. To anyone. If I were ready to commit, Vivek would've been just fine for me."

"You were in love with him then?"

"You have to be ready to fall in love. It's a mindset, and I'm not into it. There is nothing wrong with Vivek. He's a decent person. He's kind and intelligent and met all of my criteria for what I'd want in a husband—*if* I were looking for one."

"So when you're ready, you'll be able to marry anyone who meets your criteria."

She leaned back in her seat and chewed on her lip, making him lose his train of thought.

"There's no straight answer to that. My criteria may change in the future. That's why I don't want to settle down right now. I don't feel like I know what I truly want."

You and most women I meet.

"I am ready for all of it, for love, marriage and children. I thought Pooja was too, but she kept our entire relationship a secret. We never went out in public together because she was afraid someone would post a picture on social media. She refused to introduce me to her family. I had good reason to doubt whether she was as invested in me as I was in her."

"She did that because she knew that you weren't going to propose to her. If her family is traditional, they would have exploded at her bringing home an American guy. She can't go through that kind of upheaval without a commitment from you."

It was almost exactly what Pooja had said to him. "What more could I do to convince her I was committed? I was going to stop her wedding and marry her today."

"No, you weren't."

How dare you! They'd known each other for a couple of hours, and here she was, challenging him on what he was or was not going to do.

"You might have been willing to stop her wedding, but that's as far as you were going to go. If you'd really wanted to sweep her off her feet and marry her today, you would've proposed to her when you saw her and let her decide how much she really loves her husband. It takes thirty seconds to get an annulment in Vegas. But you were almost relieved that she was happy, like you were off the hook."

He narrowed his eyes. "I believe in marriage. My parents have been married for almost thirty years and they are so happy together. My brother has been married for nine. He was my best friend until he met his wife. She knows him better than I ever did. She can read his moods, anticipate his needs…" He trailed off. "My parents, and my brother and sister-in-law, are a unit. They're connected at this deep level, and that's what I want. I didn't propose to Pooja because she and I didn't have that instant understanding and connection, but then I realized that maybe that comes with time."

Or maybe it's something I can't have with a woman. Nearly all the women he'd ever had a serious relationship with had married other men. Perhaps they could intuit something in Ethan that he couldn't figure out for himself. Perhaps they smelled his desperation and didn't like its stench.

Divya leaned forward and placed a hand on his. Her touch was soft and warm, and when he looked into her dark brown eyes, a slow burn flamed its way through his body.

"Maybe you've never opened yourself up to a woman so she can really get to know you. We women can tell when men put up barriers, and we don't like being with men we don't know and understand."

He pulled his hand back from hers. "I'm an open book. I'm talking to you, aren't I?" His tone was harsher than he meant it to be. He smiled. "Maybe it's easier to talk to you because we don't know each other."

She smiled back at him. "I have a talent for getting people to talk. It's the lawyer in me. If I'd gone into criminal law, I would've gotten confessions like this." She clicked her fingers.

He smiled. Divya really did have a way about her that made him feel at ease.

"Look, I've known you for all of two minutes and I can tell you didn't really want to marry Pooja. You wanted to know if *she* was willing to marry *you*."

Her words made his stomach churn. *Divya was wrong.* He was no longer the little boy who wanted his mother's new husband to love him, or the teenager desperate to be cool enough to get noticed by the popular girl.

Kathy knocked on the door, then entered with a tray of hors d'oeuvres and their drinks. They both sat in silence, Divya staring out the window, sipping her wine, while he moved himself to the couch and opened his laptop. He had an excellent management team who handled the day-to-day operations of his company. He'd let them know that he was taking ten days off, but he knew they'd call him if something needed his attention. Checking in on things was a comforting ritual to make himself feel useful. He also issued some instructions to his assistant in the New York office.

He looked at Divya, and as if feeling his gaze, she turned her head to look at him and gave him a smile that tightened his chest. What was it about her? The last thing he needed was to get involved with another woman. This one had declared from the outset that she wasn't available, yet he couldn't help but be attracted to her. Why had he taken it upon himself to fly her to New York? He could've satisfied his save-the-day complex by giving her the jet and a credit card.

She plopped herself on the seat beside him. He moved over so their knees weren't touching.

"Look, I'm sorry if I was a shit to you. You've been really nice to me. I can't stop my mouth sometimes. My brothers always tell me that I'm entirely too blunt and I need to temper my remarks."

"When do you get to the part where you sincerely apologize?"

She gave him an affronted look. "That wasn't sincere?"

"That was you telling me that you wished you'd sugarcoated what you had to say."

A smile twitched at her lips. "See what I mean? I can't stop my mouth."

Oh boy. Try as he might, he wasn't annoyed at her. As painful as it might be, she was honest and it was refreshing. But she was sitting too close to him. That intoxicating smell of vanilla and cinnamon was teasing his sensibilities. Her eyes searched his, and he voiced the words that were rolling around in his head but he didn't want to admit, even to himself.

"I didn't propose to Pooja because I held our relationship to the same standards as my parents' and my brother's and it didn't measure up. Yesterday I realized that I can wait my whole life for something that may never happen or I can seize the little bit of happiness that's right in front of me. When we got to the wedding, it was clear that Pooja had found with Anil what I'd been seeking with her." He'd seen the glittering adoration in Pooja's eyes and the shining smile on her face. She'd never looked that happy with him.

Divya shifted on the sofa, so her body was angled toward him, her knees now touching his. "I have no right casting stones on you. I had plenty of opportunities to stall my wedding. I did not have to do it in quite so dramatic a fashion. I clearly have my demons too." Her voice was soft and contrite.

"What demons do you have, Divya?"

She shrugged. "You talked about seizing the little bit of happiness that you can. My whole life has been about letting go of the happiness I want, in order to hold on to the joy I have." She looked away from him, and the shine in her eyes tugged at his heart.

"Aside from singing at Café Underground, what do you want to do? What's on your bucket list?"

She shrugged. "I've never made a bucket list. What's the point in wanting something you know you can't have?"

Her words struck a chord in his heart.

"Well, for the next few days, consider me your magical genie. Make a wish and I'll try to make it happen." He grinned. Divya was easy to talk to and maybe she could be the distraction he needed.

She smiled. "You're serious?"

He nodded.

"I guess I could really use a friend right now. Especially one with a private jet." She held out her hand.

"And I could use a friend who gives it to me straight." He smiled and took her hand in his. It was meant to be a handshake, but he found himself holding her hand loosely, his thumb moving across the back of her hand, feeling its softness. Divya's mouth opened and he stilled, summoning every ounce of willpower he had not to lean over and kiss her. Why wasn't she pulling away? Was it his imagination or was she leaning even closer? Their mouths were inches apart.

He knew he was being impulsive again but he wanted to feel her soft lips on his, to know whether the earlier kiss that had shot zingers through his body had been real or if he'd been high on adrenaline and imagined the whole thing. He leaned forward.

Four

A second before their lips touched, she moved back. *What am I doing?* She'd almost kissed Ethan. Again. Just a couple of hours ago, she'd been about to take seven sacred circles around the marriage fire with another man. Granted, Vivek wasn't a man she wanted to marry, but it was a little too soon to get involved with someone like Ethan. *Especially Ethan.* Divya wasn't the good Indian girl her parents believed her to be. Without their knowing, she'd dated off the approved list. But Ethan was far beyond the unsuitable category.

Ethan shifted on the sofa so there was more space between them. He turned back to his laptop. An awkward silence settled between them.

He was gora. Not even in her wildest dreams had she thought about dating someone who wasn't Indian. Her entire identity revolved around her family and culture. What could she possibly have in common with an American?

What does it matter? I'm not marrying him. For the first time in her life, she was free of her parents' watchful eyes. In this moment, she was attracted to him, so what was the harm? There was no chance she'd fall in love with him.

Kathy appeared, saving them from more awkwardness. She asked what they wanted for lunch. Divya suddenly realized she was starving; she hadn't eaten anything all day. Ethan ordered a burger and she asked for the same.

"You eat beef?" he said, looking surprised, once Kathy had left.

She smiled. "Busted."

"Pooja didn't eat beef. She said most Indians, especially Hindus, don't."

"That's true. My parents would die if they knew I'm eating beef. Is it wrong that I love hamburgers? It's rare to find them in India. McDonald's serves lamb and chicken burgers."

He laughed. "I don't see anything wrong with having your own belief system. I wish Pooja had been more independent. She was always too concerned with pleasing her parents."

Divya frowned. "What's wrong with that?"

He held up his hands. "I don't mean any offense. It's just that our whole relationship revolved around the fact her parents would never approve of me."

"Did you try with her parents?"

"She never gave me a chance."

Divya chewed her lip. This was exactly why she had never fantasized about dating a *gora.* "I can see where Pooja was coming from. In Indian families, everything revolves around the parents' expectations. That comes with its bad parts, like having to conform to traditions you may not agree with. But there's also a lot of good. I've always felt loved and secure in my home. I've never felt loneliness in my life. When we were all on lockdown, it was the best time of our lives. We enjoyed being together. We stayed up playing games and having deep conversations about the silliest topics. None of us got cabin fever. When the lockdown ended, we were all sad that it couldn't go on longer." As she said the words, dread spread through her chest. *What if they don't forgive me?* "It's not about pleasing the family, it's about respecting who they are. It's a small price for the love and happiness you get in return."

He held up his hands. "I value that too. I'm very close with my family, and they've always been there for me. But they won't be dictating who I marry."

"Won't they?"

He frowned at her. "I don't understand what you're getting at."

"Did your family want you to marry Pooja?"

He shrugged. "It had less to do with my family than hers. My parents will accept whoever I choose."

"Would you be happy marrying someone who wouldn't get along with your family?"

He frowned, then shrugged. "That's difficult to answer in the hypothetical."

Bullshit. But she let it be. You could push someone only so hard into seeing what was right in front of them. Plus, she couldn't risk pissing him off.

She changed the topic. "Thank you for taking me to New York. I can only imagine how busy you must be." She gestured toward his laptop.

He shrugged. "Not as busy as I'd like. The business is on autopilot. I hired a great executive team, who in turn hired some great people, and as the business has grown, I've become more of a figurehead for important decisions. They do the day-to-day."

"Is it hard for you to give up control over something that you created?"

He gave her a wistful smile. "It should be but it's not. I like focusing on the big picture. Besides, work can only give you so much satisfaction." He sighed. "I'd canceled all my meetings and taken ten days off to get married and go on a honeymoon."

"Sorry about that."

"No, you're right. If I really wanted to marry Pooja I would've proposed to her when she first threatened to leave."

Ah, he can admit when he's wrong.

Kathy returned with their burgers and they dug in with gusto. They chatted about their favorite books, movies and places they'd been. Divya was surprised at how much they had in common: they hated reality TV and loved witty historical dramas and suspenseful thrillers. He didn't share her obsession with horror movies, but no guy was perfect.

They landed at the private aviation terminal at Teterboro Airport, right outside the city, in New Jersey. Divya knew from traveling with her parents that the main New York City commercial airports were very congested, so private jets used the smaller airports.

A tall older woman dressed in a business suit greeted them as they exited the plane. Ethan introduced her as his executive assistant Roda. Roda handed Ethan two roller-board suitcases, a small box and the keys to a Mercedes roadster.

When they were seated in the car, he handed Divya the small box. "That's for you."

She opened it to find the latest smartphone and a black American Express card in her name. "Thank you. I promise to pay you back for everything."

He waved his hand. "Please, don't worry about it. Like I said, the last thing I need is more money."

The catch in his voice reverberated through her. She knew well that money couldn't buy what anyone really wanted, but Ethan seemed to resent his fortune.

The early September air was cool but the temperature was warm. "Do you mind if we go top down?" he asked. She stared at him, open-mouthed, then he pointed toward the top of the car. "It's a convertible."

Yet another thing she'd never done in her life: ride in a convertible. "Seems like fun. Let's do it."

He grinned. "I'll warn you, it'll mess up your hair. Most women hate it."

She shrugged and twisted her hair into a messy bun. He pressed a button, and she looked up at the beautiful sky and took a deep breath. *This is what freedom feels like.*

"I have a condo in the city we can stay at," he said as he put the car in drive.

Um, no. Given what had almost happened on the plane, she didn't want to stay someplace on his terms.

"My brother is bound to check for us at any properties you own in the city. I can call in a favor." She made a call on the new phone Ethan had given her, then instructed him to drive to one of the most luxurious hotels in New York.

It took them nearly two hours to navigate city traffic, but Divya barely noticed. She took in the sights and sounds of the chaotic city and savored the feel of the warm sun and cool air over her skin. She had been to New York before, but today she could really taste the smog in the air and feel the rhythm of the cars, people and bicycles.

She sent a WhatsApp message to her contact at Café Underground and crossed her fingers that he still remembered her.

It was night by the time Ethan pulled into the hotel driveway and handed his keys to the valet. Divya strode up to the check-in counter and asked them to call Rajiv Mehra. The clerk eyed her but delivered the message.

They didn't have to wait long before an Indian man, impeccably dressed in a custom-tailored suit and French-cuffed shirt, appeared. He hugged Divya. "It is so good to see you. I called Gauri as soon as you contacted me. She insisted we have dinner tonight." Rajiv sounded genuinely pleased to see her. She caught the look of surprise in his eyes at her clothing. "And I insist you buy what you need from the lobby shops and charge it to me."

Divya hugged him. "You are such a good friend. I owe you big time." She knew he'd be insulted if she offered to pay him back with money.

Her phone pinged and she looked down to see a message from Café Underground.

"I definitely want to see Gauri and catch up with you two, but could we get together tomorrow? There's something I must do tonight."

If Rajiv was annoyed, he was too gracious to show it. "Of course. How about lunch tomorrow?"

"That would be great. Thank you so much for putting us up and keeping it secret. You know how my parents can be."

"How can I forget? You're safe here." He looked over Divya's shoulder to Ethan. "Is this your friend?" He arched his brows and switched to Hindi. "Now I understand why I wasn't your type."

She smiled and shook her head. "It's not like that." She quickly explained everything that had happened at the wedding.

Ethan cleared his throat and Divya realized she'd been rude in carrying on in Hindi with Rajiv. She introduced the two men. "Rajiv owns the hotel."

Ethan was duly impressed and said so without letting

on that his own net worth was exponentially bigger than Rajiv's. Divya liked that Ethan didn't feel the need to advertise his success. On the plane, he'd changed into faded jeans and a plain T-shirt. No one would guess that he'd just flown in on his own private jet.

Rajiv handed them over to a staff member and invited Ethan to lunch the next day. Then they were led to a suite of rooms that made Ethan whistle.

"I've stayed in some pretty fancy hotels, but this is something else." They entered a great room that included floor-to-ceiling windows with a bird's-eye view of the city. A baby grand piano sat in the center of the room. There were two different seating areas, a small dining table, a bar and a kitchen. There were two bedrooms, each with its own sumptuous bathroom. It was all done in a warm, modern style with boxy furniture, wood accents and white linens.

"Rajiv is some friend to put you up here."

Divya nodded distractedly as she responded to a message on her phone.

"Friend of your family?"

She nodded. "Yes, our parents are close. My brother helped him get started with this hotel."

"And yet he's doing you a favor."

"He owes me," she said, smiling. "I'll tell you about it later. Right now I need to go down to the shops and buy something to wear." She grinned. "The stage manager at Café Underground remembers me and said he'd put me on the list to sing tonight." Her heart raced with excitement.

Ethan grinned and pointed to one of the suitcases they'd brought. "There should be a variety of things in there you can use."

Her eyes widened.

"My New York assistant, Roda, did some shopping

while we were in the air. I guessed your size but hopefully they fit."

"That was very thoughtful of you. Thank you. I'll..."

He shook his head. "Please, don't say you'll pay me back. We've discussed this, haven't we?"

She sighed. "I know you have lots of money, but I still feel like I'm taking advantage of you. We just met today. Let me at least help you figure out your love life."

He raised his brows. "You think there's something to fix?"

You don't? She stopped herself from saying that out loud. "I'm a great matchmaker. I set up Rajiv and his wife and they've been happily married for three years now."

"He has a wife?"

She tried not a smile at the relief in his voice. Had he been jealous of Rajiv?

"I've set up nearly all of my friends and most of the men my parents chose for me."

His lips twitched. "Was Rajiv one of those men?"

She nodded sheepishly. "He was, until I introduced him to Gauri and he fell madly in love with her."

"If you're that good, why didn't you set up your fiancé?"

She laughed. "I don't have a lot of friends in the US. Had he been based in India, I would've found him a woman who'd make him stop thinking about me."

"I doubt a man could stop thinking about you." Ethan's voice was so low and throaty that her heart stopped. She looked away from his sparkling blue eyes before she lost her mind entirely and decided to add Ethan to her bucket list. "Let's get dressed and get to Café Underground."

They each chose a bedroom. Hers had a dark wood platform bed made up in white linens with low-standing side tables and a dresser. Her bathroom was bigger than the bedroom and included white-and-gray marble tile, a tall oval Japanese soaking tub and a glass-enclosed shower. She set the bag Ethan had given her on a luggage rack and surveyed the clothes. There was a deep maroon cocktail dress with a cowl neck that would do for tonight.

The assistant had even included makeup. Unfortunately, the colors were too light for her skin tone, so she just went with mascara and lip gloss. Her hands shook as she applied the mascara, and she had to wash her face and do it twice. She had dreamed of singing in a real club but hadn't really thought she'd get the chance to make her dream come true. What if she tried to sing and nothing came out? Was her voice hoarse? She practiced a few notes. Was the sound strange or was it the acoustics in the bathroom? She took a deep breath and focused on getting herself ready. Tonight might be the only chance she had. She wasn't going to waste time.

The shoes included with the dress were too large, but she stuffed some toilet paper in the toe caps. She didn't want to be late to Café Underground.

When she stepped into the shared common room, Ethan was by the bar. He looked casual but stunning in dark jeans and a fashionably untucked black shirt.

He whistled appreciatively when he saw her. "You look amazing. You're going to knock it out of the park."

"I know the expression, but I doubt it applies to me. I'll be happy if I don't get booed off the stage. This place is for hard-core artists and music lovers. The audience is serious."

He walked over to her and gently grasped her shoulders. "You'll be great, Divya. Just live for yourself tonight."

She took a breath and mentally repeated his words to herself. *Tonight is mine alone.*

The club wasn't far from their hotel, so they took a pedicab. The seat was cozy and she tried not to focus on the feel of Ethan's thigh against hers or the warmth of his body next to hers. She had a song in mind that she wanted to sing, so she went over the words in her head. It was a favorite of hers and she'd been singing it since she was a girl.

The pedicab driver skirted traffic, and got them to Café Underground in just a few minutes.

"This is where you want to make your debut?"

They were looking at a dark door with the words Café Underground flickering in neon lights above. She nodded reverently. It was exactly as she'd imagined it.

He opened the door and she took a breath as she stepped inside. The club was packed. A stage at one end of the room was empty but held a complement of musical equipment and was lit up with a spotlight. A bar on the other end was standing room only. The center of the room was dark and held high-top tables with barstools. All of the tables were full, and people crowded in between seats. The smell of stale beer hung in the air.

Divya's pulse quickened. *I can't do this.* Her parents never let her go out without a chaperone, and she wasn't used to such crowds. She suddenly felt unsure of herself. How was she supposed to handle this?

Ethan elbowed his way to the bartender to ask how to sign up for open mic. Divya stood back. Ethan was taller and more easily able to lean over the bar to hear what the guy was saying. The bartender pointed to another man seated next to the stage. He was short and wiry, with thick black-rimmed glasses, a mesh shirt and leather pants that couldn't be tighter if they were painted on.

Ethan made his way to the leather-pants guy, with Divya trailing behind. The crowd crushed around her and she found it hard to breathe. Ethan found her hand and squeezed it. They made their way to the stage and the man with the leather pants looked up. "Hey, you my Bollywood girl?"

She smiled. "Rick?"

"That's me, baby." He stood, leaned over and touched his cheek to hers. "Damn. You're even better-looking in person than on video."

"You are an even bigger flirt in person than on Zoom."

He smiled widely. "I'm gonna try and get you on when I can. It's a busy night, but chill. I got you."

Ethan navigated them back to the bar. A band onstage introduced themselves, and the lead began strumming an electric guitar. The noise level in the room increased several decibels.

Getting a drink turned out to take almost an hour. It seemed very few people left the club but more joined throughout the night. Each performer got two songs, and the performances ranged from bands singing their own songs to a cappella versions of popular hits to solo instrumental and vocal performances. Divya's feet were killing her, and by the second hour, she could barely stand.

"Your feet hurt?" Ethan asked.

She nodded. "I'll be fine."

He walked over to a table and she saw him handing over several bills. Ethan managed to get them two seats at a table where four other people were already seated. Divya knew money was no object for him, but it was the gesture that struck her. He paid attention to *her*, not just what she said but how she was feeling, how she was doing. How did an intuitive guy like that not have women lining up to be with him?

He tried to introduce them to their tablemates only to get shushed as they listened to the next band. He leaned over and whispered to Divya. "This crowd is no joke."

She nodded. "Broadway and other industry agents and scouts come here looking for talent."

A solo musician stood onstage and tuned his guitar.

"Hurry it up!" someone heckled. The musician looked to be no more than a boy of eighteen or nineteen. He fumbled with the chords and his voice came out strangled. The crowd immediately began booing, and the kid hurried offstage.

Divya's heart hammered. The room was getting hot.

"Don't worry, you'll be great." Ethan squeezed her hand.

"You've never heard me sing. I thought I could do this, but I'm not sure…" The words died on her lips as he put a finger on her mouth. She had an insane urge to take that finger and suck on it.

But just as fast, he pulled it off her lips. "I've seen your determination. You've given up a lot to be here. You can do this."

Tears pricked her eyes. Her family always told her how well she sang. Her parents paid for the best vocal teachers because she asked them to. Yet, none of them had ever believed in her the way this stranger sitting next to her did. He was still holding on to her hand, and she let his strength comfort her and calm the nervous churn of her stomach.

They sat and listened to the other musicians and with each new artist, Divya's doubts grew. The crowd was merciless, exuberant with their applause and brutal with their heckling. At least five performers were run offstage before they even finished their sets. She knew to expect this. It's what made Café Underground *the* place to test one's mettle. But now that she was here, she wasn't sure she could really do it.

Rick signaled to them. Divya looked up at Ethan, and he gave her a reassuring smile. "Go knock them dead." She knew without a doubt no matter what happened, there would be one person in the audience cheering for her.

Her feet hurt and her legs wobbled as she made her way onto the stage. The easy part of doing a vocal performance was the quick stage turnaround. No instrument tuning or setup required. The hard part was the fact that there was nothing but her voice. As she stood at the microphone, the crowd grew restless. They weren't going to be polite to her, like her family and friends. This wasn't like it had been on Zoom, when people were just glad to hear some music and connect with other people. And where Rick had had the ability to mute the crowd.

It was late into the night and the alcohol had been flowing for hours. They weren't going to be easy to please. This would be the moment when she'd find out whether she had any real talent. She'd worked hard for years with the vocal lessons; her singing was the only thing that hadn't been handed to her, and this was the moment she'd find out whether it, whether *she*, was worth anything. She took a breath and found Ethan in the crowd. He gave her a thumbs-up, and she began singing.

Five

Ethan didn't know what to expect, but even without ever having heard Divya sing, he knew she'd be great. What did surprise him was her choice of songs. She started with Leonard Cohen's "Hallelujah." It apparently surprised the crowd too, because as she escalated her voice into the first chorus, a hush blanketed the room for the first time all night. She closed her eyes as she sang the verses, varying her pitch to the crescendo of the words. With no instrumental accompaniment, her voice sounded pure and clear. It filled Ethan's soul with joy and arrested the audience into silence.

At the end of the song, the entire club burst into applause. Ethan stood, clapping as hard as he could. She wasn't just good. She was Whitney Houston, Aretha Franklin good, with a rich deep voice that was pitch-perfect. He'd never heard anything like it.

The deal had been for her to sing two songs. For the

second song she chose "Country Road," and the crowd went wild. This time she didn't stand still. She picked up the microphone from the stand and walked the stage. The crowd joined in with her, thrilled with her nostalgic choice. The other vocalists had all chosen more popular, contemporary songs.

When she waved to leave the stage, the crowd stood and shouted "Encore!" That was also a first all night. They'd liked other performers but hadn't asked anyone to stay.

Rick shook his head, but at the grumbles of the crowd he relented. "One more, but that's it," he bellowed and they all cheered.

Divya onstage was magic, her entire face transformed into sheer joy. This time she went with something more pop culture, but once again, Britney Spears's "Baby One More Time" literally hit the crowd just the way they wanted it. One of the a cappella groups joined in from the crowd, giving her some background vocals. This time Divya didn't just walk the stage, she danced too. If the audience loved her before, they were now smitten. She walked off to a standing ovation and calls for her to come back. Ethan was waiting at the bottom of the stairs, having correctly guessed that she'd be accosted the moment she exited.

Her eyes were wild with excitement, but he could feel the crush of the crowd wanting a piece of her, so he put a protective arm around her as he led her outside through a side entrance that he'd noticed earlier.

"That was great. Oh my God! They actually liked me." They had exited into an alleyway that smelled of urine and something worse, but she didn't seem to notice. She was positively giddy.

"You are amazing, Divya. You don't just have talent, you have a gift."

She twirled. "They didn't boo me offstage." The night

had gotten cooler, but she didn't seem to care about the goose bumps on her arms. Her face was aglow and it brightened his heart. "Can you believe I just did that?"

He smiled, watching her dance in the dirty alley, her laughter and happiness so infectious that when she grabbed his hand, he pulled her into his arms. She flung her arms around his neck and stood on her tiptoes to hug him tightly. His breath caught in his chest. She felt so right against him. Her exuberance reached in and sparked a long-dead fire inside him. She loosened her embrace but kept her arms around his neck. He looked down at her shining face and knew he wasn't going to stop himself this time. He needed to kiss her. He lowered his head.

"Ah there you are!"

Both of them startled at the booming voice. The club door from which they'd just exited banged closed.

A tall, heavyset man with a round face and white T-shirt approached them. Ethan was immediately on guard. The man held out his card. "Jason Brugge from East Side Records. I've been coming to this club for years, and you are the first vocalist who's gotten me to put down my drink. I want you to give me a call. I'll set up an audition, see what we can do."

Divya stood frozen, so Ethan took the card. He would have Roda look up the guy to make sure he was legitimate. Anyone could print up business cards.

"She'll call you," Ethan said, as Divya seemed incapable of words.

When the man was gone, she snatched the card and looked at Ethan wide-eyed. "People come to this club for years hoping to get a card like this."

"I'm sure they do. But they don't have your talent."

She rubbed the card between her hands. "I'm going to frame this."

He took the card from her and pocketed it. “Let’s go back to the hotel. We’ll open a bottle of champagne and celebrate.”

The alley was getting darker and danker by the minute. Divya hadn’t noticed, but Ethan didn’t like the look of the shadowy figures that had begun to make their way toward them from one end of the alley. He grabbed Divya’s hand and walked quickly in the other direction. His management team had repeatedly asked him to have a security detail. His face was well-known in the media, and they were worried that he was a target. He’d resisted the intrusion into his privacy. That, and he could only imagine how his parents would feel if he showed up with bodyguards. They already thought him too pretentious.

He saw a taxi almost as soon as they exited the alley.

Divya was still giddy when they got to the hotel. Ethan ordered a bottle of champagne and a couple of burgers from room service. As they ate and drank, they talked about the club and the other artists and the smell of beer that still clung to them.

Ethan had never had a hard time conversing with beautiful women. He’d dated his share of them. But it was different with Divya. He didn’t have to work at making conversation; it just flowed. And when there were lulls, they sat back in pleasant silence until one of them had more to say. It was easy and comfortable.

Divya walked over to the suite bar. “Oh good. They have Black Label.” She poured herself a small amount. “You want some?”

He crinkled his nose. “Mind if we skip that?”

“You don’t like whiskey?” she asked.

He shook his head. “I can’t even stand the smell of it. Bad memories.”

She poured the whiskey down the sink and came back and sat next to him. He caught her gaze and sighed.

"You know I won't be satisfied until you tell me, so spill it."

"I didn't tell you the whole story about my childhood on the plane." He let out a breath and told her about Wade. "I like to pretend that my life only started with my stepfather. I've tried to forget Wade but I still associate the smell of whiskey with him. On the day my mother walked out on him, I went to give him a hug and he pushed me away so he could take a swig from the whiskey bottle."

"Wade never came back into your life?"

Ethan shook his head. He'd never told anyone what he was about to tell Divya. "When my younger brother was born, I was barely eleven. In my juvenile heart, I thought I needed to let my mom be happy with her new husband. I felt like an outsider. So I saved up my allowance and took a bus to the old neighborhood and found my dad. He was still living in the apartment he shared with my mom. Same old drunk but with a new girlfriend." He hazarded a look at Divya, inwardly cringing at the thought of the sympathy in her eyes, but he didn't see any. She just looked at him steadily, hanging on to his every word.

"I asked if I could stay with him and he said he'd never wanted me." There was one more part to the bile his father had spewed that day, but he couldn't bring himself to say the words out loud. His throat was tight and the sip of beer he took just burned in his mouth. Why had he told Divya? He didn't want her pitying him.

"Well, I bet when he found out you're now a billionaire, he regrets it," Divya joked. It was the perfect thing to say.

"Yep, he tried contacting me through my company, and I got the satisfaction of telling him that Bill is my father.

He even tried going to the media and they dismissed him as a drunk."

"Well, it's great that Bill wanted you."

Actually, he didn't. But that was something he wasn't ready to share.

"So, what's next?" he asked, eager to change the subject.

"Now I can die a happy woman," she sighed. They were sitting on the sofa in the shared living area between their two bedrooms. The lights of the city glittered in front of them. He sat one seat down from her.

"Seriously, Divya, you were amazing tonight. You need to pursue a music career."

She chewed on her lower lip and he tried to ignore the stirrings deep in his core. "I don't want to be a vocalist. I wanted to test out my singing voice, but what I enjoy most about music is creating new songs. Fusing the rhythms of classical Indian music with Western beats."

"Why didn't you sing one of your own songs tonight?"

"First, I didn't have my guitar, but also I don't think the Café Underground crowd would've appreciated my Indian music. What I really wanted to do was sing onstage to a real audience. Thank you for giving me that chance, Ethan. Now I can go back to India and remember this happy feeling."

His heart dropped into his stomach. "What do you mean, *go back to India*? Wasn't the whole point of this to see if you had any talent? You want to give it all up and go back to your previously scheduled life?"

"The idea was never to pursue this as a career. It was something on my bucket list, and I did it."

"So tomorrow, you go back to your family and marry Vivek?" He couldn't keep the bitterness from his voice. Why had he let himself hope that Divya would be any different?

"I am not marrying Vivek, no matter what. And I'm not leaving tomorrow. I want to make sure a few days have passed so the wedding guests leave and my parents can't guilt me into continuing with the festivities. I'll lie low, do some touristy things, let the whole wedding fiasco die down, and then I'll go beg forgiveness."

"Why won't you pursue your dreams?"

"There's a difference between a career and a hobby. My music is a hobby. It can't be my life."

"Why not?"

"Because it's not the kind of existence I want. Being on the road all the time, away from my family."

How could he argue with that? It's exactly what he didn't want, either.

She leaned down and rubbed her foot. He patted the seat next to him. "Hand me that foot."

She raised her brow. "You give foot massages too?"

"I know you probably grew up with your own personal masseuse, but I'll have to do for now." He gestured again to her foot, and she swung her legs onto the sofa, adjusting her dress as she did.

"You're one to talk. I'm surprised you don't have your own personal masseuse on the plane."

He took one foot in his hand and began massaging her heel. "I didn't grow up with money. My dad is a high school teacher and my mom works at a diner. While we always had food on the table, money was tight for luxuries. I worked jobs all through high school and college to help pay for things."

He tried not to think about how delicate her foot felt in his hand or how much he wanted to run his hand up her shapely leg.

"You must be thrilled that you can give your parents a better life now that you've done well."

His heart fisted. “I wish. They won’t take money or anything from me.”

“Why?”

“I don’t know. It’s not like its blood money. I earned every bit of it. They went through some hard times when my mom’s diner had to close, and that was right around the time my company really started to take off. I know I got lucky at a time when other people were suffering…”

“Wait a minute. You shouldn’t feel guilty about your money. You invented a product that’s useful to people.”

He hadn’t said he felt guilty about his money, so how did she know?

As if reading his mind, she said, “I’ve been around wealthy people all my life. Until today, the only time I’ve seen someone carry hundred-dollar bills in their pocket and go around giving outrageous tips is in the movies. It’s like you’re trying to give your money away.”

He smiled. He donated a big portion of his wealth to charity, had even started a foundation of his own that gave scholarships to underprivileged children. And yet his mother still worked at a diner. She was sixty-four years old, his father was close to seventy, and they were still working.

“I never expected my company to become an overnight success, especially during the COVID-19 crisis. I don’t need this kind of money and never wanted it. My parents taught me to work hard for my successes. I feel like I haven’t done that. I just got lucky.”

She shook her head. “Would you say that to me if I became a famous singer and made billions?”

He stared at her. “It’s really hard to make billions from singing. Millions, maybe.”

She gave him a patient smile. “You’d say I have talent and am making money from it. The same applies to you.

Whatever's going on with your parents doesn't diminish your accomplishment."

He wanted to take her words to heart, but somehow he knew that if he was laboring away at a nine-to-five job, or perhaps if his brother, Matt, was the one giving it, his father would be more inclined to take his money. The thought burned a hole in his heart.

He switched his attention to her other foot, and she winced. He looked down to see that she had a scrape along the side of her foot. "Those heels were the wrong size, weren't they?"

She scrunched her nose. "A little bit. But it doesn't help that I've been wearing heels all day."

"Stay here."

He returned with a wet washcloth and cleaned and bandaged her foot.

"First thing tomorrow, I'm going shopping for some sneakers and maybe some yoga pants."

He laughed. "So you're not the kind of girl who wears couture around the house?"

"I'm not the type of girl who wears couture outside the house. Much to my mother's disappointment, I am a T-shirt-and-jeans type of girl."

Exactly the type he liked. She pulled her feet back and slid closer to him. "Thank you for today. Singing in front of a real audience, that's been a dream of mine. It's the only thing I've ever really wanted to do and you made it happen."

He shook his head. "You made it happen. With your voice, with your talent."

She leaned closer to him.

"Is it okay if I kiss you?"

Had she really asked him that? "What guy in his right mind would say no to a question like that from a beautiful woman?"

She gave him a slow smile. “You think I’m beautiful?”

I think you’re freaking gorgeous.

He wasn’t going to let this moment go. He leaned forward and their lips crashed together.

Divya didn’t consider herself a sex goddess, but she was confident with her romantic experiences. Then came the kiss with Ethan.

She’d leaned into the kiss, fully intending to take charge. Except it wasn’t the usual tangle of tongues and lips. Ethan took his time tantalizing her lips, sucking on them gently, flicking his tongue and letting her breathe in the heady scent of his aftershave. Her core tingled with anticipation. She pushed her fingers into his hair, eager to deepen the kiss, to bring his mouth closer. She heard him groan, and hot desire flared deep inside her. She wanted him. Bad.

He broke the kiss. “This probably isn’t a good idea.”

That was not the reaction she’d been expecting. He leaned back. “It’s been quite a night,” he said gently.

What am I doing? Maybe it was the high from Café Underground that had made her throw all sense of propriety to the wind. Here was a nice man who had helped her out and she’d put him in an awkward position by asking to kiss him. How was he supposed to respond to that? “Sorry, I shouldn’t have kissed you,” she said.

“I thought I kissed you,” he said, moving back on the couch so no part of their bodies was touching.

“Why did you kiss me if you thought it was a bad idea?”

“I…” He ran his fingers through his hair. “I…we both almost married other people today. It seems like a bad idea to jump into something new.”

It was as if someone had stuck a pin in her balloon. But she shouldn’t be surprised. Ethan was wealthy and good-looking and dated women who looked like Pooja. How could she possibly compare? Her dating history consisted of Indian men who were into her because she came from a highly desirable family. Ethan was the first man who focused on her and not what her family had to offer. Of course he was rejecting her.

"Well then, I guess we both better get to bed, the sun will be up soon."

He nodded. "Good night, Divya."

She stared at him for a beat. He looked down at his phone. Guess there was nothing left to say.

"Good night, Ethan."

Six

She spent a restless night, despite the silky sheets and firm bed. She woke up hot and frustrated and dreaming of the kiss with Ethan. She could've sworn he was attracted to her. They'd had that moment on the plane and then again in the alley, before they were interrupted. Why was he pretending like they weren't hot for each other?

She took a long shower, slipped on jeans and a T-shirt, grabbed a light jacket and put on her heels from the wedding outfit. They hurt like hell but at least they fit. She mapped out the nearest athletic-shoe store. She peeked out of her room to see Ethan sitting at the bar. A room service cart sat in the middle of the room. *So much for avoiding him.*

"Good morning," she said breezily. He was dressed in jeans and a baby blue polo that made his eyes look like the color of a cloudless sky. Her heart thumped loudly, but she ignored it.

He gave her a big smile and his eyes raked over her. Her stomach flipped.

"Good morning. I didn't know when you'd be up, so I ordered you a bowl of fruit."

She looked at the fruit and scrunched her nose. "Is there anything real to eat?" She picked up the phone and ordered eggs, pancakes and bacon on the side.

Ethan raised his brows. She gave him a challenging look. "Do you have a comment on my order?"

He shook his head and held up his hands. "I'm impressed. I don't think I've met a woman who likes to eat a real breakfast." He held out a piece of bacon from his own plate and she took the peace offering. She poured out a cup of coffee for herself. Yet another thing she loved abroad—coffee. She liked her masala chai and the instant whipped coffee in India, but there was something intoxicating about the smell of good brewed coffee.

"You've been hanging out with the wrong women."

"I certainly have," he muttered so quietly under his breath that Divya wondered if she'd heard it or imagined him saying it.

"So what's the plan for today?"

"I'm going shopping, and then I have lunch with Rajiv and Gauri."

"Am I no longer invited to lunch?"

No, you are not. I plan to ask Rajiv to help me lay low for a few days and then go home. It's time for us to say goodbye.

"You can come if you want to," she said indifferently.

"I'll plan on it. While you're out shopping, you might want to pick up something for tonight."

"What's tonight?" she asked, unable to keep the curious interest out of her voice.

"I'd like to take you out to dinner."

He wanted to come to lunch with her friends and then take her to dinner? What was he doing?

"There's one more thing." He pointed to the couch.

"What?" Her hand flew to her mouth to keep from screaming. On the couch was a Martin guitar case. Her mouth hanging open in shock, she stepped to it and unbuckled the latches. Lying inside was a handmade acoustic guitar with a maple-gloss top and rosewood back and sides. She picked it up reverently.

"This is the top-of-the-line Martin guitar. How did you even know that I play acoustic?"

"Someone showed me this trick where you look up someone on social media and then search their friends' pictures to find out information that might not be on their own pages."

"How did you get this here so quickly?"

He shrugged. "This is New York. Not a lot you can't buy here in short order."

Especially when money is no object. She ran her hands over the wood. Her guitar at home was a Martin, but she didn't have the latest model. She picked a few strings, then began tuning it with expert hands. It was only when room service showed up at the door that she realized she'd been lost in the guitar. She hadn't even thanked Ethan.

After the waiter had taken the old cart and left a new one, she stood and went to Ethan. "I love the guitar, but I can't accept it. You've already done much too much for me, and you don't even know me."

He shrugged. "Money..."

"I know, money doesn't mean much to you but it's also the time you've taken to be with me, to fly me across the country, to search for the perfect guitar for me..." Her voice cracked.

How dare he do the most perfect thing in the world for her?

"Did I do something wrong?" he asked and she felt a tear slide down her cheek.

She shook her head, unable to speak through the big lump that had lodged in her throat.

"What is it?" He reached over and brushed the tear from her cheek, his touch so light and gentle that her chest squeezed even tighter.

"It's..." She struggled to find the word in English. *Aaap-napan* was the word in Hindi. Someone who treated you like their own, someone who knew you better than you knew yourself. He seemed to understand what she needed at a level that even her family didn't.

"Would you like to hear one of my songs?"

He grinned. "I'd like nothing more."

She strummed a few strings to test out the guitar, then sang one of the love songs she'd written. Her eyes closed, and the words bubbled up from deep in her plexus. It was a song she'd written for her brother Sameer when he was in a bad place. It had helped heal him and her. Ethan wouldn't know the words in Hindi, but they were what she needed to hear.

> My heart doesn't know what to feel, my lips don't know what to say, but I'll be okay. I know I'll be okay because you're with me. I don't know what I want, I haven't for a while, but as long as I have you, I have hope of better things to come.

When she was done, there were fresh tears on her cheeks. It was as if something had burst open inside her. *Promise me, Divya, that if we get through this, we'll stop living for our parents and start living for ourselves.* She had forgotten that hospital-bed promise she and Sameer had made to each other.

"Wow, that was incredible."

She opened her eyes to see Ethan staring at her. "You're just being polite, you didn't even know what the words meant."

"No, but I could feel the pain in your melody, the hope in your voice." He paused. "What was the song about?"

She put the guitar in the case. "A couple of years ago my brother Sameer was in a bad accident. His whole body was broken. We weren't sure if he'd survive. I wrote this song for him. It is about hope and about not letting your fears stop you." She closed the guitar case and turned to him. "I think I'm going to give that record company guy from Café Underground a call. I'll ask Rajiv if he can put up with me for a few weeks so I can give this music thing a shot."

"I already asked Roda to check out that guy, plus I've put feelers out among my friends. Somebody will know an industry contact. And my jet is at your disposal. Whatever you need."

"We hardly know each other. Why are you doing all this for me?"

He shrugged, then he looked out the window like he couldn't quite meet her eyes. "Maybe it's because you're the first person I've met for whom I seem to be able to do something right."

There was so much longing in his voice that she wanted to hug him and tell him all the ways in which he was a great guy. But something held her back. He hadn't wanted her to kiss him. Maybe friendship was all he wanted to offer, and she didn't want to mess that up.

She poured him a cup of coffee from the room service cart and handed it to him. "Thank you. For everything. Now, let's eat this cold breakfast."

The rest of the morning went by in a blur as she shopped for some basic items. When she returned, she donned a cream silk shirt with dark blue–patterned pants. She let her hair loose and swiped some makeup on her face. Ethan had changed into dress pants and a collared shirt. He whistled when he saw her, and she couldn't help but smile. She'd put a little extra effort into her appearance.

They met Rajiv and Gauri in the hotel lobby.

"Divya, oh my God!" Gauri was petite, about five feet tall with large luminous eyes. Her dark hair was pulled into a ponytail. She wore a black dress and dangling diamond earrings. Divya hugged her back. Rajiv had a town car waiting, which took them a few blocks down the road to one of the most exclusive French restaurants in the city.

At first they stuck to safe topics like politics, religion and money. But inevitably, her runaway status came up during a dessert of Grand Marnier soufflé and pistachio crème brûlée.

"So what mysterious plans did you have last night?" Gauri asked, throwing a suggestive look at Ethan. He nearly choked on his espresso.

"I was tired and went to bed early. Ethan had some business to take care of." She could feel Ethan looking at her, but he kept quiet.

Gauri narrowed her eyes at Divya but didn't say more.

"So, what's the plan exactly?" Rajiv asked. "Your parents and Arjun have been calling everyone you know."

Divya shifted in her seat. "I just want some time for my family to cool off, then I'll go home. I emailed Arjun to tell him that I'm safe."

"Yes, thank you, you used the hotel business center, and he tracked the IP address to New York and grilled me. You know I owe your brother a lot. I feel very bad lying to him."

Divya felt a pang of guilt. "I'm so sorry to put you in this position. We'll leave."

"You can stay as long as you need," Rajiv said halfheartedly. "I'm only saying there may be a better way of handling things."

Rajiv and Gauri looked at each other, then Gauri spoke up. "Look, Divya, I know we've been out of touch, but we were good friends once, so I feel I should be honest with you."

Ethan stiffened next to her.

"If you two are together, that's fine. We can accept that. Rajiv's brother married an American, and our family dealt with it. But this hiding is not good. It'll be hard for your family to accept Ethan if you continue on this way. He already has a reputation, and well..." Gauri trailed off as Divya shot her a murderous look.

Ethan didn't deserve to be attacked for her decisions. "Ethan and I aren't together. He accidently crashed the wrong wedding and I used the opportunity to run away. All he's been doing is helping me hide."

Gauri raised her brows. "Then, what are you still doing together? He's done his job. You are safe with us. Why is he staying with you?"

"I'm right here, you know," Ethan said quietly, but the anger in his voice was clear. "What Divya and I do is our business. We appreciate your hospitality, but we've clearly outstayed our welcome."

Divya winced. Ethan didn't know her friends and didn't understand that they were just looking out for her. His tone had been unnecessarily harsh.

Gauri reached out her hand and grabbed Divya's, clutching it as she turned toward Ethan. "Please, don't take it the wrong way. We are only concerned about our friend. It's in our nature to speak plainly. We didn't mean to offend."

"I know you didn't, and your point is well-taken. I will think about it," Divya said soothingly. She held up her spoon, eager to ease the tension around the table. "This crème brûlée is to die for."

After they were finished with lunch, Gauri cornered Divya when they returned to the hotel. Ethan looked at Divya, and she nodded to him, so he excused himself and went to the room.

"Divya, you know the rumors going around about you and Ethan."

She nodded. She had resisted the urge to google their names, but she could only imagine the media storm that was raging.

"What are you doing with him? If this continues, you will never get a good *rishta,* and your reputation will be ruined forever. It's not like you to be running around with a strange man. Especially not a *gora.*"

Divya took a deep breath. Every Indian parent with a daughter of marriageable age was on the hunt for a good *rishta,* a suitable match for their child.

"I don't want or need a good *rishta.* And Ethan is a perfect gentleman. I know what I'm doing."

"Do you? There might not be anything going on between you now, but I see the way he looks at you. It's only a matter of time before he makes a move, and then what'll you do?"

Jump his bones. The thought of Ethan making a move on her made her warm all over.

"I can take care of myself," she said cagily.

"Listen, Divya, I know it feels good to be out and about by yourself. To not have rules or restrictions. But trust me, Ethan is not the right man for you. He's hot, no doubt, but he's not marriage material."

"Why not? Because he's American?"

"Yes, that's exactly why. Rajiv's brother is married to an American woman, and let me tell you, it's like lunch was today."

"What was wrong with lunch today?"

"We had a polite conversation. We didn't talk about anything real. I didn't get to tell you that Rajiv's parents are really upset with my sister-in-law because she traded in the family jewelry they gave her for their wedding for something more modern. We didn't get to talk about how your parents are going to react when you go back. That's how it is in my house. We talk to his brother and sister-in-law about meaningless things, like they're strangers. There is always an awkwardness when you don't marry someone from your culture. And look, when I did try to talk about something real, he got angry."

"You were a little rude."

"I was being honest. But that's how it is. If he had been Indian, he wouldn't have taken offense like that, he would have understood where we were coming from."

Divya sighed. Why was she even having this conversation with Gauri? It's not as though she and Ethan were together or that she was even thinking about him in any serious capacity. Yet she felt an anger inside her and wanted to defend the idea that they could have something real.

Gauri touched her arm. "I'm just saying think about things carefully. Your parents will forgive you. Vivek still wants to marry you. The story came out that Ethan was dating some other Indian girl, so they know you didn't really run away with him. They all know it was cold feet and will forgive you. Take it from me. I couldn't wait to get away from my parents. Now I miss them every day. We only get to go to India once or twice a year and I savor every visit with them. You don't know what you're missing until you don't have it anymore."

Divya murmured a platitude, gave her friend a hug and said goodbye. Gauri hadn't said anything that Divya hadn't thought herself, but now every fiber of her being wanted to disagree with her friend, to prove her wrong.

When she returned to the room, Ethan was sitting on the couch with his feet up and his laptop open. She went and sat in a chair across from him. She owed him an explanation. To his credit, he didn't ask.

"I didn't want to tell them about the singing."

"It's something that's yours. You don't have to share it until you're ready."

And just like that, he struck a chord in her heart and she wanted to run back down and tell Gauri that this American, the one who didn't know her culture or speak her language and had known her for all of two minutes, understood her better than anybody else.

"Gauri didn't mean to offend you. She was just being blunt." Divya kept her voice light.

"She wasn't blunt enough. What she meant to tell you is that you're ruining your life by running around with me."

"You were a little forceful too."

"How did you expect me to react?"

"With some patience. If my brother finds out that Rajiv lied to him, it'll jeopardize their lifelong friendship. He's stuck his neck out for me. You could have been a little more polite."

"So it's okay for them to be rude to me?"

"They weren't being rude. They were asking a genuine question."

"Which was what exactly?"

"Why you're still here. You aren't romantically interested in me, and yet you're buying me guitars and making wishes come true. Why?"

He looked away from her, but she wasn't going to let him off the hook. She stepped to him, bent down and kissed him hard on the lips. He opened his mouth and kissed her back with the same hot intensity. This time, she broke the kiss.

"You're lying to me and yourself if you still think there isn't something between us," she said, then walked into the bedroom and closed the door.

Seven

Divya dressed for dinner in an off-the-shoulder black dress she had bought that morning and comfortable flats. It wasn't the look for a fashionista, but with her hair curled in stylish waves and her eyes rimmed with dark eyeliner, she knew she looked good. As she stepped into the common area of their shared hotel room, Ethan gazed at her with darkened eyes. "How many looks do you have, woman?"

Divya had avoided him for the rest of the afternoon. She'd heard him moving around but had kept her bedroom door firmly shut, spending the time tuning her new guitar and practicing her songs. She'd made her move, now it was his turn.

He offered his arm and she took it, noticing the clean scent of his soap and aftershave. She resisted the urge to lean into him so she could breathe him in. They took a pedicab, and she was somewhat surprised when they pulled up to a food stand outside Madison Square Garden. The city was alive with the sounds of honking cars and people bustling everywhere. The air was thick with the smell of exhaust fumes and cooking food.

"This is our big dinner out?" she quipped, tucking her hand into his arm.

"This place has the best hot dogs ever. And then I have a surprise for you."

They ate the hot dogs, standing on the sidewalk, watching the crowds flow out of Penn Station and stream into Madison Square Garden. There was a show on tonight and the headliner was a popular hip-hop artist.

"Have you ever been to a show here?"

Divya shook her head. Ethan pulled two tickets from his jeans and Divya's eyes widened. They made their way into the arena. Ethan's tickets were on the floor, toward the middle. When the opening act was introduced, Divya realized why Ethan had brought her here.

"Tina Roy. She's an Indian artist who mixes Indian and Western music," Ethan whispered to Divya.

The music was fantastic, and the crowd ate it up. Divya watched Tina dance around onstage, wearing a short fringed skirt and a tube top. She pictured her parents sitting in the audience, watching this woman grind with the male backup dancers and thrust her hips to the beat of the music. Her family wouldn't be proud; they'd be embarrassed. Her mother didn't even like Divya wearing skirts around the house. *Appearances are important, Divya. What will the staff think of you parading around with bare legs?*

Her mother would have a coronary if Divya ever wore an outfit like Tina Roy's, let alone performed onstage in it. Her cheeks reddened at the thought of her dad seeing her in such skimpy clothes.

Tina started her second number. The music, the clothes, the special effects were all designed to rile people up and

Divya could feel the crowd practically vibrating. She closed her eyes and pictured herself on the stage at Café Underground, the energy that had pulsed through her as the audience appreciated her singing. She'd never felt that kind of power surge through her body. A crowd like the one at Madison Square Garden right now would be addictive.

Tina Roy's performance was amazing, but she wasn't a fan of the main act when he came onstage. "Do you mind if we leave?"

Ethan smirked. "This guy is no Tina Roy. Let's get out of here."

Ethan asked the taxi driver to take them back to the hotel. Divya laid her head back on the seat. Her heart raced. *Life is too short not to live it on your terms.* After Sameer had gotten out of the hospital, she'd spent all her free time working on her music. But as time went on, she'd slipped back into her mother's society life and the family business.

She looked out the window. "Can you pull up to the curb?" she asked the taxi driver. They were at Fifth Avenue and East Seventy-Second Street. Central Park stretched out on the right-hand side of the cab. "Can we go for a walk?"

Ethan paid the driver and exited behind her. They walked in silence, her hand tucked into his arm. Even at that time of night, the city was bustling. Birds chirped in trees, joggers pounded the trail, dogs walked with their owners, occasionally stopping to sniff something interesting.

"When I was growing up, my dad fulfilled my every wish. At the age of eight, I wanted a horse. I'd just read about Jhansi ki Rani, who's like the Indian equivalent of Joan of Arc, and I thought I would be great at horseback riding because I could feel the spirit of Jhansi ki Rani. My mother, who is always the realist in the house, told my father that it was a fad and not to go overboard. But of course, he didn't listen to her. He bought me a magnificent horse and hired a professional trainer to teach me how to ride. He even began renovating the ancient stables on our property. At first, I loved riding, but then as the lessons wore on, it wasn't fun anymore. It became a matter of working hard to learn how to ride. Each lesson left me sore and aching."

They walked toward the lake, which shimmered darkly against the soft lights of the street lamps on the trail. Her hand remained tucked in the crook of his arm.

"I continued with the lessons for years because I wanted to prove to my mother that I could do it. I never became a good rider. When my horse was too old to ride and retired, I was so happy. My father offered to buy me a new horse, and my mother simply turned to me and said, 'Tell him.'"

They walked alongside the lake. The night was rapidly cooling. Ethan put his arm around her shoulders, pulling her close. She didn't resist, grateful for the warmth and the feel of his solid body against hers.

"My mom knew all along that I hated riding, but she didn't say a word for ten years." She stopped walking and turned to stare at the lake. There was just enough light to see the reflection of the trees. Ethan remained quiet beside her.

"It's a lesson I'll never forget. There's a word in Hindi, *ghamand.* It doesn't have an English equivalent. It means pride, arrogance, vanity. It's being so stubborn that you cut your nose to spite your face."

Ethan turned to face her, and her heart raced. He kept a hand on her arm and stood so close that all she had to do was stand on tiptoe and she could kiss him. His hand moved up and down her arm and she felt the goose bumps, but her body was far from cold.

"Divya, I can't even begin to tell you how many times people discouraged me from moving forward with Deal Catcher. Amazon already existed and the market was flooded with apps. You have to believe in yourself. You can easily be Tina Roy one day."

She put a finger on his lips and felt him suck in a breath. Then she brushed her finger across his lips before retracting her hand.

"I'm not giving up on my singing. I loved being onstage. But that's precisely why I don't want to ruin it for me. I don't want to be like Tina Roy. I remember listening to some of her early works and they were nothing like what she performed today. I don't want to write songs that appeal onstage and end up hating music."

"It doesn't have to be that way—"

"Ethan! I have a law degree, a career, a family. I have a lot going for me. Music will remain my hobby, something I enjoy."

"But you're so talented you can do anything you want."

Was it her imagination or had he stepped closer to her? She could almost feel the rise and fall of his chest. She put her arms around him and he closed the distance between their lips.

This time, he didn't hold back when he kissed her. He pulled her close and she gave as good as she got. Their lips were in perfect harmony as they explored and tasted each other. She pressed her body to his and fire licked deep in her core. She molded herself to him, and felt his attraction, hard against her belly.

He stepped back from her, his breath heavy.

"There is one thing I really want to do that I'm not sure I can."

His lips twitched. "What's that?"

"I want to seduce you."

Eight

Do not kiss her again. Ethan wanted to tell the inner voice ringing alarm bells in his head to shut up. She lifted her chin, her eyes challenging him to take another taste of her wet lips. He could handle an affair with her, couldn't he? He knew where she stood on the topic of marriage; there'd be no expectations between them, just a physical relationship. He looked into her eyes and his heart jolted.

"It's getting late. Let's go back to the hotel."

She raised a brow but didn't say anything. They retraced their steps back to Fifth Avenue and caught a taxi back to the hotel. They were at the lobby elevators when one of the front desk clerks came rushing up to them. "Miss Singh!"

"Yes?"

"Mr. Mehra needs to speak to you urgently. He's on his way. Please wait right here."

Rajiv appeared a few minutes later, his suit still perfectly pressed, despite the late hour. "Divya! I didn't know how to reach you." He sounded frantic.

"What's happened?"

"The show you were at tonight, someone recognized Ethan." His gaze flicked to Ethan. "Arjun is tracking all mentions of Ethan on social media. He and Vivek are on a plane from Vegas."

"Vivek? Why is he coming?"

Rajiv shrugged. "Arjun didn't get into the details, but I think Vivek wants to talk to you. Maybe he feels he can convince you to get married."

Divya sighed. Rajiv gave Ethan a pointed look, then lowered his voice, as if doing so would exclude Ethan from the conversation. "I think you should be honest with your brother. Running away is not the way to handle things."

Divya glanced at Ethan. He should nod, tell her Rajiv was right, because he was. She needed to confront her family, not hide from them. Yet he couldn't bring himself to do more than blink at her.

"I can't, Rajiv. I'm not ready to face my family yet."

Rajiv pressed his fingers to his lips. "Then, I need you not to be here when Arjun arrives."

Divya placed a hand on Rajiv's arm. "I'm so sorry. Of course we'll get out right away."

"I've arranged a limo for you. A friend of mine has a house in the Hamptons where you can hang out until you're ready to go home. I'll arrange whatever you need." Rajiv gave her a pointed look and it wasn't hard to understand the subtext of his words. Divya didn't need to rely on Ethan. There was no reason for him to hang around anymore.

Once again, Divya looked at Ethan. *It was probably best that they parted ways.* The more time he spent with her, the greater the chance that he would lose his heart to this girl who was very much unavailable.

"Thank you, Rajiv, but I don't want to involve you more than you already are. I know your friendship with my brother is important."

"Divya..."

Ethan took a step forward. "Don't worry, Rajiv. I'll take good care of her. I can have my jet ready to go in an hour."

Rajiv looked between Divya and Ethan, then spread his hands. "Good luck to you." Then he turned and said something to Divya in Hindi. Her eyes widened and Ethan could've sworn he saw her blush. She responded in Hindi, then hugged Rajiv. Without a glance at Ethan, she pressed the elevator button.

Ethan didn't ask what Rajiv had said and Divya didn't volunteer. They didn't have a lot of stuff, so it didn't take long to pack. Ethan made arrangements for the jet and called the valet to bring the Mercedes.

"Are you sure you want to keep running? I'd be happy to wait and take you wherever you want to go after you sort things out with your brother."

Divya began shaking her head before he even finished the sentence. "I'm not ready for this to end yet. I'm enjoying my freedom."

"Why does it have to be an all-or-nothing deal, Divya? Why can't you tell your brother that you're ready to be your own independent woman?"

"Because that's not how things are done in my family."

The valet brought the Mercedes, and he loaded the luggage and opened the door for her. The night was cold, so Ethan didn't drop the top on the convertible. As he eased out of the hotel driveway, he turned toward her. "What're you so afraid of?"

"I'm afraid of how much I love my family. Arjun has a way of convincing me that he'll work something out to get me what I want. But it's never exactly what I want."

"What do you mean?"

"After I finished law school, I wanted a job. I was even offered this great position with a law firm, but my parents didn't want me to take it. They didn't understand why I wanted to work, given that we have plenty of money. My mom wanted me to be a socialite like her so I could find a nice husband. Arjun brokered a deal with my parents where I could work, but for the family firm. Don't get me wrong, I appreciate it was a big battle for him to get me that concession, but the whole reason I wanted a job is to have some independence from the family."

"I still don't understand why you didn't just take the law firm position. It's not as if your family would've locked you at home."

She blew out a breath, but Ethan wasn't going to let her off the hook. Divya didn't seem like the type of woman who had been cloistered all her life. She was confident and self-assured enough to get what she wanted. *Including me.* There was something she wasn't telling him.

"No, of course not. We're not that type of family. It's more that they worry and care about me, and once I see my brother again, he'll remind me of all the reasons why I should come home." She looked out the passenger-side window, clearly hiding her face from him.

"What aren't you telling me?"

"It's complicated, and now's not the time. Let's discuss where we're going."

He wanted to know more, but clearly, she didn't trust him enough to share what was really going on.

"I have something you should add to your bucket list."

She grinned at him. "What do you have in mind?"

"Trust me?"

She leaned back in the car seat. "I'm all yours."

If only that was true.

Nine

It was past midnight when they arrived at Teterboro, but Roda was waiting there. She handed Ethan several shopping bags and took the keys of the Mercedes.

Kathy greeted them warmly when they got on the plane. They ordered coffee and dinner.

He took a seat in one of the reclining chairs that faced the back of the plane and Divya sat opposite him. They were quiet until Kathy returned with their food. “We’re waiting for clearance from the tower. It might be a while before we’re ready to take off. The pilot is expecting a bumpy ride because of a weather system coming in from the south. I’ll be in the jump seat. Ring the call button if you need anything.”

They dug into their food, both of them famished. The hot dog at Madison Square Garden had been hours ago.

“You want to tell me where we’re going?” Divya finally asked.

He smiled. "Let's just say we're going to go do something that'll help you face your fears."

"Please, don't tell me we'll be in a tank full of sharks."

He laughed. "Now, why didn't I think of that?"

She leaned over until her face was inches from him. Her breath smelled of coffee and her vanilla lip gloss, and all he could think about was pulling her onto his lap and kissing her until he didn't have any air left in his chest.

"You told me to trust you," she said.

He swallowed, trying to remember what they were talking about. "Don't worry. I'll be with you." He placed his hands on her shoulders and gently pushed her back into her seat. He couldn't have her so close to him.

"You want to tell me what's going on between us?"

"Excuse me?"

"You kiss me like you're going to swallow me whole, and then you pull away. What's going on?"

He sighed, not sure if he loved or hated Divya's straight talk.

"I'm attracted to you, Divya, but just a few days ago I broke up your wedding. What kind of man runs away with the wrong bride, then gets involved with her? I don't want to get into something messy and make you feel uncomfortable."

"How chivalrous of you. First of all, I decide what's comfortable for me, and second, why do you assume it'll be messy? I'm an adult and so are you. I enjoy sex. I hope you do too. Why can't we enjoy it together?"

Damn. When she put it that way, he had a hard time coming up with a coherent answer. How did he explain to her that he felt a connection to her? Perhaps it was real, or maybe it was his traditional pattern of falling for women who were unavailable. He knew their chemistry was real, and he was afraid to find out just how explosive it could be.

He stared at her, and the fire in her eyes ignited something deep and powerful in his core. For the first time in his life, he wanted to fight his impulses. A loud warning blared in his head, but he was having a hard time hearing it. Divya's glossy pink lips were calling out to him.

"Look, there are no expectations between us. I don't think you're taking advantage of me, we've clearly got chemistry. Why not enjoy ourselves for the short time we have together?"

Because I may not just want you for a short time.

Of all the men she'd been with, none got her as hot and bothered as Ethan. Maybe because for the first time in her life, she wasn't looking at someone through her family's eyes. He wasn't a man to be evaluated for marriage. He was a man she could just be with. No expectations, no boundaries. Total freedom.

It wasn't a question of attraction. She'd felt his attraction hard and clear when they kissed. *Does he think I'm too inexperienced to understand what sex means?*

She left her seat, leaned over and pressed her lips to his. His eyes darkened and she knew she had him.

"I'd like to add the mile-high club to my bucket list."

She gave him her most sultry smile, then turned her back to him, took her shirt off and let it drop to the floor. His eyes were glued to her, but he sat frozen in his seat. She took off her lacy bra and flung it at him, then crossed her arms over her chest. She stood for a second and looked over her shoulder at him. The sharp intake of his breath made her smile. She walked to the bedroom at the back of the plane.

As expected, he wasn't far behind. She'd barely stepped into the tiny bedroom when she felt his arms around her, his chest to her bare back. The bed took up most of the space in the room. There was a mirror opposite the door.

She saw their reflection as his hands crisscrossed her waist. He kissed the spot where her neck met her shoulder, and a delicious quiver coursed through her body.

He met her eyes in the mirror. "You're a dangerous woman, Divya, but I'm no slouch in the seduction department." He ran his hands over her narrow waist and flat belly, then worked upward and cupped her breasts, running his thumbs over her sensitive, taut nipples. Her core melted and she moaned. She reached back and weaved her fingers into his hair, tugging at it to let him know he was driving her crazy as his lips worked their way up her neck to nibble on her ears.

She moved her hands down and found him hard and ready. She caressed him through his jeans and smiled as he groaned. He loosened his arm and she turned around and tugged his shirt off. His chest and hard abs had a sexy smattering of hair that was just right. She ran her hands over him, noticing the darkness of her skin against his paleness. "Wow, you are really white."

He chuckled. "I'll work on my tan."

She ran her hands down his pecs, over his belly, following the trail of sandy-brown hair from his washboard abs to the top of his jeans. She popped the button, and he shook off his shoes while she tugged his jeans off.

"Hmm, I like a boxers man."

She touched his velvety hard-on, tentatively at first, but then she took it firmly in her hand.

"Divya!" He breathed her name in a begging moan. She moved her hand up and down until he placed his own hand on hers, stilling her. She looked at him questioningly, but he moved her hands to her own waistband. He undid the button on her jeans and she slid them down. She was wearing one of her new purchases, the red lace panties. His appreciative moan told her it had been a worthwhile purchase. He touched her core through the soft fabric and she melted. She was hot and swollen and wet and she wanted him hard and fast.

She hooked her fingers in the waistband of her panties to take them off, but he stopped her.

"Not so fast." He worked his fingers over the outside of her panties, circling her tight bud, pushing his finger slightly inside.

They felt the plane gain speed as it began to taxi down the runway.

Enough. If he was going to drive her mad, she was doing the same to him. The bed was behind him. As the plane rose in the air, she gave him a hard push and he stumbled backward. She pushed him again until he was sitting on the bed. She straddled him. Her panties were wet and she ground against him, enjoying his moan of pleasure. His mouth found her breast, and his tongue licked and teased while he cupped the other in his hand, his fingers rubbing her nipple until she felt intense pressure in her core.

It was tempting to give in to her release, but she knew it would be so much better with him inside her. When he came up for air, she got up, reached into her jeans for a condom and tore off the outside packaging. She'd been prepared for this moment. She took off her panties while he watched, his sky-blue eyes as dark as hers. Then she touched herself.

"Take off your boxers."

He complied immediately, then reached over and took the condom from her. He quickly sheathed himself, and she stepped back toward the bed, spread her legs on either side of his knees and straddled him as she took him inside her in one slick motion.

He filled her just right, and the feeling was so intense, so perfect that she clutched him with her muscles, dug her fingers into his shoulders. She rocked and shuddered and shattered violently against his arousal, her climax so powerful that she screamed. He vibrated inside her and that brought a new wave of heat and pleasure coursing through her.

She rested her head on his chest, too blown away to speak. He circled his arms around her as she slid off him, pulling her close. She wrapped her arms around his chest and inhaled the scent of his soap and sweat and felt her core twitch with desire.

The plane shook as they hit a rough patch of air. She moved involuntarily and felt him harden.

Whoa. She'd had sex before. She liked sex. But what she'd had before was the kind of run-of-the-mill orgasm that her vibrator could accomplish. Ethan… Ethan was the master of finding all the right spots.

As she slid off him, he caught her wrist and she looked at him. His eyes smoldered with the same emotions that raged through her: unsatiated desire, surprise at how good it was between them, fear because of how good it was between them and perhaps a little anger that she'd brought them to this point. She gave him a half smile. Who knew what the future held for her, but at the moment, she had all the freedom in the world. She wouldn't have to wonder what it would've felt like to be with Ethan. The longing would've consumed her. Now she could get it out of her system, just like she had with her dreams of being a singer.

He let go of her wrist, stood and went to the attached bathroom to get rid of the condom. Divya stood uncertainly, wondering whether she should get dressed. Should they sit and have a naked chat? What she really wanted was to go for round two. Make sure she hadn't imagined round one.

He returned from the bathroom, tossed himself onto the bed, got under the covers and patted the space beside him. She crawled into bed and he pulled her against him, her back to his chest. He curled himself around her and she felt him getting hard, which made her own core tighten with anticipation.

"You had to do that, didn't you," he whispered in her ear, sending hot shivers down her spine.

"Would you rather I hadn't?"

"It's hard to answer that now, when the reality was better than my fantasy."

"It's better than wondering what could've been," she said.

"Aren't you the one who advised me not to go for women who are unavailable?"

She had, hadn't she? And she definitely wasn't available. Had she been so selfish in her desire for him that she hadn't noticed him developing real feelings for her? She eased herself from his arms and sat up on the bed so she could look at him. "You're not falling for me, are you?"

"Don't you have a high opinion of yourself."

"Well, I am pretty lovable."

"And hot, don't forget hot." He reached for her and pulled her onto him so that their naked bodies molded together. She ground against him, getting him harder, then leaned toward him so her breasts tantalized his chest. He sucked on one hard nipple, then the other. She was already slick. He rolled her over so she was underneath him. From there, he went on an exploration of her body with his mouth that left her writhing with pleasure. He worked his way down from her breasts to her belly and finally to her core, where he teased her with his tongue and sucked her with his lips. When she couldn't take it anymore, he reached into the bedside table, pulled out a condom and put it on, then entered her slowly. She cried out and pushed her hips up to meet him, taking him deeper inside her.

He moaned and she increased the tempo. It didn't take

long for both of them to shatter, the world exploding even more powerfully this time than it had before.

Divya gasped for breath as she finished. She lay there as Ethan took care of the condom, then returned. He slid into the bed and she turned to face him, tucking her leg between his. She wanted to stay with him for as long as possible and soak in the feeling of pure bliss. She placed a hand on his chest and traced the hair across his ribs. The men she had been with all had dark hair and dark brown nipples, like she did. Ethan's were pink and rosy and she ran her fingers over them. "There is such a difference in our skin color."

"Does that bother you?"

"It's just… I don't know."

"You know, our differences are only skin deep. We have more in common than you think." He took her hand and weaved his fingers through hers. "Family means everything to me, just like it does to you. And I know what it's like to want something so badly that it scares you to admit how much you need it."

Her heart slammed against her chest. Ethan stilled. She withdrew her hand from his and turned her back to him. "I think the day is catching up with me."

"I'm not going to let you go that easy, Divya." Ethan muttered. He put his arm around her and pulled her close.

His warmth felt so good, so comforting, that it wasn't long before she fell asleep dreaming of singing onstage like Tina Roy, with Ethan cheering her from the audience.

Ten

"Where are we exactly?" The first rays of sunlight were barely visible in the sky when they deplaned. They'd made a fueling stop somewhere, but Divya hardly remembered. She'd been so exhausted that the final descent had barely registered.

The air was hot and humid. An attendant waited with the keys to a Porsche Carrera, the convertible's top already down. Divya was wearing jeans, a long-sleeved blouse and a sweater and felt very overdressed for the weather.

She looked at Ethan, meeting his eyes for the first time since she'd slid out of bed. He walked to the passenger door of the car and held it open for her. "We're at a private airport in Key Largo. Let's get on the road. There's a sunrise view I don't want you to miss."

She lowered herself onto the hard leather seat and took off her sweater. "What about our luggage?" she asked as he slid into the driver's seat and started the engine.

"We'll be back on the plane by the evening. I have to be in Minnesota tonight. It's my parents' wedding anniversary."

"Oh," she said. Was she going with him? Did she even want to go with him? She studied his profile as he steered the car out of the private airport. He was objectively the most handsome man she'd ever been with. His jawline was sharp, his nose perfect, his lips utterly kissable. Warmth pooled deep in her belly as she thought about his mouth on her body and in between her legs. Her entire body still tingled from his touch. He was a considerate and giving lover and she knew without a doubt that she'd always compare any man she ever slept with from this point on to Ethan.

What if he's the last man I sleep with? She pushed the idea firmly to the back of her mind because it was too pleasant a thought. Had she made a mistake by seducing him? He'd been good to her. She didn't want to break his heart, but there was no way they could be together long-term. He was wrong about their differences being only skin deep. He knew her only as Divya the woman, not Divya the sister or daughter. Would he understand her commitment to her family? How would he deal with her parents? She'd seen how defensive he'd gotten with Rajiv and Gauri. Her mother didn't mince words and she didn't let anyone talk back to her. *Why am I even thinking this way?* It wasn't as if she was getting serious about Ethan. It was good sex. Okay, amazing sex. But that's all it was.

Ethan motored south onto US Route 1 just as the first rays of the sun began to brighten the sky. She gasped as she caught sight of the crystal clear water all around her. It seemed like the road was floating on top of the ocean.

"The Atlantic Ocean is to our left and the Gulf of Mexico to our right. This is called the Overseas Highway," Ethan said.

"Are we even on land?"

He smiled. "If you're impressed now, wait until we get on the Seven Mile Bridge in a few minutes. You'll feel like you're about to fall into the ocean."

As the sun burst into the sky, the scene in front of her transformed into hues of orange, red and purple. The water changed from a dark blue green to a lighter blue. There was little traffic on the road, so Ethan drove slowly. "This the most beautiful sunrise I've ever seen, I wanted to share it with the most spectacular woman I've ever met."

Her chest constricted at the thickness in his voice. She was glad she couldn't see his face and he couldn't see the tears that had suddenly sprung in her eyes. Plenty of men had told her how beautiful she was, but Ethan hadn't just meant her looks. She knew that in her heart, and that made his compliment sting. He was a good man. Had he been a *suitable boy* who her parents had set her up with, she would've been having a very different conversation with herself. But there was no scenario in which her family would accept a *gora.* Arjun had almost been disowned for wanting to marry an Indian girl who was divorced. Divya's sister-in-law, Rani, was an amazing person who spoke their language, understood their culture and traditions. Yet Rani struggled with truly fitting into the family. How could Ethan ever become a part of her world? Gauri's comments about the impersonal nature of their relationship with her white sister-in-law came to her. Ethan would always be an outsider standing next to her.

She saw the sign for the Seven Mile Bridge, and Divya leaned over as far as she could to look out the window. "Oh my God, I can almost see the fish, the water is so clear."

"We won't have time to go swimming today, but you should come back and really explore the Keys."

He'd said *you*, not *we*. Somehow, she knew she could

never come back here without Ethan. This place, this feeling of pure bliss, would always remind her of him. She lifted her face to the sky and breathed in the warm, salty air. Her home in Rajasthan was a desert, so there was always a grittiness in the atmosphere. She'd been to Miami before with Arjun to check out a potential hotel he was looking to buy, but they'd never taken the time to travel to the Keys. "How did I not know that such a spectacular place existed?"

"You have to get out of your comfort zone to find this kind of paradise."

This was truly paradise. But it wasn't real life. It didn't include the people she loved. It was a momentary escape. She closed her eyes to savor the moment and lock it away in her mind so she wouldn't forget. She took out her phone and snapped a picture of the sunrise, then reached out her arm and leaned close to Ethan for a selfie.

"Are you going to give our social media fans a honeymoon picture?" he said laughingly.

"I want to remember this moment forever."

"Why?"

What did he mean, *why*? "It's an amazing sunrise."

"Is that the only reason?"

Her stomach clenched. Why couldn't things just be easy, uncomplicated and temporary between them? "I enjoy being with you, Ethan. I love our time together and I want to remember it for when..." Her throat suddenly went dry.

"For when it ends, and you go back to your regularly scheduled life."

"It's not as if it'll be goodbye forever. We will keep in touch, stay friends."

He stayed silent, his lips set in a straight line, and her stomach flipped. He knew it could never be serious between them, *didn't he*? She'd been upfront with him that she was not the marrying type, and he wanted someone forever. He was done with jetting around and temporary relationships. She was done sitting at home and letting other people make decisions for her. Perhaps it had been a bad idea to sleep together. And yet as she looked at him, all she could think about was running her hands all over him.

Once they got off the Seven Mile Bridge, he took a right turn onto a gravel road. He pulled up to what looked like a log cabin. A hand-painted sign read Skydive Keys. She stared at it.

"You can't be serious. We're going skydiving?"

He nodded. "That beautiful view we just saw is even more spectacular from the air."

"Are you crazy? I don't know how to skydive."

"You're not going to do it alone. We're going to be strapped together in tandem."

You are nuts! There was no way she was going to do something like that. She wanted adventure, but this was extreme. What was Ethan thinking?

A man with long blond hair and a scraggly beard appeared from the cabin. "Ethan, my man."

Ethan exited the car and did some sort of secret handshake with the guy, who looked more like an overweight surfer dude than a lean mean skydiver.

"It's been a while. Plane's gassed and I got your gear laid out." Divya got out of the car and surfer dude turned to her. "Name's Buck."

He held out his fist and she gave him an awkward bump with her own. "You guys picked a nice day. Sky is clear, air is warm and you've got just enough wind to get a nice ride."

"Awesome!" Ethan said. "Let's go! Thanks for opening early. I want to get our run in before the tourists get here."

"I got you, man."

As Ethan began walking toward the cabin, Divya grabbed his arm. "Are you really serious about this?"

"Relax. I have a level D skydiving license. I've done about six hundred jumps. You're going to be strapped to me the whole time and I'll take care of the parachute pulling. All you do is enjoy the experience. It'll be like taking a roller-coaster ride."

All she had to do was strap herself to him and enjoy? That did sound good. Except they'd be falling out of the sky. Her mouth went completely dry.

As they turned a corner, she saw two long pieces of cloth on the ground attached to a backpack.

"Is that our parachute? Is that how it's supposed to be?"

He laughed. "I like to pack my own parachute and make sure it's done right. There's two main parachutes, one you'll be wearing and one that I'll be wearing. Plus we each have an emergency parachute that someone else inspects and packs. It's all perfectly safe. We only need one parachute and we'll have four between the two of us."

She looked around. There was an airstrip and a plane that looked like it had seen better days. Beyond the airstrip, the Gulf of Mexico shimmered as the sun rose higher. "Is this the only skydiving place around?" Divya asked.

He shook his head. "I know this place looks like a dump, but Buck and I went to high school together. He's a good guy and he knows what he's doing. I've been jumping here for years."

Ethan ran his hand down her arm. She turned to face him and he pulled her close. His body felt solid against her and a shiver rose deep from her core. She pressed herself to his body and stood on her toes to whisper into his ear, "You know, sex on the beach is also on my bucket list." She kissed his ear and felt his reaction push against her belly. He pressed his lips to hers, then disengaged.

"Nice try, but we're doing this."

Her eyes widened. "This is madness. I'm not into sports. I don't even play badminton."

He stepped closer and cupped her face. "At any point you want to abort, just say, 'bridesnatcher.' It'll be our safe word."

She couldn't help but laugh.

"You trust me?" he asked.

His eyes, the color of sky, sparkled like the shimmering water behind her. It was so easy to get lost in them, to forget all the alarm bells ringing in her mind. She nodded.

Things moved quickly after that. Buck returned with a tablet and made her watch a safety video while Ethan meticulously inspected, folded and packed the parachutes. The video showed her how the gear would work, how to position her body during the dive, how to open her chute and how to land. Buck then did some practice exercises with her.

"What happens if we free-fall too long and don't open the parachute in time?"

"If you open the chute too late, your descent will be too fast." Buck slapped his hands together. "You pancake if you land on the road or become shark food if you land in the water."

Her mouth fell open.

"Stop it, Buck," Ethan said. "I'll open the parachute in time. You don't have to worry about that."

Things were moving so quickly, Divya couldn't even process everything that was happening. She was exhilarated as much as she was scared. When else would she ever get to skydive? Her parents thought skiing was too dangerous a sport. She was free to do what she wanted.

They put on their harnesses and chutes, did a final safety check, then climbed into the plane. The interior of the plane was like the inside of a paper towel roll. There were no seats—it was even more basic than the outside. Ethan showed her how to scoot onto the metal floor and sit with her legs in front of her. They could see clear into the cockpit.

Ethan pulled Divya close to him, her back to his chest, his legs beside hers.

"All right, sit tight, flight time is ten minutes." Buck looked back from the cockpit, and Divya closed her eyes.

As the plane taxied and took off, Divya's legs stiffened. She was glad she wasn't sitting near a window to see how far up they were. The noise inside the cockpit was deafening, and the plane bumped around like an old railcar. Her heart raced. *What am I doing?* She was about to jump out of a plane with a man she'd known for… *Had it really just been three days?* The plane lurched and her heart went with it. A light at the front of the plane turned yellow, and there were two beeps. That was their signal to get ready to jump.

I can't do this. She had taken everything too far. In her desperation to escape her wedding and her longing to sing at Café Underground, she'd completely lost her mind. What was she doing thousands of miles away from her family? How had she abandoned all her responsibilities? What was she doing sleeping with Ethan, playing with his emotions and her own? How was she pretending that this was a vacation and when it was done, everything would go back to the way things had been? That she would be the same person?

Ethan had said that if she got to a point where she really didn't want to do it, all she had to do was say the safe word, *bridesnatcher,* and they could abort.

Ethan pulled her close and she heard him attaching the harness that would connect them, just as they'd practiced on the ground. His body felt solid against hers. "The first time I did this, I was scared out of my mind, but after this, there's nothing you'll be afraid of. It's time to let go of all the fears you hold inside you."

She exhaled. "I can't do this. I can't!" But the words were stuck inside her throat.

"I've got you," he whispered in her ear. "I'll be with you." He wrapped his arms around her tightly. Her heart rate slowed. He wouldn't let anything happen to her.

The light buzzed green and he pushed her forward until they were at the door.

"Don't worry. He hasn't lost one yet," Buck quipped as Ethan opened the plane door. A rush of air assaulted them, and she was sure she'd get blown right out of the plane. She tried to find something on the floor to grab on to, but her hands were so sweaty that they just slid over the floor. Ethan stood, lifting her up with him. She was unstable on her legs since he was taller than she was and they were now harnessed together. He held on to a strap on the ceiling with one hand and slowly shuffled them along. The cold air slammed her in the face as they got to the edge of the plane.

Her chest exploded. She was pretty sure she was having a heart attack. *Oh my God!* Wisps of white clouds froze her face and hands. She could barely see the streaks of blue below. She couldn't breathe. Her legs were so stiff, she couldn't move them. Ethan pushed her gently and her toes went over the edge of the plane. She screamed, but no sound came out of her mouth. She squeezed her eyes shut. There was no way she could do this. It was time to use the safe word and abort. She'd never been this scared in her life. Her heels were barely on the edge of the plane.

"You ready?" Ethan yelled next to her ear, and yet she could barely hear him over the rush of the wind.

He gently moved them forward, and now her feet weren't touching anything. All she felt was a tug against her harness where she was connected to Ethan. *What if he couldn't open the parachute in time?* She knew what was coming next, and that Ethan was waiting for her to use the safe word. She tried to take a breath, but she'd forgotten how to breathe. Her lungs were burning. *Bridesnatcher! Bridesnatcher!* Had she said the words out loud?

Ethan wrapped an arm around her waist and squeezed tightly. "Trust me." She took a shuddering breath, leaned forward slightly, and he pushed off with his feet. They went over the edge.

The air slapped her face and her skin felt like it would tear away. They were falling, rolling around uncontrollably, and she didn't know for a second if her heart was even beating. She was supposed to do something, but she couldn't remember what. She was going to die and kill Ethan with her because she couldn't remember the body position for the free fall.

Then Ethan grabbed her arms and thrust his body forward to force her to arch, turning them so her belly was facing the earth. Now her body was flat against the wind and she was looking straight down through the clouds. The wind rushed into her face. Her heart was beating so wildly, she could feel it in her throat. Her mouth was open, but she wasn't sure if she was actually screaming. All she could hear was the deafening sound of the wind in her ears, the sting of cold on her face and Ethan's solid body on her back.

Everywhere she looked, the color blue stretched before her; she could barely make out where the sky ended and the water began. It felt like they were in free fall forever, even though they'd told her that it would be only a minute. All of a sudden, she felt a sharp tug between her legs as the parachute opened and the harness yanked her into position.

They slowed and she gasped at the sight before her. The glimmering waters of the gulf and Atlantic stretched out endlessly. A tiny line marked US Route 1, connecting the

Keys with the rest of Florida. There were tiny specks of green land dotted with what she figured were houses and businesses. It was surreal, like she was having an out-of-body experience. In that moment, nothing mattered, not her family, not the decisions that lay before her, not even her life. The world spread out beneath her, full of possibilities.

"How do you feel?" Ethan said.

She tried to turn and look at him but could see only his hands holding on to the straps of the parachute. "I feel free. Like I can do anything in the world."

She didn't need to see his face to feel his smile. "The first time I did this was when I was a senior in high school. Buck's dad owned a dive shop in Wisconsin right across the Minnesota border. He'd been doing it for years. There was this girl who I'd been in love with since ninth grade. She'd finally noticed me, and we were both headed to the same college. I knew now was the time to finally ask her out, but I was so afraid of rejection. Buck told me that after I did this, I could remember that I'd jumped out of an airplane and nothing seems scary after that."

She laughed and they both shook in the harness. She had to admit that she'd never felt her heart beat as hard as it was now.

"I hope that the next time you're afraid to do something, this experience gives you the courage to face your worst fear." His words hit her deep in her solar plexus.

As they came closer to the ground, Ethan navigated the parachute and they could see the cars on the road and the runway they had used. The plane was lifting off. There was a green field with markings, and she knew that was where they were supposed to land.

"Remember how we practiced the landing? Raise your legs now." Divya did as she was told, and it felt like the earth rushed up suddenly to meet them. But the landing was surprisingly soft. Ethan got his footing then lifted her slightly so she was also standing. The parachute floated behind them. He disconnected them and she turned and hugged him tightly.

Every cell in her body was alive in a way she'd never experienced. "Oh my God. That was the most amazing thing I've ever done in my life."

He grinned.

She stood on her toes and kissed him with everything she had. She'd just jumped out of a plane. Ethan was right: after this, there was nothing she couldn't do. He held her close as he kissed her, and this time it was more than just her body that responded to him. Her soul reached out to touch him, to thank him for giving her this experience, to tell him just how much she cared for him. It felt like they were connected at a cellular level, like he knew her better than she knew herself, and she wanted nothing more than to give herself to him entirely.

Ethan finally broke the kiss. "Divya, there's something I need to say to you."

The catch in his voice sent a chill through her. Was this it? Was he going to tell her that they were going to part ways? They hadn't discussed how long this would last, and he certainly didn't owe her anything.

He cupped her face. "I know you told me not to go for girls who are unavailable. But I can't seem to help it. I need you to know that when things end between us, I can't be friends with you."

He said when *things end between us. Not* if. He'd already given up on her.

Eleven

"I got people coming in," a man in a yellow jumpsuit yelled out to them.

"Sorry!" Ethan yelled back. What was he thinking? They had to get off the landing field. Now was not the time to kiss Divya or tell her how he felt. They went to the shack and removed their harnesses and jumpsuits.

She was silent as he motored back onto US Route 1. He would've liked to have stayed in the Keys for a couple of days, but it was his parents' anniversary. He wanted to take Divya to meet his family. But not before he told her where he stood.

That connection he'd been searching for with Pooja, the one he thought he was crazy to want, had come to him in the form of yet another woman who was totally unavailable. But he wasn't going to let her go without a fight.

He pulled onto another dirt road. "Get ready. This is going to be one of the best meals you'll ever have," he said lightly. Divya's silence was heavy in the air, but she cracked a smile as they looked up at the sign that read Joey's Love Boat.

A bar and kitchen were set up on the sandy shore. The dining room was a houseboat. A young girl wearing a tank top and shorts asked them to wait until a table opened up. There was a small beach area next to the boat, and without discussing it, they both took off their shoes and went to dip their toes in the cool water.

"What did you mean when you said we can't be friends?" she asked without preamble.

"It's exactly what you think, Divya."

He turned and put his hands on her arms. Her body softened and she moved closer to him until their noses touched. A lump formed in his throat. "You were right Divya, when it's the right person, you don't need a lot of time to know. It took Vivek three weeks to know that you were the one for him. It's only taken me three days. I love you, Divya."

She froze, then stepped back from him.

"Your table is ready." The waitress appeared, holding menus. Ethan let go of Divya and she turned away from him. His heart sank deep into his toes. This was why he'd jumped today, to find the courage to tell her how he felt. She could choose to end things now, but he didn't want to be with her unless she knew he was in it for real.

Every minute he spent with her, he knew he'd be in free fall. He wanted to know how she felt before it was too late to pull the parachute.

The hostess led them onto the boat. There were only ten tables, each covered with a colorful tablecloth and adorned with fresh flowers arranged in beer bottles.

As they sat, the boat rocked slightly, causing a little of the water the waitress had poured into their glasses to slosh over the rims. The afternoon was hot and muggy, and he noticed Divya fanning herself. "I should've warned you we were going someplace hot so you could've dressed for it."

"You should've warned me that things were going to get hot between us."

The waitress reappeared to take their orders, and Divya asked him to order for them. He ordered coconut shrimp, fresh mahi-mahi, and as the waitress was leaving, Divya asked for a rum punch.

"Need a drink, huh?" he quipped.

"We need to talk."

While a part of him had hoped she'd tell him she loved him too and was ready to be with him, he hadn't really expected it. That wasn't how things worked for him. Like everyone else in his life, she was about to reject him.

"I need to tell you the real reason I don't want to get married."

He leaned forward. Was she finally going to trust him with what she'd been holding back?

"Remember I told you about Sameer's car accident?" A lump formed in her throat and she felt the sting of tears in her eyes. "He was hurt pretty badly, but he recovered fine, or so we all thought. Then we went into lockdown, and I noticed he started acting strangely. At first, I was worried he had the virus, but when I pushed to call the family doctor, Sameer told me that he hadn't given up the pain medications from his accident. He'd been buying them illegally and couldn't get them because of the lockdown. He was in withdrawal. He didn't want the family to know, he was so ashamed."

"So you hid it from them and helped him through it." Ethan wasn't surprised that Divya had nurtured her brother through his addiction.

She nodded. "It wasn't just about protecting his health. Arjun's wife, Rani, was pregnant, and they were in Vegas for the lockdown. Sameer had taken on Arjun's business responsibilities so Arjun could focus on his family. The last thing Sameer could do was manage a multibillion-dollar empire while going through withdrawal. I was already involved in the business, so I took over his responsibilities. No one knew that I was doing his work. My family still doesn't know."

"Is Sameer still struggling?"

She nodded. "He says he's fine. He hasn't relapsed for almost six months, but in two months, we're going to be launching a new hotel in DC, and I know what the stress does to him."

"Why can't another family member help him?"

"The only person who could handle that kind of responsibility is Arjun. But he can't leave Vegas and return to India. His daughter, Simmi, was born with a heart murmur. She's had surgery, but she needs to be constantly monitored, and she can't travel. That's why my wedding was in Vegas. It would kill Arjun to leave Rani and Simmi alone."

"What about your sisters?"

"Sameer is too manipulative for my younger sisters to handle. The last time he relapsed, it took me weeks to figure it out and I was watching him like a hawk."

"So you're going to dedicate your life to helping him cope?" Ethan couldn't keep the disbelief and disappointment out of his voice, and Divya noticed. She sat up straighter.

"That's what we do for family. We take care of each other. We give up our selfish needs to help them."

Their food arrived, which saved him from saying something he'd regret.

"If something happened to Sameer, I'd never be able to live with myself," Divya said softly.

He pushed the food toward her. They dug in, ravenous after their adrenaline-filled morning.

"Sameer isn't going to need you forever," Ethan said carefully. "He will eventually kick it."

Divya dipped a coconut shrimp in pineapple salsa. "Sameer is the reason I need to return to my family right now. But it still doesn't change the fact that I don't want to spend my life on someone else's terms. My mother was twenty-three years old when she married my father. For eighteen years, ever since she was five, she'd been studying classical Indian dance. *Bharatnatyam*. It's a real art that takes decades to learn. She was so good that she earned several awards. When she married my father, she gave that all up to take care of his household and have his children. He would never let her dance publicly. I still remember when I was a little girl I'd catch her with *ghunghuru*—those are bells you wear on your feet for classical dance. She tried to hide it from me, but I'd hear the music coming from her room and the sound of the bells as she tapped her feet in perfect rhythm. When I was older, I asked her why she hid it from me, and she said it was because she didn't want me to fall in love with something I could not have."

"That's not how it is in my family," he said gently. "I would never tell my wife what she can and cannot do." She fidgeted as he said the word *wife*, and his stomach clenched. "Come with me tonight and meet my family. You'll see that we share the same family values but a very different sense of what a marriage partnership looks like. We're not as far apart as you think."

She chewed on her lip. "Are you sure?"

"It's not as big a deal in my house to bring someone home as it is in yours. We don't even have to tell them we're involved, if you don't want."

She ate in silence for a few minutes.

"I'd like to meet your family. But I don't want to hurt you."

What she meant was that she didn't want to lead him on. "I'm clear on the fact that you don't want a long-term relationship. I understand the reasons why. I may not agree, but I understand." *And I plan to change your mind.*

As they finished their meal, Ethan stole glances at Divya. She seemed to be lost in her own world. He'd put his cards on the table. It was her turn now to decide how she wanted to proceed. She needed to figure out whether she was brave enough to love him back.

"A rupee for your thoughts."

She gave him a small smile. "Boy, you're cheap. Not even a whole dollar?"

He took the last piece of the coconut shrimp, dipped it and held it out to her. She leaned forward and took the bite directly from his hand, flicking her tongue to lick the sauce off his fingers. He rubbed his thumb on her lips, then touched her cheek.

"I don't want to say goodbye to you, Ethan."

You say that Divya, but are you going to break my heart like the rest of them?

Twelve

It was dusk by the time they arrived in Minneapolis. A Lexus sedan was waiting for them at the airport, with a big bow on top of it.

"It's a present for my parents." Ethan grinned. "My mom's car is on its last legs."

Divya pressed her lips together.

"What is it? I know you want to say something."

She sighed. "You said your parents don't like accepting help from you. Isn't this a little extravagant?"

He waved her off as he loaded their luggage and the gift bags Roda had given him in New York into the trunk. "It's an anniversary present."

There was some traffic as they got onto the highway. "My parents are in Stillwater. When we have time tomorrow, I'll show you the town. It's really cute with antiques shops, riverboats and even a park with a giant teddy bear." He loved taking his niece and nephew to Teddy Bear Park. He'd been sad when they'd outgrown it. Lately he'd had trouble connecting with them, like he used to when they were much younger and all it took to make them happy was a game of peekaboo or a ride on his shoulders. But he was hoping that the gifts he'd bought would help return his cool-uncle status. His chest constricted as he thought about how much he'd loved the baby phase with all of the kids. As they'd grown, he'd looked forward to reliving each part of their childhood with his own children.

He snuck a look at Divya. *Why do I keep doing this to myself?*

Traffic was light as he got on the highway. Was he doing the right thing, taking Divya to meet his family? He wanted her to see the love he had for them, to know that he understood her commitment to her own family. They weren't as different as she thought.

His parents lived in an old neighborhood. When he was growing up, it had been small houses like his own, with large backyards full of children. After a few large companies had opened headquarters close to the community, the home prices had gone through the roof. By the time he was in middle school, the older houses had been torn down and replaced with towering mansions with private swimming pools and tennis courts. His parents' house stuck out like a sore thumb in the neighborhood, but his father refused to sell or renovate. He wanted to keep it exactly as it was, and Ethan was secretly glad.

As he passed a particular redbrick house with a white picket fence, he slowed down like he always did. But this time he also found himself stepping on the brake, reversing back and pulling into the driveway.

"Are your parents not home? The house is dark."

"This isn't my parents' house."

She looked at him questioningly.

"It's my house. Or I should say, a house I bought."

She leaned over and placed a hand on his arm.

"Houses rarely come up for sale in this neighborhood, and my father is never selling his, so I bought it to be close to them. But I never moved in. They don't even know I own it."

"Why didn't you tell them?"

He shrugged. "I bought the place right after Pooja left me and I didn't want to hear my parents tell me that I'd made another mistake."

He reversed the car and drove back onto the road, his throat tight. Why had he shown it to Divya? The only person who knew he owned it was his accountant. Was he being impulsive in loving her? Did he want to fill this house so badly that he was clinging to whoever came his way? He took a breath to ease the constriction in his chest.

As the car crunched over the gravel driveway of his parents' house, Ethan relaxed. The sight of the gray siding, stone chimney and the two rocking chairs on the front porch filled him with comforting warmth. The house had looked this way all his life. No matter how hard a day he'd had at school, when the bus had dropped him off at the end of the street, he'd looked forward to walking up the porch steps. He parked beside his mother's old car so she wouldn't see the Lexus's bow from the front porch. He couldn't wait to give this gift to her.

His mother came outside to meet them. She looked the same as always, dressed in jeans and a knitted sweater. She was a small woman, no more than five foot four with blond hair and tired blue eyes, which reminded him of the fact that she still put in long hours at the diner. He enveloped her in a bear hug.

"It is good to see you, my boy." She hugged him back, holding on to him tightly and making him feel like everything was okay with the world. "I thought you'd forgotten."

He kissed her on the cheek. "Happy anniversary."

"Who's this?" She looked at Divya.

"Mom, meet Divya."

Divya held out her hand, but his mother leaned in and gave her a hug. "Welcome."

Ethan surreptitiously removed their bags from the car, and Divya retrieved the pie she'd insisted on picking up and handed it to Marilyn.

"Now, what's this?"

"Key lime pie from the Florida Keys," Divya replied.

His mother's eyes widened. "Now, that's mighty thoughtful of you. Well, come on in, Bill is probably wondering what's taking us so long."

They walked into a small foyer that led to a staircase to the second floor and a dining room on the right. Divya followed Marilyn into the kitchen, where Ethan's dad stood to greet them. He had dark hair and gray eyes. He was a thin man with round glasses and a goatee.

"It's nice to meet you, Mr. Connors," Divya said.

"Oh, call me Bill."

"Divya brought a pie for us from the Keys," Marilyn said as she set the pie down.

"Wow." Bill looked at the pie as if he was making sure it was real.

"What were you guys doing in the Keys?" Bill asked.

"Ethan took me skydiving."

Marilyn shot Bill a look that didn't escape Ethan's notice. When he'd been a kid, he'd hated how his parents communicated wordlessly; now he compared every one of his relationships to that connection they had.

"Matt and the kids should be here any minute. I made pot roast." Marilyn looked at Divya. "Are you okay with that?"

"I've never had pot roast, so I'd love to try it."

"Mom makes the best pot roast." Ethan leaned over and

gave his mother an affectionate kiss. "I've been looking forward to it for weeks." Marilyn leaned over and tousled his hair.

"So are you and Divya sharing a bedroom?" Marilyn asked.

Divya looked down and Ethan enjoyed seeing the twinge of color on her cheeks.

"Um, no, we're not staying in the same room," Divya said.

"We're not?" Ethan whispered to her and she shot him a look.

Marilyn looked between them and rolled her eyes. "Ethan, why don't you show Divya to your room and I'll make up the couch in the family room for you."

Ethan carried her bag upstairs and she followed.

"Is this your childhood room?"

He nodded, looking at the familiar space. The walls were covered with Star Wars posters. The bookshelf held the memorabilia he'd brought home from college. He knew every inch of this room. One of the first things he and Bill had done together was put the bed together. This had been Bill's office before he'd married his mom.

Ethan reached to the back of the bookshelf and pulled out a framed photo. It pictured a younger version of Marilyn, Wade and Ethan, when he was about four.

"That's your real father?" Divya asked.

"Bill is my real father. This is the man who cheated on my mother, drank himself into a stupor every night and took five seconds to sign away his paternity rights."

She placed her hand on his chest, her eyes shining. He lifted her hand and kissed it. "Don't feel sorry for this poor little rich boy. Bill loves my mom and he's been a wonderful father. It could've turned out very differently for me."

"I hope you know that your father rejecting you had nothing to do with you and everything to do with him."

Ethan nodded. "I know that at some level. But he wasn't always a drunk. Mom told me his drinking started after I was born."

"You didn't drive him to drink."

"I know." He hadn't looked at the picture in years, but he'd needed to show it to Divya, to have her understand that there was a reason he ran scared from relationships. But that he was ready to confront his demons, just like he'd asked her to confront hers.

"Not a lot of people know this, but Arjun is my half brother. My dad had a first wife who died when Arjun was a baby. We never knew. We found out a few years ago, and Arjun was devastated. For the rest of us, it didn't matter. He had always been our big brother and would still be. Nothing changed for us. But he started treating us differently. It was him that put distance between us because he felt like he didn't belong."

"You think that's what I'm doing?"

"I think it's time for you to realize that you're a wonderful man and there's nothing wrong with you."

He ran his hands down the length of her arms, feeling the goose bumps, and placed a light kiss on her lips. Then moved on to her neck. She brushed her hair aside and tilted her head. He'd been with a number of women in his life, but it felt different with Divya. As aroused as he was, he was also content just being close to her, touching her skin, smelling her sweet vanilla scent.

He circled her waist with his arm and pulled her closer. He untucked her silk shirt and ran his hands underneath it to cup her breasts, enjoying how perfectly they fit in his hands and how taut her nipples became at his slightest touch.

"Matt's here." Marilyn's voice came clear up the stairs, and Divya pushed Ethan away. He smirked.

"Coming, Mom." Divya quickly tucked her shirt back in and adjusted her bra. He leaned in close to her ear, kissing the lobe while whispering, "Don't worry, we'll pick it up tonight. The bed is really comfortable."

Her eyes widened. "We're not having sex."

He raised his brows. "Then, what did we do on the plane?"

She shook her head. "I mean we're not having sex here. It wouldn't be proper in your parents' house."

"You're kidding, right? They know I have sex. I'm sure my mom thinks it's silly you want me to sleep on the couch."

"But it's not okay by me."

"You're serious?"

She nodded. Marilyn called out to Ethan again. They went downstairs to see his brother's minivan in the driveway. The kids, Allie and Jake, burst out of the back, slamming the door shut in their excitement to give Ethan a hug. He held them close in a group hug, his heart overflowing with love for them.

"Uncle Ethan, you won't believe what happened at school today." He turned his full attention to five-year-old Jake, who had his mother's dark hair and brown eyes. Jake went on to give him the lowdown on the most recent recess games.

"That's enough, Jake, Uncle Ethan doesn't need to hear everything that happens in kindergarten." Allie was seven going on fifteen. She was the perfect mix of her mom and dad with platinum blond hair from Bill's side and big eyes and a snub nose from Heather.

"Nice to see you again, Ethan."

He smiled at his sister-in-law. She had dark hair, brown

eyes and a tall, slim build. She was holding two covered dishes. "You okay?" he asked, taking them from her. Heather looked tired.

She gave him a small smile. "Just the usual grind, dealing with these kids." She shot them an affectionate glance.

His brother came up and gave him a hug. Every time he saw his brother, it always surprised him that Matt was no longer the small, lanky boy from Ethan's memory. He was as tall as Ethan but with a much stockier build. Ethan slapped his younger brother on the back. It was hard to see Matt with kids of his own. Ethan still remembered the day his mother came home from the hospital with newborn Matt bundled in her arms. Ethan had stood at the top of the stairs and watched his parents become a family. And then twenty years later, he'd watched Heather and Matt become a family.

"Why does that car have a bow?" Allie asked.

Ethan grinned. He'd been hoping to wait until the morning when he could show them the car, but now was as good a time as any. "It's Mom and Dad's anniversary present."

Marilyn gasped. "Ethan! What're we going to do with a car like that?"

"Get rid of your old beater and not worry about car repairs."

Bill put a hand on Ethan's shoulders. "Thanks, son. This is mighty generous of you, but we're doing fine. This is too much—we don't need it."

Ethan clenched his jaw. "It's your wedding anniversary. I have the right to buy my parents a gift, don't I?"

"We bought them a bottle of wine," Matt said unhelpfully.

"Why don't we go inside and set the table," Heather said and took the kids inside. Matt and Divya followed.

"Come on, Mom. Accept this. For me." Ethan put on his

most charming smile and put his arm around his mom. "It'll make me so happy to see you enjoy a luxury for once."

Marilyn shook her head. "I appreciate it, Ethan, but this isn't for me. I'm used to my old clunker."

"I don't understand why you guys don't like nice things," Ethan said with obvious impatience. "I know you think my money is easy, but I earn it honestly. What's wrong with me wanting to spend it on the people I love, to give you nice things?"

"We don't need it, son," Bill said firmly. "I can take care of my family."

My family. Bill's family. Blood pounded inside his ears. It had always been like that. While Bill called him *son*, the fact that Ethan was in truth his stepson was always just under the surface in their family. He would always be the boy looking down from the staircase.

"Fine. I'll take the car back." Ethan took a breath as he walked into the house and to the backyard, where Divya was helping Heather set the table.

Jake came running toward him, and Ethan scooped him up. He was getting too big to really carry, but Ethan couldn't resist. He'd seen how fast Allie had grown up.

"Uncle Ethan, where's that Poo lady?"

Ethan caught Divya's eyes and saw that she was barely suppressing a laugh at Jake's question.

"Her name was Pooja and she won't be coming around anymore, buddy," Ethan answered. He set Jake down and the boy went in search of a soccer ball.

"Exactly how many women do you bring home?" Divya said, her voice weirdly high. He turned to her, ready to make a snarky comment, but the look in her eyes stopped him. He didn't want to tell her what he told his family each time he brought home a new woman: that he wanted them to see that he came from humble beginnings.

He put his arm around her waist and pulled her close. "It helps to have someone in my corner."

Divya gave him a kiss, and he was grateful he didn't need to say any more, that he didn't need to verbalize his insecurities. He knew from the look in her eyes that she understood.

"Did you bring us anything, Uncle Ethan?"

Ethan disentangled himself from Divya and looked affectionately at Allie. He'd had Roda pick up the latest iPhone for his niece and a gaming console for Jake. He still remembered being the kid at school who didn't have the coolest new toy.

"Of course I've got something for you." He gave them the gift bags Roda had handed him in New York. The kids excitedly opened them and squealed in delight as they found their requested items. "You are the best, Uncle Ethan." Jake beamed.

Allie screamed. "Oh my God, my friends are going to die when they see I have this."

"Ethan, we've talked about the expensive gifts." Matt's weary voice broke into the kids' excited chatter. When the kids were out of earshot, examining their toys, Matt turned to him. "Ethan, you've got to stop buying them such expensive things."

Ethan rubbed his neck. "I'm their uncle, I have the right to spoil them."

Matt exchanged a look with Heather, who shook her head imperceptibly at him, and he turned away from Ethan. Ethan looked to his parents for support, but they were exchanging glances of their own. Ethan's breath stuck. Then he felt Divya's hand on his arm.

"You've got me in your corner," she whispered.

Thirteen

Marilyn broke the tension by asking everyone to come to the outdoor table for dinner. Divya had watched the exchange with Ethan's parents and then his brother, and her heart ached for him. He was trying so hard to find his place, his role in the family, and he was doing it all wrong. He thought he could do it by being the rich uncle who spoiled the kids and provided for everyone.

The conversation at dinner was easy as the kids excitedly filled them in on the happenings at school. Ethan engaged in genuine conversation with the kids. He knew the names of their friends and their favorite teachers, and even the supersecret code name of the boy Allie liked but her parents didn't know about. They asked Divya about herself, and what it was like living in India.

It was exactly the kind of dinner her family had when they were together. There was a lot of laughter and good-natured ribbing, and the love was palpable across the table.

"Marilyn, can you pick up the kids from school tomorrow? I have to work late and Matt has a PTA meeting," Heather said.

"What's a PTA?" Divya asked.

"Parent Teacher Association," Heather responded. "Matt volunteers as the room parent for the kids."

Divya raised her eyebrows. "Most of my friends have kids, and I don't think a single one of their husbands volunteers at the school."

Heather smiled and leaned over to kiss Matt. "He is an amazing guy. When we had Allie, I was in medical school. I couldn't postpone residency, so he stayed home with Allie. Now I'm doing my surgical fellowship and my schedule is crazy. There's no way I could do it if it weren't for Matt."

"So you gave up your career for her?" Divya slapped her hand to her mouth as soon as she said the words. She hadn't meant to sound so incredulous.

Matt smiled. "I'm an accountant. I do some consulting on the side to keep up my skills. When the kids are a little older, I can easily go back to my job. It's much harder for Heather to take a break in her medical training. This is the time to focus on Heather's career."

Divya couldn't imagine her father saying something like that. She almost laughed at the thought of her father giving up his career so her mother could become a dancer. She looked at Ethan and pictured him in the audience cheering for her at Café Underground.

"Anyway, can you pick them up?" Heather asked Marilyn.

Ethan's mother sighed. "I'm sorry. I have a double shift."

"We can do it," Divya piped up.

Ethan looked at her in surprise but then chimed in, "Yeah, in fact we will pick them up and feed them dinner if you and Matt want an evening to yourselves."

Everyone looked at him in surprise. Heather and Matt exchanged a look.

"Mom, can we, please?" Jake said excitedly.

"Sounds like a great idea," Marilyn said.

"It's a very nice offer." Heather looked at Ethan and then Divya. "Are you sure?"

They both nodded enthusiastically, and under the table, Ethan squeezed Divya's hand. The kids whooped and began discussing where they wanted to go eat the next day.

Divya excused herself to go get a jacket. The evening was getting chilly for her, especially after the hot day in the Keys. As she came down the stairs, she heard Marilyn and Matt talking in the kitchen.

"You need to talk to him, Mom. A week ago, he told me he wished he'd proposed to Pooja, and now he's here with someone else. I don't know what's going on with him."

His mother sighed. "He's so damn impulsive. I knew Pooja would never marry him. The last time she was here, she pretty much told me that her parents would never accept someone who wasn't Indian. I swear, he purposely picks women who're going to break his heart."

"You know he met Divya while trying to crash Pooja's wedding? I saw it on social media. Divya was marrying someone else four days ago and got cold feet. I'm worried about him, Mom. I don't want to see him get hurt. It's obvious he cares about her."

Marilyn sighed. "He's been like this all his life. I don't know whether he's faster at falling in love or out of it. I'll try talking to him tomorrow."

Divya's stomach dropped. Marilyn had just put into words the thing she feared the most. When Ethan told her he loved her, she wanted nothing more than to say it back to him. To tell him that she had been picturing what it'd be like to introduce him to her family, to have him dress up in an Indian *sherwani* and celebrate the upcoming Diwali holidays with them. She had started thinking of things that she'd never considered before. But she'd never told anyone she'd loved them. Not even Vivek. The best she'd been able to tell him was "ditto" when he'd said it to her, and she hadn't truly meant it. For her, love was something that happened once in a lifetime. With someone that made her heart explode. That someone was Ethan. But she didn't want to be yet another girl that he was in free fall with. He'd said that he expected her to break his heart, but somehow she knew he'd be the one shattering hers.

She heard plates clinking, then the door open and close. She waited a few more minutes, then quietly slipped back into the backyard.

"Wow, this pie is amazing, where did you get it?" Heather exclaimed.

"Divya brought it from the Florida Keys."

"Mmm, why haven't you brought this for us before, Ethan?" Matt cut himself another piece. "Did you take her skydiving with Buck?" The way he said it, Divya got the feeling that it was something Ethan did all the time. Maybe it was his standard date for all those girls he'd fallen in love with.

Everyone pitched in to clear the table, and Divya liked the easy way they worked together. The kids carried the plates to the kitchen while Marilyn and Heather packed up the leftovers, and Matt, Ethan and Bill moved the extra dining room chairs back inside. Divya stood back and watched, listening to their banter, watching Ethan light up from the inside.

Matt, Heather and the kids left to get the kids to bed. Ethan began loading the dishwasher, and Bill wiped down the kitchen counters.

"Coffee, Divya? Or do you prefer tea?"

"Whatever you're having."

Marilyn started the coffeemaker. Divya watched Ethan load the dishwasher, arguing with his dad about the best way to position the dishes. Her brother Arjun liked to cook, but she'd never seen him clean. Rani was working hard to teach him how to wash dishes. Divya and her siblings had grown up with servants who did the cleaning after family meals, under her mother's supervision while her father and brothers retired to the living room for a nightcap.

Marilyn handed Divya a coffee cup, and they went to the front porch and sat in the rocking chairs.

"You know, I really don't mind you and Ethan sleeping in the same room," Marilyn said.

Divya's cheeks burned. "My parents are very old-fashioned. It wouldn't feel right."

Marilyn smiled. "I can tell your mother raised you well. Thank you helping with the kids tomorrow."

"It's my pleasure. They seem wonderful." Divya meant it. Two of her closest friends were married with kids, and while she adored her pseudo nieces and nephews, they were spoiled. Matt's kids seemed to be well-grounded, the way she'd like to raise her own kids. The thought stopped her cold. Why was she thinking about children?

Marilyn looked toward the Lexus with the bow on it. "I don't know what Ethan was thinking with that car."

Divya bit her lip. She hadn't heard the full exchange between Ethan and his parents regarding the car, but from the face he carried with him to dinner, she knew they'd rejected it, just as she'd suspected they would. It wasn't her place to say anything but what did she have to lose? It wasn't as if she was trying to impress his parents or audition for the role of his wife. She might as well help him as a friend.

"You know, he was really excited to give you the car. It would mean a lot to him if you'd accept it."

"I don't know how many times we've tried to explain to Ethan that we don't want money or gifts, and yet he doesn't seem to get it," Marilyn said irritably.

Divya's heart clenched. "Do you know that during the pandemic, he donated most of the money he earned to people who had lost their jobs and healthcare workers? He still pays the salaries of those employees who died from the virus or can no longer work so their families are okay. He goes around giving ridiculous tips. He's not like the other billionaires in the world who spend their money buying mansions." Her voice nearly cracked as she thought about how excited he'd been to give his mother the car. "He's not trying to throw his money around. He feels lucky to have it and wants to share it with the people he loves most."

Marilyn blew out a breath. "We don't want to hurt his feelings. It's just that the money seems to have changed him. He used to take the kids to the park, and now he wants to take them to Paris and London. That's not how I raised my boys, and it's not how Matt wants to raise his kids."

Divya chewed on her lip. She didn't know Ethan's parents and maybe she should keep her mouth shut and stay out of the whole situation. "Ethan loves the way he grew up. This is not about passing judgment on what you weren't able to give him. The money is meaningless to him unless he can enjoy it with you. When you don't accept his gifts, it makes him feel like he's not a part of this family."

Marilyn stared at Divya and she shifted in her seat.

"You and Ethan really only met a few days ago?"

Divya nodded.

"Then, how is it that you know my son so well?"

Divya shrugged. "Maybe because we met each other at a vulnerable time, or maybe because we're going to be together for such a short time, we don't feel the need for any pretenses between us."

Marilyn sipped her coffee. "Maybe we've been hard on Ethan. But the money seemed to change him overnight. He was never into private jets and luxury condos."

"I have never had pot roast, but after dinner tonight, I'm going to want to learn how to make it." Divya warmed her hands on the coffee mug. "I've been around spoiled rich men all my life. Ethan is not one of them. He'd give away all his money if that's what it would take for things to be right with you."

They sat in companionable silence, drinking their coffees, then Marilyn reached out her hand and patted Divya's. "You're a good girl, Divya. I hope you're not just around for a short time."

Divya dropped her gaze to the coffee cup. She tried to imagine Marilyn with her well-worn sweater and jeans sitting next to her own mother, who was always in designer clothes. She couldn't. Nor could she imagine Ethan sitting with her father in his study, dressed in a *kurta pajama*, with a crystal tumbler of whiskey.

Ethan's parents retired to their bedroom and Divya joined Ethan on the couch in the family room. He turned off the TV. "Are you tired?"

"It's only nine o'clock. This is usually when we eat dinner at my house," Divya said.

He shrugged. "My mom is usually up early to get to the diner before breakfast is served, so we've always been an early-to-bed household." He put his arm around her and she snuggled into him, enjoying the warmth of his body. "Thanks for breaking the tension with my brother. You don't have to babysit tomorrow. I can take care of it."

She touched his arm. "They seem like nice kids. I'd like to get to know them." And she meant it.

"I don't know why my brother has such a chip on his shoulder about me getting them expensive presents. Heather has some serious medical-school loans to pay off, and she's still in training, so she doesn't make that much money. With Matt not working, I know he can't afford that stuff. I'm only trying to help," Ethan said wearily.

She sighed. "My college friend has a five-year-old who I love to spoil. She asked me to stop buying him expensive presents because it undermines what she and her husband can provide for him. It's hard for them that he has a rich auntie. Think of how your brother must feel about the fact that his kids are more excited about what you give them with your spare change than what he sacrifices every day to provide for them. It's hard being the parent who has to buy clothes and books, while you get to swoop in and be the hero giving them cool toys. If you want to help, ask your brother what he needs for the kids. Give them the things they need every day."

Ethan rolled his head back and closed his eyes. She reached over and rubbed her thumbs over his forehead.

"Hmm. Is that a head massage?"

"Kind of. My mom does it when I'm stressed and angry. It calms me down."

He smiled. "It's working." He grabbed her hand and kissed her fingers. "You know, there's something else that would be really de-stressing right now."

She pulled her hands back. "Oh no, you're not tempting me into doing *that* in your parents' house."

He pulled her close to him. "They sleep really soundly." He turned her hand and kissed the inside of her wrist, then began working his way up her arm. Delicious tingles worked their way from his mouth all the way to her core.

She pulled her arm back. "How about we watch a movie?"

He let out a sigh of frustration but grabbed the remote. She placed her head on his chest, enjoying the warmth of his body and the steady beat of his heart. She was asleep before the movie even started.

She woke when she felt him carrying her up the stairs to the bedroom. He set her gently on the bed, gave her a kiss on the forehead, placed the blankets on her and left the room. After he'd left, she sat up and turned on the light. There was little furniture in the room, just a bed, nightstand and a bookshelf that held a picture of two young boys with their arms around each other, grinning widely. She picked it up. It reminded her of a photo at home of her and her three sisters, all with the same pigtails and school uniforms. Her heart clenched painfully. *What am I doing here?* She was in Minnesota, a state she hadn't even known existed a few days ago, with a family that wasn't hers and a man who made her body sing in ways it never had before and had wormed his way into her heart when she'd least expected it.

Seeing Ethan with his family just made her miss hers even more. She clicked on the phone Ethan had given her. She opened her email. There were several messages from him, her sisters and one from Sameer. Her pulse quickened as she clicked on his message.

Yo sis! Cool move. I'm pretty sure this trumps all the idiot things I've ever done. Passing my bad boy trophy to you. I'm doing well. Stay away as long as you need. You deserve a break. I'm good. Really.

PS—Vivek is a *maha* bore. Why did you ever want to marry him?

She laughed and read the message several times before deciding Sameer really was okay. The messages from Arjun and her sisters weren't as comforting. Her parents were taking things really hard. Arjun begged her to come back and promised that he would make sure she didn't have to marry anyone she didn't want to. He'd gotten rid of Vivek. There was also an email from her best friend, Hema, telling her how much she missed her. Her sisters had written long messages that spanned pages. Divya closed her eyes, unable to read them.

It was time to go home.

Ethan was not real. He was a fantasy, just like her singing career. What would life be like as a singer? It would be like the last four days. Going from one place to another, with no tether to home. Having to dance onstage wearing skimpy clothes. Maybe she'd been pursuing the wrong goals. She'd thought that knowing she had done something on her own, a success her parents hadn't bought for her, would be enough. It would fulfill her, close the hole she'd felt in her soul. But then why did she still feel so empty? Why were her thoughts full of an American man with bright blue eyes and sandy-brown hair who owned a house down the street from his parents? A world away from everyone she loved. She lay on the bed but hardly slept.

She was not going to be the woman who would make the dark, empty, redbrick house a home for him.

Fourteen

Ethan rolled his shoulders and stretched his back. The old couch had lived its life. He was tempted to order a new one, but Divya's words came back to him.

"Coffee, hon?"

He nodded to his mother, who poured him a cup and set it on the small kitchen table. It was still early in the morning, but his father had already left for work. His mother was in her diner uniform and Ethan bit his tongue to keep from asking when she'd quit.

"You know the old McPherson house?"

She looked at him, puzzled, and sat at the table, after putting a plate with eggs, toast and bacon in front of him. She'd gotten up earlier than usual to make him breakfast.

"I bought it."

She gasped. "That was you? The neighbors were wondering who the mysterious buyer was. Why didn't you tell us?"

He shrugged. "I felt silly, buying that big old house for

just me. I thought I'd tell you about it when I was ready to start a family."

Marilyn hugged her son. "You don't need a woman to start a family. We are your family."

"Then, why does is feel like I can't do anything right lately?" He reached out and took his mom's hands and she squeezed his.

She smiled sadly at him. "Oh Ethan, we love you so much. We're still getting used to your money. I guess we don't want to take advantage of your generosity. Your dad and I have always provided for our children, and we're not used to the idea of our children taking responsibility for our needs."

"There's something I want to tell you," Ethan started. It was time he told his mother what he knew. "Right after Matt was born, I went to see Wade, in our old apartment."

His mother froze, but he continued. "I needed to know why he gave me up so easily. I know he wasn't a good man, but I was his son." He paused and took a sip of his coffee. "He told me that Bill only agreed to adopt me because you made it a condition of your marriage."

His mother gasped audibly. "That awful man. How dare he say something like that to you?" She grabbed Ethan's hand. "Is that what you've thought all these years? Why didn't you say something?" She shook her head. "It's not true. I never asked Bill to take you in. He fell in love with you the first time he met you. Remember that day I took you to the park?"

Ethan did remember the day. Bill had shown him how to ride his bike without the training wheels on.

"Bill proposed to me the next day. I still joke with him that he only married me because he wanted you. Oh honey, I wish you hadn't kept this in your heart all these years."

His mother leaned over and gave him a hug and he hugged her back.

They sat in silence for a while, eating breakfast, then his mother turned to him. “I guess I could use a new car.”

His heart soared, but before he could say something, she held up a finger. “But, I want to go down to the used car lot and pick out something safe and sturdy.” Her eyes softened. “I’m sure the Lexus is amazing, but I wouldn’t feel comfortable in it.”

He nodded. “Anything you want, Mom. How about I pick you up when you get your break between shifts, and we’ll go down together.”

She stood and put her coffee cup in the sink. “About Divya…”

He stared at his plate, ready to hear the litany of things that were wrong with her. “That girl has a good head on her shoulders. She’s a keeper.”

He looked at his mother in surprise. She came over to him and kissed him on the head. “But prepare yourself, my boy. She’s going to break your heart.”

There it was. The alarm that had been blaring in his mind, that he kept silencing.

He poured a second cup of coffee and went to wake Divya. He knocked on his bedroom door, but there was no answer. He opened it to see her curled up in his bed, her dark hair across her face.

She is so beautiful.

He imagined the master bedroom in the redbrick house and waking up next to her each morning, and he couldn’t. She didn’t belong in that house. She didn’t want the life he did.

She stirred and he brushed her hair from her face. Her eyes blinked open. “Hey there, handsome.”

He smiled. “Morning, beautiful.”

“Did I sleep in late?”

He shook his head, then bent down to kiss her. She wrapped her arms around him and he inhaled her smell. He moved his mouth to her ear, then her throat and then worked his way down her body.

"Wait. Your parents!"

He had made his way down to her stomach and started taking her pajamas off. "They're gone. The house is empty. You're mine," he growled.

He made love to her slowly, savoring every inch of her body, enjoying the way she responded to him, her moans music to his ears.

When they were done, he lay down beside her and pulled her close. "Well, you can wake me up that way anytime," she murmured as she laid her head on his chest.

"Can I?"

She turned her head so she could face him. "Can you what?"

"Can I wake you this way not just for the next few days but for longer?"

She sat up, grabbed a pillow and smacked him in the chest. He sat up, startled. "Did I or did I not tell you not to fall for me?" she said indignantly.

He caught the pillow and pulled her toward him. "Didn't we discuss the fact that I have a knack for falling for unavailable women?"

Her smiled faltered. "You know we're all wrong for each other."

He took the pillow from her hand and kissed her. "I know. But that's why it feels so right between us."

She put her cheek on his naked chest. "I want to be with you," she said softly. "Can you give me some time to figure things out?"

It was the best he was going to get, and he was going to take it.

* * *

He took Divya on a riverboat ride in the morning, then dropped her at the main street in Stillwater so she could explore the antiques shops. He picked up his mom at the diner during her break and convinced her to buy a fairly new Honda Accord at the used-car dealer.

Then he went to collect Divya.

"Let's have lunch at your mother's diner," Divya suggested.

"You know what? It's a great idea." He'd never brought anyone he was dating to the diner; he usually took them to the fancier restaurants in Minneapolis.

The look in his mother's eyes when he sat down in her section with Divya made his heart burst. She didn't have to say it. She'd been waiting for him to make this move for years. His mother introduced him with pride to the regular customers, who had no idea who he was. This was the working class of Stillwater, not the people who lived in the mansions. He shook hands, listened to advice about how to be a good son and admonishments that his mother was too old to work at the diner and he should help out more. He smiled and nodded, and his mother beamed with pride.

"What should we do with the kids this afternoon?" Divya asked when they were done with lunch.

"Let's not plan anything. We can ask them what they want to do."

They picked up the kids from school and Jake asked if they could go to Teddy Bear Park. Allie rolled her eyes, but once they got to the park, Ethan noticed her climbing the giant teddy bear while he and Divya chased Jake around the obstacle course. They all climbed on the bear when it was time to leave and had someone take a picture of them.

After dinner, they bought giant ice-cream cones and

made a mess trying to finish them before they melted. Ethan savored every second of the day.

When they dropped off the kids, they hugged Divya for a long time. “You’ll come back, won’t you, Divya? You won’t be like that Poo lady?” Jake asked in a voice so sweet that Ethan’s heart lurched.

Divya got on her knees so she was eye to eye with Jake. “I’m going to do my best, little man, but I can’t make any promises. Remember, I live in India, that country far away.”

Tears sprung to Jake’s eyes. “So this is the last time we’ll see each other?” He put his little arms around Divya and buried his face in her neck.

She looked at Ethan helplessly. The kids had fallen in love with Divya, just as he had. “Jake, how about I promise that we will video chat? And I can’t promise when, but one day, I’ll come see you.”

He held out his hand and she shook it. “It’s a deal,” Jake said, nodding importantly.

Ethan’s throat closed. When she didn’t come back, it wouldn’t be just his heart that was broken.

When they got back to his brother’s house, Ethan asked to have a private word with Matt and Heather. Divya volunteered to tuck the kids into bed. He sat with his brother and sister-in-law for a long time, and Divya waited patiently. Once he was done, he drove Divya to the riverfront and they walked along the bank, enjoying the cool air. He held her hand. “Thank you, Divya,” he said.

She turned to him surprised. “What for?”

“For showing me what I’m really looking for in a woman. All my life, I’ve been chasing women who do things the way I do, who think the way I do, who want the things I want. But that’s not what I need. I need someone who tells me what I’m doing wrong. Who shows me a better way.”

She leaned over and kissed him. "Is your plane available tomorrow?"

He smiled. "At your service. Where do you want to go? What's next on your bucket list?"

"No more bucket list. It's time for me to return to my family."

Fifteen

His face crumpled. *Should I let him suffer?* She leaned over and whispered in his ear. “I want you to come with me. I think you should meet my family.”

“Did I hear you correctly?” he asked breathlessly.

She’d made the decision to go home last night. She’d been afraid of what she’d be facing when she returned, of going back to a life she didn’t want. But then she thought about jumping out of the plane. Of the raw fear she’d experienced standing on the edge. If she could do that, couldn’t she tell her parents that she didn’t want the life that they’d chosen for her?

She’d fallen asleep thinking about how to tell Ethan that she was ready to return. And extract a promise from him that they’d continue seeing each other. Not as friends but as lovers. But then she’d spent the whole night imagining herself in her bed at home, alone. It wasn’t fair to him, or to her. If she wasn’t willing to give him up, then she had to go all in. She had to see whether their love could withstand the ultimate test: her parents.

She bit his ear playfully. "Yes, Ethan Connors. Look, I'm not saying I'm ready for a permanent commitment."

"Then, what are you saying?"

"I'm saying that I am willing to admit to my parents that I've fallen in love with a most unsuitable boy. I'm willing to see where things go with us. But I'm not ready to move into a redbrick house and have three-point-five kids. Can you accept that?"

His eyes shone and her chest constricted. "We can negotiate the number. I'd be happy with two-point-two-five kids."

She slapped his chest playfully and he caught her hand. "There's a lot that I'm willing to do for you, Divya. All those women I chased… I wasn't going to give up what I wanted for them. I didn't love them enough."

She'd come to the same conclusion, but she wasn't sure if he was really willing to give up his dreams for her, either.

"I took your advice and asked Matt if there was anything the kids needed," he continued, seeming to change the subject as he brushed an errant hair out of her face. "Heather is pregnant. She's still early and they haven't told my parents. It wasn't planned and they're freaking out." A small note of pride crept into his voice at the notion that he'd been trusted with something so personal. "They admitted that their house is getting really small for them. They only have one bathroom upstairs, and it's getting hard for them to share it with the kids. There's no bedroom for another child. With the school pick-up and drop-off schedules and after-school activities, and now a baby, Matt can't go back to work. They'd pay so much in babysitters that it's not worth it for him. Heather has these massive student loans from college and medical school, and it'll be a while before she starts making real money. They can't afford to buy a bigger house right now."

"I think it's great that your brother takes on the parenting responsibilities."

Ethan pulled her closer. "I would do that for you in a heartbeat." She had no doubt he would.

"So will they take money from you?"

"I'm not giving them money."

She raised her brows.

"I gave them the redbrick house."

She gasped. "Your house?"

Ethan took both her hands in his. "It was never my house. It was a dream. It's not a house you want. It's not the life you want. And I want you."

Tears stung her eyes. "I love you, Ethan." Her voice was thick and her heart swelled in her chest. She didn't know when or how she'd fallen in love with the most improbable man, but she knew it was true.

He cupped her face. "I love you, Divya. More than anything else in this world."

The kiss they shared was sweet and salty. She didn't know if the tears were hers or his.

"Before we go back to your family, can you give me a day?"

She narrowed her eyes. "Only if you tell me what we're doing. I don't want to go mountain climbing or helicopter skiing or some other crazy sport."

"You didn't enjoy the skydiving?"

She raised her chin. "I didn't say that."

He leaned down. "Then, trust me."

She smirked at him but felt her nerves ignite at the prospect of whatever he had planned and another uncomplicated day with him.

They left early the next morning. Marilyn and Bill

both gave Divya a long hug and extracted a promise that she would stay in touch. Ethan slowed down as he passed by the redbrick house but resolutely refused to look at it. Divya's heart squeezed painfully.

He took them to Los Angeles and her curiosity was peaked. Yet another assistant met them, this time with a limo and driver. "LA traffic can be horrendous, and I want to make the most of our time together."

Why was he talking as if it was their last day together? He still wouldn't tell her where they were going, but according to the GPS, the ride would take over an hour, so they chatted about her family.

"Karishma is my partner in crime. She and I are only two years apart, so we've always gotten into trouble together. Naina is a little younger, so we usually con her into covering for us, but she's been getting smarter about wanting to be part of the fun."

"Did they know you were planning to run?"

"Karishma did. She even tried talking to Vivek for me, but he dismissed her concerns just as he'd ignored mine. She and Naina have both emailed me begging me to come back. Even Hema, who supported this plan all along, said it's time to return."

"Who's Hema?"

"She's like an adopted sister. Her parents and mine were close friends. When they died, we took her in. She was actually arranged to be married to Arjun, but he fell in love with Rani and bailed."

"So running away from an arranged marriage is a family tradition, then?"

She laughed. "I guess it is."

They finally pulled up to a building with a large fountain in front and an enormous rotating record on the roof. Divya turned to Ethan, wide-eyed. "What did you do?"

"I called in a favor and bought some studio time so you can cut a demo."

"Ethan!"

"You have a résumé for your career, don't you? Artists have portfolios. If you decide not to do anything with what you produce, consider it a souvenir of our time together."

Once again, her heart skipped. Why did she get the feeling he was preparing to say goodbye to her? Had he really fallen in love with her or was this like his love for Pooja? Now that things were getting real, was he getting ready to bolt? Was it all about the chase for him?

He hadn't just bought studio time, he'd also hired one of the best producers in the field, several technicians and background musicians. Ethan had booked her for twelve hours, which seemed ridiculous for recording the two songs she had written. But when they started, she better understood what it really took. It wasn't just about singing her songs; it was mixing in the music, fine-tuning how background music would be used against her vocals, even touching up her lyrics. The team Ethan had hired were professionals, and they worked hard without a break. Ethan went on food and coffee runs and watched her patiently the whole day. She should've been exhausted at the end of the session, but she was on top of the world. The finished masters were her songs, but they now sounded polished and sophisticated. Her voice had been amplified in the right places and the background music added the depth and symphony her guitar alone couldn't.

"You're like no woman I've ever met. And you can be like no other artist that's out there. You don't have to be like Tina Roy. You don't even have to tour if you don't want to. This right here—" he waved at the studio and the musicians packing up "—this is what making music is all about." He handed her a card and it took her several minutes to recognize it as the one that the man at Café Underground had given them. "The record label is small, but it's legitimate. I had them checked out." He pressed the card into her hand.

She hugged him, unable to find the words to say thank-you. How did he know what she needed when she herself didn't? How was she possibly falling even further in love with him?

They spent the night at his condo. Her family was camped at Arjun's hotel. Vegas was a quick flight, and they would leave in the morning. Ethan offered to take her out to dinner, but she wanted room service. They ordered hamburgers with fries and milkshakes and demolished their plates. She took a shower and wrapped herself in a hotel robe. When she emerged from the bathroom, Ethan whistled.

"Now, this is exactly how I want to see you dressed." He stood and kissed her, then untied the flimsy belt holding the robe together. He slipped his arms around her waist, and she savored the feel of his warm hands across her cool, damp back as he kissed the sensitive spot between her neck and shoulder. He moved his right hand down her back and across her stomach, then reached to touch her between the legs. "You're already wet."

Oh yes I am. "I started without you," she whispered into his ear, kissing him just underneath the earlobe, knowing it drove him crazy. "I want you inside me now." Even through his jeans, she could feel how hard he was.

"Divya," he murmured, moving his hands to her back. She unbuttoned his jeans and pushed them down along with his boxers. He took off his shirt. She pushed him toward the bed then slipped off her robe and straddled him. She rubbed her sensitive nub against him and he moaned, but she didn't hear it. Her slickness against his hardness was driving her mad. Her heart thundered in her chest and her body quivered, desperate for him.

She adjusted her position so he could sheath himself. Then she reached between her legs and pushed him inside her with a roughness that surprised them both. He tensed and stopped, his eyes checking with her to make sure she was okay. Even in the height of passion, he wanted to make sure he wasn't hurting her. Her heart burst inside her chest. For this night with him, she didn't want a parachute. She wanted to free fall for as long as they could. She moved on top of him, up and down, up and down, until she couldn't take it anymore and exploded, screaming his name as she did. She collapsed on top of him, totally spent physically and emotionally.

"Ethan…"

He put his finger on her lips, slipped an arm underneath her and pulled her close. The feel of his breath made her exhale whatever she had pent up inside her.

She'd needed the release to prepare for what was coming tomorrow.

"Ethan, meeting my parents is not like it was for me to come to your house. It'll change my life forever. It'll change my family. It will irreparably fracture the relationship I have with them. If we do this tomorrow, there's no turning back. You understand that, right?"

She couldn't remember his reply because she was so exhausted and comfortable that she fell asleep listening to the beat of his heart.

When she woke the next morning, he was gone.

Sixteen

He nearly dropped the breakfast tray he was carrying when he walked into the bedroom and saw Divya sitting on the bed with her knees pulled into her chest and her head down. She looked up when she heard him, her face streaked with tears. He set the tray on the bed and went to her. She wrapped her arms around him hard, nearly choking him.

"What's going on?"

She shook her head. "Nothing."

"Did you think I left?" The way she tightened her hold told him she had. He pulled her naked body onto his lap, trying to suppress his instant reaction. He rubbed her back. "How could you think I'd leave you like that?"

She kept her face buried in his shoulder, but he pushed her back so he could look at her. "You think I'll run away, like I did from Pooja?" She didn't answer, but the fear in her eyes told him that was exactly what she was thinking. He cupped her face. "We're going to meet your parents, and I'm going to convince them that I'm the best catch they can ever hope to get for their wayward daughter, and if they don't agree, I'm going to grab your hand like I did at your wedding and fly you away to a place where they'll never find you."

She cracked a smile. "You're not really going to do that."

He lifted his brows. "There's nothing I wouldn't do for you, Divya. I don't have any doubts. I'm not afraid. I love you and I'm going to be there for you."

They ate breakfast and dressed quickly. Divya wore black pants and a blue silk blouse. Her hair was styled and her face painted with almost as much makeup as the day they'd first met. She looked stunningly beautiful but not at all like his Divya.

It was early in the morning, but it took them nearly two hours to get to the airport in rush hour traffic. Once they were seated on the plane, Divya texted him a number.

"What's this?"

"It's my father's number. You're going to call him and tell him that you're bringing me back."

"Like you're a runaway teen?"

"Like you're the hero who finally talked some sense into his rebellious daughter."

"I don't need to lie to your parents to win their approval."

"Oh yes, you do. Things with my family have to be done the proper way. Right now, you are the asshole who crashed the wrong wedding and fled with the bride. My family will say that you're the kind of man who changes women like he changes clothes."

His stomach turned at the way she said this.

"Step one is to reverse your bad image. Our story is that you were helping me get away from what you thought was a forced marriage, because I lied to you. Once you understood that I just wanted to run away, you felt duty bound to return me."

"Have you considered writing screenplays for Bollywood movies?"

"Shut up. We don't have a lot of time to get our story right." She took a sip of the coffee she'd ordered from the flight attendant. "My family will thank you profusely and expect you to be on your way. Next, you're going to say that you have business in Vegas and ask my brother for a hotel recommendation."

"Doesn't he own the Vegas hotel?"

She slapped her hand on her forehead. "Of course he does. That's why he's going to feel obliged to offer you a room. He has an apartment there, where he stays and where my parents and siblings are also staying. This will give you an excuse to stay close to me, and their Indian hospitality will require them to offer to take care of you while you're in Vegas, as a thank-you for returning me safe and sound."

"But I haven't returned you safe and sound. I'm pretty sure I've marked my territory." He wiggled his eyebrows and reached for her, but she slapped him away.

"Pay attention. You're going to spend time with my family and get them to like you. Then I'm going to tell them that I've fallen in love with you. They are going to freak out and try to convince me that you are totally unsuitable. They will spend all their time trying to prove that you are a player, and they'll bring up the whole Pooja situation. It'll get ugly. Under no circumstances will you be rude to them. If you are, there's no turning back."

"Yes, ma'am!" He gave her a mock salute. "So how do I convince them I'm not just some ass taking advantage of their daughter?"

"You are going to go and buy the biggest, most outrageous engagement ring you can find in Vegas." She put the black American Express card he'd given her on the table. "Use this if you have to," she winked at him. "Money should be no object."

"I get it. This is a con, isn't it? You've been with me to get me to buy you an expensive ring that you'll hawk later. I bet your family isn't even rich. I bet they're drowning in debt, and you're going to sell the ring and save the family business."

"Ethan!" She was trying to give him the stern look again, but he noticed her lips twitching. He had absolutely no doubt in his mind that even if he followed her plan to a T, it was all going to go to hell.

"Are you really ready to get married?" He tried to keep his voice light. He wasn't sure which part of her plan was real versus a joke.

"It's not a serious proposal! In my family, showing up with an engagement ring is like asking permission to date me. You need to show my parents that I'm not just some hot piece of ass that you're after. The ring shows how serious you are."

"And this is the part where they'll tell me that I'm not worthy of their daughter and to go back to the trailer park I came from."

She shook her head. "My parents would not know the trailer-park reference."

It was his turn to roll his eyes. "I've seen this movie, Divya, and it's not going to end well. This is where the parents drug the daughter and fly her back to India, where they lock her in the house and marry her off to a bald guy who is twenty years older than her."

Divya laughed. "First of all, I'm quite a catch. My parents would not have to stoop to getting a guy twenty years older than me. Second, if my parents tried doing that, my brothers and sisters would make sure I escaped and reunited with you. Bollywood romances always have a happy ending."

"Do they also have hot sex in the heroine's brother's hotel?" he asked hopefully.

She crossed her arms. "No sex anywhere near my parents. They find out we've been sleeping together and they'll lose all respect for you and me."

He reached out and touched her hand. "We need to play this straight, Divya, tell them outright how we feel about each other and convince them of our love."

She shook her head. "In my family, you don't date unless there's a prospect of marriage. At least, the women don't. The boys are allowed to do whatever the hell they want." The bitterness in her voice was palpable. "But one problem at a time. I don't want them to see our relationship as frivolous. I need them to respect you and understand that we are both serious about continuing our relationship."

"Are they really going to be okay with you being with me?"

"I'll tell them I'm doing it anyway. But this is where you're going to make sure that you charm and disarm them. That's the key to this whole thing."

"And how do you propose I do that? Do you have a ten-point plan for that? Maybe some tips from a Bollywood film?"

She shook her head. "Be yourself. I fell in love with you. They will too."

She pointed to his phone. He took a breath and dialed the number she'd texted him. "It's going to voice mail."

She cursed under her breath. "Hang up."

She held out her hand and he gave her the phone. She punched in another number. "That's my brother Arjun."

This time someone answered, and Ethan recognized the distinct voice of Brother Number One from the wedding.

"Mr. Singh? This is Ethan Connors." There was silence on the line. "As you know, your sister and I have been traveling together."

"Where is she?" The voice on the other end was so quietly cold that Ethan shivered.

"She's on my jet and we're inbound to Las Vegas. I'll bring her directly to the Mahal Hotel. I expect we will be there in about one hour." Arjun was silent. "Look, Mr. Singh, as you know, me crashing the wedding was a big misunderstanding. I was under the mistaken impression that Divya was being forced into the marriage and just wanted to help her. Now that I realize she has to work out her family issues, I'm bringing her back, safe and sound."

Divya raised her thumbs.

Silence on the phone. "You're an idiot. We'll be waiting for you in the lobby." Arjun hung up.

"Well, that went well." He told Divya what Arjun had said and she frowned.

"Maybe we should've left a voice mail for my father. Arjun is a tough nut to crack."

Ethan shook his head. She wasn't going to understand, no matter how he explained it to her. They had to face the firing squad and see if there was anyone left standing when the shooting stopped.

The Tesla was waiting for them when they arrived at the airport. He loaded their suitcases and got to the hotel in record time. His pulse quickened as they pulled into the driveway of the Mahal Hotel. He handed his key card to the valet and resisted the urge to tell him to keep the car close.

Ethan thought he was prepared for what greeted them when they arrived, but he was so wrong. Where normal hotel lobbies bustled with people, this one was empty. Divya's entire family stood in the center of the entrance, in what could only be described as a scene from a mobster movie. Brother One, whom he now knew as Arjun, stood front and center. An older version of Arjun stood beside him with his arms crossed. A woman who looked remarkably like an older version of Divya narrowed her eyes at him. Brother Two, who he assumed was Sameer, stepped from behind Arjun. Behind them stood ten Men in Black–type guys with their hands on their hips as if they were just waiting for the mob boss to give the signal and they'd pepper the place with bullets.

"Divya!" her mother cried and came rushing toward her. She enveloped Divya in a hug and held on to her while letting out a stream of Hindi that Ethan didn't need a translator to understand. He stepped forward and held out his hand. Arjun took it first and, to his credit, didn't try to squeeze the living daylights out of it, even though his eyes shot daggers at Ethan.

Divya's father was next. "Thank you for bringing her back," he managed with practiced politeness.

Sameer kept his arms crossed, so Ethan retracted his outstretched hand.

"I know we have so much to talk about," Divya gushed. "I'm sorry I upset you all, but I need you to know that Ethan was just trying to help."

"I'm sure he was," Sameer muttered.

Divya powered on. "Ethan, I can't thank you enough. What are your plans?"

Oh boy, that doesn't sound like a practiced question at all. He tried to appear nonchalant. "I have some business in Vegas so I'll be staying a few days."

"Where are you staying?" Divya asked.

"I'll ask my assistant to book me into a hotel."

Silence.

Divya looked pointedly at Arjun. "I can make some recommendations," he said. Ethan suppressed the urge to laugh, not at all surprised at Arjun's response. He was seeing right through Divya's charade.

"*Bhaiya*, Ethan was very generous in lending me money to buy necessities and the like. Surely we should show him some hospitality."

"How much do we owe you?" Arjun asked coldly.

Ethan shook his head. "It's no trouble at all. Divya and I have become friends. I was happy to help."

Divya glared at him.

Sameer stepped up and whispered something to Arjun. Ethan got the distinct impression it was the Hindi version of "keep your friends close but your enemies closer."

"Why don't you stay here a night while we sort it all out." There was absolutely no warmth or welcome in Arjun's voice.

"Thank you," Ethan muttered.

"My staff will show you to a room. Come on, Divya. We have some catching up to do."

And just like that, her family whisked her away and Ethan was left in the lobby, holding both of their suitcases. He had a sinking feeling that the luggage was all he'd get to keep of Divya.

Seventeen

"Chai for everyone," her mom ordered as soon as they entered Arjun's apartment. It had a beautiful two-story great room in the center and a second-story balcony that wrapped around the space. Rani had designed the apartment, and it felt exactly like their home in Rajasthan. When Divya's parents weren't here, it was serene and private. But her parents came with her mother's attendants, who bustled about making sure everyone was constantly fed, whether they were hungry or not.

Rani came down the stairs holding eight-month-old Simmi. Her sister-in-law looked more beautiful than ever. Motherhood agreed with her. Her hair was held up with a clip in a messy ponytail and she wore a shirt with spit-up on the shoulder. Divya automatically held out her hands for her niece, and Simmi gave a little cackle and came to her. She hugged the baby tightly to her chest, enjoying the feel of the warm, squishy body and the smell of milk and diaper cream. They'd spent a lot of time together in the last several weeks while her wedding was being planned. One advantage of dating America-based Vivek was that Divya had gotten a chance to get to know her sister-in-law and niece. For a second, she wondered what her and Ethan's baby would look like. Would he or she have his beautiful blue eyes?

Karishma and Naina raced down the stairs and enveloped Divya in a hug so tight that the baby protested.

Arjun plucked Simmi from her arms. "You, young lady, have a lot of explaining to do." He pointed to the center of the room where two grand couches and chairs were set up in a square. No matter where she sat, she'd be in the hot seat.

She straightened her back and chose the couch. As predicted, her parents and Arjun sat across from her so she was sitting alone. All eyes were on her. Then Karishma and Sameer plopped down beside her, and she took each of their hands and squeezed gratefully.

One of her mother's maids came around with a tray that held tea served in cups with saucers, along with snacks. Divya refused the tea, craving coffee.

She'd thought a lot about how she was going to approach this meeting, but her mouth was completely dry, and her heart thundered so loudly in her ears that she couldn't hear herself think. She closed her eyes and thought about Ethan, about him holding on to her as they jumped off the plane.

She pulled out the phone Ethan had given her, scrolled to the audio file she needed and played the recording she'd made in LA.

"What's this nonsense?" her mother exclaimed.

"This is my music. Songs I wrote and recorded."

"It's really good," Sameer chimed in. "Who knew you had this kind of talent, sis. You should audition for *American Idol, yaar.*"

"Oh yeah, or that new Indian reality show about rich kids who give up their parents' wealth to pursue their dreams," Naina hollered, clapping her hands.

"Shut up." Arjun glared at Sameer and Naina. "This is why you ran away?"

Divya waved the phone. "I left to explore a dream you would never support. Now I know this is what I want to do with my life. I want to work on my music, be a singer. I never wanted to marry Vivek, and if you guys had listened when I tried to tell you before, I wouldn't have had to run away."

Silence settled over the room, broken only by Simmi's fussing. Rani took the baby and went upstairs, sending a sympathetic look at Divya.

"What is wrong with you, Divya? You are going to throw your life away to become a cheap bar girl?" Her mother's voice was full of fury.

"Being a musician is not like being a bar girl. Look at Lata Mangeshkar."

"Girls from our family don't engage in such professions. You don't want to marry Vivek, fine. We'll find you another boy to your liking," her father said. "Is this the reason you shamed us all by running away from the wedding *mandap*? Do you know all the horrible news stories that circulated about you?"

"I don't want to get married," she yelled, then took a breath. "I want to be independent. I want to make my own decisions, about who I marry, about what I do. I love all of you, but I feel smothered. I can't breathe. I had to run away because none of you would listen to me when I tried to tell you I didn't want to marry Vivek. You forced me into a choice I did not want to make. Now I am telling you what I want, what I need."

"And do your new needs include that *gora*?" her mother asked, her voice dripping with disdain.

No, no, no, this is not the time to talk about Ethan. She didn't want the focus to be on their relationship right now. She wanted to establish her independence with her parents and let them get to know Ethan before bringing him into the picture.

"Divya, it's best to tell them the truth." Divya looked at Arjun. He'd had a similar conversation with his parents when he'd fallen in love with Rani, and she knew he'd struggled with choosing between his family and the love of his life. He nodded encouragingly.

She took a breath. "Yes, Ethan and I are in love and I'm going to keep dating him."

Clank! Her mother set her teacup down with extreme force on the coffee table, cracking the saucer. "This girl has gone mad. Mad, I tell you! You have known that boy for, what, five, six days, and you think you are in love with him?"

Divya looked to Arjun. "How long did it take you to realize you were in love with Rani?"

Arjun looked toward his parents and then at Divya. She silently pleaded with him to help. He'd always been her ally with her parents.

"Americans are not like us, Divya. An Indian boy understands that when he dates a respectable girl, it's with an eye toward marriage. American men date for sex. You will not cheapen yourself like that," her mother said matter-of-factly.

She wanted to tell her parents that their views of Indian men were antiquated, and the realities of modern Indian dating were that men and women pretended chastity in front of their parents and enjoyed themselves behind closed doors.

"How about we invite the dude to dinner and find out

what he's thinking? We all know Divya's a little…" Sameer circled his finger near his head and whistled. "Maybe he finds her just as annoying as we do."

Divya gave Sameer a grateful smile. Ethan would follow the plan she'd laid out and show her parents that he was serious and respectable.

"I don't think we should encourage the boy any more than you already have," her father said coldly.

Divya shot Arjun a desperate look, silently pleading with him. Arjun met her gaze and sighed. "I think we should invite the man to dinner, get a feel for him and sort things out."

Her mother looked like she was going to explode, but Arjun stood and put his hand on her shoulder. Divya knew that Arjun would talk to their mother and calm her down before dinner.

Divya stood. "I'll go invite Ethan."

"You just got here," her father said quietly. He stood and stepped up to Divya, holding his arms out.

She got up and collapsed into his arms, hugging him tightly. The tears she'd been holding back flowed down her cheeks.

"Please, don't leave again, *beti*. Each day you were gone felt like years to me. Like I was missing a piece of my heart, a chunk of my soul."

Sobs choked through her as she settled onto her father's chest and he held her tight, running his hand over her head, like he used to do when she was a little girl and had fallen on the playground. All of the emotions, the pent-up stress, bubbled over, and she felt unable to hold herself up. Sameer wrapped his arms around her from behind, and Arjun, Karishma and Naina joined in. They all held each other for a long time, crying. Divya soaked in their love. *How did I ever think I could live without them?*

When they finally untangled, Divya looked at her mother, who was still seated, drinking her chai. "You must be tired, Divya. Go rest. We will talk tonight at dinner." The firm set of her mother's jaw told her that the night wasn't going to be easy.

"I'm going to go talk to Ethan and let him know about the plans for dinner."

"No need. Arjun will call him and personally invite him. Your sisters have been crying themselves to sleep, missing you. You can wait a few hours to see your *aashiq*." Her mother almost spat out the Hindi word for lover.

"But Ma…"

Her mother held up her hand and cut her eyes to Karishma, who gently took Divya's arm and led her upstairs. Divya's feet moved of their own volition, her eyes glued to the look of anger and disappointment on her mother's face.

They went to the room she'd be sharing with Karishma, who talked nonstop and insisted on getting all the details. *Five hundred rooms in this hotel and we all have to stay in the same apartment.* But there was an advantage to sharing with Karishma: she could sneak off to go spend the night with Ethan and Karishma would cover for her.

Naina and Sameer joined them, and her siblings filled her in on everything that had happened immediately following her wedding escape.

"I swear, Divya, I thought Dad would have a heart attack when Arjun and Sameer returned without you after you ran out of the hotel gardens," Naina said. Divya's stomach soured. "But that was nothing compared to what happened after the social media posts started and they found out who Ethan was. I love that BrideSnatcher hashtag."

Sameer chimed in. "There were all kinds of conspiracy theories. Somehow the Indian media latched on to the idea that you and Ethan were planning a secret takeover of our family business to overthrow Arjun."

Divya gasped. Such a thing was unfathomable, but she could see how the media could get out of control. Family feuds were the bedrock of Bollywood movies.

"Arjun and Dad had to fly overnight to India to calm the shareholders," Sameer said, his voice suddenly quiet.

Divya's head hurt. How could she have been so irresponsible? If she'd stopped to think about her actions, she would've seen all this happening. Arjun hadn't gone to India for Karishma's college graduation because he didn't want to leave Simmi, yet he'd had to leave his wife and baby because of her. Her chest was uncomfortably tight. She barely heard everything else her siblings had to say.

"I should check my email," Divya said weakly.

Sameer nodded. "That would be good. We've had some problems with the contracts for the new hotel in Washington. I could use your help."

Knowing that she had a lot to catch up on, her siblings left as soon as she opened her laptop. She turned on her regular phone, which Karishma had thoughtfully plugged in. There was no way she could possibly get through all of the text messages, but she sent replies to Hema and her close friends, letting them know that she was okay and promising to talk to them soon.

As she immersed herself in her work email, she didn't notice the buzzing of the phone Ethan had given her. She'd discovered that Sameer had downplayed the disaster he and Arjun had to deal with. Investors were threatening to pull out of their new project in DC, and several urgent contracts that she had prepared before the wedding remained unsigned. Sameer had been worried about her and hadn't been able to focus on the work. She'd seen this pattern before: first his work suffered, then the pressure of catching up got to him. If she didn't take over now, he would spiral, and once that happened, recovery took months. She had to stop it before it got worse.

I've only been thinking about myself.

Karishma reappeared, holding a tray of tea and snacks. "We'd better start getting ready for dinner."

Divya gasped as she realized that hours had gone by. She guiltily grabbed Ethan's phone to see several missed messages from him. "I need to go see him," she said to Karishma.

"Div, dinner is only an hour away. You can wait that long, can't you? Or are you all hot for him?" She hugged herself and made kissy faces.

"Stop! I need to talk to him before he comes over here. Cover for me." With that, she stepped outside to the balcony and looked down at the great room to make sure the coast was clear. Ethan had texted her his room number and she went straight down. Arjun had given him one of the best suites in the hotel.

As soon as she arrived, Ethan pulled her into his arms and held her tight. "I was afraid you'd forgotten about me already."

Tears stung her eyes. "We need to talk."

Eighteen

Ethan didn't need her to spell it out for him. He saw it all over her face. She'd been sucked back into the family fold.

"I love you." It's all he had left to say to her.

She sniffed. "And I love you. Change of plans."

"We're switching from a Bollywood plot to a Hollywood one?"

She rolled her eyes but couldn't help smiling. "I need to prep you for dinner with my parents. They know we're involved. They are going to grill you about—"

He kissed her. "Divya, I got this."

She stared at him. "You don't understand. Things have to be…"

He looked into her deep dark eyes, trying to tell her without words that he'd do anything for her, that he finally understood what it meant to love someone. She had shown him how real relationships worked. She'd brought him closer to his family; now it was time for him to do the same for her.

She looked at him uncertainly. He cupped her face, then bent his head and pressed his lips softly to hers. "I'm ready."

One thing was clear: if Divya was going to be happy with him, her family had to accept him.

Divya put on a conservative black dress, did her makeup and added the right amount of jewelry. When she went downstairs, it was clear that her mother approved. She was the last one to arrive. Everyone was dressed somewhat formally. Even Simmi was wearing a cute red dress and had a little bow in the few wisps of hair on her head.

Divya's stomach churned. She'd forgotten to tell Ethan to dress up. His standard-issue jeans and polo would not go over well. She rubbed her temples. *This is going to be a disaster.*

The table was set for dinner, and waiters stood in the corner ready with a tray of *samosas* and *pakoras*. She looked at the time and cringed. Ethan was a minute late.

The bell rang and she rushed to answer it, but one of the staff beat her to it. Her heart stopped when she saw him. He was wearing a perfectly fitted black suit with a French-cuffed shirt. *Wow.* Even though she'd just seen him a half hour ago, she needed to touch him. To make sure he knew that she loved him.

Arjun stepped forward to greet Ethan, and her heart swelled at the sight of her brother shaking Ethan's hand and slapping him on the arm. Her parents were standing by the living room couches, and Arjun escorted Ethan to them. "I don't think we formally introduced everyone," Arjun said good-naturedly. Divya guessed that Rani had talked to Arjun, perhaps reminded him how difficult it was for them when they first announced their love.

Ethan stepped to her parents and bent down and touched

their feet. Divya gasped. She hadn't briefed him on *pairi pauna,* an Indian tradition where you touched the feet of your elders as a show of respect and to get their blessings. She'd never expected Ethan to understand an archaic custom like that, nor had she felt comfortable asking him to do it. Rani had told her all about the first time she'd met Divya's parents. Arjun had asked her to do *pairi pauna* and Rani had felt disrespected. Being Indian, she didn't agree with the custom. Divya never expected Ethan to understand.

She leaned against the wall to steady herself, her knees suddenly weak. A hushed silence fell in the room. Her mother's hand instinctively touched Ethan's head in blessing, just like it would when Arjun or Sameer touched their feet. Divya could almost see her mother's heart melting.

"What would you like to drink, Ethan?" Sameer broke the stunned silence.

"A beer would be great." Divya did a mental face palm. She'd forgotten to tell him about the family drink.

"I'm sure room service has some," Sameer said easily.

"Whatever you're having is fine," Ethan amended.

Sameer handed Ethan a tumbler of whiskey. Ethan gallantly took a sip and tried not to grimace as he swallowed. Divya noticed Sameer also had a tumbler in his hand and she frowned. He wasn't supposed to be drinking. While he was addicted to painkillers, his therapist had warned her that any substance use could cause a relapse.

The waiters circulated with the appetizers, but no one seemed hungry.

"He's really hot, especially in a suit. I hope you've seen him without all those clothes?" Karishma whispered. Divya shushed her before their mother's owl ears caught wind of their conversation. Her parents still thought she was a virgin. It had always galled her that they never had that expectation of her brothers, but now was not the time to dwell on the gender hypocrisy in her family.

"Tell us, Ethan, how is it that five days ago, you professed your love in front of all of us, thinking Divya was another woman, and now you're here to convince us that we should trust our daughter to you?" Apparently her mother wasn't going to give Ethan a chance to settle in.

Divya silently pleaded with Ethan to go with the story she'd concocted: that Pooja was his best friend and had asked him to save her from the wedding. Ethan was facing enough judgment just being American.

"There's this notion of love at first sight. It seems irrational to believe in something like that. It feels like it only happens in films. I was indeed trying to break up my ex-girlfriend's wedding, but that's because I'd talked myself into wanting to love her. I'd lost hope that I'd find the kind of love I was looking for. And then I met Divya."

Divya sighed. She knew Ethan meant well. He was trying to be genuine, but he had no idea what he'd just done.

"*Wah!* Karan Johar couldn't have written a better line." The sarcastic comment came from Divya's father. Ethan had no idea who Karan Johar was, but now was not the time to ask.

Divya had warned him to expect her parents to be blunt, and they clearly weren't wasting time. Not even a minute or two of polite small talk? He didn't want to play the games Divya had suggested. He wanted to be honest with her parents. If he and Divya were going to have a future together, he needed to develop a relationship with her parents too. He'd spent his entire life feeling like an outsider in his family; he would not be the man who created a rift with hers. He would win them over. He had to.

"How do you know this time it's real, and you're not mistaken again?"

"Dad," Divya said pleadingly.

"Why don't we sit down to dinner?" The soothing compromise was offered by Rani, who was struggling to hold on to her wiggly baby while carrying a bowl of baby food.

Divya took the baby from Rani's arms, expertly turned Simmi around and settled her on her hip, giving her a kiss on the head, all in one move. The baby giggled and extended her pudgy little hands to touch Divya's face. Ethan's chest constricted. Everything he ever wanted was right there next to him. He just had to be strong enough to get it.

Rani took the baby back from Divya and settled her into a high chair. She waved for everyone to take their seats. Divya motioned to Ethan, who took a seat next to her and grabbed her hand under the table. She quickly pulled it out of his grip. All eyes were on them.

"If the whiskey isn't to your liking, we can order some beer," Arjun said, nodding towards the still-full tumbler Ethan had set down on the table.

"It's great," Ethan responded and lifted the glass to his lips, his stomach curling at the smell of the whiskey. He could almost see his dad sitting at the dining room table, glass in hand, barely looking at him as he signed the papers disowning him. His own father hadn't wanted him. How did he expect Divya's family to accept him?

Six waiters appeared, each carrying a different dish. They went from person to person, ladling food onto their plates. Ethan swallowed the bitter-tasting whiskey.

"So, tell me, Ethan. Why do you want to date a girl from India? Surely there are plenty of American women who'd be interested in you. Someone you have more in common with." Divya's dad's tone was friendly but his eyes stared Ethan down.

Ethan took a breath. “Divya and I have a connection, we understand each other. Where we’re from doesn’t matter as much as how we feel about each other.”

“That is a very naive view of the world. Do you think it won’t matter that you two come from very different worlds, that your culture, your traditions are nothing alike?” Rani’s mother could freeze lava with the ice in her voice.

“Culture and tradition don’t define who we are. Our values do. I was also raised in a very close-knit family. No matter where I am in the world, I always go home for all family birthdays and special events. My parents have an incredible relationship, and that’s what I want.”

“How long did your parents date before they got married?” Divya’s father was not cutting him any slack, but Ethan was no slouch. He hadn’t built his company into a billion-dollar empire by being a pushover. But the stakes had never been this high.

“How long did you and Mrs. Singh date before you were married?” He knew the answer to that question, which is why he asked. Divya’s parents had an arranged marriage. They had never gotten the chance to date, but from what she’d told him, her parents genuinely loved each other and had built a successful life together.

Divya’s mother didn’t miss a beat. “Our marriage was based on a firm grounding of shared values and expectations. Our families knew each other. We were raised with the same traditions, wanted the same things out of life, understood how our lives would work.” She took a breath. “Tell me, in which country will you live? Where will you raise your children?”

“Ma, we’re only dating. We haven’t even talked about marriage. These details aren’t that important right now,” Divya said, exasperated.

“No, Divya, these are the decisions that tear families

apart. This is exactly why we prescreen boys for you. We have generations of experience in these matters, but you kids only think about today. Now you are dating, tomorrow you will want to get married and then you'll have children. Will your children be raised Hindu or Christian?"

"We will teach them both of our religions," Divya said.

"I'm agnostic," Ethan answered at the same time.

"You see. These are not trivial things," her mom said smugly.

"Ethan, why don't you tell us a little more about your family," Arjun said diplomatically, and Ethan released a breath, glad to be on to a safe topic.

When he was done with describing his family, Divya's siblings asked him impersonal questions about his business, clearly trying to ease the tension around the dinner table. At some point, Sameer and Karishma deftly moved the conversation to easy topics like movies and politics. Without thinking, they slipped between English and Hindi as they spoke, Divya included. When they weren't grilling him, the family had an easy way with each other, and he had to keep himself from staring at the beautiful smile on Divya's face when she looked affectionately around the table.

At one point, Naina asked him a question, and he had no idea she was speaking to him. Divya elbowed him. "I'm sorry, I didn't catch that."

Naina smacked her head. "Sorry, Ethan, we don't even realize when we're speaking Hinglish."

He smiled gamely. He was used to being the odd man out, the one who didn't fit in. He took another bite of chicken. It burned his throat, and the whiskey soured his stomach.

"You haven't eaten much, Ethan. The food not to your liking?" Divya's mother asked.

He knew it was irrational, but he could swear she could read his mind. "The food is great. I'm just enjoying the conversation."

She scoffed. "A conversation you only half understand, just like this family. You've only seen one side of Divya."

Anger surged through him. It was one thing to question his motives but another to insult him. He turned to Divya, expecting her to stand up for him, to say something to her parents, but she resolutely avoided meeting his gaze. A familiar ache settled into his chest. Divya didn't know it right now, but she was going to reject him, just like all the other women in his life.

Nineteen

"Let's have dessert in the kitchen," Rani suggested. Divya shot her sister-in-law a grateful look. It hadn't been easy for Rani to fit into the family, but she'd found a way to take control of her house. It would eventually be okay with Ethan too. *Wouldn't it?*

The kitchen island was far more informal than the dining room table and it would help Ethan relax. She'd felt the tension in his muscles all through dinner. She'd tried to warn him about how difficult her parents could be, had told him how to handle things. But he was ignoring her advice. Did he want to sabotage this dinner?

It was a large island with several counter chairs. Rani excused herself to put the baby to sleep. The staff served chai, coffee and *kheer*, an Indian rice pudding that Ethan seemed to enjoy. Divya made a point to keep the conversation in English. She hadn't realized just how much they spoke in Hindi. Sameer made a gallant effort to keep the conversation on neutral topics. It felt stilted, as it had at dinner. Divya thought about Gauri's comments about her American sister-in-law. Would it always be awkward to have Ethan around her family?

After dinner, Arjun directed Divya and Ethan to the study for a nightcap. From the look on Ethan's face, he would rather have drunk more whiskey. The study was cozy with book-lined shelves, a couch and two leather chairs around a coffee table.

Ethan and Divya were left alone. She didn't need to hear what was going on outside the study to know that her siblings were being dismissed and her parents were plotting.

Ethan reached for her hand, but she eyed the door. "While I'd like nothing more than to throw you down on that couch and kiss you senseless, I know PDA is not okay. I just want to touch you for a second."

She smiled and took his outstretched hand. He pulled her closer to him.

"You're doing great," she said.

He smiled. "You're a really bad liar."

She looked into his impossibly blue eyes. "You can do this."

"And what if I can't?"

"You have to." She'd meant it as a joke, but her voice held a high, desperate note. He placed his forehead on hers and she leaned into him.

"Divya!" Her father's shout as he and her mother entered the room made Divya jump away from Ethan like he was radioactive.

She took a seat in the leather chair, forcing Ethan to take the other chair. He couldn't resist touching her, and her mother's eagle eyes wouldn't miss how physically comfortable they were with each other.

"So, Ethan, what do you know about Divya's new singing career?" Her mother could teach a class in making a loaded question sound friendly.

Ethan exhaled while she tensed. He had no idea what was coming. "I think she's incredibly talented."

"Do you think it's a respectable profession?"

Ethan frowned. "I think it's a legitimate career, just like being in business. Entertainers in this country are highly valued."

"So you'd be okay with Divya wearing skimpy clothes and dancing around a stage while drunk men ogle her."

Ethan took a sharp breath. "That's a stereotype of entertainers that doesn't have to be true. Divya can do what she's comfortable with, and I'll support her."

"So you're the one who's been encouraging Divya to pursue this crazy plan to give up her law career and become a singer," her father said accusingly.

"He helped me understand what I wanted. He generously bought studio time so I could explore my musical abilities," Divya interjected.

Ethan turned to her parents. "Divya has an amazing talent and deserves our support to pursue a new career."

"Singing is a hobby. Divya, if you really want to pursue this, we can buy you all the studio time you want." Her mother leaned forward. "You had your fun. It's time to come back to real life."

Divya bristled. Her parents didn't get to decide what she wanted for her *real life*. "This is something I have to do for myself, Ma. I want to live my life on my terms. The way I want."

"Just a few days with this American and you've forgotten your whole upbringing," her mother muttered.

"Mrs. Singh, I respect your culture and your point of view, but Divya is an intelligent, independent woman. She has the right to make her own decisions, to choose what she wants to do with her career and whom to date."

"And as her parents, we have the responsibility to protect her from bad influences," her father said pointedly. "Look, Ethan, in our family, you don't get to *date* our daughter. We believe in old-fashioned values. You talk about respect. A man who cares about our daughter would show more respect for her family traditions."

Ethan's jaw clenched.

Divya tried to catch his eye, silently telling him that now was the time to pull out the engagement ring she'd asked him to buy and ask her parents for her hand in marriage. After a heavy silence that seemed to weigh them all down, her mother turned to Ethan. "Let us get to the point of this conversation. What is your relationship with our daughter? What are your intentions toward her?"

He straightened and looked both her parents in the eyes. "I love your daughter."

Divya breathed a sigh of relief. She knew that the romantic way to do things was to propose to the girl on bended knee, but that's not how it was done in Indian families. Ethan knew what a big deal it was for her to introduce someone like him to her parents. They needed to see that he wasn't a stereotype, that he held the same values her family did.

"I hope we'll have a future together. With your permission, I'd like to keep seeing her."

Divya glared at him. *What is he doing?*

"Excuse me, Mr. Connors, our daughter is not someone you try out to see if she is to your liking," her mother said icily. "Clearly, you don't understand or respect our family values."

Ethan stood. Every muscle in his body was rigid, his hands clenched tightly at his sides. "Excuse me, Mrs. Singh,

Divya is not your property, and she does not need to put up with this. You have no idea what we share, and I will not let you insult her like this."

Divya jumped from her seat and looked from Ethan to her parents and back again. *What are you doing, Ethan?* They had talked about this very scenario, and she'd reminded him that under no circumstances could he be rude to her parents.

Ethan had done everything she'd asked him not to do. It was as if he was purposely sabotaging the whole thing. Then it hit her.

She thought back to something Rajiv had said to her in New York. Now the words haunted her.

It's not that he's American. It's that he doesn't take relationships seriously. For him this is a game, an amusement.

When he'd gotten to Pooja's wedding, he'd realized that he had been impulsive and didn't really want to marry her. The same thing was happening now. He'd done what he always did when things got real. He'd pulled the safety parachute.

This was the moment when he'd find out whether their love could withstand the ultimate test. He had come with every intention to win over her family, but now he was clear on the fact that he would never win her parents' approval. Not only that, it wasn't the right environment for her. She loved singing; the day they had spent at the studio had energized and exhilarated her. Divya wasn't a corporate lawyer, and if she stayed with her family, they would crush her spirit.

But could she stand up to her family? Could she give them up for him? If she had to choose, would she choose him?

He held out his hand to her. "Come with me, Divya. My

plane is ready to take you anywhere you want to go, and I'll be with you. I'll take care of you."

Time stopped. Their eyes locked and he tried to tell her how much he loved her, how badly he wanted her to choose him.

He didn't know if it was a few seconds later or several minutes when Divya slowly shook her head and backed away from him.

"Divya, now's the time to take a stand. Run away with me. Again."

Her eyes shone. "Ethan, I can't." Her voice broke, and along with it, his heart shattered.

She'd made her choice, and it wasn't him.

Twenty

Divya set her bag down and sat wearily on the old couch that she'd gotten at a yard sale. At least the temperature in New York City was much cooler than in Rajasthan.

She looked around the small apartment. Her bathroom at home was bigger than the entire five-hundred-square-foot efficiency, which included a galley kitchen, bathroom and bedroom/living room. The entire closet wasn't even big enough for her shoe collection, but luckily all she'd come with was a suitcase worth of stuff and a Martin guitar.

This was the best she could afford right now, and she was fine with that. Arjun had offered to give her money, but she'd refused. Rajiv and Gauri had invited her to live with them. They were centrally located in Manhattan, and it would've made her life easier than commuting into the city more than an hour each way on buses and the subway. She had a small advance from the contract she'd signed with East Side Records, and for now, it was enough to pay the rent on this small place in New Jersey.

She ran her hand over the guitar. It was her only connection to Ethan. After he'd walked out on the dinner with her parents, she'd gone knocking on his hotel room door only to find the room empty. He wouldn't answer her calls, texts or emails. Why wouldn't he even give her a chance to explain?

The answer was plain as day. He'd realized he'd been impulsive again and done what he did best: give up.

It had been six months since that fateful dinner and not a day went by when she thought about whether she should have gone with him. *But how could she have?* She'd seen Sameer drinking that night at dinner, and she couldn't leave without making sure he was okay. Her worst fears had come true when she'd found Sameer in bed the next morning, clearly hungover. She'd hoped it was just alcohol but knew enough from her research about addiction to know that he was in trouble. She had returned to India with her parents and siblings, to wallow in self-pity and watch over Sameer. Her parents assumed that she had come to her senses regarding Ethan. She'd slipped into her old life like a familiar pair of jeans that went with everything but felt a little too tight.

She searched Ethan's name on Google every day, and while there were articles about his company, he had disappeared from public life. It was as if he'd been a figment of her imagination. Then a month later, the Martin guitar had showed up at her house in India. There was no note, but she knew what he was trying to tell her.

She'd been miserable in her regularly scheduled life. The work of lawyering brought her no joy. Her mother dragging her to social events made her want to scream. Then the guitar had arrived, and she'd realized that just because Ethan was gone didn't mean that she had to go back to her old life. She had fled her wedding in search of her dream. A dream that could turn into reality. It was time to follow through.

She'd sent her demo to East Side Records and they had asked her to come to New York.

Sameer had still been lying to her about his addiction, and she'd finally called Arjun and told him what was going on with their brother. With typical take-charge efficiency, Arjun found the best rehab facility in the United States and flew Sameer there in the family jet. Sameer's continued relapses had finally made her realize that she had done him a disservice by trying to manage his addiction herself.

She'd packed her bags, left her parents a note along with a special item for her mom, and bought an economy class ticket on a commercial plane to New York.

The album with East Side Records was being released next week.

Her phone buzzed with a video call from Sameer. She clicked and greeted her brother. Sameer had stayed in the facility for ninety days and had been out for two months. "How's the next Beyoncé settling into her new space?"

She grinned back at her brother, noting how great he looked. He'd been sober for five months, and she had nothing to do with it. "It's a little basic, but I don't need much." She turned the camera to show him.

"Basic? Div, our servants live in better quarters than that. I don't understand why you won't use your bank accounts. Ma and Dad haven't cut you off, you know. Stop being stubborn and call them. I'm sure they'll come to the launch party if you personally invite them."

"I sent them the invitation."

He shook his head. "I don't know who's more stubborn, you or them."

"I will not be held hostage emotionally."

Her parents' plan had almost worked. The entire time she'd been back in India, her parents had reminded her of her responsibility and duty to the family. If Ethan hadn't sent the guitar, she would've slipped further into her old life. But leaving India made her realize that she'd faced her worst fear, and she was fine. As Arjun reminded her, he'd been forgiven for wanting to marry Rani, and eventually Divya would be forgiven too. She had to wait out their parents.

"Well, I am not staying in that dump when I come next week, but I do have a surprise for you that should be arriving any second."

As if on cue, someone knocked on the door. She opened it and a deliveryman handed her a giant box from Naeem Khan, one of her favorite designers, known for his Indian-influenced dresses. She squealed and set the phone on the coffee table so Sameer could see her unbox it. "You didn't!"

"My sister is not going to launch her first album wearing something off-the-rack."

Divya pulled out the beautiful gown. It was pale pink with a sheer black layer embellished with intricate embroidery. She excused herself to put it on and it fit perfectly. The asymmetric neckline was striking, and the hem was just the right length for the heels that were included in the box.

"Oh my God, I love it." She twirled in front of the phone's camera for Sameer to see.

"I asked Ma to contact your tailor in India to send your measurements to the New York boutique. I think she's ready to forgive you."

Divya ignored his comment. "This dress is way too tasteful for something you would pick out and way too risqué for Ma's tastes."

"I had help," he said slyly.

She narrowed her eyes. "Sameer, are you already dating? You know what the therapist said about taking time to be by yourself."

He rolled his eyes. "She's just a friend. Relax." Then his voice became serious. "You don't have to worry about me, Div. I'm really good this time." She believed him. He sounded different—stronger, more confident. "Arjun and Rani have been amazing in supporting me, and Karishma's really stepped up with the India office. She's way better than you were."

Divya smiled. She hadn't given her younger sister enough credit for being ready to step up. She'd always see her as the little girl who pulled her pigtails and stole her toys.

"Karishma is so good, she actually got the family jet for her and Naina to come to New York for your launch party."

Divya's heart filled with love for her siblings. They'd banded together to support her, and yet it felt like a piece of her soul was missing.

"Have you invited him?"

Sameer didn't have to say who he meant. They both knew. She shook her head.

"Want me to invite him?"

"Don't you dare. I've tried contacting him. If he wanted to talk to me, he knows how to get hold of me."

"Have you ever thought about the fact that he was right in running away? You didn't exactly stand up for him with Ma and Dad. Even I wasn't sure that you really wanted to be with him. You seemed to be unsure of what you wanted."

"It's what he does, Sam. He decides to take something on full steam ahead and when it gets real, he runs away. It's best I forget about him."

"You don't seem okay," Sameer said.

She pasted a smile on her face. "Of course I am. I'm just jittery getting ready for the record launch." After she hung up the phone, she ran her hands over the guitar. She wasn't okay. Her parachute hadn't opened and she didn't know what to do. She was hurtling toward the ground, and Ethan wasn't there to pull the cord.

Twenty-One

Ethan stared at the phone, unwilling to believe what his mother had just said.

"Divya's mother specifically said Matt, Heather and the kids are included in the invitation to Divya's record launch."

Divya's mother had called his? He rubbed his neck, looking out at the view of the Hudson River from his Upper West Side condo.

"The kids are really excited to go. They've been asking about Divya."

"You can use my plane," he said flatly.

"Hon, there's got to be a way to patch things up," his mother said.

No, there isn't. He had changed his cell phone number and email address, closed all his social media accounts. He didn't want to weaken and answer Divya's call. Yet not an hour went by when he didn't think about her, when he didn't worry about her, when he didn't miss her. He had consoled himself with the knowledge that she'd be happier without him in the long term.

"Mom, you weren't there that night. You should've seen her face when I stood up to her parents. Her heart broke right in front of me. If we stayed together, our love would be a constant battle in her house. It would ruin the amazing relationship she has with her family. She'd feel like a part of her was missing. I don't want that life for her. Marrying an Indian woman means marrying her family."

"Mrs. Singh invited you too."

"Are you sure?"

"I think it's her way of reaching out to you."

He still couldn't believe that Divya's mother had called to invite his family to her launch party. Six months had gone by. He was sure by now they'd have found her another Vivek to marry.

"If you ask me, I think she sounded incredibly sad. We talked for over an hour. She asked me a lot of questions about you and about our family. She sounded really nice."

"That's why I'm wondering if it was really her," Ethan said.

Marilyn chuckled. "You know, Ethan, ever since middle school, I've watched you crush on one girl after another. You always cancel the relationship before it really begins, because you're so afraid the girl will break up with you."

He looked at the picture sitting on his kitchen counter. It was the only personal item in his otherwise sterile condo. A picture of him and Divya and Allie and Jake on a giant teddy bear. It was exactly what he wanted.

He remembered what Divya had told him the first day they met. She wanted to be independent; she didn't want to get saddled down with a husband and children. Now that she was on the way to achieving her dream, he wouldn't be the one to hold her back. She deserved to get everything she wanted in life.

Out of habit, he touched the little box in his pocket. It was the ring he'd bought for Divya when they'd arrived in Vegas on the day he was scheduled to meet her parents. He carried it with him everywhere he went, unable to let it go.

"You should all attend, but I won't be coming," he said to his mother, a note of finality in his voice. "Tell Divya I wish her well."

It was her night. She looked amazing. She stood backstage, waiting for her cue to make a grand entrance. She should feel nervous, excited, maybe even scared, but all she felt was empty. What was the point of this success if she couldn't share it with the people she loved? Maybe she had been too stubborn. She should have called her parents. She should have called Ethan.

"There she is."

Divya turned to see Arjun making his way toward her with Karishma, Naina, Rani and Sameer right behind him. Sameer stretched out his arms to pull her into a hug, but Karishma slapped him away. "Do not ruin her makeup or hair right before she goes onstage. Look how perfect she looks."

"You do clean up nice, sis," Sameer quipped.

It had been four months since she'd left home and seen all her siblings together and her heart swelled. "Did Ma and—?"

"We came."

Divya turned to see her parents step toward her from the shadows.

"How could we miss this?" her father said.

Divya didn't hesitate. She ran into her father's outstretched arms and buried her face in his chest, not caring whether her hair and makeup were ruined. He put his hand on her head. "*Beti,* we are not going to agree with all the decisions you make, but that doesn't mean we don't love you. And it does not give you the right to cut us out of your life."

She turned to her mother, who looked brilliant in a royal blue saree with silver thread woven through it. Diamond solitaires glittered in her ears. She held out her hand and Divya took it, squeezing it tightly.

"Ma, our family means the world to me. But I don't want the life you've chosen for me. It's okay if you don't accept Ethan. We aren't together anyway. But I need you to support me in my career. You have to trust that you raised me right, and I wouldn't do anything to embarrass myself and or my family."

Her mother dabbed at her eyes. "You know, your father went directly to your grandfather and asked to marry me, and my father said yes. I was so angry that he made this decision without asking me that I ran away."

Divya's eyes widened. Her mother was always so proper; she'd never imagined her doing something so rebellious.

"Someone reminded me what it's like to be forced to give up something you love to do." Her mother's voice cracked, and she pointed to her feet. Divya looked down and her mother lifted her saree. She was wearing the *ghunghuru,* the little bells Divya had bought her right before she'd moved to New York.

Tears prickled Divya's eyes. "I never told you this, Ma, but my love of music started when I listened to the sounds of your *ghunghuru.* I used to watch you from the crack in the bedroom door and sing to the sounds of the bells on your feet."

Her mother wiped a tear from her cheek. "I guess I'm to blame for this whole singing thing, then."

Divya smiled. "And also the running-away thing."

"If you guys are all done being sentimental, we should head out to the party and let Divya get ready for her big performance," Sameer said.

They all wished her well. When her mother was out of earshot her father turned to her. "You know, Divya, there was someone I loved before I married your mother."

She looked at her father. It wasn't a secret, but he never talked about it. "Arjun's mother," she whispered.

He nodded. "I know what it's like to fall in love with someone your parents don't approve of, and I know how it can rip your heart into pieces. When Arjun wanted to marry Rani, we stood in his way because I thought she would tear this family apart. Instead, she's helped us see that it isn't the worst thing in the world to have an American son-in-law. The worst thing is losing you. You don't have to give up your music, and you don't have to give up Ethan."

She smiled for her father's benefit. She hadn't given up Ethan. He'd given up on her.

Ethan stood outside the ballroom, listening to the sounds of the party inside, knowing that Divya was just beyond the doors. Allie texted him every few minutes, giving him a play-by-play of what was going on inside. They'd met Divya's parents, whom Allie described as *totally cool.*

He hadn't intended to come. Wasn't even dressed for the occasion. But he hadn't been able to resist. All he wanted was one look at her. A last look.

"Ethan!"

He looked up to see Rani emerge from the ballroom. "What're you doing out here?"

He smiled, but his throat was so tight he couldn't speak. She looked at him kindly, then motioned to the armchairs in the hallway. He took a seat and she sat next to him.

"You know, when Arjun and I first got together, his

mother convinced me that our relationship was doomed to fail. I almost didn't marry Arjun because of his parents."

Ethan looked up in surprise. Rani seemed to fit in so well with the family.

"They're not bad people, it just takes a while to open their minds. They're like ice cream when you first take it out of the freezer, cold and hard and unyielding. But give it enough time, and they melt into sweetness."

"Thank you, Rani. But it's not about your in-laws. I don't want to hold her back. She ran away from her wedding because she didn't want to get saddled with marital obligations. She's finally found her freedom and voice. It's time for her to live her dream. I don't fit into her plans."

"But you fit with Divya, and that's all that matters." She put her hand on his. "I'm not saying it all works out, but when you love someone, it's worth the sacrifices."

"I don't want to hold her back."

She looked toward the ballroom doors where the CEO of the record company had just started speaking. "When Divya wants to do something, I've never known her to let anything stop her. Don't you think you're holding her back by making decisions for her?"

He sighed. What was the right answer here?

Rani put her hand on his and he looked up at her. "Do you love her?"

He didn't hesitate. "More than anything."

"Then, tell her."

He smiled. "Would you help me with something?"

Twenty-Two

Divya stood on the stage in her beautiful gown as East Side Records's CEO introduced her. She ran her hands over the wood of her guitar. She didn't need the guitar—there was a quartet of musicians onstage to provide the instrumentation for her song. She needed to feel the wood beneath her fingers, to remember Ethan's faith in her.

The ballroom had been decorated with sarees and lanterns to celebrate her Hinglish songs. Sameer waved from the front of the crowd, and her heart soared as her mother blew her a kiss.

She searched frantically for Ethan. *He has to be here, he has to be here.* She mouthed Ethan's name when she caught Sameer's eye, but he shook his head and her heart sank into her toes. *He really isn't coming.*

When it was time to sing, she stepped up to the microphone. Her stomach churned and her legs felt like wooden posts. A sea of people stared at her. Cameras flashed and bright lights shone down on her. She knew her performance was being broadcast live. It wasn't just the people in the room who'd be watching her.

The musicians started the instrumental introduction to her song. There was no voice in her throat. *I can't do this.*

Then the ballroom door opened and Ethan entered, his eyes focused on her.

Her breath released from her chest. He raised his thumb, and she began to sing the song she'd written for him. She sung her heart out, needing him to feel her voice, to understand that she loved him with every fiber of her being.

People burst into applause and she performed two more songs. She lost track of Ethan in the crowd, but she knew he was there. She could feel his presence and that was all that mattered.

When she was finished, the roar of the crowd was deafening. The CEO was back onstage. It was her cue to leave so he could make his closing speech, but he motioned for her to stay. "Before you leave, Divya, we have a special presentation."

She looked in surprise as her parents and Ethan walked onto the stage. He stood in front of her and looked at her with such longing that her legs threatened to buckle underneath her. He dropped to one knee and a hush fell over the crowd.

"I'm sorry I was such an ass and didn't realize how much you meant to me."

They were the same words he'd said when he'd crashed her wedding.

"Must you always show up in such a dramatic fashion?" Tears stung her eyes, and her heart felt like it would burst if he didn't touch her soon.

"I've been an idiot."

"Yes, you have."

"I don't need a house. I don't need children. All I need is you."

She shook her head. "I need at least three-point-four children, but not now, in a few years."

He pulled out a ring box and opened it. "I bought you the biggest ring I could find in Vegas."

Vegas? He'd bought the ring months ago? Tears streamed down her cheeks. She didn't know whether she wanted to kiss him or punch him.

"I'm a poor musician now. I'm going to sell that ring for cash."

He held his hand out and she placed hers on top of it.

"Will you marry me for my money?"

She shook her head. "I can make my own money."

He stayed on his knee, his eyes so impossibly blue, so full of love that her heart burst in her chest.

"I love you, Divya. You make me a better man, you give me strength and I want to spend the rest of my life becoming the man you deserve. Will you marry me?" He'd said the words in perfect Hindi.

She couldn't speak through the lump in her throat, so she nodded as hard as she could. He slipped the ring onto her finger.

He stood and she fell into his arms.

"Kiss! Kiss!" the crowd chanted, and he obliged. She drank him in, her knees suddenly unable to hold her up, but she knew she wouldn't fall. He'd hold on to her for the rest of their lives.

Her mother stepped forward and placed a hand on his shoulder. Divya looked at her, silently pleading with her not to ruin the moment. "Ethan, welcome to the family."

Her mother joined her hands together in silent apology. Then Divya was hugging her parents, and before she knew it, her father and her siblings and Matt and Heather and the kids were all onstage, and she and Ethan were in the center of a giant group hug.

"Run away with me?" she asked.

"My jet is waiting."

* * * * *

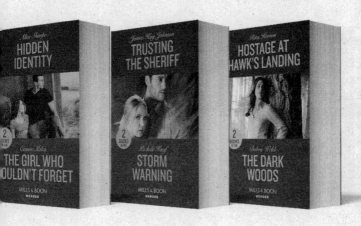